The Angels' Lament

Etched in Granite Historical Fiction Series – Book Two

Mj Pettengill

Copyright © 2017 Mj Pettengill

Cover Photography © Mj Pettengill
Author Photograph © Brenda Ladd Photography
Cover Design -- Mj Pettengill
All rights reserved.
ISBN: 1979557020
ISBN: 9781979557023

I dedicate this book to my parents and a young girl named Maria—a pretty little dancer who never gave up.

Preface

THE CIVIL WAR ended. It was a time of radical social and economic change in America—a time for expansion, discovery, and healing. For some, it meant piecing together the fragments of their lives, rebuilding families, homes, and communities. For others, it was time to leave the safety of their small towns and venture into nearby, rapidly growing cities, to prosper and find their long-awaited independence as industrial wage earners.

This transition was not new. In the late eighteenth century, with men at the forefront, the Industrial Revolution in America began to take shape. By the 1830s, women and children started flocking to the mills. While many of the obstacles that the workers faced are still present in today's workforce, most labor practices were horrific beyond measure.

The Angels' Lament is the second book in the *Etched in Granite Historical Fiction Series*. It was not enough to recover the names of 268 souls buried anonymously in a long-forgotten pauper cemetery. It was not enough to pen a historical novel about those who lived and died there. And, it was not enough to place a monument at the burial site to acknowledge them. Yes, these events served a higher purpose, but it was the beginning, not the end. Many untold stories are begging to be unearthed and acknowledged.

In *Etched in Granite - Book One*, we come to know the inmates, workers, and various individuals connected to the County Farm. We are afforded a brief glimpse into the life of Abigail Hodgdon's sister Sarah, who follows her dreams, departing from the deadening effects of farm life in the rugged New Hampshire landscape, and goes to the textile mills of Fall River, Massachusetts. There are many possibilities for one who has never seen the ocean and only read about cities in well-worn books.

Why Fall River? Throughout the process of my ongoing research, I have learned that my passion lies in the unveiling of that which has been consistently hidden, and in some cases, banned from conventional sources. Challenge motivates me. The less material available on the surface, the more determined I am to dig.

I chose Fall River, located in the southeastern part of the state, because, between 1820 and 1840, information pertaining to the mills is abundant. However, there is little mention of what transpired a few decades later in Fall River.

In the 1870s, Fall River became the second largest producer of cotton cloth in the world. Manchester, England was number one. During this time, along with the rapid increase of wealth for the few families that dominated the industry, a massive surge of immigration occurred, changing and reshaping the labor force, and altering the roles of men, women, and children for generations to come.

Insight brings illumination. The most profound narratives are tucked away in rare books— considered controversial in their time—yellowed newspaper articles, diaries, and letters. This extraordinary information consistently pulls me deeper into the complex structuring of our social history while broadening the spectrum of varied strands available to weave into the fabric of who we are today.

My initial research focused on the torment and adversity of women in the workplace while crammed into filthy tenements, rising up to the meet the challenges of daily life. During my analysis, a natural shift occurred, bringing my attention to the children, work conditions, general management, and labor practices.

It was my examination of the power struggles within the political, economic, and cultural development that sparked a desire to acknowledge the lives of immigrants. It is impossible to focus on one group and not the others. As divided as they appeared to be, they were often bound by their afflictions. Setting aside their differences, they came together to stand up for their rights. They were agents of change. This civil unrest has been a work in progress now for almost two centuries. Looking back, it may appear as if much has changed. However, it is wise for us to examine their efforts through a more transparent lens and refocus.

Seeking that which never existed, workers traveled to mill cities from lands across the sea, neighboring farming communities, and Canada. They became victims of social and moral collapse due to public neglect, incalculable abuse, and corporate greed, unknowingly paving the way for the future.

With empty promises of a prosperous life, wealthy factory owners lured immigrants to America, where they suffered cruel punishment, and endured hard labor while under life-threatening conditions. In an effort to adapt to their new world, the lives of thousands of men, women, and children disintegrated. With hunger and disease rampant, their wretched circumstances persisted, seemingly without end.

Within this high-charged environment was an ever-present undercurrent—conflict between gender, race, ethnicity, social class, and religion. All of this existed in the face of oppressive paternalism, the growth of corporate power, and textile capitalism.

As with Nellie in *Etched in Granite*, the narrative spans generations, reaching back to the shores of Ireland during the Great Hunger—mass starvation and exile— a catastrophic historical event, systematically deemphasized and misunderstood. The harrowing world left behind followed these immigrants as they boarded coffin ships, embarking on a perilous transatlantic voyage, to a world that did anything but embrace them.

The characters are fictitious, intended to bring voice to actual historical events.

Sarah makes her way down to the textile mills, bringing us into a spinner's world while living in filth, in a cramped tenement unfit for humans. Her sheltered background could have been a fatal weakness. Her determination to stand firm contains many valuable lessons.

August Wood shares his experiences as a street kid in New York City, in and out of the Children's Asylum, and on a westbound Orphan Train.

Bess Adams, pianist extraordinaire, daughter of an influential corporate lawyer, and surrounded by servants, seems to have it all.

My background as a cornetist and Civil War Music Historian is a significant resource. The element of music propels the story, forging a strong bond between the characters.

I am grateful for the courage required to enter into these dark places, providing the opportunity to discover what once was; for the fortitude necessary to stay with it, when the somber truth threatens to overwhelm; and for knowing when to walk away, allowing information to seep in so that my work is effective.

For her expertise and ability to ignite my critical thinking skills, I offer my deepest gratitude to my editor, Mariel Brewster; David W. Cooper, Jr., for his continued support, making things possible; and Shelby J. Trevor for countless hours of conversation, sifting through grim discoveries. For inspiration, I thank Anna and Miles Trevor; Alan Richardson for his valued feedback; and Brian Height for his technical computer skills.

Finally, for facing the unthinkable, this story honors my maternal grandparents, their children, and current and future generations. It is through my learning of their experience that I came to understand the significance of intergenerational healing. The umbilical cord is not severed; although invisible to the naked eye, it continues to grow.

—Mj Pettengill

Chapter 1

Sarah Jane Hodgdon
August 30, 1872
Ossipee, New Hampshire

OUR MOTHER HAD come undone. The Irish stoicism, bred in us for countless generations, was a myth. While a euphoric birdsong softened the edges of her cries, she lay on the platform in a pitiful heap. Once again, God turned away.

She rose to her feet, pausin' long enough to catch her breath. When her beggin' resumed, I remained uncommonly rigid and cold. The slightest indication of givin' in would have been to surrender. I would do no such thing. She dug her fingers into my arm, first pullin' and then pushin' me away.

We shared our disbelief, hers born of the idea that I had abandoned her, the way Papa did, and me wonderin' if she had no shame. I was the one headin' into the wilds of the unknown and climbin' aboard a beastly train. Where was her courage? I had prayed for the possibility to depart with a light heart and a kind word. God ignored that part of my prayer.

I looked into her green eyes, hoping to find a trace of the woman who taught us how to snuff out any and all emotions, especially those that were unpleasant. She wasn't there. I kissed her on the cheek, broke free from her grip, and said a simple goodbye.

I walked away, leavin' her curled over in despair, unaware of the people inside the station with their hungry faces pressed against the windows, watchin' without shame. Her usual kindliness, fortitude, and ability to fight in the face of adversity was dead. She had unknowingly crawled into her own coffin—her daughters givin' the final push.

My sister Abigail stood taller than me, yet I knew that her soul withered within her small, sturdy frame. She waited just a few steps away from our mother, smilin' to overcome the fear. I embraced her. It was possibly my turn to come unraveled, but I remained intact.

"Do you have everything?" she asked.

Somehow managin' to function without takin' a breath, I nodded. It was time to leave. My body was prepared to do so, but my heart would not have it. I had no choice but to keep movin'.

I hurried over to Eb Burrows, the station attendant. "Did you carry away my trunk and bags? I need my small bag and bandbox for the trip." I tightened my grip on my lunch-basket.

Eb was rather unpleasant with his yellow-stained teeth and a guaranteed dribble of tobacco on his whiskered chin. He was never a man about town until he got this job, and suddenly he was of great importance.

"I can get yer bag if you want," he said, lookin' past me at my sister, who innocently triggered a deep longin' of the flesh amongst most of the men, both young and old, in town.

The train whistle blasted three times causing me to hurry and stumble on the steps. Being so far north of Boston, there were only a few stragglers onboard. I went towards the back and slid into the seat, immediately positionin' myself near the window.

"Sarah Hodgdon?" Eb walked towards me with my smaller bag.

"I'm here," I said with a bit of disgust, as we knew each other well.

I supposed that it was with too much disgust that I snatched my bag away from him. It was not the fault of that poor, simple fellow, but he became the object of my discomfort.

Relieved that he would disembark, I didn't answer him when he wished me well. I had known this foul little man for all of my life. He was simply another reason why I needed to leave.

The train car rolled ahead with a jolt, hesitated, and then started in again. The steam whistle blew harmoniously as the mighty engine chugged and hissed, propellin' me into my bright future and away from my home that was cradled safely within the breast of the familiar mountains.

I took one last look. Eb had joined Abigail in liftin' my mother off the platform floor and bringin' her to our sturdy, old cart. I opened my bag and without taking my eyes away from the changin' scenery, ran my fingers along the stitches of the small leather case. I rested my hand on it. I was prepared to go anywhere.

Against my better judgment, I took yet another look and waved to my sister as she stood motionless with her eyes locked onto mine. Mother pushed Eb out of the way and started to run after the train. I tried to look away, but I could not. Abigail raced after her, finally catchin' up, but Mother struggled against her as I knew she would.

My sister never gave up. She always tried and always failed. I thought of dashin' down the aisle and leapin' from the train while it still moved at a crawlin' pace. I bit my finger through the glove and waved with my other hand as if it were a joyful departure, lyin' right up to the last moment. The sun formed a bright golden outline around them, makin' it impossible to see Mother's scowl, but I knew it was there. As much as I denied it, my sister was right. I was our mother's favorite.

I had become quite weary of the task of seekin' the right words. Even the gentlest expression spoken in a kind manner would not soften the blow that I delivered to my mother and sister a week before my departure. They chose not to hear me, disregardin' my deepest desire to leave our dreary little town and strike out on my own. The young women were expected to embrace the shackles that kept us enslaved to our crumblin' farms and the awfulness of waitin' to be chosen by a wounded soldier or an uneducated, toothless farm boy, to endure a tedious life, one which held no promise of happiness or abundance.

I found it unhelpful to complain, knowing that dark thoughts would simply bring about more of the same. However, it had become an urgent matter when Abigail was obsessed with Silas Putnam, following him around, hidin' in the shadows, quick to deny it. We used to share all of our deepest thoughts, but she was no longer present in the realm of our sisterhood. I had lost her to love.

<hr />

When Papa died in the war, we had to carry on. I believed that our willful determination to do so was our way of avoidin' the unimaginable pain and finality of his death. Mother only cried in secret, and when we talked about him, she quickly hushed us as if we were cussin' or mentionin' somethin' forbidden. Perhaps in her mind, it actually was forbidden. We were expected to hold our feelin's inside at all times, which is why there was so much confusion over the small things that we often magnified to a higher degree.

It was cruel to instill a love for someone or somethin' only to steal it away. Being quite naive and unworldly, I failed to comprehend the full risk of Papa goin' off to war. The fanfare at the train station was unrivaled by any other gatherin' that I had attended.

It was a predictable November day, one that brought a deep chill and offered no hope for comfort. We were thankful for the frozen ruts that just a day earlier were endless puddles of muck, threatenin' to swallow the wheels of our carriage, keepin' us stuck in a place in which we never wished to return.

I stood still within the dense crowd, denyin' the ache that most others accepted as a way of life. It was the silent acceptance of bloodshed and despair, loss, and troubled loneliness—a peculiar call to patriotism.

His regiment, the Sixth, mustered with other New Hampshire infantry regiments. They were settin' out to fight for the Union. There were well over one hundred soldiers biddin' farewell to their loved ones. We were driftin' in a sea of blue woolen coats, muskets, canteens, and weeping women with their desperate children.

Like many others, Mother and Abigail were overwrought. Just as I began to feel that very same distress, the brass band started in playin' a familiar quickstep. My heartbeat quickly assumed the rhythm. I temporarily lost sight of the reason for our bein' there and aligned myself with the remarkable strains of what I would later learn was a soprano cornet. I stared at the young man's fingers as they gracefully and quickly danced on the paddles of his lovely silver horn. His sound was as sweet as chocolate and as smooth as cream. I thought for certain that I was dreamin'.

After his farewell kisses, Papa made promises that, unbeknownst to him, he could not keep. Oh yes, he did return, only in the most grievous manner, nailed shut inside of a blood-stained pine box. From Mr. Wood's gruesome account, I was able to conjure up an image of his lifeless body, shot in the heart while breakin' up a rebel camp at Roanoke Island.

"Goodbye, Papa!" My sister cried, wavin' her handkerchief and squeezin' my hand. I joined in with the other women and children and waved my handkerchief, secretly watchin' the cornetist play a rendition of Yankee Doodle that didn't seem possible.

The familiar curves of the mountains diminished into lesser rollin' hills as we left the fertile and inexhaustible valley and headed south. The sun was warm on my face, and the constant swayin' of the train car rocked me like a sweet lullaby.

My thoughts drifted to Weston Jones, a handsome boy I fancied in my younger days. I had hoped that he would have taken an interest in me, but my attempts to capture his affection fell flat, until one day last year when he finally seemed to notice me. I realized then that my attraction to him had become nothin' more than a habit. He just didn't have anything interestin' to say. I supposed it was all for the best, as he was like the rest who had no desire to expand his world beyond the narrow confines of Ossipee and the struggles that came with it.

Many of the girls who left to work in the mills penned detailed letters, sharin' their stories of the new world—Fall River—and other mill towns that had been thrivin' in the cities south of us. We heard stories of travelin' circuses, people from far away lands, and the thrill of bein' away from home. There were some who returned, claimin' that the work and general lifestyle were too demandin' because they were probably weak in mind, body, and spirit.

I was prepared to work hard. After Papa died, and except for Grandpa Wills, Mother, Abigail, and I managed the farm on our own. The only outside help we required was for the repairs on the house, barn, and fences, and the cuttin' and splittin' of firewood. We were very capable of the stackin' ourselves. From time to time, we requested aid in the birthin' of a calf, shoein' our horses, and breedin' the pigs, but this was not unusual for any farmers in good standin'.

My sister and I were nothin' alike. Abigail spent countless hours with Lizzy, our favorite milker, dawdlin' in and about the barn and pasture. She was a dreamer and had no interest in readin', schoolwork, or sewin'. I, on the other hand, was swift with the chores, gettin' to the business of it all so that I could study, read, and practice my cornet.

The passengers began to stir, rummagin' through bags and fidgetin' with their tickets. The skies were exceedingly disagreeable, swollen with gray rain clouds bearin' down on the city. Thick smoke billowed out of giant smokestacks from the mills, perched along the river's edge. The wheels screeched as the locomotive slowed down. I had never been to Manchester before. Not only did it lack mountains, but even the hills had vanished into a dull, flat landscape. The lush greenness was glaringly absent.

Although we were still in motion, folks quickly filled the aisles, eager to disembark. I held tight to my things and continued to stare out the window. All I had to do was find a train headin' to Boston. My heart raced. What if I boarded the wrong train? If only I could have stashed away in my trunk and let the porters get me to Fall River, I would have had no worries. I chased away my doubts and sat up straight. I lied and told myself that it would be easy, somethin' I knew better than to do.

The conductor announced our arrival, and the passengers poured out of the train. As soon as I stepped onto the platform, a young man rushed by, almost knockin' me off of my feet. He didn't even stop to assist me or offer an apology. I searched for a sign for Boston and was bumped again, first by a large, burly man and then by another man with a slight build. People were dashin' about in every direction. I tightened my grip on my belongin's and followed what seemed to be the general flow.

I paused when I spotted a girl about my age standin' on the sidelines. At first, she looked to be one of those types from the County Farm, underfed, a shabbily dressed sinner. But Mother taught us to take a moment to release the urge to pass judgment and if possible, lend a steady hand.

She had reddish-blonde hair, a fair amount of freckles, and a lovely face. Her bleak dress—gray, somber, and void of any and all warmth—matched our surroundin's. She appeared to be unruffled. I was certain that God had shined his light upon me when we made eye contact.

"Ya goin' to Boston?" she asked.

"Yes, yes, I am," I said.

"Well, I am too. We best be headin' that way." She pointed towards a platform where most of the others were goin'.

"Have you been there before?" I asked.

"Of course!" Her laugh was like that of a child.

"I'm on my way to Fall River. I've never been this far south."

"I'm goin' to Fall River, too!"

"Really? What great fortune to meet up with you." I hurried along to keep up with her.

"So it's ya first time, eh?" She picked up the pace.

"Yes, I left my home up north to go to work. I've been lookin' forward to it for a long time. I'm Sarah, Sarah Hodgdon."

"I'm Mary. Pleased to meet ya."

Suddenly the crowd stopped, and we were at the end of a long line of people waitin' to board another train, one that was much longer and fillin' up quickly. She set her satchel down in front of her, unfolded her ticket, and dabbed her forehead with a dirty cloth. Beneath the grime was a pretty girl. I felt safe with her.

As the line dwindled and we approached the train, we passed by a young boy standin' on the edge of the tracks beggin'. I caught sight of his holey boots and shabby hat, covered with half-sewn patches, and thought that I could spare a two-cent piece. I rooted around frantically in my reticule.

"Ya won't be givin' away ya money now, would ya?" Mary asked.

"I—I thought that…"

"Never mind. You'll be workin' your backside off and wishin' for it back in no time," she said.

I forced myself to look away from the young boy, pulled the drawstring tight, and boarded the train. "I'll accept your advice this time, but it's always best to give to the poor."

She laughed. After the conductor checked our tickets, we made our way towards the back and found an open seat where we could sit together. There was an air of desperation as folks scrambled for seats. The constant rushin' around was unsettlin', but I was beginnin' to expect it. Some of the men were tippin' their flasks without any shame and took to playin' cards. I had heard cussin' before, but it seemed to be the common language of many of the passengers headin' to Boston. Even the women were cussin'. I saw one or two of them spit right out by the tracks as if they were chewin' tobacco.

Once we were in motion, I reached for my lunch-basket. With all of the commotion, I hadn't eaten anything since breakfast, which was barely enough to sustain me. I fixed a biscuit with fresh strawberry jam and felt Mary's eyes upon me.

"Would you care for a biscuit?" I asked.

"No, no, I wouldn't want to take your food," she said.

"I have plenty here. I'd love to share with you. After all, you made it easier for me to find the train. I insist."

"Ya woulda' found your way. You're a smart one," she said and smiled.

"Please? Mother would be insulted if you passed on her strawberry jam. It's from the recent crop. It's most pleasin'."

"Fine, if you insist. I could use some nourishment."

We ate our biscuits along with a hearty piece of perfectly aged cheese. If there was somethin' that gave me satisfaction, it was the sharp yellow cheese from the wheel at Tibbetts' store. Like a field mouse, I took small bits throughout the long afternoons that I spent workin' there. Of course, Mr. Tibbetts didn't mind, and he encouraged me to eat as much as I wanted, an offer that in spite of my wish to be humble and polite, I couldn't refuse.

"What's so special in that bag of yours?" Mary asked.

"Oh, nothin' special."

She grinned. "Ya sure 'bout that? I can tell it's somethin' by the way ya hold onto it."

"It's really nothin' of interest. Some things that my mother insisted that I take," I said, uncertain of the need to lie.

"Suit yasself. I don't mean to press," she said. "I'll git me some sleep. You should try to do the same." She fussed with her shawl, fashionin' it into a pillow.

Sleep had become a lost friend. I was in much need of it, but it was nowhere to be found. The combination of tobacco and wood smoke burned my eyes and stung the back of my nose and throat. The scent of damp leather and oil hung heavily in the air, takin' me back to the rainy afternoons when I sat on the sawhorse watchin' Papa work in the barn. I was content to be a bystander, unlike Abigail who insisted on helpin'. I wasn't one for doing a man's work, although I did learn to do much of it after Papa's death.

Once again, I found comfort in the soothin' rhythm of the train car as it clicked and rocked along the tracks. The more I tried to quiet my thoughts, the more they rushed in, keepin' me alert. I tried to suppress the overwhelmin' urge to move my legs, to get up and walk about.

At that moment, there was nothin' more intriguin' than the young woman sleepin' beside me. I couldn't help but stare at her peaceful, dirt-smudged face. She could have been an elegant princess had she been born in another place and time. How cruel and unfair to be birthed into a life based upon the circumstances of our parents.

She stirred, restin' her head on my shoulder and pullin' her tattered shawl up under her chin. Although the seams had come apart, she held tight to her blanket. Pinned to the inside of the frayed hem was a piece of baby blue fabric with the initial "M" embroidered on it. I wondered if perhaps she too had left her mother behind at a train station, or on the busy docks, where great steamships come and go. She seemed so unafraid, at ease in the dusty shadows of the train station where herds of vulgar people pushed their way through it all. I closed my eyes.

Heavenly Father, Spirit of Love and Truth, I thank You for sendin' this angel. It was through Your divine guidance that she arrived to bring me safely to Granite Mills, memorized a section of Concerto No. 5, which had become my favorite. Mr. Todorov insisted that I do so. If it weren't for him and my long afternoons at the conservatory, I would have gone mad.

I was careful not to allow uninvited tears to spill onto the keys, possibly spoiling my slightly imperfect, yet brilliant performance. I would not give in. I would play through it, through the grief of having to leave my home, my friends, and more importantly my music. Yes, there would be music in Fall River. Yes, a well-known teacher eagerly awaited my arrival. Father had promised me all of that. However, my dreams of staying on to pursue my studies at the conservatory had vanished. Everything that I loved was in Boston.

Although they would gain me no sympathy, my tears were finally liberated. I played with more passion than I knew existed. Mr. Todorov would have been pleased. It wouldn't have mattered that my playing was driven by pure rage. How unfortunate he never knew the fullest extent of my capabilities, for he was a distraction, and I played much better when he was not in the room.

When I got to the part where I usually stumbled, I did not falter. The clanging and shouting in the background were no longer a part of my world. I leaned in closer to the piano, leaving no separation between us. The shaking that began in my hands had reached that passionate place within, nearer to my heart, bringing about a burst of energy that transported me even further away from the present situation. The crescendo finally exploded. In fact, one may have called it a tantrum. Over the years, I had learned how to use fury to my advantage.

A lock of hair fell from my favorite tortoiseshell comb, and my cheeks were aflame. For an instant, I regretted that my dress, freshly cleaned and ironed by Tempy, was damp. I stared at my hands, frozen in place, unwilling to release the last note. *We'll have an Irish washerwoman in Fall River.* I exhaled. *Tempy will be free.*

"Excuse me, Miss." The younger man in the group was the first to break the silence. Three other men stood behind him, staring at me, not knowing whom to fear more, my mother or me, something that I grappled with as well.

Keeping my eyes down, I folded my hands on my lap, unable to move from the stool.

"Miss, it's time to move the piano," he said.

Mother walked into the room, muttering and fussing. She stopped when she saw me. Her tone softened. "Bess, the men are going to move the piano now."

I couldn't find a word, not one word. Even though it was a sultry day, and I had become quite heated in my playing, I was chilled.

"Now, now, dear," she said, ushering me away from the piano. "Everything will work out just fine."

I caught sight of Tempy and dashed down to where she stood in the middle of the empty kitchen. She turned and gave me a look that I relied on and craved, a look of reassurance.

"What is it, child?"

"I can't go through with this," I said.

"Ah course you kin go through with dis... and you will," she said, crossing her arms.

"No, no I can't." I started to cry. "Why can't you see that this is horrible?"

"Ah, Miss Bess, you can't know dis is horrible 'til you been there," she said. "You ain't even left the house, and you made up you mind dis is bad. Then it will be bad if you say it is so."

I had hoped that she would agree with me and complain about how unfair it was to be moving away, but she was of no help.

"I will never be able to play music like I do here," I cried.

"That's right. You will not have anything like it is here because you will be there. You don't know what it will be like. Cryin' makes it worse."

"How do you know?" I asked.

"Because I've been here, and I've been there. It is what is in here that will bring you happiness or sorrow." She pressed one hand upon my heart and the other upon her own. "You will decide and trust in God."

Tempy would never lie to me. She had lost everyone in her family. Her father drowned in a river before she was born. When she was six years old, her brother and two older sisters were sold, leaving her in Georgia with her mother. Although she and her mother were sold together more than once, they were finally separated when my grandfather purchased Tempy and took her to Virginia.

Because he was a doctor, Tempy learned a bit about medicine. Following his death, she was sent north to live with us. Mother told me that she was always free to go, but she preferred to stay on, becoming a superb house servant, with her most vital task being to relieve my mother of her nurturing duties.

"We're waiting, Bess," Mother called.

Tempy cradled me in her arms. "It's gonna be fine."

Hand in hand, we left the kitchen. I decided, once again, to trust her, that what was coming next would be up to God and me.

Dismissing any sad thoughts that chased after me, I followed Mother down the stairs. I turned back, looking one more time. The piano was the last to go.

Chapter 3

Sarah
August 31, 1872
Boston, Massachusetts

I DREAMT THAT I was dreamin'. The fact that I awoke with a start was the only proof that I had slept at all. Other than Mary's shawl rolled up in a ball, the seat beside me was empty. I took a quick look around. I thought that my eyes had tricked me when I saw her clustered around a crate, playin' cards with three crude men. She had a serious look about her as she tossed her cards down. The men paused at first and then all of them started in swearin'.

With a broad smile and her face aglow, Mary swept the coins from the table into her pouch.

"It was a great hand. Thanks to ya, gentlemen. I'll be off now."

"Wait a minute. Ya surely cheated to get that straight flush." An older, portly man with a clouded eye and jagged face grabbed Mary's arm.

"Ya callin' me a cheat?" She broke free and glared at him. "It was a fair game."

"Jest leave her be. It weren't for high stakes or nothin'." A handsome young man with thick ginger curls and clothed in rags stepped in.

"Never mind, Brian. I can take care of myself," she said. "I don't need your help, and I can take care of Mr. Sullivan, too. It ain't 'bout the money. He's cryin' 'cause he was beat by a woman. Ahh… It shatters my heart to be the one." She broke into vicious laughter and headed towards our seat.

"You played cards for money?" I asked.

"Well, ya saw with ya own eyes," she said. "I only do it from time to time."

I knew firsthand of the menfolk who played cards at Tibbetts' Store and from Mother tellin' us about the others in town who gambled. From the back room of the store, I could see those scoundrels shufflin', cussin', and tuggin' on the jug, willin' to lose their hard earned money. Of course, it was an outright sin.

"For the love of money is the root of all evil: which while some coveted after, they have erred from the faith"—I cleared my throat— "and pierced themselves through with many sorrows."

"You're quotin' the Good Book here… and at me?" She stared at me. Her eyes were bright green, the color that I imagined my mother's to have been in her youth, before all of her vibrancy faded with the loss of her one true love.

I admit that I was somewhat surprised at my response. The words simply spilled out from my lips without a thought. Although I was quotin' the Bible, it seemed more like I was quotin' my mother. I blushed and looked out the window. "I'm in need of a bath and a good cup of tea."

"We'll be pullin' into Boston shortly. There's plenty to eat and drink there, and we'll have to wait for the next train," she said.

I knew that I relied on her in Manchester, but I wondered if it was a wise choice for me to keep company with such a wild one. I feared that she had become an unsocial companion. Perhaps one to lead me astray. She seemed completely comfortable in the company of vile, wretched men, and what was worse, willin' to take their money in a card game. Who knew what she would have done next on this dismal train, so devoid of light and spirit?

"I don't know. I still have some merries in my lunch-basket." My voice had become surprisingly meek.

"I can return your favor and buy ya' a cuppa," she said, "and maybe a cinnamon roll?"

"You don't owe me anything."

"I think ya got nerved up at me playin' cards." She laughed. "Even quotin' the Bible."

"I don't mean to judge, but gamblin' is considered to be a pastime of weak and devious men. I was shocked to see you engaged in it."

"Ya find me playin' cards to be a shock? Ya got quite a road ahead."

A potent, unfamiliar scent washed over me. At first, it reminded me of the food scraps that we fed the pigs after it had set for a few days, but it was nicer than that. I didn't feel the need to pinch my nose. It was similar to gunpowder or maybe when Grampa Wills made fish chowder a few times. It was a weedy, pungent odor that commanded my full attention.

Then, the ocean came into view. I leaned towards the window to see the harbor, bustlin' with ships of all sizes, goin' in various directions. The risin' sun glimmered, wave upon wave, like a million jewels. I could not take my eyes away from the scene and held on tightly as we rounded another sharp corner in time to see the silhouette of a grand train station surrounded by many buildin's, more than I had ever seen.

"This must be Boston?" I asked, quietly.

"Sure thing! We're pullin' in," Mary said.

"Boston! Boston Station! Boston! Boston Station!" The conductor called as the whistle blew. I looked back out over the harbor.

"It's quite the busy place. I don't mind stickin' around and takin' ya to the next train," she said. Her earlier untamed look had transformed into one of grace and beauty. Perhaps I had been too harsh. After all, it was a new journey, and along the way, I would meet others who were not at all like those unworldly folks from home.

"I would like that. Thank you," I said.

"And we'll get a cuppa and a bun." She rifled through her satchel. "Maybe two, thanks to Mr. Sullivan."

I joined in her laughter, not at the expense of old Mr. Sullivan, but because I was in need of a cup of tea and to stretch out my legs. As I watched the scene unfold, I was convinced that I would get gobbled up in the crowd and fall between the multitude of endless train tracks. I needed Mary to get me through it.

"That sounds lovely," I said, holdin' tight to my bag and basket.

"By the way, the verse that ya preached?" She looked me square in the eye. "Timothy 6, verse 10."

The pink mist vanished, revealin' a pumpkin sun as it rose up behind the tall buildin's. I had seen pictures of cities in library books and newspapers, but this was much grander to the naked eye. From afar, it appeared to be serene, just awakenin' to the new mornin'. My senses—dimmed from smoke and oil, filthy faces, and harsh language—had suddenly become heightened. I had anticipated that moment and dreamed of a new land, abundant with adventures. I prayed earnestly to leave the old behind, maintainin' impenetrable faith that God was good and would not have led me there if it did not hold promise. Lookin' out over Boston, renewed my faith. Indeed, God was alive.

It was well before the brakes squealed when most of the passengers, packed tightly in the warm filtered sunlight, swayed together in the aisle. They leaned and looked out the windows with their sad strained eyes, eager to escape the congested car. Mary and I sat patiently in our seats, clutchin' our bags, and knowin' that it was not worth the tramplin'.

We finally made our way through the dwindlin' crowd and onto the platform. I stopped, frozen in place, and looked up at the largest buildin' I had ever seen. It was fit for royalty, hardly what I expected of a railroad station. There were many pale wanderin' souls, driftin' about, rushin' quietly, flowin' around me as I had become an island.

"Whatcha' waitin' for?" Mary tugged at my sleeve. "Let's go!"

"I've never seen anything like this," I said while she ushered me through the herd.

There were rows of pleasure carriages lined up with men and women of high character gettin' in and out of them. Some of the women's dresses had high bustles and delicately ruffled designs that I had not even seen in the newspapers. The men wore smart black suits and carried leather bags. Quite a few colored men scurried about, protectin' them all from possible mishaps.

Small, sweet birds darted in and out of the eaves, while pigeons strutted about, peckin' away at pebbles and debris. The scent of coffee and bacon merged with an assortment of exotic foods, causin' a rumble in my stomach. There were long lines of people waitin' for tickets and others asleep in random lumps along the walls of the station.

I stopped when I noticed a little boy with only one arm. I could feel his heavy little heart as he sat with a tin cup in front of him and his gaze fixed upon the many feet that hurried past.

"We should see if he needs help," I said.

"And what about him? And him? And that one over there?" Mary said, pointin' to three other boys with dirty faces, dressed in rags, with tin cups by their feet.

I stumbled along after her. "We cannot simply think that they should starve or die? Surely, we can help?"

"We hafta' begin by helpin' ourselves. It don't make us bad. When we find our way, we'll return. But for now, we gotta' move along."

"But that one has lost his arm. How can he look after himself in such a sorry state?"

"He is likely one of the mill boys that met with an unfortunate accident. You'll get used to it. They get along jest fine and swear like grown men. Some are even bold enough to use the pennies from their cup to go into a beer store and drink," she said.

"What kind of unfortunate accident would take his arm?" I asked, knowin' full well what the answer might be.

"Their lil' hands and arms get caught in machinery. It can happen to anyone," she said.

It was hardly possible that I would suddenly doubt God. I had just decided that He lived and that He was good. "There must be a way…"

"Look! A bakery!" she shouted.

We entered a small shop where, without question, the scent of Heaven overflowed. A growin' line of people meandered towards the door. We stood behind an older woman, once lovely in her youth, in a much-blessed state. She held the hand of a young boy with beautiful yellow locks. He looked up at her and smiled, the sort of smile that could bring the world to laughter, upliftin' my own weary heart. The wild-eyed urchins that sat in hollow places beyond the walls could only dream of such warmth and joy. The door opened and closed in a flurry, with people comin' and goin', payin' no mind to the wounded and untamed children only a few feet away. I wondered why all people would not weep at such a sight.

A plump, laughin' girl stacked shiny rolls, gingerbread, and small white cakes on top of wooden shelves. Her ease at puttin' in an honest day's work was expressed fully in her graceful movements. Without lookin' up, she asked in a rushed manner, "What pleases you today?"

After two cups of strong black tea with lemon, a large piece of braided sweet bread, and a conversation filled with riddles, Mary paid the girl with some of the money that she won in the card game. I insisted that she needn't do so, but she would have it no other way.

Without success, I tried to look away from the sad-eyed children wanderin' about with various injuries, arms filled with rags, and some sellin' newspapers. Clutchin' my bandbox and basket close to my chest, I was unable to comprehend where I would find the energy to carry on. I admit that the thought did pass that it would be easier and safer to wake up in my own bed, ready to face a day of farm chores and siftin' through the usual problems of the day. I concluded that easy was not the answer; it was not the way. I would dash those notions should they enter into my mind again.

"We have a lil' time before our train comes. Do you want to look in the shop windows?" Mary asked while continuin' to rush at least two steps ahead of me.

"Yes, yes, I would like that very much," I said.

I continued to follow behind her, stoppin' now and then to reposition my bags. The shops that lined the streets went on in every direction and as far as the eye could see. In front of them were open markets with people speakin' languages that I had never heard before. Dark skinned men and women with black eyes and perfect white teeth sold their wares, stacked upon barrels and crates. Ragged women hung out of windows, callin' out to their men and children, scoldin' and wavin' their hands. The flutter and cluckin' of nervous chickens and pheasants added to the riotous sights and sounds. Although she did not return the gesture, I smiled at a petite Chinese woman, who from a wheelbarrow, was sellin' mismatched stockin's with large holes that had been darned. There were even some negroes siftin' through the ash barrels very quickly, mergin' fine ash with the spicy smoke pourin' out from a buildin' that had large sausages hangin' inside the doorway.

I laughed aloud when I recalled our little feed store, Mr. Tibbetts', the seedy tavern with clouded, cracked windows, and the random shops scattered about Ossipee. I blushed at the thought of Abigail and me, primpin' and fussin' in case we bumped into one person of marginal importance durin' our weekly trip into town. Who would have believed that a magnificent place such as this existed? How could one not want to see the outer world?

Carriages and horses clattered against the cobblestones, swellin' with the emergence of the new day. As I picked up my pace and walked beside my new friend, my previous doubts gave way to a surge of hope and excitement.

There were what seemed to be endless side streets lined with stalls and carts filled with vegetables, fowl, fish, and everything a girl could imagine. A well-kept gentleman stopped abruptly in front of us, almost causin' me to take a spill. He looked out over the crowd, takin' it all in.

"A lot of faith, he has... stoppin' like that in the middle of it all," Mary said, elbowin' past him.

"Excuse me, sir." I blushed and raced to catch up with her.

"We ain't got the whole day to flit about without aim," she said. "Hurry up."

"You don't have to be rude."

"Rude? There ain't time to stop for silly conversation."

The throng of people that were movin' in the same direction came to a sudden halt. A man wearin' a full-length black coat and fancy hat stood on a platform shoutin' and surveyin' the onlookers.

"Step forward! Anyone who has an ailment or illness of any kind. Come up and try Foley's Brain Tonic and Pain Relief!"

The salesman's eyes met mine, and I quickly looked away. I would never try anything of the kind. I stared down at my feet and almost fell over when a man from one of the fancy carriages bumped into me with force. Had a rough man of about the age of twenty not grasped my elbow, I would have fallen. I tried to hang onto my bags, but everything tumbled to the ground in disarray.

The man who prevented me from fallin' helped me gather my things. I found myself to be quite frozen, and my face heated with an unwelcomed blush.

"Here you go," he said.

"Thank you," I replied, not certain why I felt so small and helpless.

"You should be careful," he said. He had chocolate eyes and butterscotch hair, and he wore a smart, yet faded black cap. He appeared strong with an air of confidence, unlike anything I had seen before. I was about to thank him again when he vanished.

"You seem to attract trouble, girl," Mary shouted from behind.

For a moment, I thought that I had lost her. And though she delighted in peckin', I was happy to see her.

I scanned the crowd. "Did you see where that man went?" I asked.

"Of course I didn't. Why would I do such a thing or care?" She started in walkin' again.

Determined to avoid another calamity on the wild streets of Boston, I kept a tighter grip on my bags.

We seemed to walk in circles. I had had my fill of cryin' babies, tobacco smoke, and vendors endlessly callin' out to passers-by. It did not occur to me that I was one of them. Somehow, I felt removed as if I were an observer, only aware of bein' part of the chaos when Mary pulled me into it with her demands.

We made our way back to the train station, where due to the echoin' inner walls, the hollerin' got worse. The red-faced conductor called out train numbers like a well-rehearsed song. Mary was so far ahead of me that I feared I would lose her. She stopped and looked my way with what I expected to be a frown, but she was smilin'. It was time to board the train. I intended to sleep. No swearin', joltin', or sharp corners would prevent me from gettin' the rest that I needed before arrivin' at Fall River.

Chapter 4

August Wood
August 31, 1872
Boston, Massachusetts

The dingy blue cape covered most of her face, but I could still see her eyes. She hugged me and said somethin' that I couldn't understand. I always thought that I'd remember, but never did. I heard footsteps comin' from behind. When I turned to look, she was gone. I stared at the church steps with that old feelin' in my gut. I didn't know which direction she went, but I knew that she was gone.

The shriek of a baby from a nearby window pierced into my dream. The sun lined up just right, blindin' me when it burst into the alley.

The others stirred, nestlin' deeper into the safety of each other, pressed up against the brick wall, under the partial shelter of the fire escape, covered with a blanket that we found. I pushed Aaron off to the side and got to my feet. He was the youngest of the boys, probably about nine. He rubbed his eyes and rolled back into the heap. The city had awakened; the sounds of carts, shops, and tenements made their way out into the streets to begin another day. The baby's cries blended in with the commotion.

I headed down the long alleyway and looked back at the pile of sleepin' boys, feelin' lucky that the rain held out for more than a week. Although it was not what I had hoped for, I had become a father figure to 'em, somethin' I didn't much want, but I couldn't turn away. I can't say that I blame 'em for not wantin' to be placed out, and the Children's Aid Society was surely gonna put 'em on the next train.

I picked through my rusted tobacco tin and found my comb. It weren't really nothin' fancy, but it had enough teeth to tidy up so that I would look presentable. I reached into my pocket only to find that I had fewer coins than I recalled. My first thought was that one of those rascals helped themselves while I slept, but then I remembered that the smoked sausage cost a bit more than expected.

I put on my cap and went to the rain barrel near the slanted gutter. I was sure that it would fall one of these nights, but it hung on tight. It was nice that we didn't have to sleep in the rain, but we had surely reached the bottom of that barrel.

I splashed some of the murky water on my face and swished a good mouthful, before spittin' it out. The only person in sight was an old man carryin' a small load of potatoes, so I took to relievin' myself, aimin' for the same spot every time. I was ready to make my way down to the train station.

I turned the corner, the place where folks gathered around to hear about snake oil and all those other remedies. I usually spotted someone with a kind heart who was lookin' for directions, who would buy coffee, tobacco, or beer for a poor wounded soul like myself. It wasn't as easy in Boston, but it would do until I got to the next place.

I tried to grab money or watches, but I always lacked the nerve. Although it was easier when I was a youngster, it usually worked to roll up my sleeves. One look was enough to get 'em searchin' for a coin unless they were the type that ignored things that made them squirm. I couldn't dwell on that. I was after the folks that refused to look away. They'd likely toss a coin.

Just as I was about to move closer to the center of the crowd, a carriage driver stepped out in front of a young woman, nearly causin' her to go down right in front of me. When her bags went flyin', I reached out and caught hold of her arm. She was a pretty thing, and I wondered what errand brought her to the station as it wasn't her place. She was scared and brave all at once. Yeah, she was strong all right, but not from the streets. Her wildness came from somewhere else.

I helped her gather her bags, gave her a kind word, and thought it best to move along. It seemed that she was keepin' company with one of those Irish girls. I had enough of the likes of them in Lowell.

I supposed I could have gone back there, but I didn't much like the place. Workin' the streets in Boston was gettin' too hard with all those other wanderers scroungin' for scraps. It made the most sense to do a good bit down at Fall River, work in some mill for a time and see what came next, then maybe go back to New York or somewhere I had never been before.

Chapter 5

Bess
August 31, 1872
Boston, Massachusetts

I REFUSED TO give them the benefit of my tears as I stared out the window, saying a silent goodbye to my beloved Boston. Mother chatted incessantly while Father nodded without hearing so much as a word. It was their way of connecting without actually connecting. I fought the urge to leap from the carriage and run back home. If my piano were not en route to Fall River, I might have considered doing so.

Tempy looked at me, nodded, and smiled. If I gave in to fear and anger, I would be betraying us both. I fidgeted with my bonnet and took a deep breath. After all, it was my choice. I must adhere to the positive thoughts that would clear a pathway for an illuminative experience.

I held onto the edge of the seat as we came to an abrupt stop and lined up with the other pleasure carriages at the station. People scurried about. Could they not calmly approach the platform and walk steadily to their seats?

The ruckus was too much. Perhaps I was spoiled by the endless beauty of string music pouring out of practice rooms at the conservatory. I could not tolerate being on the edge of sanity while people pushed and shoved, shouting about this tonic and that miracle-cure. I concluded that I required a cure for the consequences of such insulting behavior.

As our driver was about to offer his hand, a woman in front of us lost her balance. I stepped back into the carriage and waited until the upheaval passed.

"Come now, Bess. Ignore the crowds." Mother said. "Stay close to me."

I hadn't spoken a word all morning, and I wasn't sure if I would ever speak again. I held onto my parasol and followed my parents, Tempy, and Father's longtime driver and assistant—a friendly negro named Davis Logan—through an unruly crowd, looking away from the filthy little beggars as they tried so desperately to reach the strings of my heart and purse. I wondered what we had come to with such blatant poverty before us at every turn.

"Young Lady! Come up and try Foley's Brain Tonic and Pain Relief!"

CHAPTER 6

Sarah
September 1, 1872
Fall River, Massachusetts

I AWOKE WITH my head on Mary's shoulder and her arm around me as if she were my own mother, not a girl that I had met just a few days before. She stirred when I sat up and fiddled with my things. There were still quite a few people jammed in the train car, and there had been many stops throughout the evenin', bringin' chaos into my dreams. Although it was not the sort of rest that I was accustomed to, I was oddly refreshed and flooded with anticipation.

The buildin's in Fall River did not possess the grandeur of those in Boston, but it was a thickly settled area. Tall smokestacks rose up from the mills as far as the eye could see. The crowds of people appeared ragged, lackin' the energy of those in Boston. There were fewer fancy carriages and more general confusion.

"Mary, Mary..."

She buried her face into her shawl and shooed me away.

"Mary, wake up. We're here," I said.

I looked out the window for my friends Rebecca and Mercy Porter. Their mother promised that because it was Sunday, they could greet me and take me to the tenement where we would share a room.

I should have been more concerned about Mary, who decided to pretend to be asleep rather than join me. I had no patience for her puzzlement. I tried to stir her and get her to come with me, but my eagerness propelled me to disembark. I trusted that she would appear once I gathered my trunk and met with the others.

When I stepped off the train, I was immediately assaulted by the foul stench of filth, unlike the aromatic blend of exotic food and salt air that wrapped itself around me in Boston. Until that moment, I had never given much thought to what fresh mountain air meant to me and how I took it for granted.

"Sarah! Over here!"

How was it possible to have felt so much joy upon seein' the faces of the Porter sisters? Rebecca was a few years older than me, and Mercy was a bit younger. Of the two, I preferred Mercy as Rebecca had a mind to intrude and gossip.

I ran away from my waitin' spot and embraced Rebecca. She was awkward and perhaps the tallest woman that I had ever met, towerin' over most of the boys in town. Her gray eyes were sunken in and her hair, which was usually neatly curled and dressed with ribbons, was quite matted. Her unwell appearance was undeniable, but I could not allow worries in on such short notice. She was, after all, good and well-meanin'.

Mercy, on the other hand, looked fine. She was clear and happy. Her cheeks were flushed, and there was a sparkle in her eye. I always gravitated towards the ones that brought about a smile and genuine laughter.

"I finally arrived," I said.

"We're so pleased that you're here," Mercy said, ignorin' the nudge from her older sister. "It seems as if we have been waitin' all day."

I glanced over at the man takin' trunks and such from the train. "Excuse me. I must get my things."

"Wait!" Rebecca shouted.

When I turned to look at her, my mouth went dry. I searched for comfort in Mercy's face. It was no mistake that her cheer had quickly evaporated.

"I have news," Rebecca said, with an odd look about her.

"News?" I asked.

"I do," she said.

"Well, what kind of news do you bring on such a special day?"

She looked away from me and began wringin' her hands as if somethin' awful had turned up.

"Go on," Mercy said.

"It's your mother," Rebecca said.

"My mother?"

"Yes."

"Are you Miss Hodgdon?" The railroad man stood before me with my trunk at his feet. "I believe you have only one trunk. Is that right?"

I ignored him and searched Rebecca's face. "What about my mother?"

"For God's sake, will you tell her?" Mercy pleaded.

"She's gone," Rebecca said, wipin' away a tear.

I tried to hear her words, but they seemed far away. "What do you mean, she's gone?"

"There was a fire…"

There is no word for the pain born into that moment. I could not swerve from the truth. I could only let it crash into me, leavin' nothin' recognizable in its wake or that which would resemble what existed before that moment.

"Ma'am," the railroad man interrupted what I hoped was a dream, "your trunk."

All colors, sights, and sounds blurred into one as an unendin' flurry of people passed by, the way they always did at train stations. I felt the man's eyes on me, but I couldn't move. I knew that he only wanted to be done with me. He had a job to do. So, I pushed him aside and sat on the old, reliable trunk that Mother had given to me. She was proud. After all, it had belonged to her beloved Daidí.

Suddenly I thought that I would vomit. My insides were churnin'. I was both hot and cold.

"Sarah, there was a fire at your farm. Your mother perished. We received a telegram yesterday tellin' us to have you turn around and go back if you want to attend the funeral. Moses Blake paid for your train fare." Mercy spilled it out all at once.

"Abigail?" I could only utter her name and even then, was uncertain if it came out.

"Abigail is fine," Rebecca said.

"Fine?" I went from bein' a confident seventeen-year-old who had boldly struck out on her own, to a helpless child. "What do I do now?"

"We'll have your trunk delivered to the tenement, and you'll take the train back home," Rebecca said.

I closed my eyes and imagined Mother wailin' on the platform and how I just turned away. I remembered Abigail tellin' me that she would not be able to carry on without me. An image of our home in flames came to mind. Suddenly, I was sobbin', rockin' back and forth on the trunk. It was my turn to come undone at a train station.

Rebecca leaned over and tried to hug me. I pulled away and screamed, "This cannot be! You've made a terrible mistake!"

She stepped back. "Mercy," she said. "Do somethin'... anything."

"I know this must be a shock. I don't know what we can to do help. But, you should hurry and catch the northbound train. Abigail needs you," Mercy said in her kindest voice.

I paused long enough to catch my breath and wipe away my tears. It was hard to believe that I was so nervous about catchin' a train in Manchester. It was all so trivial. My mother was dead. There had to have been a mistake. I searched Mercy's face for answers, for her to tell me that it was a dream and that it was time to go to our room. However, the anguish that she wished to conceal was clear and unbearable.

The rest of the mornin' was a muddle. Somehow I managed to get back on the train carryin' only two bags, while my trunk and basket went to the home that I would not see until my return.

Everything was blurred, and when folks tried to speak to me, it was as if I were in a foreign country. I had a response for no one. I had no desire to eat, drink, or even sleep. I could only look out the window and visualize the face of my mother, engulfed in flames.

It wasn't until the train pulled out of Boston Station that I remembered that I had not seen Mary.

CHAPTER 7

August
September 1, 1872
Fall River

THE SCREECHIN' BRAKES woke me with a jounce, causin' me to roll into a rumpled old man who I had never met. There were usually many familiar faces in the boxcars, but as time marched on, there seemed to be even more of us ridin' the rails.

"Look where you're goin' for Chrissakes," he said.

I thought about respondin', but he had already turned away and pulled his coat up over his head. I brushed the hay off myself and got my comb outta' my tin. I always tried to look presentable, even after a night of travelin'.

"You gettin' off here, August?" asked my old friend, Jacob, a decent soul, always offerin' to lend a hand in some way or another.

"Yep," I said, "sure am."

"What's in Fall River that you're lookin' to get?"

"I'm thinkin' about millwork. I've been travelin' for a while, and it's time for a break."

He laughed and picked strands of hay from his bushy gray beard. "You still got some time 'fore the cold sets in," he said.

"Oh, I know," I said.

"Didn't you work up ta Lowell?"

"I did," I said.

"So why'd ya leave?"

"I dunno. It just wasn't where I was supposed to be," I said.

He grabbed his sack as we slowed down to a crawl. "Good luck, son. I'm sure I'll see you 'fore too long."

A few others followed him, and one by one they hopped off the train before it came to a stop. The ones who were stayin', burrowed deeper into the hay and behind random boxes to avoid gettin' caught. Most of us knew where the bulls were, and Fall River was one of those places.

I headed for the openin' when someone shoved me aside. I swung around ready to fight for my spot when a slight girl continued on by and rolled out onto the embankment. I tucked my bag under my arm and thought of how lucky she was that I didn't cold-cock her because that was my aim. I never hit a girl and didn't want that day to be the first.

I got off the train without incident and didn't catch sight of a bull. They would take you out and beat you senseless if they found you hidin' in a car. I only got caught once, and that was enough for me.

After sprucin' up, I walked towards the station where the payin' folks were gettin' off the train. I didn't see any easy targets, which was always the case for me. Long ago, I figured that out. Fall River was nothin' like Boston. There were some well-to-do folks, but not as many. Most of the people were millworkers and had nothin' to spare.

A high-pitched scream sliced through the usual chatter. Somethin' wicked had happened. I couldn't help but be as curious as the next one. I walked a little closer and there—all torn up and sittin' on a trunk—was that same pretty girl I'd seen in Boston.

I had my eyes fixed on her when a fancy pleasure carriage came within inches of me, so close it brushed against my trousers.

"Clear out of the way!"

I spun around and raised my fist. No driver with a swelled-up head would threaten me. I thought about firin' off a few cuss words but stopped short when the curtain in the back of the carriage was pulled aside, revealin' the eyes of a woman.

Chapter 8

Bess
September 1, 1872
Fall River

I STEPPED OFF the train and into what seemed like a thousand beehives. The smoke and peculiar odor caused me to choke. With my handkerchief covering my nose, I glared at Mother who offered a look of apology. There was no need for words, for I knew that in her heart, she was as sad as I was to leave Boston. She did protest some when Father accepted a partnership at the new law firm. It meant a better life, but at what cost? As far as I was concerned, we had been doing quite well.

I fixed my bonnet and tried to smooth out the wrinkles in my dress. Then I remembered that there was no need to fuss. Who was there to impress in such a dreary place? The landscape proved to be as expected with many large buildings boasting smokestacks, devoid of any character. Even the trees appeared to be haggard, with glaring features hanging over fences that never saw a paintbrush.

"Bess," Mother said, "over here."

I turned to follow her when I was interrupted by a woman's scream. I got a chill and fought the impulse to look at what I sensed to be quite unnerving. Perhaps she too had to leave her home and loved ones and was appalled at the place before her.

The cries got louder, making it impossible to ignore and oddly enough, I sensed a flutter in my soul. I finally looked over my shoulder to see a bedraggled woman of about my size, sitting on a trunk with her head in her hands, shaking and sobbing beyond all description. Two unsightly young women, looking quite helpless and distraught, stood before her.

"Bess!" Mother snapped. "Mind your affairs."

"I'm coming," I said.

I climbed into the carriage, but not before taking another look at the disturbing trio. I hoped that it was not an indication of what was ahead. I took a deep breath and leaned back into the seat. It was clear that all was not well, far from it. I wondered what would have caused such an outcry, and in public at that.

"You'll love the house," Mother said, hoping to provoke a reaction.

"I'm sure it's nothing like our grand home in Boston."

"You must be more agreeable, and give it a chance," she said.

Her unrelenting optimism did not convince me. I knew what was best for me. Being in a run-down mill city crowded with pitiless foreigners, who could not string together enough words to make a clear sentence, was not my idea of betterment.

"Tempy, I think that you'll like it too. I heard that there are a lot of markets," she said.

"I'm sure, ma'am," Tempy replied.

Father spoke with our driver and finally got into the carriage. With his new hat, polished buttons, and impressive suit that had somehow escaped getting wrinkled, he settled into the seat. He avoided looking at me and did not hide his guilt. I would not allow him to forget that he ruined my life, that my world had crumbled.

He tapped on the end of his walking stick, and his knee jiggled as it often did when he was wallowing in unpleasant silence. "It's a beautiful day," he said.

"It certainly is, dear," Mother replied.

At that moment we lunged forward, narrowly missing a man in the street. Our driver shouted at him, and he raised an angry fist. I peeked out the window and got a better look at the ruffian.

Surrounded by the riotous conduct of so many that lacked schooling or anything of real value, it only took a few hectic moments to realize that I was doomed. Oh, how I missed Mr. Todorov and the others, how I longed to be in the company of those with uncommon talent and bright minds.

CHAPTER 9

Sarah
September 3, 1872
Ossipee, New Hampshire

IT WAS JUST after daybreak when Moses Blake—a long time family friend and man about town—fetched me at the train station. Not asleep and not awake, I had full command of my senses. Once again, I inhabited my private, inexplicable world, the hidden door to my heart, the place where I felt whole. I went there durin' difficult times. After Papa died, I found myself there often, for it was my only hope in findin' spiritual refreshment and revival of faith. It had become the secret breathin' of my soul. It wasn't somethin' that I talked about, really, but I found great comfort there. Although removed from the outer world, it was the only time I wasn't woefully alone.

Moses stood before me with clouds of smoke curlin' about his face, matchin' the thick swollen clouds overhead as if they were goin' home. The pained look about him would surely be the cause of unendin' tears to flow from my own eyes. I am not certain of how I managed to walk, but I did.

"Sarah," he said, "how was your trip?"

If I had responded, I would have fallen into a careless state, losin' all respect that I had guarded for a lifetime. I could only stare at him, ponderin' whether I was breathin' or not.

"I'm sorry," he said as he drew on his pipe. "This ain't easy, I know. You must be tired and hungry. Come on, your sister's waitin' on ya."

Somewhat wobbly from bein' on the train for what felt like weeks, I made my way to his cart. Bein' the gentleman that I knew him to be, he offered his arm for support. I thought that leanin' upon him in any way would be the end of me. Refusin' help, even the simplest kind, was a weakness in my nature. In spite of my weariness, I reached for the backboard and pulled myself up.

He gave me a look, yet all I desired was for the strength to endure. I looked away from him and did what Mother taught us to do in the face of fear. I screamed at God, but only in my head.

God, where are You? It is Your guidance and protection that I seek in my needful time. It is Your support that I call upon in my distress. Please forgive me for leavin' Mother and for my disobedience and wildness which stirred up my pure mind. Do shine Your light as I walk in darkness. I must pay for departin' from the right way. I am unworthy to utter Your name. Although I feel much anguish of spirit, I will trust in Thee, Amen, Amen, Amen.

"We couldn't help your mother, poor soul, but Abigail acted in a way that most men couldn't have done. That girl saved most all the critters in the barn all by herself." He shook his head.

"She did?"

"Yep, she rounded up the chickens, pigs, and that favorite cow of hers," he said.

"Lizzy?"

"Yep."

"Is there anything left?"

"Not much, I'm afraid. It was quite a blaze."

"Did she get Old Gray?"

"Is that her horse?" he asked.

"Yes, yes it is." The memory of my sister ridin' with a spirit that could never be broken brought about a weak smile.

"Ayuh, the horse is fine."

"How did it—"

"I don't know what happened, why your mother didn't get out," he said. "Abigail did hurt her ankle and got some burns, but it coulda' been worse."

I squeezed my eyes shut and tried to ignore him. When we turned down Brown's Ridge Road, I wondered how it was possible that I was still alive, because takin' a single breath required strength that I feared I did not possess. In the awfulness of that moment, I thought that I would die right there on Moses's cart, less than a mile away from my home that I dared not look upon.

"Stop!" I cried. "Stop! I cannot go any further."

He stared at me.

"Did you not hear me?" I screamed. "Let me off." I lifted my skirt, about to jump.

"Whoa!" He yanked on the reins, and we came to a halt.

"I cannot and will not," I said, jumpin' down from the carriage.

"Sarah," he said, "you can't jest get off here. Your sister is waitin' for you at the house. We gotta' get to the church for the funeral."

"I can't," I said and continued walkin'.

The rain didn't bother with even the briefest introduction, it slammed us with a sudden surge, rushin' to overwhelm.

He toked on his pipe, starin' straight ahead into the punishin' rain. "Sarah, I know this must be painful, but we gotta' do what's right. Now, come on."

"No!" I started to run.

He jumped off the cart and chased after me. When he grabbed my arm, we both almost toppled over. I paused and looked into his eyes, this time seein' beyond the grit and into the kindness.

"It hurts now, probably like nothin' you ever felt. I know you girls was close to your mother, but you have to accept it. You have to be there for Abigail, too."

He embraced me, which I feared would hinder my strength to resist him. It was at the moment of embrace, of compassion and love, that my soul would be overwhelmed. I knew that he was right. I had to reject the fear and pain and go with him.

Again, without words, we approached the cart. I allowed Moses to help me onto the seat—a pool of rainwater. How muted I was, as my heart refused to be comforted. We rode in silence. I screamed inside, that is until the charred ruins of our farm came into view, and the scream made its way to my lips.

The cart nearly spilled when we struck a deep, water-filled rut, and a rather large crow fluttered and squawked, almost collidin' with me. It flew to a nearby branch where it perched, knowin' and waitin', watchin' with a forbiddin' eye. The tempo of the rain increased, poundin' like never before.

"Mother…" I reached towards the wreckage of my whole existence. As fast as they came, my tears stopped. My eyes followed the thin lines of smoke that rose upwards from the blackened debris, fightin' to remain, swirlin' and vanishin' into the rain as if nothin' had happened. I looked up at the crow as if it somehow held the answers to questions yet to be asked.

It wasn't long before we arrived at Moses's farm. He had wrapped his coat around my shoulders and was goin' faster than what would be considered safe in such dreadful conditions. I had completely surrendered to all that wished to consume me and graciously accepted help to disembark and make my way to his house.

Lookin' more disturbed than usual, Mrs. Blake met us at the door. "Oh, child! Come in, quickly. You'll catch a fever if you don't shed them wet clothes."

I searched the room with my eyes, hopin' to see Abigail while Mrs. Blake yanked on my blouse, which had become one with me.

Mrs. Porter, a pleasin' sort, rushed into the room with a black dress draped over her arm. She stopped in front of me, wordless as it seemed.

"Mrs. Porter?"

"Sarah, I'm so sorry for the tragic loss of your mother," she said. "Annie was such a dear."

"Thank you," I said, tryin' to stay with it.

"I have a dress here for you. It was Mercy's mournin' dress that she wore when my beloved husband passed. You look about her size."

"Thank you." I wilted when I realized that I had already removed most of my clothes in front of everyone in the room. I quickly snatched it away from her and held it in front of me.

"Did you get to see my girls?" she asked.

"I did, indeed," I said.

"Are they well?"

"I saw them briefly at the train station. They were the ones who informed me of Mother's death. They look to be in good spirits and well-kept."

"I worry about them, bein' so far away and without motherly guidance."

"They took my trunk to our room and await my return. I don't have much news to share," I said.

Mrs. Blake came at me with a sackcloth petticoat and undergarments that looked to be too big. "Here, this will have to do. We haven't much time to waste."

I dressed in the rags that she gave me, dismissin' any usual modesty and choosin' to forget that Moses was nearby. The women started in cluckin' about the pies and such for the gatherin' after the funeral. I looked around the kitchen and finally noticed the abundance of food, as if there were somethin' worth celebratin'.

"Where's Abigail?" I asked, wonderin' why she was not the first order of business.

"She's upstairs takin', her time to get ready. It's gonna be a long day."

As Mrs. Blake spoke, I heard clumsy footsteps on the stairs. There was Abigail leanin' on the rail, makin' her way towards me. Although burdened with much pain, she was the most gratifyin' sight of the day.

I ran to the bottom step, and she fell into my arms. The wave of tears that washed over us could not be measured. She smelled of smoke and appeared to be quite broken.

"Sarah," she cried, "Mother is dead." She fell in such a way that I could not support her. I sat beside her on the floor, pushin' away the desire to escape into my private world while somehow commandin' my own tears to cease. There was no sense in all that had happened, and the agony of knowin' that we were about to bury our mother weighed heavily upon us. Unable to avoid the unchangeable truth, I passed through the hidden door to my heart, where it was safe.

CHAPTER 10

August September 3, 1872 Fall River

EVER SINCE I left the train station, a young deaf boy had been followin' me. Due to my habit of payin' too much attention to 'em, I had a way of attractin' the young ones, holdin' together body and soul. I recalled my early days of wanderin' and knew that without companionship and tender sympathy, and if you weren't strong, you'd surely lose the fight.

Like all of us, he had a mother and father somewhere, but no one claimed him. And, no one would own him as long as he avoided the asylum, workhouse, and mills, and especially the likes of men like Smitty, who would get him to commit wicked crimes. Bein' deaf and all, he'd be perfect for beggin', peddlin', and if he were good at it, stealin'. He was just another scamp like the rest of us, and his fate was in his own dirty little hands.

"Come on," I said.

He sat on an unstable crate lookin' past me. I knew he was afraid, but tryin' not to let on. I reached for his cap, and he let out a whoop and grabbed it, finally makin' eye contact with me. He wasn't lettin' that go. Everything else was up for negotiation, but not that.

"Aw, I wasn't gonna steal your hat," I said.

He clutched it to his chest and looked away. If his shirt were any more worn, it wouldn't have resembled a shirt. Out of the corner of his eye, he watched me comb my hair.

"You want to use my comb?" I asked.

He looked away again.

I approached him with the comb in my hand. He stared at my arms.

"Oh, it's nothin'. It doesn't hurt anymore," I said.

I was used to people's discomfort. It used to pain me, but it was what I knew. It made me strong, and I rejected pity. And although I didn't earn a healthy wage, I was a pretty good type, right smart for bein' on the streets. I knew that if I tended to myself, that I could pass as a store boy or somethin' of the like.

Chapter 11

Bess
September 3, 1872
Fall River

I TRIED TO recall my dream. However, as always, the moment I opened my eyes it was gone. I stayed beneath the blanket, ignoring the persistent calls of my mother. The rain beat hard on the roof, threatening to crack it open. On that morning, there was no need to rise. I was feeling poorly, without a way to pinpoint its origin. I was utterly miserable with a deep craving for that which was undefinable. I was in need of being lifted from the loathsome pit that was my new home.

When such things happened upon me, I had to stop listening, looking, or sensing the world. It was a cue to close my eyes and stay within the confines of my own soft darkness. It enveloped me and lulled me to sleep as if I were swaddled tightly in a soundless womb.

If it were possible for rain to have a choice, on that day it chose to offer comfort over irritability. Sometimes, the outside noises became muted familiar voices, unable to decipher, yet oddly comforting.

"Bess, dear..." It could have been moments or perhaps hours when my mother shook me out of the safety of the womb.

"I want to sleep," I said.

"I understand, dear, but there is so much to do," she said.

"It can wait until tomorrow."

"I want you to meet some new friends who will be sitting with us. We will paint a set of porcelain. I heard that it is straight from Bavaria." I was always aware when she was on a mission to sway me or get me to do something other than what I wished to do. I did enjoy china painting, but it was not the time for it.

"You are inviting them here today? What about all of the trunks and clutter everywhere? We are not ready for guests," I said, reluctant to make eye contact with her, knowing that it meant the end of a peaceful retreat.

"Well—"

"And, what about the piano? It's not even in place," I said.

"It will be situated by tomorrow morning."

"You promised that it would be here waiting."

"We have to be patient, one step at a time. Now, come and join us for breakfast. You'll feel better after nourishment, dear."

"I may feel better when I can sleep." I put the pillow over my head.

"Just this one day, I will allow you to stay in bed for as long as you see fit."

I waited until I heard her footsteps on the stairs before removing the pillow and returning inward to my mind and finding my way back to the refuge of the unlit womb.

Chapter 12

Sarah
September 5, 1872
Ossipee, New Hampshire

OVER THE YEARS, memories of my mother's funeral appeared in fragments, only to quickly vanish into limitless gray clouds. I questioned the substance of what was real and what was an illusion. The only possible comfort existed in my hushed inner world. From the time of Papa's death, it was as if no time had passed. I slipped through that hidden door to the place where nothin' else existed.

Through my tears, I was able to see that the sad and shadowy event of her death had brought the town folk together, somethin' that a small community required from time to time in order to remain intact. It was my mother who taught me to find the lesson in everything, so for that, I was grateful.

If my sister and I had been unable to lean on each other, it would have been impossible to endure. Incapable of hearin' Pastor Leighton's words, and for once, able to ignore the clumsiness of his wife's organ playin, I drifted into my inner sanctuary. Without real success, I tried to imagine my mother's blackened remains—her ash-clad body—lyin' in the coffin. Until she was returned to the earth, I simply could not begin to accept her fate.

I wasn't bothered, but found it odd, that Weston Jones was overly attentive to my sister. However, it heightened my sorrow to witness the blatant show of affection between Silas Putnam and Jessie, the new girl in town. If it were true that Abigail was with child, he would have no choice but to share the blame and own his wickedness. If it weren't a somber occasion and if there were room for it within the walls of our grief, I would have brought about a quarrel. But, Abigail promised that she would tell him of her news, and I took her for her word.

Followin' a large gatherin' at the Blake's farm, Abigail drifted in and out of piecin' together the events of the night and how it came to be that our mother was dead. Of course, she blamed herself. After all, she did sneak out to meet up with Silas, and if she had stayed at home, it wouldn't have happened. However, I believed that it was no fault of hers, as she had such urgent news that needed sharin'.

It was I who was to blame. I had left Mother in despair, dismissin' her screams with a gentle wave of the hand and continuin' down the tracks as if she mattered not. If she were not in such a state, she would have had the mind to escape the fire.

Again and again, we went over the story and assured the other of our blame, dismissin' the other's claim. Just before daybreak, we finally surrendered to sleep. The nature of the circumstances provided me with a disturbin' buzz of energy, promptin' me to carry on. I knew that returnin' to Fall River was of the utmost importance, but I found myself to be unstable and in helpless need of prayer.

Followin' a full day and night of driftin' between my sanctuary and into the bitter surroundin's of where my mother was no more, I knew that it was not a time for idleness. Although the Blakes and Abigail urged me to stay longer, I dismissed their pleas. I saw no purpose in dwellin' in a place of desertion and sorrow. It was my solemn duty to leave.

It was absurd to think that I could remember all that Mrs. Porter asked me to relay to her daughters, but I assured her that I would not forget a word. Bein' tenderly attached, I found it in my best interest to refrain from lookin' into my sister's eyes. In addition to her gravely broken state from the fire, there was the woeful condition of her bein' with child.

After a tearful goodbye and the rejection of any and all emotion, Moses took me to the train station, where I no longer feared gettin' on the wrong train. I could travel anywhere, knowin' that whatever transpired would work out. Much to my dismay, I was eager to board the train.

It was a bright day, the kind of day that typically reminded me of how grateful I was to be in it. The slight breeze was busy erasin' earlier signs of the torrential rains that accompanied our tears when we buried our mother. When the sun warmed my face, I stopped a smile from risin' up to my lips. Perhaps it was too soon to show anything but unrelentin' grief.

I took notice of the green pastures tucked into the slopin' mountainside. I was wise enough to pull my cape completely over my face before even a hint of the remains of our farmhouse came into view.

When it was safe, I looked towards the cemetery. "Moses, will you please stop?"

He pulled back on the reins, slowin' down the cart. "At the cemetery?"

"Yes."

"Well, I s'pose we could stop, but not for long. You have a train to catch."

He drove the cart up the hill towards the fresh grave. I reached behind me and fetched my case.

"Whatcha' got there?" he asked.

There was no need to answer when he saw my cornet. I blew into the mouthpiece to warm it up a bit.

"I won't be long," I said while hoppin' down from the cart.

Undeterred by the risk of hurryin' over the wildly uneven ground, I made my way past the poor people's graves and over to where my parents were laid to rest. Drawin' a deep breath was more difficult than anticipated. I realized that it may have been hopeless to play a note under such conditions. I was unable to move until I heard a faint rustlin' comin' from within the pine grove. I saw the vague silhouette of a woman. I gasped when she parted the branches. It was the old Indian woman who roamed about town. We held our gaze while my breathin' slowed, and I gathered my senses. She gave a nod, and with my eyes closed, I played "Home Sweet Home."

The first note was shaky, almost apologetic. I was sure that I would sink beneath it. I took another gulp of air, and with a much-divided heart, I played. I must confess that I had never played for such a vast and diverse audience—on both sides of the fence—it mattered not that they were, in fact, dead. I knew that Mother and Papa heard the sweetness of my notes as they spilled from the bell of my horn.

A shiny black crow ruffled its feathers and looked down from its perch—a long jagged branch—above where the old Indian woman stood just moments before. I strained to see her, but she was gone.

When I returned to the cart, Moses quickly turned away so that I would not see that he had shed a tear.

CHAPTER 13

Bess
September 7, 1872
Fall River

THE SUNLIGHT POURED in through the window, bringing about radiance without casting a glare on the music. I contemplated practicing scales, but I skipped straight to Bach's Preludes. The thought of Mr. Todorov scowling and crossing his arms made me giggle. Not that I enjoyed his protests, but because I craved his guidance.

"It's nice to hear you play," Mother said. "It certainly didn't take long."

I didn't answer. For there was no need. I continued to play, focusing on a passage that I had yet to get under my fingertips. I longed to believe that I could thrive if I looked inward rather than seeking comfort from external sources.

"Would you like some breakfast?" Mother asked.

I played louder. I wondered if the day would ever come when she would just be and not try to manage every situation.

"Tempy baked a lovely blueberry cake that I'm sure you will relish," she said.

I stopped. "Mother, do you mind if I play through this piece once without interruption? Then I'm confident that I will have whipped up enough of an appetite to devour some cake."

She walked away, talking under her breath. She meant well, but I couldn't concentrate with her hovering around like a bee to a flower. Her fretful ways usually left me feeling unanchored. I regretted pushing back, but I knew of no other way. I wanted to go after her and sit and eat blueberry cake and sip tea, but the conversation would undoubtedly consist of the usual fussing and asking countless questions. My sharp tongue often left us both in a state of regret and me of deep unworthiness.

I tried to focus on the music. I failed, and the fault was my own. I knew better than to try to do anything before sharing breakfast tea with my parents. Laying aside my frustrations, I got up from the piano and pulled back the curtain.

Sitting by the garden wall, were a couple of tramps, probably brothers. The older one, a golden-haired man of rugged physique, was doing all of the talking. He was quite handsome for an ill-bred street urchin and too young to be a father. They were sharing food. I pitied those like him who would never delight in reading a book or playing music, let alone partake in a hearty meal or sleep on fine linens.

I stepped away from the window when he looked my way. I could still see him through the curtain, but I was confident that he could not see me. My eyes lingered for another moment before I hurried off to the kitchen where my parents sat across from each other, picking at their cake, sipping tea, and not speaking a word. Father glanced over his spectacles at me and then quickly returned to his newspaper.

"I changed my mind. Fresh blueberry cake sounds delightful, and I'm quite hungry after all," I said. "All is not gloom. I'll be sure to practice even harder than I did before. There is nothing I desire more than to be the finest pianist in Fall River."

Mother, my greatest fan, glowed as if she were already in the front row. Father cleared his throat and rattled his paper, once again, unaware of his transparency and how it no longer mattered.

CHAPTER 14

August
September 7, 1872
Fall River

OF COURSE, I had no way of knowin' the boy's name. But, ever since he took a chance and stole a fish from a street cart, I decided to call him Finn. He was better at stealin' than I ever was, but it was no way to live. Beggin' wasn't much different from stealin'; it was simply a theft of the heart. It was best for us both to earn an honest wage, maybe work at one of the mills. I'd even take him with me and act like an older brother and get him a job too. He wouldn't have heard the doffer's bell, but he could have been a sweeper.

You woulda' thought he was part of the circus the way he stumbled around wearin' two right shoes, held together with butchers twine. He needed a sturdy pair—both a right and a left. I saw a decent pile of shoes in front of a church down the street.

Havin' a few cigarettes to offer in trade wouldn't help. But, I supposed that if I rolled up my sleeves and put out the tin cup one more time, we'd get enough coins to buy a shirt for Finn and maybe even a sausage.

He sat on his crate lookin' through the broken window in the back of a dilapidated shed that we called home. Other than a poorly patched roof, it served us well. The bell tower clocks struck again, and the other folks were wakin' up and slowly makin' their way out into the streets. The millworkers had already been gone for a good hour, startin' in before sun up.

"Come on, Finn," I said. Course, he didn't look up, because he never heard a word I said. So, I went over and tapped him on the shoulder causin' him to whoop like he did.

"Didn't mean to scare you. I don't know about you, but I sure could use somethin' to eat." I put my hand up to my mouth. "And, maybe we can find you some shoes. Ones that fit."

He looked down at his feet and smiled. I reached over and ran my comb through his hair. Again, he whooped.

"Hey! Don't you want to look your best? Maybe we'll find work today."

He smiled and ran his fingers through his hair, makin' it messier than it was before I tried to comb it.

We left the cool shadows of the alley and entered into the warmth of the sunlit street, instantly dodgin' a honey cart and a stream of people who weren't lookin' where they were goin'. I was too hungry to wait, so we went to the place that had three good sized sausages hangin' in the doorway.

No hagglin' with the Portuguese. They weren't ones to make a deal. We settled on the one in the middle—the thickest one. We went up the hill a ways, where the houses were grand, with fountains, big old trees, and nice things that I usually only saw from afar.

We sat together in silence, devourin' the spicy meat, thankful to be in a place where we could draw a fresh breath. The birds twittered about, and fragrant flowers hung over a freshly painted fence. Then, my heart almost stopped beatin'. I never heard anything quite like it before. I mean, there was the organ-grinder and his monkey, but this was somethin' else. I knew that it was a piano, and it was loud and deliberate. Course, Finn kept right on eatin'.

Chapter 15

Sarah
September 7, 1872
Fall River

It was hot. Lint swirled in the air like a dream—an enchanted snowy day— only instead of meltin', it stuck to your skin, clothes, and hair. You didn't try to catch it on your tongue. While standin' amidst this peculiar blizzard, I realized that I had become further removed from home, because usually on days like this, we made snow angels. One was never enough.

I kept on runnin' and tried to ignore that my shoes were drenched from splashin' in the shallow, murky puddles that oozed out from beneath endless rows of tenements.

I gagged at the sight of rotten food and other sour things that were carelessly strewn about. The vile odor strengthened as we crawled deeper into the maze. I tried to keep up my pace while rummagin' through my reticule for my handkerchief.

"Will you please slow down?" I hollered defiantly against the relentless roar of the mills.

I stumbled around the corner and found myself facin' a cluster of outhouses and open sinks. I backed away cautiously, nearly bumpin' into a young girl fillin' up her pail at a pump. Her dress was nothin' more than a collection of scraps held together by a thread that was about to let go. A grungy, tattered ribbon attempted to rest neatly on her strawberry colored hair, which was carelessly chopped, barely reachin' her small shoulders.

The squeakin' stopped when she turned to face me. "They went in there." She nodded in the direction of a narrow gap between the buildin's. "Ya gonna' follow 'em?"

I stared at the outhouses and then at her. "Uh, yes... I am," I said.

Without expression, she started in pumpin' again, and the steady squeakin' resumed.

Rebecca and Mercy did not listen, in fact, they ran faster. I stopped in front of a pile of discarded odds and ends and slowly looked up. Patched linens and threadbare garments hung on pulley lines from open windows, strung between the buildin's, goin' all the way up to the roof and flappin' in the slight breeze.

Meanwhile, the girls entered through an already opened door. I held tight to my bags and followed. Met with an unexpected stench of fried fish, boiled cabbage, peppery soap, smoke, and general foulness, I quickly covered my nose with my handkerchief. It still smelled like home.

A pale, ragged girl of about our age, clearly expectin' to give birth at any time, stood in a doorway with a baby perched on her hip. Behind her was what looked like a common kitchen and dinin' area. I squeezed by her and nodded, but may as well have been invisible, as she remained expressionless, even when her red-faced baby squirmed and started in cryin'.

There was an awful lot of commotion comin' from a darkish nook under a flight of stairs. I gasped and nearly collided with a group of children pitchin' pennies. They barely noticed me and continued to play.

Mercy burst in through a door at the end of the hallway and stood inside with outstretched arms and a smile brighter than a hundred candles. "Welcome to your new home."

"It ain't much, but we make do," Rebecca said, standin' erect with her hands folded at her waist and her eyes dartin' about.

Surprisingly winded and damp with sweat, I stopped abruptly when I detected at least one source of the filth that I had smelled earlier. I scanned the room for any sign of welcome, validation that I had made the right choice.

A single ray of light streamed through a hole in the wall at the end of the hallway. The only window in the room had been nailed shut with boards on the outside. Along with three beds haphazardly shoved in a corner was a long crate stuffed with musty hay and covered with a soiled bedtick. A swarm of flies buzzed around the oily surface of a small desk that sat squarely in the middle of the room. Basic cookin' utensils, a rusty tin coffee pot, a jar of sugar, and a stack of unclean dishes were scattered about on a little pine table. A washtub was turned over, covered by a torn gray cloth with a well-worn Bible in the center of it, lyin' open, and set beside it was a crumpled tobacco pouch. There was a single rocker, much like that of Mother's, beside a small barrel that served as a table with a lamp upon it. Although fragile and a bit queasy, I refrained from sittin' on the nearby chair without a back, fearin' it would collapse beneath me.

Mercy pointed to the bed closest to the worthless window. "This is where you'll be sleepin'," she said. "You can share with Rebecca and me. We washed it up 'specially for you. Cora slept in with us before. She up and left more than a week ago, and we've heard no mention of her. The police came by and took a statement. I'm not worried though. I think that she left with the boy she'd been meetin' for a time. In fact, I believe that they were familiar, but it isn't right to say. She was blacklisted, so it's likely that she won't return. All that matters is that she's gone, and should she come back, she'll have to make other arrangements. It's your bed now. I mean, we'll share it of course."

"You don't need to go into such great detail," Rebecca said.

"Never mind," Mercy said. "Let's put your things away."

She pulled back a sooty patched curtain, revealin' a stack of three trunks with mine bein' on top. "Take your time. You must be so tired from all that travelin' and the emotional toll of losin' your mother. As you recall, it wasn't long ago when Father passed."

The combination of putrid scents and the lack of decent light emphasized that it felt more like a grave than a home.

"I don't know how I feel. Everything happened so quickly. Someday, I may finally realize it all," I said.

Rebecca looked down at her feet. "We're in a bit of trouble," she said.

"What trouble?" I asked.

"We left the spinnin' room to bring you here. When we met you before, it was on Sunday, so it was of no consequence," she said. "Mr. Aldrich gets annoyed, and when I asked to leave, he said no. He reminded me that it was up to our agent, Mr. Colby, to meet you, but we just had to be here. I tried to explain that your mother died and that an agent would never do, but he was unaffected. So, when he was out of sight, we left—a dreadful decision—but I'm prepared to beg for forgiveness. Of course, we knew that our absence would be detected at once, but our loyalty to you left us no choice. And besides, we promised Mother that we'd be here. We'll accept the punishment, which will include a loss of pay. He's more even-tempered than the other overseers, and I'm confident that he won't dismiss us."

Unable to find a word to reply to this uninvited confirmation of worriment and guilt swellin' up in my chest, I stood in morbid silence. There was no room for self-loathin'. Bein' called away by the death of my mother was enough.

"Generally, we have very good attendance. I stayed with Mercy one day last winter when she was sick with the fever, and we returned to the spinnin' room the next day, even though she was still burnin' up. It's not the loss of wages that's a burden, but the shame and tongue lashin' in front of the others. We don't ask for favors and have earned Mr. Aldrich's praises."

She fumbled with the buttons on her unwashed blouse. "Also, we're required to work harder when we go afoul. I was waitin' for my chance to leave the spinnin' frame, to start trainin' to be a drawin'-in girl, but now I'll have to wait." She bit her fingernail and glanced at the door. "No worries."

"Well, you should go back right away. It's early, and there are still a few good hours left in the day," I said.

The baby's wailin' had become much too loud and seemed to be comin' from an adjoinin' room. I peeked through a crack in the wall that was so wide, I could see clear into the next room. Piles of clothin' were flung about, and more mattresses jammed even closer together than the ones in our room. There was a broken chair beside a partially boarded up window, affordin' much-needed light. I leaned in to get a better look when my eyes met with those of another. I gasped, forgettin' where we were in our conversation.

"Don't you agree?" Mercy asked.

"I'm sorry," I said. "What?"

"All that matters is that we stay together at work and in our quarters, makin' it as cozy and safe as can be," Mercy said.

"I'm all for it," I said. "Now go back to work before more comes of it. I'll get settled—"

I froze at the sound of a hearty fit of laughter comin' from outside the doorway.

"Mary!"

I rushed over and embraced her. Although I had known the Porter girls for as far back as I could remember, Mary was more like the longtime friend that I yearned for.

"I thought it was you that I heard," she said.

"What are you doin' here?" I asked.

"I spoke with an agent and signed up for Granite Mill. I decided to give it a go." She pulled a tobacco pouch from her pocket.

"I start Monday. I hoped to see ya again, but there weren't no sign of ya when I got off the train. Seems we'll be together after all," she said.

"I'm meetin' with a Granite Mill agent, too," I said, no longer carin' that she was the rough girl on the train who beat the men in a real poker game and was about to roll a cigarette.

Rebecca's bottom lip quivered. "So you have a friend here besides us?"

"It's quite remarkable. I met Mary at the train station in Manchester, and we were together for the rest of the journey. When we arrived at Fall River, we were separated. I was in a state, went back home, and never knew what happened to her."

"Ya did what?" Mary asked.

I hesitated as Rebecca headed for the door. She glared at Mercy, who unlike herself, was eager to hear what the new girl had to say.

"We have to get back," Rebecca said. "We're already in a tangle, a world of humiliation, and who knows what other punishment will befall us. We'll hear their stories tonight, Mercy, providin' we can keep our eyes open."

The door slammed behind them, and they hurried away, clompin' down all of those steps, interruptin' the cries of the baby, but only as long as it took for them to pass by. Rebecca's naggin' voice quickly faded into the ragin' din of heavy machinery and the shouts of men brawlin' outside.

Mary's hair was pulled back into a single, neat braid, and she looked as if she may have had a bath since I last saw her. She was a sight with her faded blanket draped over one shoulder, a patched, draggled skirt, and her toes stickin' out of the holes in her stockin's.

"Why did ya go home?" she asked.

I searched for a chair, forgettin' for a moment that this new place did not afford the things at home that we simply took for granted. I pulled a quilt from the bed and spread it out on the floor. We sat in between stacks of boxes and an array of rags, eatin' the rest of the apple bread that Mrs. Blake gave me for the trip. I didn't fuss or even think of quotin' Mother when Mary smoked a cigarette.

I told her about the fire and of Mother's death, sorrowfully remindin' her of what she had lost. My pain was raw and fresh, while hers was merely a way of life. Hardship was her loyal companion. Bein' newly orphaned, I had much to learn from this girl, whose memories of her own mother had been stolen away by time.

After Mary left, it was time to settle in. I realized that in my haste, I was possibly runnin' away from regret. I dismissed the idea that I had not even settled in, and I was homesick. Everything happened at once. I knew that if I slowed down, I would have been keenly aware of the wretched condition of the room and that the constant clatter and drone of the mills would have caused my heart to faint.

I rummaged through various bundles of rags, rusted tin cans with broken hinges, and other waste. I considered usin' a shelf beneath the boarded-up window that offered hope in the middle of the hodgepodge. I summoned the courage to look beneath a yellowed newspaper, where tiny flies circled around two spoiled tomatoes and a questionable apple. I quickly wrapped them up in the paper and wandered in a full circle, searchin' for a place to discard them. Everything was either broken, rotten, or filthy. It was impossible to know what to do.

Our home was in order. Mother had no patience for clutter. I gasped at the thought of her charred remains and our beloved farm. All I wanted to do was flee from all that had happened. I slid down onto the floor and watched my chest rise and fall. I closed my eyes, findin' my way to that hidden door inside, where I felt complete and where calmness resided.

I only wanted one spot where I could place my things. After all of that, I decided that it was best to keep my possessions in my trunk and bandbox.

For several minutes, I stood in the middle of the room with my leather case tucked under my arm. I noticed a gap—a loose board—in the wall. After brushin' away the dirt and cobwebs, I wiggled it free. My case fit inside that wall perfectly, and I was able to replace the board to keep it concealed. Ignorin' my tired body, I found a well-used broom and brushed up the place.

The bells from a nearby tower rang out, rattlin' every part of me, penetratin' the walls of my emptiness. It wasn't time to stop. If I failed to continue movin' about and keep a busy mind, I would surely falter.

I went over to the wall and retrieved my case. The medley of children's laughter, shoutin' women, boorish men in the alley, and the howl of the mills, assured me that I would go unnoticed. I could not attract even the slightest bit attention.

I grabbed one of the least spoiled rags from a pile, and with cornet in hand, left the room. I lingered at the bottom step of this unfamiliar place, listenin' for signs of life. It was dark except for a thin line of sunlight streamin' in through a window from above. I made my way to it. There before me was an attic alcove that, like everything else, was cluttered with offensive waste.

I cleared away the random debris to uncover a dirty, yet functional, chair. After cleanin' it up, I set it by a small window, caked with a layer of fine, brown dust. All it took was a good scrub, and the room exploded with new light.

Droplets of sweat gathered on my brow as I pondered the risk of tryin' to open the window. In the name of secrecy, I chose to endure the heat.

My pulse raced as I stuffed a rag into the bell of my horn. I paused. A vision of my parents' graves filled my head. *Will this broken heart live to play another note?*

The mouthpiece felt cool against my lips. I hesitated long enough to tame the thoughts that scurried about, refusin' to allow them to be the enemy of my soul.

Although bittersweet, and as muffled as it sounded with a rag crammed into the bell, playin' my horn was a relief. I started warmin' up, all the while decidin' which song would be the most appropriate for such an occasion. After all, it was to be the first song in my secret room—an odd contrast between Ossipee and Fall River. *How well will I hide my passion?*

I was grateful for the whir of spindles that rang out mercilessly from the streets below. Combined with the undefinable, cheerless sounds that filled the tenement, it became a coarse ballad that cloaked me in safety.

The sun disappeared behind the loomin', black chimneys—the mountains of my new landscape. I had quickly warmed up to the idea of my escape into the attic rafters. I played the sweet strains of "The Ashgrove," one of Mother's favorite songs, a passageway for the tears that allowed me to weep bitterly and finally surrender.

Chapter 16

August
September 8, 1872

I FELT HER smile. There was no need to see it. Knowin' was enough. She peeked out from behind her blue cape. I never knew anyone with eyes as green as hers. She hugged me and whispered somethin'.

"What?" I asked.

She spoke again, but it was unclear. I almost knew what she said. I looked in the direction of the footsteps comin' up from behind. Why did I always turn away? When I spun back around, she was gone. Tears filled my eyes. I didn't know which direction she went in, or how she got there to begin with. She was gone.

Covered in sweat, I bolted upright. It took a few minutes to shake off that dream of mine and remember where I was. I studied the pile of discarded clothes that I used to make a bed for Finn, and he wasn't in it. I scrambled to my feet and looked outside.

Sunday mornin's were different from the other days. The mill folks that usually marched down the streets, lookin' straight ahead with their vacant eyes while holdin' onto their dinner pails, were home doin' chores and gettin' ready for church. Due to sheer exhaustion and knowin' what lie ahead, their only day of leisure lacked appeal.

I rifled through our rag piles until I found my other shoe and then ran my comb through my hair. I thought of Finn runnin' off. He didn't have a chance on his own. He'd end up wanderin' 'til they took him back to where he came from, put him in reform school, or on a westbound train to be placed out. I wouldn't wish any of those things on anyone, 'specially Finn. They'd see that he was deaf and throw him away.

We were told that they were doin' us a favor, placin' us out and all, but most of those families just needed help workin' and buildin' up their land and farms. When they were done, if the placed outs hadn't already fled, they were tossed out with nothin' to show for their hard work 'cept for blisters and a broken spirit. I was gonna see to it that Finn had better odds.

When I looked back on it, there was no question that I did the right thing. For nearly two hours, I was with dozens of others on that platform at the train station in Ohio, but I felt alone. The whole time, those folks prodded and poked at us, tryin' to see which one of us boys would work the hardest, be the best bargain. Sure, there was some lookin' to adopt, but it was mainly about the labor.

At first, when I wasn't so strong, the folks who met the train passed me by and went for the others and a few of the girls who would be good for housekeepin'. When I asked the reverend why there weren't many girls bein' placed out, he told me that by the time he got to them, they were beyond redemption. When I saw them lil' wanderers—girls or even someone like Finn—I wondered if redemption was possible and how I coulda' helped.

After goin' up and down the line a few times and askin' a lot of questions, Mr. and Mrs. Brown said that they wanted to take me to their home for a picnic, to get to know me. Reverend Phillips kept track of everything. He scribbled somethin' next to my name and sent me off with the Browns. "Now don't you go takin' off again, August. Next time you do, you'll end up back at the asylum, the one you don't like," he said.

I turned my attention towards the couple who was sizin' me up. Mrs. Brown seemed decent, yet generally worn out, with her well-dimpled face and pleasin' smile. Mr. Brown didn't have a look of kindness anywhere to be found. The lines of worry and disapproval were carved deeply into his forehead and around his small dark eyes. Unlike the others, he didn't even pretend to be a pleasant sort in front of the reverend.

I lost my footin' when he grabbed me by the back of my shirt collar and dragged me off to their crude cart. I felt the reverend's eyes on me and pictured him checkin' over that list of his. No one ever said a word. They just loaded up the trains and posted those signs—*Charity Begins at Home*—and did it all over again.

Once we got to their place and no one was lookin', Mrs. Brown took charge. "Go over there and pick up that saw and start cuttin'."

I studied the small pile of boards stacked up and headed for the sawhorse. Mr. Brown shoved me from behind. "You heard her, son."

I purposely slowed down and shrugged him off. He was much bigger than me, but it never stopped me from fightin'. When I was little, I was a dirty fighter—quick and mean. I'd come up with somethin' unexpected, like a good claw on the face, and then I'd run like hell. I'd rather fight and lose than take any guff from the likes of those folks.

Ready for the unthinkable, should the need arise, I picked up the saw and glared at him. "Do you want them to be the same length as the others?" I asked.

He knew. He knew that I was prepared to take him on, and I think that he liked it. "Yes, we're usin' these boards to build a shed."

I wailed on that saw. I cut so fast and precise that I even surprised myself. I stacked them boards in a neat pile and was almost sorry when he told me that I could stop. It was that old twisted thing that happens when you're stranded on the wretched side of life.

My thoughts returned to Finn. Which would be worse, reform school, the trains and bein' placed out, or the streets? I remembered New York and Smitty, and how he would use Finn's deafness to make a profit. He'd put him out there on the street and yell out to the crowds about how this boy, a mere child, was a victim of an evil factory accident that left him deaf, and he'd ask how any decent man or woman could walk by without takin' pity on him. Then, at the end of the day, after a half a bowl of thin broth with the only protein comin' from a long-dead cockroach, Smitty would beat him. He'd take away his money, and show him to his narrow canvas cot, strung up between the rough beams alongside the other boys, where he hoped to live to see another day.

Damn him. Damn Finn for runnin' off. How could he not have appreciated that I was there to help deliver him from a violent end? I kicked at a crumpled paper and headed down the street, stoppin' to pick up a half spent cigarette. I straightened it out, lit it, and startin' in coughin' immediately.

Swarms of people filled the streets, makin' their way to church. They huddled together in tired groups, driven by common needs and bound by their afflictions. I continued walkin' and puffin' on that cigarette when I felt a tuggin' on my arm. I turned around, and there was Finn, all pleased with himself, carryin' a loaf of bread and a small brick of cheese.

"Where have you been?" I pulled him aside, out of the flow of people. "I've been lookin' for you. I thought somethin' happened. Don't you have any respect?"

He raised his eyebrows, pushed the bread towards me, and raced off. His newly torn shirt exposed familiar letters stitched under the collar, typical attire for the children's homes. I grabbed his elbow and led him up the hill towards the nice houses. The next thing was to get him a new shirt so that the officials wouldn't spot him. Maybe he did have folks after all, and they were inmates in the almshouse. Either way, I was gonna help us both find somethin' better.

"Let's sit here. I need to talk to you, Finn." We sat in the shade of that thick old tree by the house of music.

"If you get caught stealin' or just wanderin' the streets, they'll take you away. I don't know if you've already been in any of these places, but you don't need to end up—"

"—No exceptions!" A woman, more interested in the feather in her hat than a response from the person she was shoutin' at, strutted towards a first-rate pleasure carriage.

I grabbed Finn, and we ducked behind some tall orange flowers. A smartly dressed, colored driver helped the couple into the carriage. It seemed that no one spotted us, but we waited 'til they were well out of sight before sittin' up straight again.

I was about to resume my talk with Finn when that piano music started. It was loud and fast. I had no choice but to listen.

We stayed right there in the mornin' sun, and although the bread was stale, we ate it up in no time, savin' the cheese for last. The birds had joined in singin' with the piano, and the flowers were bright and fragrant. I had to convince myself that it was time to go back down the hill and into the filthy streets where we belonged.

"Finn, it's time to go now. We're very lucky to be able to take a short walk up this hill and find such a pretty spot," I said.

He had his back to me and was inspectin' a rock. He smiled and put it in his pocket. I tried to imagine what it would be like without hearin' music, birds, and the tower bell. I knew that if I let him out of my sight, he would get into trouble. I was sure that he fled from the children's home or the almshouse. There was a reason for everything. I promised myself that I would keep him safe.

I tapped him on the shoulder and pointed down the hill. "Time to go," I said.

We walked off together, Finn in his over-sized shoes and me with my ideas about how we would go to the mill the next day and set out for an honest wage.

The crowds thickened as we approached the mills, tenements, and busy streets. A tiny old woman, with a gently lined face, sang out sweetly, "Apples! Apples for sale! Come and get your sweet apple right here!"

Finn stopped and stared at her with his face all lit up. He tugged at my sleeve.

"Not now. We can't get an apple now. We just ate," I said.

"The boy wants an apple. You should get him an apple," the woman said.

"We had a hearty breakfast. He can wait," I said.

"Why don't you buy him an apple for later?"

"We'll come back and buy an apple when we have the money," I said, turnin' away from her and pullin' Finn along with me.

It was easy to spot the pickpockets and little thieves that worked in pairs. I prayed, in case God was listenin', askin' Him to help me avoid the temptation to steal or to roll up my sleeves and toss out my hat. By the time we got to the place where I had seen the pile of shoes, there were only a few left, and they didn't match. The shopkeeper told me that to get shoes there, we had to arrive early, and even then, there was no guarantee.

I stepped into a narrow alleyway, where they sold shirts out of the back of a store. There were piles of them tied together next to a woman who was sittin' on a crate with two young children hangin' off of her.

"You don't want to buy them shirts. They was taken right off the dead. People who died from yellow fever," she said.

"How do you know that?" I asked.

"That's what they do in here. They buy things that no one else would touch, and they mend them and sell them, makin' a good profit," she said.

The door opened, and a husky man walked over and grabbed her by the arm. The children toppled to the ground. "I tole you not to talk to strangers and to stop tellin' 'em things."

"It's the truth. You're goin' to Hell for this. If you stop, there's still time to get into Heaven," she said while starin' him down.

I took Finn by the hand and headed back out into the streets in search of somethin' else. It got hotter as the day wore on. I couldn't help myself, rolled up my sleeves, and sat down. I patted the ground beside me, and Finn came right over and joined me.

I tossed my hat out in front of me with a few coins in it. "Please help us. Please help. I was burnt in a factory fire, and I'm takin' care of my deaf brother. Can you spare a cent or two?"

Folks had the usual quizzical look about them and came in closer to examine the horrid scars that covered my arms. While some walked away, I collected a few pennies and a two-cent piece in my hat. One man stopped and said a prayer, and a young tramp ran up and tried to steal my hat. By the end of the day, we were able to get Finn a shirt, not one from a dead person, but from a woman who sold mended garments from a wheelbarrow. I also had enough money to buy a new black clay pipe, and we found the apple lady and bought us each an apple for later.

We were on our way back to the shed when a middle-aged man walked straight into my path. When I tried to walk around him, he blocked me again. I wasn't one for a fight, but it seemed we were headed there for no good reason.

"Get outta' my way—"

"—I saw ya sittin' there beggin'," he said.

"What's it to ya?"

"I'm a lamplighter."

"And…"

"I need a few hands." He wiped his brow with a rag.

"What does that have to do with me? With us?"

"Are ya interested in a job, or do ya wanna beg for ya suppah?"

"Can both of us do it?"

"Yep, I could use both you and ya brotha'," he said.

Finn was busy emptyin' all the rocks out of his pocket and linin' them up on the ground. I wanted to work every day and not have to sell cigarettes or beg. I didn't like it in the mills but was ready to go back and try again. After Lowell, I shoulda' known that it wasn't for me, but I had to do somethin'.

"You need us every night?"

"Every night unless the moon is lightin' up the sky," he said.

"What do we have to do?" I asked.

"Follow me. I'll show you where the ladders are kept, and you can meet the boss. I'll put your names on the list at the Street Department, and we'll talk about your route and how it's done," he said, "Name's Francis, Francis Murphy." He extended his hand.

I took right ahold of it and shook hard. It wasn't every day that someone came to me for somethin' good. "I'm August Wood, and this is my brother, Finn. He doesn't talk or anything. He's been deaf since the day he was born. He's smart and knows what to do, and I'll keep an eye on him."

"As long as he can carry a ladder and go from one lamp to the next, it doesn't matter."

CHAPTER 17

Bess
September 8, 1872

Even the birds were ecstatic. It was not my imagination; there were far more chirpers than usual and singing forte at that. I wanted to celebrate, as I did not have to primp and preen. No rushing about with Mother at my heels and Father pacing and looking at his timepiece with a predictable frown.

I would not have been required to sit up straight in a dreadful pew, pressed shoulder to shoulder between my parents while listening to a well-intentioned reverend lift up the lowly by promoting temperance—the virtue of good health and vigor. I was spared from the reading of the scriptures, which I did enjoy if read by one who shows appropriate passion and inflection when speaking. I supposed that it was unfair to not even give him a chance, but I had endured many monotonous readings. Why would this have been any different?

However, I did wonder about the missed opportunity to sing hymns with a new congregation. I was quite curious about the organist and if they even had a choir, although I knew that it would pale in comparison to our lovely church in Boston. There was no point in attending church at all if there was no music. Churches were built for music.

Thankful that Father decided to have mesh screens installed, I sat by the open window. The air was crisp and sweet, and the canopy of sun-filtered leaves from the oak tree provided an abundant veil. I questioned the need to go to a particular building to connect with God, requiring a man in a black frock to be the messenger. My bond with the Divine was resilient and ongoing, as I was fulfilling my duty as an instrument of God.

Even my less than perfect music was the voice of the angels. We would be better off if we understood our own power. When I expressed these ideas to Mother, she became flustered and left the room. When I mentioned them to Father, he just looked at me as if I were speaking in a foreign tongue, before finally telling me that I was out of line. Tempy, on the other hand, was the one who consistently pointed out that my music was a creation of God. *You are His instrument. Your songs are from the angels. Never stop, child.*

The sound of Tempy humming one of her old spiritual songs, filled the hallway, begging me to follow. I was much absorbed in the familiar melodies that she sang as far back as my time in the cradle and whenever I felt poorly. I stopped in the doorway and watched her clean the candlesticks. She was always up at least two hours before the rest of us, claiming that it was necessary to do her dirtiest work without interruption. After she was finished with those chores, she would change into a fresh white linen apron, brush any dust from her hair and tidy up her locks, to appear, as she would say, respectable.

"Look at what came in with the mornin' sunshine," she said.

"Don't stop humming. It sets the tone for the morning. Please, carry on," I said.

She smiled in a way that only she could smile, in a way that nestled into my heart. "I'm sure you're hungry. I can't hum and sing all day," she said.

"You just want me to beg," I said.

We shared in our laughter, until she stood up, wincing and placing her hand upon the pain that had settled into her back. She began humming again while preparing a breakfast of fresh blackberries and cream, buttered toast, sharp cheese, and tea.

I sat at the dining room table with Mother and Father, allowing Tempy's quiet melody to be a solo that rose over and above their small talk.

"I know that I've been giving you time away from our usual activities while we get settled in," Mother said. "I want you to be comfortable in your new surroundings. So, staying home from church is only going to happen this once."

Father looked up for a brief moment, just enough to pretend that he was part of it all, before returning to his stack of papers.

"I understand. I wish to be ready for my new teacher. I want to impress him, which should not be hard in this place," I said, breaking my rule of not being drizzly and disappointing.

"You must give him a try—"

"—I know, I know," I said, ignoring Tempy's expected look of disapproval.

I moseyed into the parlor and rifled through a box of music. My first piano lesson was scheduled for the following Wednesday. A certain Mr. Carver was coming by. There was no need for me to leave the house, for there was no conservatory in Fall River. I made a promise to myself, Tempy, and to God, that I would give this man a chance, that I would give Fall River a chance. However, it was not easy when I missed Mr. Todorov horribly every day.

As I was about to select my etudes, I detected movement by the garden wall. I glanced out the window, and there was the brother duo, sitting in what was becoming a favorite spot. I sat down, and once again, ignored the etudes and started in playing notes that needed to escape. They screamed from my fingers and onto the keys without my approval and with little thought. My unseen guide whispered for me to keep on going. Stopping was not an option.

CHAPTER 18

Sarah
September 8, 1872

I AWOKE TO the sound of a shriekin' rooster. *What was Pearl doin' here?* I pushed Mercy's arm off of my chest and listened carefully. Surely, it had to have been a dream. The rooster crowed again. I thought of our own rooster and how he crowed exactly one-second before the sun appeared, no earlier, no later.

The others barely stirred as the bell tolled seven times. I looked around the room at the empty lunch pails and clothin' draped over fragments of furniture and a cracked washtub. My stomach rumbled. Other than the leftover cake that I had shared with Mary the day before, I had not eaten. The other girls came home the previous night and had little, if anything, to say to me. One friendly girl, Norah, offered me some sort of meat pie, but my insides, agitated and distraught from all that had transpired, rejected the idea.

Ruby, a slim girl with kinky red hair, sat on the floor right in the middle of the room, rolled a cigarette and drank rum straight from the jug. She started in swearin' and complainin' until Addy, the pretty one, interrupted her.

Poor Ruby, her arms were badly scarred from an accident that happened some months prior in the mule room. Apparently, the sleeve of her blouse got caught in some gears, but she escaped possible amputation and a near-fatal tragedy when a man was able to stop the machinery and pull her arm out in time. She suffered deep lacerations and, unfortunately, was beaten for her sloppiness and sent home.

It was clear that Addy was the oldest and seemed to be in charge of everyone. Her shiny black hair, blue eyes, and fair skin were set off by rosy cheeks. She reminded everyone that hollerin' and swearin' were prohibited after nine o'clock. Until then, she made sure to do both at every opportunity.

Clara was the sickly one. She was about my age, with pale blonde hair, gray eyes, and a sorrowful face. She had many scars around her hairline and behind her ear because, accordin' to Mercy, she suffered from a horrible accident a few years earlier.

It is said that when she was a doffer, she got her hair caught in the back shaft and was pulled into the machinery. Although the speeder was shut down quickly, it required a great deal of time to extricate her hair and parts of her scalp, which were tangled up in the mess. She was taken home where the mill doctor and her lovin' mother tended to her wounds.

Rebecca said that in some places, her brain was exposed and had she not been cared for by a particular doctor, would have perished from such a terrible injury. It took many months for her physical wounds to heal, however, the fear lived on and could be seen in her eyes.

I thought that I might have liked Norah the best. She had a noticeable light about her when she smiled and was the only one who acted courteously. She sat in the rocker, lit the lamp and read, only lookin' up when one of the others swore, and then she rolled her eyes and returned to her book.

Clemmie was the last to trail in. Much like Clara, she was sad and quiet, with no visible signs of wounds, because hers were of the spirit. Bein' the youngest of us all, and hitched together by one button, she stood before me. How could I have not embraced her? I learned that her father was stabbed to death two years before durin' a violent disturbance involvin' discontented millworkers, and her mother and brother succumbed to cholera. At one time, they all lived and worked together, but only she remained. In spite of her much-neglected state, she was quite beautiful with her warm brown eyes and thick, curly hair.

A silent cloud of melancholia hung over us. Because they left the mill without notice, Mercy and Rebecca dissolved into an outpourin' of tears, exchangin' their previous happiness for woe and regret. They were told that if they did it again, they would be blacklisted. They had already received a cut in pay, and Rebecca was sent to another room to work, away from Mercy and the others. I tried to console them both, but I had no way of knowin' what to say since it was my fault.

So, that mornin', after the rooster crowed and the bell rang, one by one, the girls awakened. The heat had already started to rise, but I still donned my cape and followed Ruby, Mercy, and Norah down the stairs, towards the bangin' outhouse doors and squeaky pumps. Folks either stood in line for a turn in an outhouse or held onto a bucket, waitin' for the next available sink.

I quickly learned not to look anyone in the eye. People moved about slowly as if there were no thought involved. The stench had risen to heights I could not comprehend, nor would ever want to. As the line moved, we stepped over stagnant pools of indescribable slop.

The line was movin' along faster when Norah turned to me with a smile. "Look! There's the milk cart. After we wash up, let's go to the market and fetch some." She disappeared into an open outhouse, not waitin' for a response.

I flinched when the door slammed. I envisioned my sister sittin' on the milkin' stool, singin' one of her silly songs to our beloved cow Lizzie while I collected the eggs. I ignored the foul odor that may have prevented me from imaginin' a breakfast of fresh milk along with some of Mother's eggs and bacon from our own pigs. I looked up to see a small, older woman wearin' a simple gingham smock. She was the only soul to acknowledge my presence. She looked me in the eye and smiled, revealin' one lonely tooth in the middle of her head. Her sparse gray hair swirled around her face like wild ivy, flowin' slightly in the damp mornin' air. She made it a point to hold the door open for me.

"Thank you," I said.

It happened very quickly. I spun around and vomited in the hole. I closed my eyes, and a river of hot tears streamed down my face. Leanin' against the door, I wiped my mouth with the sleeve of my cape. *There is no hope here, no hope in an outhouse. There never is. Pull yourself together.*

The bangin' of doors got louder. I had no choice but to make sure that I was actually breathin'. My cape still smelled like home, which was only comfortin' for a brief moment until I remembered that home was just a memory and not a place where I could return.

I jumped when someone banged on the door. "Watcha' doin' in there?"

I could not determine if it was a voice that I knew or not. There were so many people in one place, so many girls and women of all ages, it was impossible to know if it was one of my new roommates.

I managed to squat down without touchin' the wet, stained plank of wood while thinkin' about usin' the outhouses before the crowds came, before the ruckus. How could I have ever complained about anything from home? Yes, it was often cold and filled with spiders, but it was not vile. It was private. There was never someone hollerin' on the other side of the door.

I started to hurry while fixin' my sackcloth, but I stopped. I refused to be rushed. I had waited in line for a very long time, inhalin' a putrid odor that I could never describe. I wouldn't allow anyone to pressure me. I flung my cape over my shoulders and stepped outside, findin' myself face to face with Ruby.

"What the hell took ya so long? We ain't got all day," she said.

"Don't listen to her. Take all the time ya want," Mary said from a ways back in the line.

"Mary!" I dashed over to her.

"How was ya first night? Ya ready for church?" she asked.

"I might wait until next week. I'm still gettin' things sorted," I said. "Are you goin'?"

She laughed loudly as she always did. "Course I ain't goin'. Why would I start that now?"

"Well, I thought that you might want to go to church. Most folks do, and I read that it is expected of us to find a church of our likin' and that we should attend," I said.

"I'll spend my day off of work the way I see fit. I can talk to God anytime I want," she said.

"Well, we're goin' to the market and—"

The door of the next available outhouse flew open, and she raced up the steps without another word.

The lines dwindled, and fewer people gathered around the sinks. The puddles grew from the drippin' spouts and mixed in with the street garbage. I found an available sink and splashed tepid water on my face, finishin' up with a long drink. I knew that it would not be as clear and fresh as the water from the mountain streams at home, but it was water, and I was in much need of it.

Feelin' somewhat refreshed, I returned to our buildin'. There was a large crowd in the common kitchen. They were discussin' what they would have for breakfast, who would cook, and who would go to the market. Everyone shouted as they did most of the time. Even when the mill machines were not in use, there was a hummin' in my ears. The bell rang every hour so that we always knew the time. There was no quiet, no silent spaces where I could retreat.

I made my way up the creaky stairs and into our room, where Clara was still layin' upon her straw pallet. The girls came and went, payin' her no mind. It seemed that other than food and goin' to church, nothin' else mattered at all.

I stood over Clara. Her skin was so pale that I could see her veins. I imagined that she would have been a lovely girl had she not become disfigured and frightened from the accident. Even in sleep, her brow was furrowed.

Suddenly her eyes popped open, and she sat up with a gasp. "I must get dressed and go to church." She scrambled out of her crate and left the room.

"Don't mind her. She's always like that," Addy said. "The girls either go to the Methodist Church, Freewill Baptist, or St Mary's. You can make up your own mind."

Like so many others here, she didn't wait for an answer. I decided to tidy up myself and my things and be ready for the next day—my first day at Granite Mill. I was excited to finally be workin' for a wage.

After a short walk to pick up the milk, a loaf of crusted bread, and a thick chunk of aged cheddar cheese, we returned home and had our breakfast with a special, pungent tea that I had never tried before.

All at once, the streets filled up, only this time the people were more handsomely dressed, headin' for their various churches. I watched out the window as they moved together with occasional, smaller tributaries breakin' off in different directions.

When it seemed safe, and there was no sign of Mary, I fetched my cornet and went to my secret attic alcove. It was by far the hottest day, but I didn't mind. I was ready to sit, to pour forth my soul, as then more than ever, I was in need of it.

Chapter 19

Sarah
September 9, 1872

The first mornin' bell shattered my already troubled slumber, chasin' away a vague dream of my sister and me. I tried to hold onto it but was further distracted by the high-pitched crow of the neighborhood rooster that came about too late, when it no longer mattered. His determination summoned an unexpected smile. He could have learned a lot from the roosters back home.

The girls tumbled out of bed, not speakin' a word as they rummaged through piles of clothin'. Mercy and Norah headed straight for the outhouses. I grabbed a bucket for washin' and caught up to them. I looked out over the yard and stopped. The lines were even longer than the day before.

"Don't worry," Norah said, "it goes by quickly on workdays."

After goin' about my business, I went straight to a free sink, filled the bucket halfway, and hurried back to our tenement. I passed by many grim and expressionless girls on the stairs and vowed never to become like them.

"There is water here if anyone wishes to bathe," I said.

"We don't have time for that, Sarah. You need to hurry, or you risk bein' late for the second bell," Mercy said while pullin' her dress over her head.

The words echoed in my head. *No time for washin'?* I hurried and got dressed, suddenly worried that I would be left behind to find my own way.

Entombed in anxious silence, the girls gathered their dinner pails, which they had prepared the night before. Although I had savin's tucked away, I was grateful that the girl before me had left her well-used pail behind. Rebecca, Addy, and Clemmie cooked simple meat pies the night before. We ate some for supper and saved enough for us all to take in the mornin'. That, along with an apple and two slices of bread, would get us through the day.

The screechin' machinery was set in motion, vibratin' my eardrums in the most frightenin' manner. I was aghast when I realized that so quickly, I had become like the others, crushed and silent. I understood. It was too early in the mornin' for hollerin', and my thoughts were generally scattered.

So away we went, herded together, with heads slightly bowed and downcast eyes. I broke the spell and looked up to scan the crowd, hopin' to see Mary, but she was nowhere in sight. I realized right away that goin' against the flow meant takin' the risk of bein' trampled or separated from my friends. The yard gates magically opened as we turned off of the street and approached the courtyard. Not missin' a step, we made our way to the entrance situated in the central tower of the monstrous buildin'. Men, women, and even small children entered swiftly and quietly through the doors. I held onto Norah's elbow.

"Go over there," Norah said, pullin' away. "That man in the front, the one wearin' the hat, is Mr. Colby. He's the agent, and he'll get you settled."

While most of the folks scattered in different directions, a group gathered around the agent. I approached him and began to read the many signs posted on the wall. Most of the information described various positions, what they entailed, and the rate of pay. Other signs referred to conduct, hours, and what was expected of us in the community. Along with the bell schedule, there was mention of a curfew, an emphasis on the fact that gamblin' and dishonesty were not tolerated, and that goin' to church was required.

"I didn't mean to disobey. I was tendin' to my ma. I won't go without leave ever again. I promise. Please ask Mr. Aldrich to let me back." A plump young woman with tears runnin' down her face stood before the agent.

"You know the rules, Miss O'Reilly," the agent said, lookin' past her at the next one in line.

"Wait. Please? I need to work now more than ever. With Ma sick, we're not able to make our rent payment. Please, please?"

"Not only will you be done, but I could also blacklist you right here and now," he said, smilin'.

"I will do anything. Please talk to Mr. Aldrich. Please?" She cried and pulled at her hair.

"Step aside, and we'll make arrangements to speak with Mr. Aldrich," he said.

"Thank you. Oh, dear Lord, thank you," she said, dabbin' away her tears with a ragged sleeve.

I wanted to embrace her, to be a tower of support in her time of distress. To watch a humble woman beg for forgiveness because she was carin' for her sick mother was disturbin'.

"Excuse me, miss," Mr. Colby bellowed. "What's your name?" He stared at me with a look of great perplexity, as if he had already asked me several times. His greased, black hair was gray at the temples, and his pencil-thin mustache was waxed quite well. He was flushed and had already sweat through the neck, chest, and back of his shirt.

"Yes, I'm Sarah Hodgdon from—"

"—I got you right here, Miss Hodgdon. Welcome. These are your options."

"Thank you," I said.

He scribbled on his paper. "I gave your name to the paymaster. You'll have to sign his book before you leave and check in every day. Do you have an idea of where you want to work? Do you have any questions?"

I glanced at the board again and remembered that the girls mentioned spinnin'.

No sooner had I opened my mouth when he was already usherin' me towards the stairs. "It says here that you have experience spinning."

"Well, I, I..." the roar of spindles reached a higher pitch as we neared the stairwell. I didn't know what he thought of my experience. I had never worked in a mill, and like most of the girls in Ossipee, had only spun at school and at home on our modest wheel.

"Everyone has some experience, and it doesn't take much to learn. We'll get you started up here and see your strengths and—"

"—Excuse me?" I shouted. The racket was even louder and gettin' worse as we continued up the stairs towards what I learned was the spinnin' room. He held open the door to reveal a sight that would be forever imprinted on my soul—a sea of spindles, looms, and machines that I could not identify. People reached, twirled, and moved about as if they too were machines, locked into a frenzied dance. I turned to ask him what was next, and he was gone.

The lint flew about like grand a nor'easter. Small children stood barefooted on and around giant equipment, and women worked very large looms. Husky men with sweat covered muscles maneuvered oversized carriages, and there were clusters of young boys nearby, some carryin' boxes of empty bobbins and others had brooms.

A man, tryin' to conceal that he was lame in one leg, limped towards me. "Did Colby send you up?" he hollered.

"I think so," I said.

"Speak up! You need to speak up in here! Now, what's your name?" Shoutin' did not become him. Thick purple veins pulsed across his shiny temples, and his foul breath hung in the air.

I attempted to speak, but nothin' came out of my parched mouth.

"I can't hear you." The droplets of sweat that had clung to his brow before let loose.

Suddenly, I became fearless, rememberin' that cowards—weak, small-minded men—shout at women. I resisted the urge to slay him with my tongue. I would not give him the benefit of exhibitin' any sign of emotion. It was a job. Nothin' more. Nothin' less. I knew that I could rise up to meet any challenge set before me. I stared back at him, unblinkin'.

"Sarah Hodgdon." It wasn't a shout, but it was clear and strong. It cut through the din and clatter. It caused him to blink. Out of the corner of my eye, about three rows away, I saw Mercy and Ruby.

"Follow me." He turned down the aisle and stopped beside them. At first, they pretended not to notice, but Mercy's smile was not discreet. He paid them no mind as he whistled and motioned for Addy to come and join us.

Even under the circumstances, Addy was clearly the prettiest girl there. She stopped what she was doin', pushed her loose hairs into her snood and made her way over to us. "Yes?"

"This is Sarah. Show her how to run the machine. She ain't done it before, so teach her right." He looked her over from top to bottom with his greedy eyes brazenly lingerin' on her breasts. "I'll come back to check on her."

"Yes, sir," she shouted.

When he spun around, he brushed against her, almost causin' her to lose her balance. Together we watched him hobble off into a maze of spinnin' frames.

"Goddamned pig," she said.

"Do you think he's worse than Mr. Colby?" I said.

"Colby is a little better than Aldrich, but they're all bastards," she said. "Now let's get to work. How lucky I am to get to show you the way."

Other than our breakfast break, we spent the mornin' workin' the spinnin' frames. Addy was quite skilled. She inspired me so with her agility and graceful movements. The children—doffers and sweeps—were the nicest of the lot. There was one particular back boy, scantily dressed and quite lanky, who caused me to tremble more than once as he dashed in and about the workin' machinery, exhibitin' his skills and varied responsibilities. I marveled at the very young bobbin boys and girls, who at the sound of a bell, rushed in and fetched the full bobbins, replacin' them with empty ones as their honest smiles waned throughout the day.

The windows were blocked, and the swelterin' heat clashed with the eerie winter scene—a frenzied increase of cotton lint flyin' about, stickin' to our sweaty skin, damp clothes, and accumulatin' on the floor. Within an hour of arrival, many of the men and boys were stripped down to their waist, and like the children, most of the women were barefooted. My eyes were bleary, breathin' had become a challenge, and my temples throbbed. Dinner ring out was at twelve o'clock, noon. There was a buzz in my ears when the machines died down, and we gathered our pails.

I was somewhat queasy and did not know how to find my way or make time to go to the outhouse. When I mentioned it to Addy, she laughed and said there was no time for such things, only after ring out, and even then we only had a few moments to spare.

I may have taken the wrong pail, but there was no time to fret. I ate very quickly, not entirely convinced but thinkin' that the meat pie and bread tasted quite good. Rebecca advised me to eat my meat pie durin' the dinner hour, or it would spoil and have to be thrown out. I saved my apple for later, for the walk home.

Addy said that I was a natural at tyin' a smooth knot when the thread broke. You had to do it quickly for the machinery to stay up and runnin'. It required rapid finger movement, which made it easier for me because of my skills as a musician.

It seemed as if the day would not end. When I tumbled into a state of weakness or instability, I prayed silently, only to ask for my own forgiveness, as it was my dear sister who dwelt in the shadows and needed His comfort most. It was she who was surrounded by the ashes of our dead mother and carried a child in sin. How could I have asked for anything other than what He required of me in service? When I imagined the face of my sister—unshaken and hopeful—I became lost in my own unworthiness, but the notion of returnin' was too much to bear.

At the end of the day, my posture was bent, and my shoulders and back throbbed in pain. In spite of praise for swiftness, my fingers were raw. My feet were swollen from standin' so long, but my soul was bowed in profound gratitude to have completed my first day.

Much like when we came in, the herd filed out of the mill, only the silence was sharp and the shared thought body more dense and rigid. Every now and then a mother would snap at her husband, a child would cry, or a man would let out a curse word. There was a low level of mumblin' that blended with the ringin' in my ears. There was a certain numbness that took over as I walked through the yard gates and headed for my new home, where there was much to do in preparation for the next day.

The sun was about to set in the smoke-filled sky. The lint continued to float eerily in our midst, but it had become a squall and not the blizzard that it was inside. The sweat had dried on my skin, and even though it was still humid, the dampness on my blouse felt cold. Had I been at home, I would have persuaded Abigail to go for a quick swim. I didn't know if there was a spot for swimmin' in Fall River, but I intended to find out.

We were almost home when we passed by the lamplighters. A young boy with red-patched trousers stopped his struggle with a small ladder and offered up a tender smile. His meek and quiet spirit restored my hope.

There were a handful of women—worn out, young mothers—who did not go to the mill but stayed home with the babies. They tended to the coals in the kitchen stove for cookin', and if, in the rare instance durin' the week, someone wished to heat water to bathe.

When we entered our room, there was some squabblin' as to whose turn it was to cook. Norah proposed to write a schedule, but no one bothered to listen. I left the commotion behind and went to the sinks in the yard to fill a bucket. I had spotted a white ironstone pitcher and washbasin set upon a wobbly washstand in the corner of our room. I was in much need of bathin'. My heart leapt inside of me when I remembered the small cake of rose soap that mother had made durin' the summer and wondered if it was better to save it.

I plodded down the steps on feet that felt as if they belonged to another. Very few people wandered about, and I was the only one at the pump.

"Where have ya been?"

I winced in pain and turned to face Mary with her radiant smile, damp curls pressed into her forehead and covered in a fine layer of lint.

"I was there… At the mill. Where were you?" I asked, ignorin' the obvious.

"I was too. Ya were ahead of me in line, and I shouted before ya walked away with the agent," she said. "Ya didn't even look."

"Oh, I didn't hear you."

"Where did ya end up workin'?" she asked.

"In the spinnin' room, fifth floor."

"I'm on the fourth floor," she said. "We must find a way to spin together!"

"I don't know how to manage that," I said.

"We can manage anything we put our minds to," she said.

"Mercy and Rebecca wish to work their way up to the attic. Rebecca wants to be a drawin'-in girl, and Mercy likes to be where her sister is," I said. "But they're bein' punished for goin' home without leave, and now it'll take longer. I s'pose it's my fault, for which I feel horrible. But how was I to know?"

"Ya worry too much about others," she said. "Just worry about ya'self and to hell with everyone else." Her laughter echoed off of the buildin's in the alleyway.

"That's not very nice." I was tempted to quote my mother.

"Ya can't be responsible for everyone," she said. "You'll be gobbled up in no time."

She followed behind me, waggin' her tongue. I couldn't understand why she was not depleted from such a long day and where she had the energy to go on so.

I went into the kitchen, where the girls were choppin', stirrin,' and mindin' the stove. When I reached for the kettle, Ruby slapped my hand. "What the hell are you doin'?"

"I'm goin' to heat the water so that I can wash up," I said.

"The water in here is not quite heated, and it's for me." She glared at me.

"It's a large kettle, perhaps we can share the water, and I can refill it after," I said.

"You think you have an answer for everything," she said.

"I'm just tryin' to work together and make it easier for us all."

"If you wanted to make it easier for us all, you'd stay out of the way." She nudged me with her hip and stood in front of the stove.

"I don't know who ya think y'are," Mary said, "but no one talks to my friend that way."

"And who are you?" Ruby asked.

"Just stop. Please." I pushed my way in between them. "I only wanted enough warm water to fill one pitcher for the wash basin. I can wait 'til the cookin' is done." Although it was a lie, I couldn't tolerate another moment of peckin'. I took the bucket and left the two of them standin' speechless in front of the stove.

When I entered our room, I suddenly realized that washin' up with cool water would be refreshin', even better than warm water. I had become so heated and drenched in sweat, which had dried off and on throughout the day, that it mattered not. At first, the sharp odor of all those around me was distasteful, but as of that first work day, I had become a part of it. We reeked together in unison.

I fetched the pitcher and basin and went to my corner of the room. Typically, I was modest and would never expose my nakedness to anyone other than my sister. I was even shy around my mother. However, that night, I didn't care. I peeled off my damp dress and smiled when just like the others, I tossed it across the room.

I decided to save Mother's rose soap for a special occasion, which had nothin' to do with the moment that I was in. Just as I had accepted the notion of a simple rinse, I spotted a well-used, flattened soap ball behind the wash basin. I pried it off of the stand and held it to my nose. It had an unusual scent, not quite flowery, almost like an orange. I used a meager amount on my hair and with my small linen, washed the parts of myself that were in much need of it. I had never loved a bath as much as I loved that one. The girls hurried in and out of the room, none payin' attention to the other. We were together apart—functionin' separately within our strange union.

Barely covered by my linen, I stood in front of the window, thinkin' for an instant that I would throw out the water, and then I remembered that it was nailed shut. So, I emptied my bath water into the bucket, lugged it down to the end of the hallway, and poured it out the open window.

When I found my summer nightgown, I pressed it into my face, tryin' to detect the essence of home. Any trace of hunger that I had before vanished at the onset of the heaviness that rested upon my heart. I pulled it over my head and stood quietly, countin' my breaths. After a moment or two, I was able to comb through my tangled hair and twist it into a bun.

"If you want to join us, we're havin' supper and fillin' our dinner pails for the morn'," Clara said.

"Thank you."

"And, this is for you. I got it from the apple woman," she said, handin' me a shiny red apple.

"That's so sweet, Clara," I said. "Thank you."

She blushed and reached for my hand. Together we went, down the hallway and stairs that led to the common kitchen. Except for the scrapin' of utensils and clatter of plates, it was eerily quiet. None of the women or girls—all standin' in line holdin' onto a plate—looked up when we entered. We got our plates and stood at the end of the line.

Once we all had our food, we found a place to sit at one of the splintered pine tables. Finally lookin' beat, Mary sat across from me. I kept my eyes fastened on her, but she continued to stare down at her plate—a strip of dried pork, a few carrots, and a quarter of a potato. There was a shiny bread wreath in the middle of the table and a bowl of light-colored gravy.

A plump woman, who had not yet uttered a word, rose up from the table and broke the silence with her strong Irish lilt.

"Heavenly Father, may this food provide strength and energy for our tired limbs, and good thoughts for our weary minds. Let this drink revive our souls, quench our spirits, and warm the hearts here that have become cold. Protect us. Keep us safe and unharmed, and guide us as we work and slumber side by side. In return, we give thanks, Amen."

The meal was not flavorful, but it satisfied my hunger. Other than crude acknowledgment, very little, if any conversation took place.

Norah managed to get a sign posted near the door. Overlookin' the crude penmanship, one could decipher whose turn it was to do the kitchen chores. It was my night to wash up the pots, while each of us took care of our own dishes. Addy poured hot water in the tub in the sink closet, and there was plenty of soap.

Clemmie, Clara, and some of the girls from other rooms that I had not met, sorted through the food that we would put in our dinner pails for the next day. Much like the machinery at the mill, yet quieter, we all worked together—well oiled and finely tuned.

Although my body screamed, and muscles that I did not know existed before that night pounded, my mind was sharp and filled with many thoughts, too many to abandon. I found it impossible not to get my cornet, even if it were only for a handful of notes. If I kept my promise to myself, to stay regimented with my playin', then my heart would be still.

I waited until some of the girls were busy with activities such as readin', fixin' their bed sheets, brushin' each other's hair, or just packin' their dinner pails, before goin' to get my cornet. First, I put a candlestick and matches in my pocket, rememberin' the brass holder on a crate in the attic.

"What are you doin'?" Mercy asked.

"Oh, nothin'. Just thinkin' of gettin' a little fresh air before goin' to sleep," I said.

"I'm too tired for that. Did you like your first day?" she asked.

I responded, perhaps too quickly, "Yes, it was good, now if you'll excuse me—"

"—Leave her alone. She'll be comin' to bed before you know it," Rebecca interrupted as she often did.

How fortunate for me that Rebecca drew her sister into her tangled web of complaints and fretfulness. I was able to collect my horn and slip away.

I stopped at the bottom of the stairs and contemplated my ability to feel my way up the steps in the dark. A candle would have drawn unwanted attention.

Once at the top of the stairs, I gasped at the sight before me. The lamps on the street had been lit, and all of the mills, tenements, and shops had their soft lights glowin' in the windows. It was hard to believe that this was the filthy place that I had been out paradin' in with hundreds of others only hours before. I wished that my sister could have seen the magnificence of it.

I blew into my mouthpiece to get it warmed up as best I could. I didn't have the luxury of a proper warm-up, and I felt as if I was stealin' each note.

I stopped when I heard a crash. I was not alone. After a few moments, when nothin' came of it, I returned to my horn.

I stuffed the rag into the bell and played "Come Where My Love Lies Dreaming," another one of Mother's preferred pieces. Most of her favorite songs were about such things. She loved through music, a secret world that we almost shared and never mentioned—a hidden, tacit language that so few in our intimate world recognized or appreciated, rarely spoken, leavin' everything of consequence unsaid.

Chapter 20

August
September 9, 1872

It was a rare, cloudless Monday. Other than Sundays, when the mills were closed, a thick blanket of smoke hung over the city. Eager to begin our first night as lamplighters, Finn and I set out for the Street Department, where Francis Murphy waited.

We stopped at a row of outhouses and open sinks. Of course, Finn squirmed and tried to pull away from me, but I managed to splash water on his face. Luckily, I collected enough money to buy him a pair of second-hand shoes and trousers with thick red patches on the knees. They were somewhat large, but he had his cord suspenders and plenty of time to grow into them.

We hurried down the street, which other than a few stragglers, was vacant. Ring out wasn't until six o'clock. Aware of those moments when Finn had the look of a pickpocket, I kept a close eye on him.

When we arrived, I paused. It wasn't until two young men exited the buildin' with a ladder and lamp stick that I knew it was the right place. We entered through the front door where it was bustlin' with men and boys, gatherin' up their ladders and equipment. Mr. Murphy met us with a warm handshake and brought me over to meet the shift captain.

The portly man blew cigar smoke in my face and looked right past me at Mr. Murphy. "You always round up the tramps, dontcha?"

"You know me, Cap, I like to give 'em a chance," he said.

He looked at me and raised an eyebrow. "It's jest like baseball, boys, only you don't get three strikes. You're out at the first wrong move." He turned and walked away.

"Don't worry, lads. You'll be just fine so long as ya watch what ya doin'," Mr. Murphy said. "Now let's get ready."

We followed him into an adjoinin' buildin' that reeked of gas, where ladders and long brass-tipped staffs were stacked up against the wall, along with many hand-lamps on the shelves.

"Ya know, it's an honor to bring light and comfort to folks," he said. "Once ya get used to it, and if you're a reliable sort, some of 'em will give ya gifts. I know of one lamplighter who gets a pound of pork sausage every Christmas and another that gets fresh sweet bread at least once a month."

He picked up a ladder. "Finn, come here and hold onto this," he said.

Finn had his back to us and was lookin' out the window with a big smile on his face. I tapped him on the shoulder, causin' him to whoop a little, before bringin' him over to Mr. Murphy.

"Was your brother born like this? Or was there some kinda' accident?"

"Uh, he was born this way," I said.

"Are ya parents still—"

"—Our parents are dead, and I've been takin' care of my brother for a few years now."

He paused. "As long as ya do what needs to be done, it'll be fine." He handed Finn the ladder. It was smaller than a typical ladder, and Finn was able to pick it up without a struggle.

Next, he got me a staff, wick cutter, hand-lamp, and matches. He pulled a strap off the top of one of the shelves and showed me how to wear it so that I could carry all of the necessary equipment to light the street lamps. So, it was up to Finn to manage the ladder and for me to do the actual lightin'. We were assigned to the Granite Street district, which wasn't too far from where we were squattin'.

"Even though we'll have moonlight tonight, it sets at midnight, so we still need to light the lamps. We have a few days before the moon is bright enough and will set just before sunrise," Mr. Murphy said, "and then we consider the weather. If it's clear, we don't light the lamps. But, ya need to show up here, and we'll decide. Don't make that decision on ya own."

I nodded, all the while watchin' Finn as he ran his hands over the ladder with his eyes ablaze. I wasn't sure how much he understood about our new job. It was better for him to be with me out in the streets than in a factory where he couldn't hear the bells that warned of danger.

We weren't far from our district, so we were able to walk, which we did, in a line, with Mr. Murphy in the lead and Finn trailin' behind me. Havin' a tendency to dawdle, Finn wandered off now and then to look at somethin' while Mr. Murphy kept right on walkin', makin' it tough to get where we were goin'.

He stopped near where we had used the outhouses.

"This is ya startin' point. You'll go down this street and over to the next three streets before makin' your way up the hill." He pointed in the direction of the piano music that I liked so much.

The last bell of the workday rang out, and the yard gates screeched as they swung open. The streets quickly filled up with workers. They moved in our direction, and Mr. Murphy kept right on talkin'. I strained to hear him while keepin' a watchful eye on Finn. No sooner had Mr. Murphy handed me the stick, when I saw that girl again, the one who cried and carried on at the train station. She was about to close in on me, so I turned away, givin' Mr. Murphy my full attention.

Lightin' up the city was somethin' that I could be proud of. I had planned on goin' to work in a mill, but for some reason, meetin' Finn changed all that. Deep down, I didn't like the way the overseers treated workin' folks, but I thought I'd try again.

At first, Finn wasn't good at keepin' the ladder steady or bein' close by when I needed him, but it didn't take long for him to learn to follow me. We had the makin's of a sturdy team.

CHAPTER 21

Bess
September 9, 1872

"WHAT WOULD YOU do if I told you that I might run away?" I stared at Tempy in the looking glass, knowing that the answer in her eyes would differ from what she would actually say. Our talks were often about something else, an unspoken mystery in search of a missing satin ribbon, pearl button, or the other side of a locket. There was always something else.

"I'd make sure that you had plenty of food in your sack," she said, without changing her expression.

She pulled the brush through my hair and continued to braid it into two, shiny, smooth coils on each side of my head, a style that pleased mother but seemed a bit frumpish to me.

I frequently talked to Tempy about running away, and she told me that she would help me pack. "You don't believe that I'll go?" I asked.

"You got too much to stay for," she said. "Besides, you haven't given it a chance like you promised."

"My piano lesson with my new teacher is at three o'clock. So, this morning we have time to go into town to see what the shops are like. Will you accompany us?"

"Oh, I don't know," she said.

I stood still while Tempy tended to my undergarments. I liked how she tied my corset because she was not concerned about it being too tight. It was hard enough to move about with hoops and now bustles. It was especially troublesome to sit at a piano bench with all of that apparatus, but I did what was expected of me. While at home, though, I did not wear my shoes unless we were expecting guests.

Mother was particularly bothered by my dislike of dressing up at all times. She required perfect neatness in every detail. I was to be tidy all the way down to my feet. It was as if God Himself was going to come down from Heaven and inspect us in our daily lives. I had no use for such glaring perfection unless of course, it pertained to music. Then, I was a purist.

"Bess, dear," Mother called from the parlor. "Are you almost ready?"

"We're coming!" I shouted while Tempy pulled the blue dress over my head.

I studied my reflection and wondered if I should leave the house wearing such a dark color on a bright day. Soon it would be fall, and then winter, and I would be wearing dark clothes for months. I decided that I should wear lighter colors while there was still time.

"Tempy, this is too dark. In fact, it's out of season. Let's look for a lighter color." I avoided using the word bright, which was inappropriate for a walking day dress. Mother would not hear of it, but I didn't see why there was such a stir.

Her eyes widened. "We shouldn't take too much time decidin', Miss Bess. Your mother is gettin' impatient."

"The light green, plaid dress suits me." I wiggled out of the dress and left it on the floor.

I knew why she sighed and rushed to the closet. She knew better than to argue with me about dresses, especially when I was in a perturbed state of mind. But, she often reminded me of the harmony of colors. Her idea of harmony was of the eye, while mine was of the ear. I could not live without her.

Tempy opened the band-box that held my green bonnet and gasped when she saw that the crown was crushed beyond repair. "You'll not be wearin' dis one no more."

"It must have been damaged during the move." I gave it a quick look and tossed it aside. "I don't have another green bonnet, but I do have a maroon one; it'll match a strand in the plaid."

She returned to the closet and opened boxes until she found the maroon hat. I had already decided that it would never do. I could not wear that one, because I envisioned something brighter—not too elaborate.

This was to be my first trip to the shops. I couldn't have settled for anything less than a perfect match. I knew that it wasn't bad, but I could not afford to wear such a submissive hat. Someone with a keen eye would be quick to note that green was more suitable and that something was amiss for me to have chosen maroon. It would have been obvious to me, and if I didn't notice, Mother would have pointed it out, whispering behind her white-gloved hand.

I wondered if it were truly possible to be fashionable and becoming, and if so, was it even worth it? Sometimes, I envied the plain mill girls that I saw on the streets. Their dresses were made of cheap, flimsy fabric. They carried on without worrying whether or not a bonnet was right or if what you were wearing was of good taste.

I removed the green plaid dress and flopped it on top of the dark blue one.

"Whatever are you doin?" Tempy asked.

"I can't wear the other bonnet. It simply spoils the look of the entire dress," I said.

Mother rapped on the door. "Bess! Tempy! Davis has pulled the carriage out to the front; he's waiting!"

"He'll have to wait. I'm not quite ready."

She entered the room and stood before me wearing her classic frown. "What's taking so long?"

"It would take too long to explain. Nothing seems to be coming together today. You'll have to wait for me to find the appropriate dress, or you can go without me," I said.

"Of course I will wait. I do favor the green—"

"—don't even speak of that. Somehow, the matching bonnet was damaged during the move, and the other bonnets are dreadful."

Tempy stood quietly, until mother did what she always did, which was to mumble something incoherently and walk away.

I waited for the door to close before returning to the predicament at hand. "I have given it more thought and will be happy with the light calico dress." I set the maroon bonnet on the bed.

"I'll get it," Tempy said, remaining quite calm.

"The simple straw bonnet is a good match," I said, pleased that I would be wearing a proper walking dress that did not cry for attention and was appropriate for a crowded shop.

By the time we made it outside, Davis was asleep on the front seat of the carriage, and Mother was sitting beneath the shade of one of the big trees by the fence, fanning herself.

Davis grabbed his hat as it fell from his lap, and Mother jumped to her feet when we approached.

"Are you sure you won't come with us?" I stood with my back to them both and looked longingly at Tempy.

"I have a lot of tendin' to do," she said.

I watched her limp—completely dragging one leg—until she was out of sight. She was about the same age as my mother but had suffered greatly in her youth.

Although lacking in charm and selection of those in Boston, the shops of Fall River were somewhat quaint and would do. There was no hope of getting used to the need to raise one's voice to be heard above the horrific noise of the mills. At one point, and without much thought, I transformed one of the repetitive clanging sounds into the bass and percussion section of a full orchestra and found myself humming the melody.

I imagined that the close proximity of the mills was the reason for the broad assortment of richly colored fabrics. I enjoyed flitting about and browsing.

Mother continued to tug at me to buy this or that, but I found that her pushing kept me from even looking at her suggestions. I often thought about it at night when I couldn't sleep, this need to keep her at a distance. We were locked into our very own waltz. Generally, I was not unkind; I simply could not allow her in, even though the same old step, which never moved or varied, was tiresome.

Although I did fancy one red dress with beautiful lace that would have been lovely for the holidays, I did not purchase a thing. I could only think of my afternoon lesson with Mr. Carver. I was not in the mood for a fitting, especially without Tempy's assistance.

As hard as it was, I looked away from the street urchins and little wanderers, like the two brothers who sat outside by the fence with a meager picnic, listening to my music. Under such circumstances, one could not be picky about an audience.

We returned home in time for a late lunch. After removing my shoes, which had become more uncomfortable with each moment, we enjoyed cucumber sandwiches and fresh mint tea.

"You must go into town with us next time, Tempy," I said. "The shops are different from the ones in Boston, and yes, it's noisy and dusty, but it's cheerful just the same."

"Mmmhmm." She poured a second cup of tea for Mother.

"Please, slow down, Bess. You're eating too quickly, talking too much, and your arms are on the table. You don't want to develop bad habits," Mother said.

"I can't slow down. I want to get ready for Mr. Carver," I said while stuffing the remainder of my sandwich into my mouth.

"I understand that it's an important day, but we must always pay attention to our manners, even when it is only us at the table," she said.

"Yes, Mother." I glanced at Tempy who was smart enough to avoid eye contact with me, for I may have made a face that was unbecoming of a young lady, and that's what it was about.

It seemed as if three o'clock would never come. I washed up, paced back and forth across the parlor, sorted through my music, and placed it neatly upon the desk for Mr. Carver's convenience. Unable to erase the image of Mr. Todorov's face, I sat at my piano bench and began playing scales.

"Good aftahnoon, Mr. Carver." Davis's voice drifted down the hallway.

"Good afternoon." The depth of his voice was almost startling.

"Do come in, and let me take your umbrella. Miss Bess is in the parlor and has been waitin'," Davis said.

I sat frozen with my fingers resting lightly on the keys. I had only studied with the finest piano teachers in all of Boston. I was confident that I was perhaps a better player than Mr. Carver himself.

"Miss Bess, Mr. Carver has arrived." Davis entered the room while one of the tallest men I had ever laid eyes on followed him through the door. He had a head of unruly brown hair and a curly beard that was much too long for a young man of his stature. He smiled and peered at me through his spectacles, which sat crookedly upon his nose and had one cracked lens.

"Pleased to meet you, Miss Adams," he said.

"Call me Bess, and the pleasure is mine," I said, rising up and offering my hand.

"I see that you've been taking lessons with the great Ivan Todorov in Boston?" he asked, quickly letting my hand drop.

"Yes, that's true," I said.

"Meeting his standards will be a test of my skills," he said, "but, I like a challenge."

Not knowing how to respond to his frankness, I turned to the desk. "Here is my music library. I was working on this sonata when we left." I handed him Scarlatti's Sonata in A minor.

His eyes narrowed as he looked over the music. He smiled. "I should have expected nothing less."

"These are the etudes that I am presently working on." I gave him two thick, heavily marked books.

He sat down, running his fingers through his beard, looking over each page, considering each note and marking. The ticking of the clock echoed in the room, and I could feel my heart pounding in my chest.

"Well, then," he said, finally breaking the silence, "let's hear you. Show yourself."

Unprepared for his sudden request, I fumbled through the music at hand and found my position on the bench. After clearing my throat and taking several breaths, with almost uncontrollable, trembling hands, I began to play the sonata. I felt his eyes on me, on my every move. I wanted to bang on the keys and ask him to leave. He was too close. I thought that I felt his breath on my arm. I decided to pretend that he wasn't there.

I played and played, waiting for him to stop me and complain when I played the wrong note or when my counting was wrong, but he sat patiently with his head cocked to the side, watching me as if it were the first time that he ever saw someone play the piano.

I made my way to the end of the piece and waited. Again, he did not speak. I looked at him out of the corner of my eye thinking that perhaps he had died and that I would have to scream for Davis to fetch the undertaker.

"Well?" I asked.

"What do you think?" he asked, not moving at all.

"What am I expected to think?" I crossed my arms. "You are the teacher. What do you think?"

He laughed and leaned back in the chair.

"Well, what do you think?" I raised my voice.

"I think that you have played through your fear and that you must go back to the beginning."

The nerve of that man! How dare he come here and laugh at me, humiliate me in my own parlor. I'll show him.

CHAPTER 22

Sarah
September 15, 1872

OH, THE AWFULNESS of an unreliable rooster, one that missed daybreak and crowed relentlessly about its incompetence! Although I was quite uncomfortable with Mercy's elbow pressed into my back, and needin' to visit the outhouse, I didn't move.

Several minutes passed before I rolled over and took in the sight of my new family, the girls in my room who were poor beyond description, yet rich in sheer determination and strength.

I thought about the women who stayed at home with the babies and very young children. I decided that after church, I would pen a letter to my sister, to enquire about her condition and to offer clarity through clouds of uncertainty. Time would not wait. My fears for her mounted. If given a choice, I would have chosen to be barren rather than the mother of a bastard child—scorned for a lifetime. For Abigail, the window of righteousness continued to close. All would know of her weakness, her inability to resist temptation, and the consequences would live on.

Such images were enough to bring about a flurry of panic with an onslaught of questions that only God could have answered, or Mother, who was at His right hand. In order to prevent waterin' my pillow with tears, I closed my eyes and swiftly retreated into dark silence—my hidden world. The girls were stirrin' and movin' about, so I tried hard to ignore them.

"Are you gettin' up?" Mercy said, tuggin' at the blanket.

"Leave her alone, Mercy," Rebecca said. "And get out on this side."

"She missed church last week," Mercy said.

"Never mind," Rebecca said. "She's got plenty of time."

In danger of bein' forced out of my much-needed solitude, I pulled the blanket over my head.

Heavenly Father, All that I seek is peace in this moment. Thoughts of Abigail and Mother are a blow upon my heart. I wish to find a gleam of hope, that I may have the strength and fortitude to walk in the purity and grace that comes to me when I am afforded time in my quiet refuge. For this, I bow in humble thankfulness and refrain from dwellin' in the shadows that loom above me. In the Lord's name, I pray, Amen.

Except for Clara, who slept soundly in her crate, the girls arose from their beds and set out for the outhouses and sinks. The rooster, which was fadin' fast, and the creaky stairs were a delightful alternative to the sounds of whirrin' spindles. I lingered within the beautiful, serene darkness long enough for the comfort that always found me, to do so once again.

I finally rolled out of my saggy bed, ready to experience church with throngs of millworkers.

"Good mornin'," Clara said and met me with a meek smile.

"Good mornin'," I said. "Which church do you attend?"

"I go to the Methodist Church," she said.

"I see," I said, tryin' not to stare at the jagged scars on her hairline, which were more visible than usual.

I blushed in shame, as she quickly mussed with her hair. When we weren't at the mill, she often wore a straw bonnet with a blue ribbon, coverin' her scars well. She turned to face me again, this time with her scars hidden behind a clump of her thin blonde hair.

"We can have a modest breakfast, and you're welcome to join me," she said.

"I'd love that," I said. "I must wash up now. Will you accompany me to the yard?"

She reached out her hand, and once again, we walked together to the outhouses. My time with Clara was brief and deliberate, and although with much different intentions, our union served us well.

The Angels' Lament

It seemed that even the sky took pity on us, broodin' before finally givin' way to tears. I welcomed a break from the glare of the milky sun, peerin' through the smoke and soot that pumped out of the factory chimneys. However, I was worried about the stench of the puddles and pools, what lurked in that which overflowed.

Because we were a little later than the others, most of them were already in the kitchen havin' soda bread, tea, and a slice of aged cheddar. I saved myself the effort and splashed water on my face straight from the pump. Clara looked on, perfectly satisfied with not washin' up at all.

"I s'pose ya gettin' ready for church are ya?" Mary said, sittin' on the edge of a nearby sink, smokin' a cigar stump that she probably found on the street.

"First I'm havin' breakfast, and then it will be time," I said. "How about you?"

"I tole ya, I don't go to church," she said between puffs.

"I think it's required of us. Perhaps you should go and—"

"—and sit there so that the agent don't report me?"

"Well, somethin' of that nature," I said.

"I'm not afraid. Nothin' will bring me to a church. So, I'll just enjoy me a mornin' to myself."

Clara tugged on my arm. "We'll see you later?" I asked.

"I'm sure," she said. "Ya never know."

After breakfast, I rifled through my trunk and pulled out a maroon skirt with black trim and a cream colored blouse that Mother had given me. I had a matchin' Bolero jacket, but it was much too warm. It only mattered that it was not soiled and did not need mendin'. I decided that from that day on, it would be my official outfit for church.

Everyone fussed and worked with their drab dresses to come up with somethin' presentable. I took pride in bein' the nicest dressed of us all.

"You wait. You think you're all fancy now. In about six months, you will be as tired and faded as the rest of us," Ruby said as she tucked her hair up into her green bonnet.

"That's uncalled for," Norah said.

Ruby dabbed her whiffy cologne on her wrists.

"The truth is never uncalled for," she said. "We all felt that way when we first got here and unpacked our dresses. It won't last forever."

⋅⊷⊜⊶ ⊷⊜⊶⋅

Just as we walked together to the mill, we walked together to church. At the end of the street, the Irish went to the left, and the Canadians went to the right, while the rest of us continued on straight towards the Methodist Church. I had to shake free from Clara's hand to open my umbrella. Much to my surprise, many of those walkin' in the rain did not carry umbrellas as if it were a sunny day.

A fancy pleasure cart sped by, splashin' through a puddle and drenchin' me from my waist down to my feet. My umbrella flew out of my hand and clattered to the ground, and I caught myself before fallin' into a murky puddle. The putrid, dark water dripped from the bottom of my skirt. It was clear that I was no longer one of the finest mill girls set out for church.

"Oh dear!" Clara cried. "How rude!"

I picked up my umbrella, not takin' my eyes away from the back of the head of the negro driver, who did not even flinch as he ruined everything about my day. Perhaps God mocked me, makin' sure that my boastful ways, even in thought and not words, could be overturned in an instant.

The girls circled around me. Ruby did not hide her pleasure. Clemmie, who almost never spoke, tried to dab away the black slime with her handkerchief.

"Stop," I said. "I mean, thank you, Clemmie, but don't be spoilin' your handkerchief. I must go home. By the time I get there and sort out my clothes and hurry back to church, it will be too late, and I can't go like this."

"That's true," Rebecca said. "You should go home and clean up and get started on your launderin'."

"Do you think God really minds if you have mud on your skirt?" Mercy asked.

"Don't be foolish, Mercy! Of course, God don't care, but what will all the others think?" Rebecca tossed her head in disgust at her sister's brilliant assessment of the situation.

I stopped. She was absolutely correct. Who cared? God or the people sittin' in the pews with all of their sins stuffed down inside of their reticules, pretendin' to be saintly?

"We'll speak on your behalf if the agent questions as to why you are not on the church roster," Rebecca said.

"You're not in good favor with him now, Rebecca," Mercy said, flinchin' in anticipation of an outburst.

"You're right," Rebecca said.

"That won't be necessary," I said.

"What? Surely, you aren't goin' to church like that," she said.

"Yes, I am," I said. "I agree with Mercy. Do you think that God cares that I am covered in foul mud? What kind of God would care? It would be better to think that I would be favored for goin' to hear the good word, than to dash home and cry, missin' much-needed fellowship."

What would Abigail have done? She was the brave one, and I was known to be proper, at least for a farm girl, which I learned quickly would not serve me well on the streets of Fall River.

I straightened myself up and stood tall. Mother would have been proud. She might have insisted that I go home and launder my clothes, rather than be in the House of the Lord dressed in clothes that had been mucked up by some reckless driver. She would have seen the goodness in me and given me praise. I smiled and grabbed ahold of Clara's hand. "Come now, let's go pray and sing praises unto the Lord."

The carriage that had splashed me in carelessness passed by again, this time goin' in the other direction. My eyes met with the negro driver before he quickly turned away.

"You should go chase after them and give them a few words," Mercy said.

"What's the use of goin' to church if you have to spend the whole time askin' for forgiveness?" I asked, continuin' to smile.

"It would be perfectly acceptable though," Rebecca said.

"Is it an eye for an eye? Or, turn the other cheek?" I continued. "I prefer to turn the other cheek, even though it's smudged with a little mud."

Clara squeezed my hand and laughed. "I agree. Too many people's angry all the time. We ain't got time. We ain't got time," she said.

We arrived at the church, and like we did at the entrance of the mill, stood in a crowded line while members of the upper echelon of Fall River were guided to the front and ushered inside.

I got to thinkin' about our little church in Water Village. We did sit in the same pew for the most part, but in the winter, we tried to wiggle ourselves into the back row to be closer to the wood stove. Mother often scolded us, because if we were of high enough stature to sit near the front in the spring, summer, and fall, we should accept that the price for such a luxury was to wear an extra layer of clothin' durin' the winter months. She always reminded us to be grateful and humble.

It was impossible to sustain my forced smile when people began to whisper and point at me. The women did not spare their harsh looks of disapproval and walked by with their heads held high. At first, I was certain that I could have joined in with the congregation. Whether dressed in the finest or shabbiest attire, we were all the same in God's eyes.

The need to make a point slipped away, and I considered runnin' home. Then I thought about my sister and knew that she would have laughed in their faces. Mother would have been in an unsettled state, and I would have joined in the laughter. Pastor Leighton would have stuttered and blushed, and his wife would have pretended not to notice as she played that old organ. Effie Morrill would have been the one to speak out inappropriately, which would have forced Mother into defendin' me and even splashin' a bit of mud upon herself as a show of solidarity, which I knew was just a fanciful dream on my part.

CHAPTER 23

August
September 15, 1872

BECAUSE OF THE fair weather and the risin' and settin' of the moon, we didn't work much durin' our first week. We showed up every day as expected, and Francis Murphy told us whether to work or go home. In the past, when I worked, the thought of bein' sent home would have been welcomed. I had to get used to my eagerness, not only for an honest wage and bringin' light to an otherwise dark city, but to keep Finn out of the children's home.

One of Francis Murphy's friends gave us an old stove. It was good for cookin' and would keep us warm into the latter part of fall, at least 'til we found a more suitable place to live. I had my eye on the cellar of one of the tenements.

I brought my steamin' coffee up to my lips and smiled, grateful to have found an abandoned pot on the street. Soon, I would go to the market and buy a sausage from my new friend, Tiago. Come to find out, the day that Finn was missin', he stole bread from his sister. Although it wasn't much, when we were paid at the end of the week, I made Finn pay for the bread. Accordin' to Tiago, most people who had stolen from them got away with it. I s'posed I was thankful that Finn was a lil' thief because through his actions, I made a friend.

When I opened my tobacco tin, the small blue fabric fell onto the dirt floor. I stared at the familiar letters on the bottom corner, *I-l-o-v-e -m-y- s-o-n*. I vowed to hang onto that little piece of cloth. Maggie—a girl from Five Points— told me what it said. The nuns taught her how to read. They taught me some too, but she knew nearly all of the letters.

After countin' out enough coins for the market, I carefully pressed the fabric back into the bottom of the tin.

Wrapped in the heavy cloak that I found beside the coffee pot, Finn slept soundly on his straw pallet. Like me, he seemed to enjoy honest, hard work and started to sleep late in the mornin'. I gulped my coffee and wondered whether or not I could trust him. If I left, he might have run off and gotten into trouble, but he coulda' slept too.

Just as I made the decision to leave without him, he stirred. "You want to come with me to the market? We'll get sausage and milk." I was in the habit of talkin' as if could hear me.

Payin' me no mind, he sat up and rubbed his eyes. I knelt down in front of him and put my hand up to my mouth like I was eatin'.

He smiled and took off to the back of the shed to relieve himself, which was better than a week ago when he did it right there on the street while people walked by. I combed my hair, thinkin' that we'd take a walk up the hill. He liked the flowers, and I liked listenin' to the piano.

Our hopes of goin' up the hill were quickly washed away by the rain. Luckily, I had collected extra wick, a half jug of gas, and a small hand-held lantern that Francis Murphy said I could bring home. I decided that if it were gonna rain, I'd look at the book that I found in a train car. It was torn in some places, and the back cover was missin'. There were pictures and a lot of words. Someday I planned to read every one of 'em.

Chapter 24

Bess
September 15, 1872

The day began with the threat of rain, but the skies did not open up until we were in the carriage and well on our way to church. I fiddled with my reticule and thought about how much I preferred to stay at home, but Mother wouldn't hear of it. In order to fulfill my social and moral obligations, I had to resume my schedule or accept that I had become a neglectful creature.

The unfortunate ones scurried about, huddled together under their shared umbrellas. Some didn't have umbrellas at all and held their capes over their heads, dashing off in different directions, just as I imagined chickens in a barnyard. However, the ones that I admired carried on as if it weren't raining at all. I preferred that to the panic that set in at the sight of the first raindrop. After all, unpleasant weather does not last forever.

I sighed heavily and shifted my attention to my parents, who sat across from me, not speaking. Father tapped on his walking stick and checked his timepiece as if signaling Mother to scowl. We arrived painfully early at most of our engagements, and she was displeased when we had to wait until the proper time to make an entrance.

The crowds thickened when we turned onto the main street. It was quite obvious that these people had no cares about making room for carriages. They seemed to lack common sense and the many worries and cares that we faced in our daily lives. They did not have to mind the servants or follow countless rules of etiquette while being closely observed by those who reprimanded and fussed, or worse, be the target of those, who behind closed doors, spoke with a spiteful tongue.

I gripped the edge of my seat when Davis drove the horses faster than what felt safe in a crowded street. We headed straight for a large puddle beside a group of women walking ahead of us. I covered my face, still managing to peek through my fingers, as we barreled through a deep, murky puddle, causing a giant splash, specifically drenching a woman, one of the few who carried an umbrella, which was of no use.

"Davis!" I shrieked.

"Never mind, Bess," Mother said. "These people are like swarms of unthinking ants. It serves her right for walking so close to where the carriages pass."

Although I couldn't see her face, I got a glimpse of the girl. She was surrounded by her friends. How troubled I would be if I was splashed like that and my dress spoiled. She must have been on her way to church. I glared at Mother. How was it that she possessed such an unfeeling heart?

"You should remember how fortunate you are. These regrettable things rarely happen to a young woman of your stature. You would never be in the streets on such a foul day. And, if you were, you would have the sense to walk away from the carriages."

"If I were a driver, I would take into consideration the number of pedestrians in our midst, and I would drive cautiously," I said.

"But, you are not a driver," she said.

"That's enough." Father finally had something to say, and of course, it was to keep us in line.

We pulled into the carriage line, and Davis came around to assist us. Aware that I disapproved of his recklessness, he looked away. Only Tempy understood my attempt to be kind to those beneath us. I was not a fool but had much more compassion than my parents, who seemed to think that the entire world was there for their convenience and to serve them. Even though Mother and Father were very generous and donated to charity, they did not mingle with those who they helped. There was a difference between us, and it was up to them to establish and maintain the separation. I was scolded on more than one occasion for fraternizing with those who my family deemed commoners.

With Davis's assistance, Mother stepped down from the carriage. When he reached for my hand, I ignored it. He cleared his throat, accustomed to my ways, and he helped me position my umbrella.

"Davis, you must learn to drive more responsibly. It was luck that you ran into a puddle, only soaking an innocent girl and not killing her," I whispered loudly.

"Yes'm," he said with his eyes darting about.

Father took his time getting out of the carriage. We headed towards the front doors of the church while the rain came down harder and the wind picked up. I started to run.

Mother promptly grabbed my elbow and squeezed.

"Do not try to raise your dress, Bess. It is better to soil it than to raise it. In any event, you are a sight, determined to splash in the mud. You should not have worn such a light shade on a rainy day. Now Tempy will have to scrub this one extra hard to return it to its pristine state." She spoke a bit too loudly, causing heads to turn.

"Mother, did you forget? We're getting a washerwoman next week, straight from Cork, I am told. Tempy will not have to do the scrubbing, so there is no need to worry. You can walk slowly with your skirts dragging. I wish to get indoors promptly. We differ in that way," I said.

Seized with dismay, she stood under her umbrella waiting for Father, with her eyes ablaze. I knew better, but I could not help myself. I possessed an abundance of sharp words, and they were readily available. Even if she did invite them in, I often felt a pang in my own heart after releasing them.

I waited in the church vestry, which was much larger than I expected and very crowded. Most of the people were wearing their best clothes and were, for the most part, clean. The millworkers were the exception. If you stood too close to one, you would be overcome by a distinctive, disagreeable odor. And, I feared that many of them had the crawlies.

Mother and Father joined me just as the deacon approached. Father proudly gave his name, and we were ushered to a pew near the front of the church, where others like us were seated. The organ was fairly large as was the choir. I kept my eyes down and listened to the somewhat skilled organist as he played prelude music. His playing indicated that he had decent training, but that he lacked the discipline to practice, which was evident as he fumbled through certain passages in hopes that no one noticed.

I kept my eye out for the girl who had been splashed. Although, she may have been heading to another church altogether, and the only way I could identify her would be by her muddy attire. I could not help but pity her and her lot in life. I imagined that she could not show her face under such circumstances, and perhaps she returned home to her shabby tenement and in her shame, sacrificed a morning of worship. People continued to shuffle in and take their places in the pews. I closed my eyes.

Dear Lord, Please keep me from falling prey to the many rules and etiquette of those scattered in my path. Guide me away from the prideful and arrogant. May I be clothed in humility and truth, grow in grace, and have compassion for others, for those who do not have riches and goodness in their lives. May the girl on the street, and others like her, find strength in poverty as You lead them to a righteous path, Amen.

CHAPTER 25

Sarah
September 21, 1872

I AWOKE BEFORE the bell tolled or the rooster crowed. The girls around me slept soundly. I wished that I had my pendant watch. Unless it was in our treasure chest at home, it was lost in the fire.

I thought about the poster at the market. There was to be a fireman's parade on Sunday afternoon, featurin' the Fall River Cornet Band. I was scheduled to prepare supper and leftovers for Monday's dinner pails, but if Clara agreed, we could trade days.

I drifted back to that day in 1863—about a year after Papa's death. I was eight years old and unaware of bein' on the brink of a miracle. Jonas Eldridge let me try his horn. It had been played by his Uncle Edward in a regiment band durin' the war. It was somewhat crude, but it played nicely. And, with a few adjustments made by Grampa Wills, was almost as good as new.

Used for solos and the most intricate variations, it was known as a soprano cornet. Jonas played it often, in school, and on special occasions at church. He took pride in his playin' and, other than a few noticeable mishaps, was generally good.

We were at a church picnic, enjoyin' a day of uninterrupted sunshine. Jonas was away from the crowd, sittin' on a log, playin' as softly as possible. I took it upon myself to sit on the other end of the log. He squirmed a bit from the awkwardness of my presence. To afford him a level of comfort, I looked away, but he continued to falter.

I told him not to be embarrassed. He played beautifully. Of course, he didn't believe me and said that he would never be as talented as his uncle. I tried to encourage him, but he had always been a defeated sort of boy.

He challenged me, not thinkin' that I knew a thing about music. I was not a polished performer, but I had become somewhat skilled on the piano. In addition to what Mother knew, Patience Cook had taken lessons for a few years, and she showed me some notes and basic chords.

My grandfather was a gifted fiddler. I was told that his music and sensitive heart remained in Ireland and that he was never the same after their journey across the Atlantic. However, Mother inherited her melodious voice from her own mother, one of the finest singers from their hometown in Ireland. We never met, but Mother spoke of her often.

Grampa Wills gave us a piano that, until the day of the fire, lay in ruins in the back of the barn. It was not completely unplayable. I spent many cold days sittin' at that piano, playin' until my fingers were too numb to cooperate. It was only when Mother shouted for me to come into the house that I did so unwillingly.

Jonas's uncle taught him how to play his cornet and gave him lessons whenever he visited. When I asked why his uncle didn't play, he said that playin' brought up all those memories that he wished to forget. It seemed that durin' the war when he wasn't playin' music, he and some of the other musicians tended to the sick and wounded, a difficult time indeed.

Pushin' his unpleasantness aside, his uncle was kind and taught Jonas how to play. I told him that I would have thanked God every day if I had that opportunity.

So, Jonas smiled and gave me a chance to blow into that crumpled horn of his. I jumped to my feet and wrapped my hands around the cool silver, spendin' the remainder of the afternoon makin' sounds that invited Abigail to make faces.

While all of the guests played simple games and plied themselves with baked chicken and merries, I sat with Jonas. At first, I sounded like a goat, but within a short amount of time, I was able to make a decent sound.

Mother approached with Abigail. *What have we got here? A buddin' musician?*

Reluctantly, I handed the horn over to Jonas as my cheeks fired up. Even though Mother and Abigail had no interest, I talked about the horn all the way home. I savored the distinct scent of silver and oil on my hands—a scent that forever brought me back to that moment of discovery.

For the next few months, Jonas and I met in the back of the barn, where he showed me how to play the cornet. I was filled with inspiration, lookin' forward to each lesson, only to reach the depths of despair when he packed it away and went home. I knew that I could have been a better player if I had a cornet of my own. I would have practiced daily and become quite famous, at least in our little town.

I read an article about a conservatory in Boston that admitted women. It was a dream that propelled me to find a way to raise my level of playin', to get a horn of my own.

In exchange for lessons from Jonas, I baked him merries, and since I was so good with the needle, I offered to do his mendin'. His mother had six other children to look after, so it was appreciated. Mother frowned upon it, but my relentless beggin' caused her to cave in. She knew that I could not go on without my lessons, and she wanted what was best for us.

After six months of lessons, I persuaded Mr. Tibbetts to allow me to work two afternoons a week in his store. He was apprehensive with me bein' so young, but because of his affection for Mother, I knew that he would agree.

I pitied him because she accepted his niceties, offerin' nothin' in return. I supposed that in many ways, I was just as guilty for allowin' such circumstances to help me to wiggle my way into a job. It was the only way I could have saved money for my own cornet.

My tasks varied. Whenever shipments arrived, if possible, I unpacked and sorted the lightweight goods. I brushed up and dusted every shelf. Sometimes, if they were havin' a time of it, I helped folks find things. Eventually, I was able to save enough money to buy a mouthpiece. At that rate, it would have taken a lifetime to buy an entire cornet.

As luck would have it, and without my knowledge, Jonas spoke with his uncle about my plight. Bein' a well-respected musician in his regiment, he still maintained many valuable connections.

My heart fainted within me when Jonas mentioned that his uncle wanted to attend one of our sessions. He said that he would like nothin' more than to hear me play. Besides, he planned to move up from Concord and buy a plot of land near us on Brown's Ridge.

I fretted for a full week, even persuadin' Jonas to allow me to keep the horn so that I could prepare. I practiced scales and learned "The Last Rose of Summer" to the best of my ability.

I waited for them in the back of the barn. Over time, I had transformed the space into an actual music room. I kept the piano clean, took care to preserve the last workin' keys, and placed chairs directly beneath where the sun streamed in through the transom window. Abigail helped me hang old curtains over the empty stalls, where we kept the other horses before Papa died. I even placed dried flower arrangements on various beams to add a hint of sophistication.

I was stunned to look upon Uncle Edward's handsome face. He was much younger than I had envisioned. His skin was clear, his eyes brown, and his dark hair was thick and wavy. I didn't ask about it, but I noticed a visible limp when he made his way to the chair.

When Jonas introduced us, I curtsied and then blushed when I remembered our place—a barn behind the chicken coop. First, Jonas played a song that he had written himself. In spite of the fact that the endin' was somewhat uncertain, we were all pleased.

When it was my turn, I wanted to flee. It was one thing to play in front of Jonas, or our cow, Lizzy, but this was different. I became lightheaded and began to wither.

I took the horn. Although I had memorized the music, my mind went blank. When I begged for a moment to collect myself, Uncle Edward smiled and told me to just have fun.

I was about to respond when one of our roosters crowed. We burst into a fit of laughter. I was finally able to breathe, a definite requirement for a cornetist.

Fixin' my eyes on the large bundles of mint that hung from the burnt amber beams, I pretended that I was alone in the room. I played a simple scale. It was much too fast, but I knew what I needed to do in order to perform my best. I became separate from myself.

I reached a dreaded passage and broke into a sweat. A surge of anger got me through it. *Why did God give me the desire to play, but not afford me a cornet of my own?* I managed to perform with such ease and determination that I surprised myself. I played the last note ever so sweetly. It was, after all, a song about a rose—delicate and innocent, under the guardianship of thorns.

Uncle Edward beamed, and Jonas himself was unmistakably surprised. Greatly exhilarated by my new air of confidence, I took a deep bow.

When I told Uncle Edward that I had been playin' for just over a year, the color drained from his face. He admitted that he hadn't touched his horn for a long time.

I couldn't imagine how he felt. He was in the war for a few years. Somethin' dreadful must have happened for him to come home and walk away from his music.

I pushed for him to play. If not for us, for the horn itself, which I realized was somewhat silly. I wondered where I summoned the nerve to push like that. But, it worked. After accusin' me of bein' stubborn, he took the horn.

With his head down and eyes closed, he stood very still. Again, a rooster crowed, and some of the hens clucked and fluttered on the other side of the wall. There was no laughter. I waited patiently, willin' him to play even one note.

He took a deep breath. He wobbled at first, and then suddenly, the barn was filled with vibrant, pure notes. The more he played, the more magnificent the music became. His discomfort transformed into serenity, and his playin' seemed effortless.

The last, silvery note lingered in my mind for many years to follow. After hesitation, I asked him the name of the song. With a profound look of sadness, he set the cornet on top of the piano and explained the meanin' of "The Vacant Chair."

When a band member died, they set up his chair as if he were still present. Of course, he was there in spirit. Sometimes, they placed a candle on the chair to honor what he brought to the band and how sorely he would be missed.

We spent the rest of the afternoon tryin' new songs and listenin' to stories about the encampments, battlefields, and other places where music was integral to the war experience.

Incredibly inspired, I continued to work for Mr. Tibbetts and save my meager earnin's. Along with his mother and sister, Uncle Edward moved to Brown's Ridge, where they built a modest home. I was fortunate to enjoy weekly lessons, as he slowly reclaimed his horn. Weather permittin', our lessons took place in the music room in the barn. Jonas often joined us.

One cheerless March afternoon in 1865, when there was talk of the war windin' down, Uncle Edward showed up at Tibbetts' store. He was quite flustered, limpin' his way over to where I was stackin' flour, urgin' me to drop everything and accompany him. I was not done with my work, but he insisted that I leave immediately and follow him.

I wiped the flour dust from my hands and told Mr. Tibbetts, who had become somewhat dependent on me and always had more work than I could manage, that I had to leave. I promised to work harder the next day, to finish what I had started.

We rode through the icy rain to Uncle Edward's, makin' good time. I followed him into his house, where his mother hovered over a stewpot, hummin', and stirrin', and payin' us no mind. He asked me to wait as he dashed out of the room.

Hello, Mrs. Taylor.

Hello, Sarah. I s'pose you're here for that horn.

I don't know what I am here for, actually.

Well, ever since we came here, Edward has done nothin' but play music, 'cept for when you or Jonas have his cornet, and then he broods and spends time locked up in the back room. Who knows what he's doin'. I wish he'd—

Uncle Edward burst into the room with a bundle tucked under his arm. He pulled out a kitchen chair and made me sit and close my eyes.

Tryin' to ignore the odd sensation in my stomach, I sat down.

He set the bundle on my lap and placed my hands upon it.

It was somethin' wrapped in a blanket.

Unfold it.

I carefully pulled the blanket away to find a well-crafted leather case with a clasp on the front. My mouth went dry.

What's inside?

Open it.

I opened the case and set my eyes on a new silver cornet.

Take it out.

I reached in and touched the cold metal. I nearly lacked the courage to continue, thinkin' it was a dream. I wondered if this meant that he would give me his horn and that I would no longer have to borrow it. My mind was aflutter with questions but mostly overwhelmed with the immeasurable beauty before me.

It was nickel silver with three string rotary valves. Engraved on the bell were the words "Made by Hall & Quinby, Boston" inside of an exquisite floral design. Of course, it was a soprano cornet, which is all that I knew of at that time.

It's a miracle.

Try it.

I held the cold mouthpiece tightly in my hand and then blew into it a few times before slippin' it into the lead pipe. I looked at him, still unsure if the moment was rooted in reality.

Play.

The first note caused me to jump, as the sound was brighter than the other horn. I adjusted my posture and took a very deep breath and went on what one would consider a journey. It was as if the little cornet played itself.

I stopped.

Wait. Where did you get this?

It's yours, Sarah. It's for you.

What? Is this a trick?

He handed me a letter.

Dear Friend Edward,

After a considerable amount of time, I have finally found you. It is with great sorrow that I must share the news of the death of my beloved husband, and your friend, Elijah. He always spoke very favorably of you, and together in our youth, we three shared many bright days.

My dear Elijah suffered from typhus and, according to Captain Davies, put up a brave fight. He was eager to return home within a few short months. Sadly, it was not meant to be. Elijah succumbed. I find it most difficult to consider that so many heroic men lost their lives in battle, while many more died from sickness.

It was my husband's wish to have a new cornet, specifically from Hall and Quinby in Boston. He made arrangements for it to be delivered and planned to join the serenade band here in Concord. How sad that it never touched his lips.

He penned a letter from his sick bed, requesting that upon his death, I should send his new cornet to you. I am honoring his wishes and ask that you play with him in mind and become the caretaker of this instrument. Remember him when you play, and when you pass it on, do so with clarity and awareness and that the one who blows so much as a note into it will honor it as you both would.

I expect to take care of myself as best as possible during this time of sadness. I am pleased to carry out the last wish of my dearest Elijah. I hope that you are in good spirits.
Your friend,
Margaret Curtis

CHAPTER 26

Sarah
September 22, 1872

THE DAY SPARKLED with promise. Forced to ignore the bitterness of my spirit, I returned to the church with somewhat stained, yet much-cleaned attire. I spoke with Clara about tradin' my Sunday kitchen obligations for her Wednesday. Not only did she agree, she even offered to do so without trade. Although some would, I would never take advantage of her good nature.

Not bein' a muddy spectacle afforded me the opportunity to make a better judgment about my new church. Like everything else in Fall River, it was crowded, leavin' barely enough room to fit comfortably in the pew. The choir was decent, and the organist—a gray-haired man with a sour face and clouded spectacles—played well, but exhibited no connection to the music.

I blushed when the reverend approached the pulpit. In the midst of my catastrophic circumstances of the previous week, I did not comprehend his handsomeness. Amidst a sea of red cheeks, I was not alone in my observation.

Hand in hand, Clara and I rushed home. I had attended parades in Ossipee, but I was sure that they paled in comparison to the parades in a city the size of Fall River.

While the others seemed to possess no feelin's, I felt a pang when all but Clara and Ruby set out for the parade. I stopped in the kitchen.

"Thank you, Clara," I said.

"You're welcome," she replied. Her smile was broad, always comin' from the kindest heart of any person that I knew.

"You will tell me all about it when you get home," she said.

"I will," I said on my way out the door, hurryin' to catch up with the others.

The streets were awhirl with excitement and seemed to be even more crowded than when we marched to and from work. In addition to a multitude of mill-workers, there were people from all stations of life wanderin' along both sides of the street.

Red-faced patrolmen waved their arms, directin' both carriages and those on foot. And of course, the tramps and beggars could not miss an opportunity and roamed through the crowds with their tin cups. Although there were many other options, the apple woman showed up with her cart. There was even a hand-organ and monkey, and a little tambourine girl dancin' and singin' with all of her blessed heart.

We walked until we found a good place to view the parade and to avoid the pickpockets. My stomach fluttered, and my eyes watered when I heard the brass band in the distance.

"I think it started," Clemmie said. We leaned forward to catch a glimpse.

Followed by the Cascade Fire Company, The Hook and Ladder Company led the parade with their grandest engines, equipped with various ladders and bells, boastin' tanks and hoses. Proud firemen dressed in bright red tunics accompanied their engines and waved to the eager crowds that lined the streets. Teams of chestnut-colored draft horses, decorated with majestic harnesses, were a fine example of strength and fortitude as they hauled the heavy engines.

About fifteen policemen followed the fire apparatus. Some were on foot, others on horseback and carriages.

We cheered at the sight of the group of night watchmen, lamplighters, and their boys, who marched behind the police department. The sounds of bells and steam whistles blended in with the strains of the organ grinder and the fast approachin' brass band.

Just when I thought that my heart would faint within me, my eyes met with the young boy who, only days before, I had seen on the street. With his face aglow, he waved wildly as if we were familiar. Of course, I waved back.

"It looks like someone has an admirer," Norah said.

"Me?" I asked while maintainin' our gaze.

The young man who accompanied him looked me straight in the eye and smiled, not a big, toothy smile, but the secretive kind. It seemed as if I knew him, but it was not possible. I only knew the girls in the tenement or folks at work, and surely, he was not from Ossipee.

When he removed his cap, his butterscotch hair fell out, causin' quite a stir. I remembered. It was him, the one who helped me at the train station in Boston.

I barely regained my composure when the Fall River Cornet Band came into full view. I could have done nothin' to prevent the tears that poured forth from the deepest part of myself, as both the past and the present collided.

There were about thirty men. Except for the bandmaster in his distinguished frock coat, they wore traditional blue sack coats. The men with over-the-shoulder horns carried them with pride and good posture. Like badges of honor, many of the horns showed signs of wear and experience, while some of the cornets looked shiny and new.

"Fire! Fire! Fire!" they shouted out in unison and then returned to playin' the lively quickstep—a tune that stayed with me.

When they marched by, the drummer boy was so close that I could see the sweat tricklin' from his brow and feel his drum in the pit of my stomach.

The last time I had experienced such emotion, I was at the train station wavin' goodbye to Papa. However, I was no longer an innocent child. I knew music. I felt the hunger. It would always be there until I sat down at the feast that was spread out before me.

CHAPTER 27

August
September 22, 1872

FRANCIS MURPHY INVITED us to march in the Fireman's Parade, an honor that I never expected. I'd been to many a parade in New York, but only as a spectator.

After strugglin' to get Finn up and ready, we rushed to get our mornin' sausage from Tiago. The streets were already busy with people headin' to church. We worked our way through the crowd. It had been a while since we visited our favorite spot on the hill.

I grabbed Finn and pulled him out of the way when a pleasure carriage sped by, narrowly missin' us both. I recognized the driver. He came from where I was goin' to listen to the piano.

We brushed off the street dust and sat down by the fence to eat our breakfast. I was grateful to be amongst the bees as they went from one flower to the next, away from the noisy streets below. I waited patiently. Then, the gentle bee song was interrupted, not by the usual strains of the piano, but the earthy sound of a woman singin' in the garden.

Finn was on his hands and knees watchin' a trail of ants, blissfully unaware of her exquisite voice. Beyond a row of tall pink flowers, was a somewhat older, beautiful woman with shiny black skin. She wore gold earrin's, and her long silver hair was wrapped in a red bandana.

She stopped singin'. "Thank you," she said, bringin' a blossom up to her nose. "You gave your life to grace our table."

She went back to singin', stoppin' every few feet to inspect the flowers, give thanks, and fill her basket.

I ducked behind the wall when she turned in my direction. It wasn't until she started in singin' again that I knew I was safe. Finn continued to watch the ants, puttin' sticks in front of them to change their path. If only he could have heard her sing.

⟶⇥◉ ◉⇤⟵

On our way home, we stopped at the sinks to clean up before the parade. I even had time to fix the loose boards in our shed with a handful of nails that Francis Murphy gave me. He was a kind man. He wasn't one who pretended to be your friend and then took you off to Randall Island, or put you on a train to be placed out. Francis Murphy made it possible for me to earn my bread instead of stealin' or beggin'. It was all I ever wanted but never had a real chance. The mills weren't for me. Seems that the overseers had it out for us. My temper was too quick to survive it.

Finn and I made our way over to the street department where everyone was dashin' around gettin' ready for the parade.

"There ya are," Francis Murphy said.

"We wouldn't miss it," I said.

All the men and boys were loadin' up and headin' for where the parade was to assemble. We rode on the back of a police wagon, which made Finn smile like I had never seen before. We rode through the crowds and at times were at a standstill. We finally went to where the steam engines, hook and ladder trucks, and brass band members were gettin' in line.

The Grand Marshal blew his whistle to command order. We were placed in front of the brass band, for which I was pleased. Once we got started, I found myself marchin' with the tempo of the band. They played lively marches and quicksteps, some were familiar patriotic tunes, and others were new to me.

The people on the streets cheered and were uncommonly happy, and when one woman tossed out peppermint candies, Finn to stop too long, almost causin' the band to stumble into us.

We waved and marched, waved and marched. I had never felt so many eyes on me. When I looked out at the spectators, I saw her, the girl overcome with grief at the train station here and before that, in Boston. Well-clothed and with her cheeks blossomed afresh, she looked to have a happy heart and stood out in the drab crowd. I could not take my eyes away from her and smiled when she caught sight of me.

Chapter 28

Bess

September 22, 1872

After a typical morning at church and a ride along the waterfront, we returned home for lunch. At first, Mother insisted that I go to the Fireman's Parade, claiming that I would never make new friends if I refused to socialize. I convinced her that practicing was critical because my piano teacher said that if I was prepared, I could participate in a recital in November.

I was repeatedly reminded that nothing stayed the same. We had a new cook, who was somehow related to the washerwoman. She was plump and red-faced, the type who did not make eye contact when she spoke to you. She prepared a hearty pot roast for lunch and fresh blackberry pie for dessert. I preferred it when Tempy cooked. It meant that she would be in and around the dining area at mealtime.

"Where's Tempy?" I asked.

"I don't know. In her room, I suppose," Mother said.

I excused myself from the table and followed the sound of Tempy's voice to the parlor where she was arranging flowers in a crystal vase.

"I prefer dem outside, but your mother asked me to bring some in," she said.

"I prefer them outside too, but they are quite charming," I said.

"Well, enjoy dem," she said and started to walk away.

"Wait, Tempy. Where are you going?"

"I'm going to see if your mother needs anything else before they go to the parade," she said.

"You're not going?" I asked.

"No, I'm not."

I smiled and thumbed through my music until I found the Mozart and held it up. "How would you like a concert?"

She looked towards the kitchen where my parents were arguing about whether or not they should go early to get a good spot or wait. "Of course, I'd like that very much."

"And we can sit in the garden after and enjoy a glass of cool cinnamon water," I said.

"It's a perfect day for that, Miss Bess," she said.

Tempy was my favorite audience. She was honest and polite. She did not compliment me without thought. She listened intently and told me what was genuinely pleasing to her ears. She knew when I did or did not play with my whole heart and that was how she judged the quality of my performance.

Chapter 29

Sarah
September 25, 1872

THE USUAL BRIGHT skies ushered in by September were absent from Fall River, as the lint continued to flurry about. Although the heat of summer had vanished, it was stiflin' hot in the mills because the doors and windows were intentionally closed. It was imperative to the overall operation that the conditions be as warm and humid as possible.

I managed to adapt to my schedule, sometimes gettin' up before the mornin' bell to get ahead of the lines at the outhouses and sinks. Somehow, Mary found a way to work with us on the fifth floor. When asked how she was able to get Mr. Aldrich to cooperate, she skillfully changed the subject.

After a full day at the loom, I could barely lift my feet to walk home. But, the Fall River Cornet Band inspired me. When I reached the top step, entered the attic, and looked out at the city lights, I was ready to play.

I tried not to think of Abigail, but she was on my mind, as I wondered why I had not heard a word about a weddin' date. With each passin' day, she stepped closer to a life of doom. An unborn child does not wait for you to do what is right. The townspeople would condemn her, and I could not be of help. I could only give her love from afar and then only through letters.

"Sarah! Are ya up there?" Mary shouted from the bottom step.

"Shh! Yes, please be quiet."

She rushed up the stairs and stood in front of the window.

"So, this is where ya been hidin'. I thought ya was outside sneakin' a smoke," she said.

"You know I don't smoke," I said.

Her eyes widened when she saw my horn. "That sure is pretty," she said. "Ya play?"

"Yes, I play. What else would I be doin' with it?"

"I always knew ya was hidin' somethin'. Why have ya kept it a secret?" she asked.

I sat in silence. The truth was, I didn't know. I shrugged my shoulders.

"Well, play somethin' for me," she said.

"I don't like to play under those circumstances," I said.

"What circumstances?"

"With someone sittin' real close, waitin'."

She moved to the other side of the alcove. "Is this better?"

"Yes," I said, stuffin' the rag into the bell. I decided to play a few measures of the "Nellie Gray Quickstep."

"That was amazin'!"

"No, it wasn't at all. I should have warmed up first, but you interrupted me," I said.

"I promise I won't tell nobody," she said. "But, if I played somethin' like that, I'd be showin' off."

"I would be grateful if you kept it a secret," I said.

"I promise. Ya wanna go share a smoke?"

"No, I told you I don't smoke. It's bad for you," I said.

"Ya sound just like…" She looked out the window. "Never mind."

She turned and left the attic. I waited until she closed the door at the bottom of the stairs and thought to play again but stopped. I didn't know why I kept it a secret. I just did.

I curled up in the chair next to the window. I was about to relax when I spotted the two lamplighters on the street below. I leaned forward to get a better look, and the older one glanced up at me. I quickly blew out the candle and sat in the dark. Other than a terrible go of a quickstep, I did not play at all. My music was no longer a secret, and the lamplighter saw me. There was nowhere left to hide.

CHAPTER 30

August
September 25, 1872

WE HAD ONLY lit the lamps on two streets when I realized that we were bein' followed by two men and a woman. I didn't usually mind such nonsense, but they were careful to stay just two lampposts behind, and whenever I looked at them, they turned away.

Other than an occasional outburst from them, it was generally quiet. They stuck together. The woman was writin' in a book, and one of the men had a large magnifyin' glass.

I tried to concentrate. I didn't think that we were in danger, but not knowin' what they were up to was gettin' the best of me.

I decided to approach them. They were huddled together and didn't bother to look up.

"Why are you followin' us?" I asked.

The woman laughed, and one of the men walked towards me holdin' somethin' in his hands.

"No need to be worried. We're findin' specimens," he said.

"Specimens?" I asked.

Finn rushed right up to him and inspected the giant moth that he was holdin'.

"We're naturalists, bug cranks," he said. "We find beetles, bugs, and moths that are drawn to the lamps, and we take notes."

"This is a Luna moth," he said, "one of my personal favorites."

I moved in and got a closer look. It was a beauty, indeed. I had seen them on the walls at the train station. "Well, isn't that somethin'. I never knew what they were called."

"So, you might as well get used to us. We try to come out a few nights a week until it gets cold. Some of the specimens are worth money," he said.

I thought about how we could use more money, but I didn't know much about bugs. Finn ran over to see the other moths that they had collected. He gave a whoop and tried to wiggle away when I went to fetch him. He gave in, knowin' that darkness followed close behind, waitin' for no one. We had many more lamps to light.

"James Morrill," he extended his hand.

"August Wood," I said. "Have a good night."

After cautiously placin' a small dead moth into his pocket, Finn and I carried on.

They followed us for another hour or so and then fell further behind, after a beetle that they found caused quite a stir. Although uncommon for me to think in such a way, I was relieved that Finn could not hear the excitement.

Because we were so good at our new job, Francis Murphy offered to take me to the nearest dealer's cellar and share a pail of beer. Of course, I declined. There was nothin' but trouble in such places.

He added three more streets to our route on the hill, so together Finn and I received $1.18 more per week. I thought that the fancy homes were beautiful durin' the day and enjoyed the gardens and music, but at night, those same homes, bein' all lit up, were magnificent in an entirely different way.

I fixed it so that the last street was the one with the piano. Finn and I sat down to enjoy the apples that I had bought from the apple woman. Then, to my surprise, the piano music started in. It was different that night, not as wild, but just as powerful. While Finn examined the moths that fluttered around the lamp that we had lit only moments before, I ate my apple and listened to each note.

"Bravo!" The applause came from about three or four people.

I inched a little closer to the fence so that I could hear more of the conversation.

"I shall slay the audience!" the woman said, followed by a burst of laughter.

"Bess! Remember, rudeness repels, and courtesy attracts."

"Oh, Mother! I'm not annoying anyone here in my own home. Besides, Tempy loves it. Right?"

"Miss Bess… Course I like it. You played it right from your heart."

There were shufflin' sounds and words that I could not understand, and the lights in the room were lowered. I approached Finn, who had at least four dead bugs and moths lined up on the wall.

"Time to go."

He pocketed the dead ones and cupped his hand around the one that was still alive. Without mishap, he managed to carry the bugs and ladder all the way to the outhouses and sinks. We had just washed up when I caught a glimpse of a face at the attic window. There before me was the girl from the parade. Even though she may have thought that I was spyin' on her, the way I kept turnin' up and all, I couldn't help but smile. She extinguished her candle and vanished into the darkness. I stood there for a moment, hopin' for a reason beyond my understandin' that she would reappear.

Chapter 31

Bess
September 25, 1872

Mr. Carver provoked me in a way that brought out a higher level of musicianship in me.

"Stop right there," he said.

I thought that I was doing fine, but of course, I paused. "What is it?"

"What are the markings at measure 180?"

"Pianissimo," I said.

"Do you think you were playing pianissimo?"

"Well," I crossed my arms, "no."

"Go back to the beginning," he said.

"All the way back?" I took a deep breath and started to play and immediately realized that my annoyance had sparked me to play loudly, so I quickly adhered to the appropriate dynamics.

After a good spell of playing with sharp focus, Mr. Carver stood up to leave.

"You're making progress. You're headstrong and often take matters into your own hands, ignoring how the music is intended to be played. Once you decide to concentrate on the entirety of the composition, I believe that you'll shine."

I'll shine? I am shining now. What is wrong with him?

"Work on the final movement and the three etudes that we covered, and next week we'll decide if you're ready to perform at the recital. I think that you'll be ready, but it's up to you." He gave a nod.

"Yes, I'll polish this and take care of the trouble spots. I assure you that I'll be ready to perform." I accompanied him to the hallway where Davis was waiting.

"I can show myself out," Mr. Carver said and slipped out the door.

I spent another hour practicing and realized that I had developed a habit of playing faster and louder when I made a mistake. Knowing this made a significant difference in my overall ability to perform.

Both mentally and physically exhausted, I finally stepped away from the piano and did my needlework. I was making a pocket-handkerchief for Tempy but had not touched it since we left Boston. I had a few weeks to complete it.

Later that evening, I invited Mother, Father, Tempy, and all of the servants, including the new ones, to join me for fresh lemonade and to hear me play Mozart. I would not stop until my performance was perfect—until the people of Fall River were whispering my name upon their lips as one of the finest pianists to grace their stage.

CHAPTER 32

Sarah
September 27, 1872

ALTHOUGH MY FINGERS were sore and my body generally ached all over, my skills had improved. I understood why so many of the girls wanted to go upstairs for drawin' in, cardin', and the other jobs that required more expertise and offered an increase in pay. A spinner's work was much too tiresome.

I looked up briefly to see Mr. Aldrich whisper into Mary's ear and walk away. At first, she laughed, but when she spotted me, her expression changed to one of solemness. The noontime bell rang out, the machinery squealed to a halt, and the workers swarmed towards the long rows of dinner pails.

I tried to catch up with Mary, but I could not see her anywhere. I joined Clara, Norah, and Addy, and we sat out in the yard and ate our bread and cheese. Typically, by Friday afternoon, our conversation had lulled, as we saved our strength to endure the day, silently lookin' forward to Saturday's ring out at 4:30 and knowin' that we had all of Sunday off.

I was jammed in the middle of the other workers climbin' the stairs when I realized that I left my dinner pail in the yard. I managed to turn against the crowd and make my way to the first floor.

"You'll be late!" Addy shouted.

I didn't bother to respond. I refused to spend money on another pail if I didn't have to. I would take my chances with Mr. Aldrich. I ran out and grabbed my pail. When I returned, the last of the workers had returned to their stations. Drenched in sweat, I raced up the stairs. Just as I feared that my heart would cease to beat, I stopped. I decided that I would have to pay the consequences for bein' late anyway, so I took my time. I had not been in trouble but witnessed when others were late, as Mr. Aldrich screamed obscenities, shamed them, and then cut their pay.

I had two more flights to go when I heard groanin' comin' from the dark space beneath the steps. I went around to see if someone needed help. There was Mary with her skirt pulled up and her back pressed against the wall while Mr. Aldrich was havin' his way with her. He was unaware of my presence, but Mary stared at me with her wide green eyes as I backed away.

I supposed I should have been grateful for her sinful, lusty behavior because, other than Addy and the other girls, no one took notice of my lateness. By the time I reached my station, I was in a tizzy.

Within moments, Mary entered the spinnin' room with her cheeks ablaze, and Mr. Aldrich followin' close behind, smokin' his black clay pipe. I kept lookin' her way, hopin' that she would exchange a glance, but it took time for her to summon the courage. When our eyes finally met, I glared at her the same way that Mother would have, the glare of knowin' the truth. It mattered not, for she smiled at me and continued workin'. She had no shame.

Once the evenin' bell rang out, we stepped away from the looms and collected our pails. With our tired heads bowed, we headed for the door. Wordless and hand in hand, Clara and I walked home, appreciatin' the cool air dryin' the sweat on our skin.

"Wait, excuse me, Miss?"

I continued to walk, and Clara tugged on my hand and whispered, "That boy is talkin' to you."

I turned around, and there was the lamplighter with the ladder boy stopped, forcin' the people to split and walked around us.

"Me?"

"Yes," His cheeks reddened. "You dropped this." He handed me the pocket-handkerchief that my sister saved from the fire. It matched hers. I stared at the crudely embroidered butterfly that I made as a child when things were simple.

"Thank you," I said, "I didn't even realize that I dropped it." I took it from him, surprised that I felt faint when I touched his hand.

"You're welcome," he said.

He was more handsome up close. I dropped Clara's hand and stood speechless before him.

"I've seen you around here a lot," he said.

"Really?" I crossed my arms. "I don't recall."

"I helped you at the train station in Boston, and I've seen you here on the street by your tenement. My name's August, and this is Finn."

"Oh—" I felt the need to hide. "—I think I recall droppin' my bags and someone helpin' me. Boston was hectic… So, that was you. Thank you," I said.

"I'm always glad to be of service. What's your name?"

"Uh, I'm Sarah," I said. By then, Clara was gone.

"Well, I kept seein' you around, so I thought I'd introduce myself," he said. "We have to go light the lamps. Have a pleasant night, Miss Sarah." He lifted his cap, tapped the ladder boy on the shoulder, and they left.

I watched until they disappeared, and then I walked the rest of the way home. I found my way to the kitchen. After another meal that consisted of dried corned beef and cabbage, we packed our dinner pails for the next day. I washed up and went to the attic. The twilight had surrendered to darkness. I looked out over the city, feelin' strangely satisfied that the lamps were lit by someone I knew and that his name was August. I had never met anyone with that name or with eyes that smiled without the need to utter a word.

After a few moments of sittin' with it, I played my cornet for a good hour, until I was interrupted by someone on the stairs. I stopped and peered down, and there was Mary.

"I thought I would find ya here," she said.

I looked out the window.

"You're not shocked to see me with Mr. Aldrich are ya?" she asked.

I continued to look out the window.

"He's been after me since I started. If I didn't give in, I wouldn't be on the fifth floor."

"You didn't need to sell your soul to be up with me," I said.

"I did it because I wanted to be with ya and the others that I know. But, also, what would he do if I refused?"

134

"You should have refused. It's repulsive. And, to think that he has a wife and maybe children. Did that enter into your mind when you lifted your skirt? Where is the strength in your soul? Are you a slave to your weakness?"

"It means nothin' to me."

"He looks at others with hungry eyes. You're not special to him, just easy prey."

"He gave me a favor and moved me up to the fifth floor," she said.

I remained quiet. First, it was gamblin, then smokin, and swearin', and then lettin' the overseer have his way with her. I feared that I would have to pray for answers.

"Well, I got this for ya. I'm not sure what it says, but I know it's about that band that ya liked so much. Maybe they're playin' again." She slid a piece of paper onto the crate and left.

After she was gone, I did, in fact, turn to the Lord.

Heavenly Father, Teach me I pray, to be a good friend to Mary. I ask that You cleanse her tarnished spirit, and wash away her sins so that she reaches a pure state. May she become a devoted follower and crave the guidance that she needs to be at Your right hand. Show her the way before she falls deeper into darkness, and do forgive her, Amen.

I relaxed in my chair, about to doze off when I remembered the paper.

Auditions - Fall River Cornet Band - Sunday, October 20 - 2:00 PM
The Concert Hall Auditorium
Open to any man with experience in the following:
Eb and Bb Cornets, Alto Horn, Bass Saxhorn
Registration 1:30
Bandmaster, Victor Daniels

Chapter 33

August
October 6, 1872

The nights were cold and the days short. The idea of bringin' light pleased me. I knew that it was not my light to keep but to carry with me into the darkest corners of the city.

I felt smart in the red flannel shirt that I got from Tiago's mother. I traded her for a locket that I found. The photos inside were spoiled, so I had no way of findin' the owner. Finn's collection of oddities that he found on the trail grew bigger every day. I let him keep almost everything, but if somethin' had great value, I used it for barter or tried to sell it.

One of my best finds was a timepiece. The cover was cracked, but it worked. 'Tho I had always relied on the tower bells, it helped to know the time in between the hours.

I took every opportunity to pass by Sarah on the street. And, whenever I could, I caught sight of her in the window. At first, when she saw me, she quickly blew out her candle, but after a bit, she gave a smile before blowin' it out. Bein' it was the last place we went to before goin' to bed, I took her smile with me into the world of dreams.

Dependin' on the moon and the weather, it was possible to miss nearly a week of work at a time. I wanted to see her whenever I had the chance. She was different from other girls. She was a little quiet, but only because she chose to be, not out of fear or self-importance. She was a thinker. Bein' a thinker myself, I liked that. She seemed to have a good upbringin', but not like the fancy ladies that went to market with their drivers and servants.

After I ate my bowl of porridge with bacon fat, it was time to go out. Sunday afternoon, we liked to go to Tiago's to play marbles and checkers. Finn played with kids in the neighborhood as best he could. It bothered me when they teased him, but they learned to get along.

Tiago's sister, Maria, invited Finn inside to play with her son, givin' me some time to myself. To show my appreciation, I gave her a nice sandalwood fan that I found up on the hill. Other than one small crack and a tiny piece missin', it was in good shape.

As expected, the people filed out of the Methodist Church. I was bold that day and waited by the steps. She pretended not to notice me, and when Clara elbowed her, she tried to look surprised.

"Hello, Sarah," I said.

"August!" she said, laughin'.

"What a perfect day, may I walk you home?" I asked.

"It's a fine day, indeed," she said.

Clara caught up to another group of girls.

"Perhaps you would join me next Sunday, and we could walk to and from church together, and you could attend the service," she said.

I thought about Finn and how I would worry about him sittin' in church for so long and that someone might recognize him and try to take him away. "I don't know."

"What is there to know?" she asked.

"Someone would have to take care of Finn," I said.

"Bring him along."

"It isn't that easy. Well, he's deaf and sometimes has these outbursts and—"

"—no excuses. Maybe it would be good for him to be in the house of the Lord."

"He can't hear. He would fidget and squirm," I said.

"I understand. I thought that it might be good for both of you."

That look in her eyes meant that I was not worthy of her unless I went to church. Those days were gone. I didn't trust church people, any of them, always tryin' to catch us to take to the island. I would never return to church.

"Where are your parents?" she asked.

"They've been gone a long time," I answered. "Where are your parents?"

She took my arm and led me away from the crowd. "They're both dead as well. My father died in the war, and my mother—" her eyes filled with tears, "—well, she died about a month ago."

"I'm sorry," I said, thinkin' that's why she was so distraught at the train station.

"It's like a nightmare, and I think that I'll wake up and be able to go home to see her."

"Where is home?"

"It's a small town—Ossipee, New Hampshire."

"Why are you here? I've heard that New Hampshire is beautiful and has lots of mountains and lakes."

"Ever since I was a child, I planned to travel and see the world. And, I'm independent. Everyone back there stays on the farm, generation after generation, repeatin' the same simple lifestyle. I want somethin' else."

"Do you have brothers or sisters?"

"Yes, I have a sister, Abigail. She's a year younger than me."

"So, she likes bein' on the farm?"

"Well, it's complex. But, yes, I mean no. I don't know. She is there and is supposed to be there. Perhaps she'll join me one day. Enough about me," she said. "Where are you from?"

"Oh, that would take a long time to explain," I said.

"How could it be that difficult?"

"Well, sometimes these things are."

She gave me that look again, the look of doubt. I scrambled for the right words.

"Well, I'm from New York City, a place called Five Points," I said.

"Sounds interestin'. How did you end up here?"

"Why does anyone end up anywhere?" I knew that I shouldn't have answered her question with another question. My face was red, and I wanted to talk about somethin' else.

"I didn't mean to bother you."

"No, it's not that. Like what you said about your sister, it's complex."

"Where you're from is complex?"

"No, I mean… sort of."

"Well, it can be simple if we think in terms of nature. We come from our mothers," she said and laughed.

"Well, yes." I imagined the blue linen tucked into my tobacco tin, and then I thought about Finn. "We come from our mothers, and we are all worth redemption."

"Uh oh." She looked up at me and smiled. "You're not runnin' from the law. Are you?"

"No, no, it's nothin' like that. I've been around and seen a lot." I wanted to back up and start the conversation again. She was gettin' all the wrong ideas. How would I tell her about the steps, the asylum, Smitty, and the trains? It was too much all at once.

Together, in silence, we strolled back to the yard, where the women were hangin' clothes on the lines strung between the tenements, yellin' across to one another. I tried to find the right words, but there weren't any. We stood on her doorstep, and I thought about kissin' her. I knew better, especially in front of so many people and in the daylight. She seemed proper.

"Well, I hope to see you soon," I said.

"I'm sure of it," she said.

I was convinced that I was a strong man, but when I looked into her blue eyes, all of that came into question. It was as if she could see right through me. I thought that I liked it but wasn't sure if I could accept that kind of truth.

CHAPTER 34

Sarah
October 6, 1872

When I played music in the barn, I left my troubles at the door. In Fall River, I left them on the bottom step that led to the attic. I played so quietly that I was unsure if I would ever be able to blow into that horn appropriately again. I did what was necessary. To stop playin' music was to die a slow death, for no matter how tired I was at the end of the day, music breathed the life that had seeped out, back into my bein'.

I dragged myself from here to there, wonderin' how I would endure the next phase of the day, but I managed. I viewed my music as a reward. However, I had to be careful. Without a timepiece, I stayed up too late and dreaded the sound of the first mornin' bell.

Except for Mary and August, no one knew about the attic, and Mary was the only one who knew about my cornet. So, when I did go to bed, I thought about how I would keep my secret and wondered why it was a secret to begin with.

I took another look out over the city, and I saw August and Finn makin' their way down the street. In case he got the notion that I was waitin' for him and to avoid questions, I blew out the candle.

When I closed my eyes, I saw his face, which was quite pleasin' to me. It was hard to believe that I knew someone from New York City. I could add it to the list of others that I knew from faraway places, includin' the other side of the ocean.

I wondered why he had so many secrets. I laughed. Who was I to talk? I didn't even comprehend my own secrets. All of this left me feelin' uneasy yet curious. I would find the answers. Until I knew more about him, it was best to keep a safe distance.

I waited for the girls to go to bed before I put my horn away. I was about to go to the sinks when someone came up from behind.

"Wait, Sarah!"

There was Mercy, breathless, rushin' to catch up with me. Even though we worked together and shared the same crowded bed, we didn't talk much. Rebecca kept her under close watch. Clara and Mary, who had become an unsolved riddle, were my loyal companions.

"Are you goin' down?" she asked.

"Yes."

"I'll go with you." She giggled and ran along beside me. "Where do you go at night?"

"Where do I go?" I should have been prepared. "Oh, I just like to walk around, go out to the yard, and sometimes visit with Mary."

"Mary was playin' cards with the girls in our room tonight."

"I know. I went out and looked at the sky, hopin' to see the stars, but it's too cloudy."

"It's always cloudy in Fall River," she said.

"It doesn't hurt to check."

"Mary said that you might be sneakin' out to smoke." She knew very well that I didn't smoke. She was purposely stirrin' up a nest of bees, for which she was very good at doin'.

"She did? Well, she could not be more wrong. I would not do somethin' like that. I simply like to have my private time," I said.

I slammed the door to the outhouse, rippin' my sackcloth, before sittin' upon the cold splintered seat. All I could do was wish her away.

I tried to keep feelin's of bitterness from creepin' in, but it was impossible. No, Mary did not tell about my music, but she offered up a dark story instead. I desired peace, an anchor to my soul. I would not break my promise to Mother. I assured her that I understood that music did not perish. People perished. They perished when they ignored their true callin'—the reason for a beatin' heart.

CHAPTER 35

Sarah
October 20, 1872

THE TRUTH WAS forever lost. For weeks, I prayed endlessly. I had no tolerance for fibbin' and looked down on those who made it a habit, but this had become my road to survival.

Norah slipped on her shawl and hood. "Enjoy your visit with your cousins."

"Thank you. I will," I said, just wantin' them all to leave.

Clara kissed my cheek and followed Norah out the door.

"We'll miss you at church. Hopefully, no one will report you," Rebecca said.

"She's allowed to have family visitors," Mercy said. "I wish someone would come visit us."

"Never mind. Let's go, or we'll be late," Rebecca said, rollin' her eyes.

I waited until I knew that they were well on their way. My stomach churned, and I didn't know if I could follow through. I hardly slept at all, but I did rest. In the absence of the usual chatter and commotion, the agitated cries of the babies were heightened. The mothers never paid me any mind, so I was confident that I could leave without incident.

I rushed to the attic, where the pitcher and wash basin were already set up, and I sat in the chair. I wasn't hungry, and the thought of food caused a stir. I could not go without fuel. I unfolded the linen and forced down the bread and cheese.

I slowly uncoiled my braid. Of course, at such a time it shined in perfection. I considered wearin' a cap, but once inside the buildin', I would have had to remove it.

The shears were cold to the touch. I didn't take too much time to think, as I would lose the courage required to follow through.

With my braid in my one hand and shears in the other, I began to cut. Gettin' through the thickest part was hard. After I snipped the last few hairs, I was able to fully exhale. Abigail and I took great pride in our hair, and Mother was very good at fixin' it.

Overcome by an unexpected calm, I stood very still with my long, black braid in hand. I wrapped the thick end with twine, rolled it into a small rag, and put it in my bandbox.

I covered my fingertips with Rowland's Macassar Oil and slicked my hair back the way Mr. Aldrich did. Then I dabbed a slight amount of coal ash over my top lip and around the lower part of my chin, roughin' it up to look as if I was in need of a shave.

I sifted through the pile of clothes that I had scavenged from discarded debris alongside the tenements. I spent many a night washin', hangin', and mendin'. I buttoned the light brown trousers, thankful that they fit without the need for suspenders. I took ahold of the strip of an old bed sheet and carefully wrapped it around my torso, coverin' my breasts while makin' sure that I could still breathe appropriately.

Then, I slipped into the tan work shirt. I had to remove the buttons from the bottom and sew them onto the top. The scuffed shoes that I found behind the church, mixed in with a pile of rags and other shoes, were too big, but suitable when I stuffed paper into the toes.

I trimmed the bottom of my hair as best I could before slickin' it back again, perhaps usin' too much oil, makin' a mess. The last thing to put on was the black sack coat. It fit me better than anything else and completely covered my upper body.

Before runnin' down four flights of stairs and out the door, I thought it wise to look out the window one more time. It was clear, so I ran until I reached an unfamiliar street.

The twelve o'clock bell rang. I had a few hours to spare, so I continued to walk, steppin' aside whenever anyone came in my direction. I stopped and stared at my reflection in the butcher shop window. I did it. If I had come face to face with myself, I would have sworn that I was a young man.

A red-faced man opened the door and shouted, "Entre ou vá embora!"

I fled, missin' the opportunity to try my masculine speakin' voice. Had the man spoken English, I may have stayed, but there was no time to think of such things. I could only respond to the part of me that had taken over, someone other than Sarah Hodgdon.

I ran so fast, and for so long; I lost track of time and direction. I slowed down and walked, tryin' to catch my breath. I had adapted to the large shoes and found them to be more comfortable than my own. And, to my surprise, I enjoyed the comfort of trousers.

In my head, I rehearsed what I would say. I imagined a handful of scenarios and prepared several responses. It was important to remember what Uncle Edward told me from the beginnin', that we were all goin' through the same thing, and to just play.

After a time of walkin', I arrived at the auditorium. It was much larger than any buildin' in Ossipee. Unable to move, I stood near the front steps. Again, my breathin' became labored, so I walked over to a cluster of bushes to gather my wits. I closed my eyes.

Heavenly Father, I come before Thee, meek and mild, to ask for the unspeakable privilege of playin' music to the fullest extent of my ability. There is nothin' more that would satisfy my humble longin' spirit than to be a Divine instrument of You, Father, to soar in the highest realms with the gifts that Thou hast bestowed upon me. Please guide me so that I may serve You and answer Your call. In the Lord's name, I pray, Amen.

When I saw three young men walkin' together up the steps, laughin', and talkin', I dismissed the fear that tried to nestle into the deepest part of me. I reminded myself not to look too far ahead, but to take each moment as it came.

My strength and logic lasted for but a moment when I stopped again, frozen on the top step. I got a chill, and my shirt was damp with sweat. The young men's voices echoed, almost promptin' me to run, but I had come too far.

I entered the reception area and followed the sign: "Auditions, this way," towards the unmistakable sound of brass instruments screamin' throughout.

I finally reached the auditorium, where a group of men huddled around a table in the back. About a dozen chairs were placed in a semi-circle on the stage and more chairs scattered on the main floor with cases and coats hastily flung about.

Men stood with their backs to each other, facin' the walls and playin' their instruments as if they were the only ones to consider. *Breathe. Just breathe.*

"Excuse me!" A plump, older man with white hair and sideburns hobbled towards me. "Are you here to audition?"

I opened my mouth, but it mattered not, for he was already speakin'.

"If you are, then you need to go see Mr. Daniels and register." He turned his attention to the next man, who was wanderin' about with his huge saxhorn perched on his shoulder.

I approached the table and stood in line, waitin' for that moment that would define me—a strong, confident man or imposter? If my secret were revealed, I would be forced to leave Fall River in deep shame. Doomed forever, my unworthiness would never permit me to return to New Hampshire again.

I flinched when another rather stout man shouted, "Next?"

I cleared my throat and paused. For an instant, I could not find a word. I took a deep breath. Surely, they knew. Someone else spoke from inside of me. "Yes, I'm here to audition."

He slid a paper across the table and handed me a pen. "Fill out this form. I see that you have a cornet?"

How did he know that I had a cornet? He stared at me, and he stared hard. I was convinced that he knew about my breasts, hidden beneath my sack coat. I would be taken away, screamin' and kickin'. All I wanted was a chance to play. No one needed to know. No matter what else happened at that moment anywhere on earth, I had to respond.

The quiet in the room was unnatural. I knew that someone had sneaked away to tell the police that there was someone present who was not in her right mind. I would then be whisked away to an asylum or poorhouse, like the Carroll County Farm, where those who were not right in the head were taken, never to be seen or heard from again. No one would ever know what became of me. I would have to tell Abigail, and others at home, that I had been committed.

With my head drooped forward and my well-oiled hair coverin' my face, I was about to confess, prepared to take my punishment. Suddenly and without warnin', I had to suppress the urge to laugh. I wondered if I would laugh or cry. Of course. Of course, he saw my small case. It was fine. A tall string bean of a man broke the silence with an edgy, sour blast from his cornet.

"Yes, sir... it's a cornet." I kept my eyes down and began to write on the paper, immediately wantin' to hide my small, delicate hands, but it was too late. Everyone had seen them. Again, the room fell silent, and the ones who had been blarin' into their horns just seconds before stopped. The tall cornetist stared at me while he emptied his spit out onto the floor. The first man that I spoke with, the one with white hair, whispered to the man seated beside him. Behind thick grubby hands, they continued with their private discussion, glancin' up at me out of the corner of their eyes.

I dropped the pen on the floor. When I bent down to pick it up, I looked towards the hallway. Everything slowed down when I realized that the sweat on my forehead and under my nose threatened to clear a path through my hand-crafted whiskers. I rubbed my fingers over the sweat, hopin' to keep it adequately blended.

I broke into a coughin' fit, even thinkin' that I might die if I didn't catch my breath. When everyone stopped to stare, I held up my hand to signal that I was alright. With all eyes upon me, I returned to the table and signed up as Jonas Smith, from Fall River, Massachusetts, a millworker lookin' to play the E-flat cornet.

Mr. Daniels stared at me, and I stared back, just like any man would look another man straight in the eye. He read over the form and slid it back across the table.

Breathe. Breathe. The horns started in blarin' again. I steadied myself.

"You forgot your address," he said.

I couldn't receive mail as Jonas Smith. I quickly made up an address—unlikely to have existed in Fall River—and wrote it down.

"Okay, Jonas. Go over there and warm up. You'll get called when it's your turn. Here's what you'll be playin'." He thrust a sheet of crumpled-up music into my chest and turned to the next man in line.

I made my way across the room, finally darin' to look at the music that I held in my sweaty hand and almost came undone: "We Are Coming, Father Abra'am"—one of my favorites. Uncle Edward gave me his own copy, and we played it often.

Barely able to contain my excitement, I found a chair, fetched my cornet and warmed up. I knew the piece well. I didn't even need the music, but that was another secret.

"That horn's a real beauty!" A very handsome man looked at me and smiled.

I blushed. "Thanks. It means a lot to me." I screamed in my head. A man would never blush or say such words.

"I can see why." He reached out to shake my hand. "Elton Colby."

"Jonas Smith," I said, makin' sure that I squeezed as hard as I could.

"Gentlemen, line up and be ready for when you're called!" Mr. Daniels shouted.

Scared white, I stood in line, tryin' to watch and avoid watchin' each person audition in front of the four men at the table.

"Jonas Smith!"

I stood tall and walked to the front of the room.

"You got an E-flat cornet there?"

"Yes, sir." I placed the music on the stand before me.

"Begin with a C-scale."

I nearly choked. Beads of perspiration trickled down from my brow, and my knees weakened. I had a choice. I would rise or fall. Risin' up meant to be amongst the angels, playin' music the way it was supposed to be played, or fallin' into a place of darkness—the angels' lament.

They spoke amongst themselves while I waited in horror. I believed that it was as perfect as could be. The first note was weak, but I corrected it and moved on. My temples throbbed, and I looked at the doorway, plottin' an escape. I was about to run when the pot-bellied, white-haired man spoke.

"Sorry to keep you waiting," he said. "Now, you have "Father Abra'am" ?"

"Yes." My mouth was dreadfully parched. Makin' me wait and wonder was a trick. I was angry. They had their friends already chosen, and the audition was just a formality. How dare they expect one to endure such humiliation. I was prepared to storm out.

"When you're ready, you may begin." He sat back with a smug look about him.

Please, God. Lift me up.

I brought my cornet to my lips and played. I did not need the music, for I had collected and saved every note in my soul when I learned to play it with Uncle Edward.

The final note warm and sweet, resonated throughout the room, bringin' about an unexpected hush. Every eye was upon me. I had to stop myself from takin' a bow.

"Thank you, Mr. Smith," The pot-bellied, white-haired man said. "Come back here on Tuesday to see if your name is posted on the new roster."

"Thank you. I will. Good day," I gave a quick nod and went to collect my case.

"Jonas, wait a moment." It was the alto horn player.

I stopped. "Yes?"

"Where did you learn to play like that? It was superb."

"Thank you. My uncle used to play in a New Hampshire Regiment Band. He taught me everything."

"Well—"

"—I'm sorry, but I have to run. Folks are waitin' for me." I turned and fled as fast as I could without trippin' on my shoes.

When I returned to the tenement, everyone was in the kitchen about to have supper. I went straight to the attic, where I fell into many pieces. My shakin' came from deep within. I took off my clothes and hid them behind the crate.

With the small amount of water left in the pitcher, I rinsed the oil from my hair and washed the black from my face. Wigglin' into my skirt and blouse required more energy than I imagined. Before settin' out for the kitchen, I pulled my braid out of the bandbox, stuffed it inside of my snood, and attached it to my head with hairpins. I was prepared to answer questions about the cousins I had never met, who didn't make it across the Atlantic Ocean, but in my mind, had become my greatest allies.

CHAPTER 36

August
October 20, 1872

FINN WASN'T IN his bed. It had been over a month since he ran off and stole bread from Maria. I opened the door, and there he was, sittin' on the back step, with his hair hangin' in his face, mesmerized by odds and ends—a cracked monocle, three coins, assorted dead bugs, and a belt buckle—spread out before him. When I patted him on the head, he looked up and smiled.

I went back to makin' coffee and readied myself for the day ahead. When I set out to get my comb, my tobacco tin was gone. I rummaged through our things, but I couldn't find it. I raced back outside, and there it was, on the ground beside his feet.

I grabbed his arm. "Don't you be stealin' from me, you little thief!"

He broke free and ran inside. I chased him into a corner. I never believed in violence, but he needed a good lickin'. I raised my hand but stopped short when I saw the terror in his eyes.

"You can't be stealin', especially from me. I got you righted around, and we're doin' good together. I coulda' let them take you away, but I didn't. You can be redeemed. I know you can!"

He stared straight ahead with tears rollin' down his cheeks. I didn't want to be angry, but I couldn't have him stealin' either.

Luckily for Finn, none of my money was missin'. I counted out enough to go to the market. Since we had a stove, I was able to fix us some meals—stirabout, eggs, and soup.

If I hurried, I would make it in time to see Sarah. Keepin' a close eye on Finn, we rushed through the streets, thick with churchgoers, and made it to the market before they ran out of milk.

After breakfast, we went to see Tiago, and even though I didn't have somethin' to trade, his sister invited Finn to stay. I was eager to talk to Sarah, to see her pretty face. Her laughter made me fall over my words. I had to admit that I was smitten.

I leaned against the fence with my hands in my pockets, listenin' to the organ music, ignorin' the eagerness that waited like a cat ready to pounce. The air was filled with chatter as a wave of parishioners emptied out of the church. I lit up at the sight of Clara, thinkin' that Sarah would be at her side, as she usually was.

"Hello, August," Clara said.

"Hello," I said.

"You're lookin' for Sarah?"

"Yes, I thought I'd walk her home."

"She didn't come to church today. Her cousins are here for a visit." She smiled. "I'll tell her that you were lookin' for her," she said, before runnin' off to join the others.

She disappeared into the crowd. My disappointment was much more than I expected. Heck, I hardly knew her and wasn't sure if havin' such feelin's was right for me. I walked back to Tiago's store to help him fill the smokehouse in exchange for a cut of meat. That way, Finn could play a little longer before we went to work. It was good for him to know someone like Maria. She nurtured her children and treated Finn as if he were her own.

I had almost reached the store when I heard Tiago. He was wavin' his arms and shoutin' at a young man. I was ready to chase after him, in case he was a thief, but Tiago shook his head and laughed, which was fine with me because that man could run much faster than me.

CHAPTER 37

Sarah
October 23, 1872

It was cold, and everyone around me slept in unbroken stillness. As usual, Mercy was pressed into my back. My head was crowded with uninvited images—the list and the pot-bellied, white-haired man—swirlin' about in the spindles of my dreams. I was not entirely present when others spoke to me. Sometimes, I thought they knew, while other times, I was sure that I had tricked them. Not knowin' was far worse than knowin'.

Upon the final ring out, I rushed ahead, pushin' my way to the front of the crowd. I told Clara and Norah that I had a surprise for them and that I would share it when I got home. I planned to stop at the market and buy chocolate, hopin' that it would be enough to keep them from pryin'.

I tried to figure out a way to change into my trousers, but there wasn't time. The risk was too great. I waited until Wednesday, a day after the results were posted so that there would be fewer musicians at the music hall.

With all the mills ringin' out, the streets had become crowded, but I managed to move through it. When I reached the auditorium, I noticed a group of young men gathered on the steps, so I continued to walk. They laughed, smoked, and told jokes. It was just a convenient stop, they had nothin' to do with the band.

The idea of sufferin' through another day of unknowin' was frightful. One of the boys looked at me and smiled. I nodded and walked past him. When I noticed a poster nailed on the inside of the window frame, I broke into a sweat and slowed down. The boys left, so I raced back to the window.

The tears started in. I put my hand over my mouth to stop myself from cryin' out and drawin' unwanted attention my way. *How could this be?*

When I heard footsteps behind me, I ducked my head and scooted off to the side of the steps.

"Excuse me, ma'am." It was the alto horn player who had spoken to me at the audition.

I didn't respond. I returned to the street, pickin' up my pace so that he would not catch up with me. I finally stopped when I reached the market, where we bought milk and bread on Sundays. I watered my handkerchief. I could not stop. Everything in my whole life that had ever crushed me came forth in tears.

"Sarah!"

I hid my face in my hands.

"Sarah, what happened? What's wrong?"

"August, I hate for you to see me like this," I dabbed my eyes. "I am greatly grieved. I have not taken the proper amount of time to mourn the loss of my mother. I have worked very hard, withholdin' the sadness that I did not otherwise express."

He pulled me into his arms. I felt safe and even loved, which was not what I called for. I found myself embracin' him, clingin' to him, sobbin' shamelessly.

"Now, now, go ahead and cry. Of course, you miss your mother." Just when I thought that my heart could not soften more, he held me closer and stroked the back of my head.

I backed away. I could not risk my snood fallin' off. "Thank you for your kindness. I will be all right, really. You must go. The daylight is almost gone."

Empty handed, I ran all the way home. The girls were almost finished with dinner, and they did not even turn their heads when I passed by on my way to the attic.

I collapsed in my chair. There were no tears, for they had flowed like a swollen river, once frozen deep within the safe, dark womb of the mountain, and set free in the spring.

Chapter 38

August

October 23, 1872

We stopped at the outhouses and sinks before makin' our way to the Street Department for check-in. With each day, Finn was gettin' better at followin' instructions, and we had created hand gestures to communicate. He was less jumpy and hardly ever whooped anymore.

The bug cranks continued to follow us, and although the woman was a bit surly, the fellows were agreeable. They shared their findin's with us, and Finn learned which ones were worth savin', so his own collection was impressive.

On our way to work, I was distracted by the sound of a woman. I thought that I spotted Sarah, and she was cryin'. I hurried over, and without pause, took her into my arms. The feel of her slight frame pressed into mine was natural. She was so close, I could taste the sweat on her neck.

Within' moments, she went from sheddin' tears over her dead mother, to pushin' me away and runnin' off. She kept me at a distance, and I never knew when I'd see her. She usually walked to and from the mill with her friends all around her, like guards, yet she continuously occupied my mind.

Finn tugged on my arm, as I watched her walk away. It was time to bring light. We began in the lower section of the city and worked our way up the hill. We stopped at our favorite house, where I listened to music, and we ate from a dinner pail that I found in the street.

The music room was bathed in a golden glow, and just as we sat down to eat, someone began to close all of the windows. It was indeed gettin' cold, so I had to accept that the music would be tucked away for the winter.

I moved beyond the wall and into the garden, inchin' my way closer to the house. Finn sat there drawin' on the edges of the newspaper with the pencil stub that he found, not botherin' with me. Although barely loud enough to hear, the soft strains of the piano satisfied my longin'.

CHAPTER 39

Bess
October 23, 1872

REGARDLESS OF WHAT was written in the music, when my mind wandered, my fingers tended to get away from me. I knew that there wasn't any reason why Mr. Carver would not invite me to play at the recital, but I was tormented by the unknown.

"Well?" I looked at him and smiled.

It seemed he was not paying attention. He fiddled with his beard and stared up at the ceiling. I was about to shout, anything to get his attention.

"Hmm..."

I wondered if he was satisfied. I fantasized that he reacted as Mother did, by jumping to his feet and clasping his hands together. Then again, it was only because she was my mother, she did not have a valid concept of the quality of music performance.

"Are you not pleased?" I asked.

"Oh, yes, yes," he said. "I am. I'm trying to decide whether you should play the entire piece or one movement."

I could not help but smile, which was quickly extinguished when I thought of only one movement. I was about to protest when he spoke again.

"I think that you're prepared to perform the entire piece."

"This is marvelous news!" I restrained myself, as I imagined throwing my arms around him.

"Yes, you're ready. There is talk of a music school being built here in the future, and we are showcasing our finest players. You'll be an excellent addition to the program."

"What time is the recital? Do give me the details," I said. "Wait… Mother!"

The door flew open, and there she stood, wallowing in endless nosiness, already aware of what had transpired. "What is it?"

My cheeks reddened. I wanted to tell her that we all knew that she heard every word, but I played her game. "I'll be performing at the recital. Mr. Carver said that I'm ready."

"We'll have our next lesson at the music hall. That way you can get a feel for the room. Do you know where it is?" he asked, looking at Mother.

"Yes, we do." She looked somewhat troubled.

"Will you please write it down? Just to be certain."

The lines in Mother's face disappeared when he scribbled on the paper.

"We'll see you next week at the music hall," he said. "At the same time. Continue to practice as you have been. You've made significant progress."

Mother walked him to the door. I didn't hear a word of their conversation. I had just over a week to buy a new dress.

Chapter 40

Sarah
October 26, 1872

Saturday's four-thirty ring out could not have come soon enough. I was good at makin' it to the front of the line and pushin' my way past the others. Once outside of the yard gates, I held tight to my cape and fled.

"Sarah! Sarah, wait!"

I looked back over my shoulder at August. "Not now! I'll see you tomorrow after church!"

I hoped that he would change direction, because the girls believed that he was the reason for my frequent absences. I didn't have a care about my reputation, for there was no one of value to look down on me. The pastor of our church had hundreds of parishioners and was too busy to notice each one in his flock. The agent only paid attention if you were in trouble, and the overseer was an evil man who had his way with many of the girls. It was every woman for herself.

I ran up the attic stairs and emptied the crackers, cheese, and apple out of my satchel. I had saved bits of food so that when Saturday arrived, I would be able to take nourishment. I ate the apple and watched the girls on the street below. Except for Mary, who sat on the stoop to smoke her cigarette, they entered the tenement.

I made sure that I would not have kitchen duty that night, so there would be no problem if I were missin'. Just as I finished the last bit of cheese, Mary glanced up at the window. I leaned back into the chair. I swore that she knew things. Things that other people could never figure out.

I unpinned my snood, and with my retired braid, tossed it into the bandbox. I had been wearin' a nightcap to bed and snood durin' the day. I planned to announce that because of Clara's accident, I would cut my hair.

After becomin' Jonas, I waited for the distinctive clatter of forks against plates, before dashin' down the stairs, out the door, and into the back alley.

It was impossible to comprehend that Jonas Smith's name was printed on that poster and that I would play my cornet with a real brass band. As long as I remained quiet, my secret was safe.

The sound of brass sliced into the night. I took my place in line, where the potbellied, white-haired man was checkin' names off of his list. I kept my head down.

"Jonas Smith," he said. "E-flat cornet."

"Yes." I could have lowered my voice some. I cleared my throat in case there was a need to say more.

"Go on over," he said. "Frederick will show you where to sit."

I nodded and walked over to where men of various sizes were sprawled out in chairs, each engrossed in his own individual world, makin' everyone aware of his self-proclaimed greatness. *There is no room in the world for a timid cornetist,* Uncle Edward told me whenever I retreated into a place of shyness.

It was clear that most of these men knew this vital secret, yet it was no secret at all. It was also evident that the cornetists were leaders when it came to puffin' and preenin', like roosters in the barnyard.

A tall, slender man approached. "Jonas?"

"Yes," I said, wonderin' if the shadow on my face was convincin', or if I looked like I worked for the coal company and did not bathe. Either way, when my cheeks caught fire, everything was at risk.

"Welcome to the band," he said. "You'll be sittin' here." He pointed at a chair in the front row.

I nodded and without a word, sat down in my chair. I blew into my horn, careful to not produce a note, caught between a world of project or protect.

Play like you mean it, or don't play at all! Uncle Edward's words resolved my conflict. I closed my eyes and began to go up and down the scales. No one noticed, or if they did, it was to secretly observe the competition. It seemed that we were there to prove that we could do it and that we were the very best. To openly listen to others, was to risk bein' challenged, or mistaken as a weakness. We were required to stay within our boundaries and show that we were invincible.

Frederick handed a stack of music to me. "I wrote out the shorter pieces for you to keep, and we can take turns bringing the longer ones home to practice."

I nodded. "Thank you," I said, realizin' that if I continued to nod throughout the evenin', they would think somethin' was amiss.

Mr. Daniels approached the podium and clapped his hands. "Gentlemen, gentlemen! It's time to begin. We welcome our newest members and congratulate you all. When I mention your name, please stand up, so we may get to know one another."

"Jonas Smith!" He pointed at me.

I wasn't expectin' to be called first or perhaps not at all. My legs trembled. I faltered, and by the time I rose to my feet, he was on to the next name. I sat back down and thoughtlessly ran my fingers through my hair. I stared at the sticky oil on my hands and quickly wiped them off on my pants, leavin' a dreadful stain.

I heard none of the other names. To my horror, I realized that I was the only one who sat down. All of the other new band members continued to stand, beamin' with pride.

"Take a seat, gentlemen. Let's tune our instruments, beginnin' with the cornets."

I went in and out of an uncertain dream state. Whenever I drifted too far away, I remembered Uncle Edward's wisdom and stayed with it. Playin' the music was a welcomed challenge. It was natural, an unquestionable confirmation of knowin' where I belonged, but only as a young man named Jonas. Sarah was not allowed.

CHAPTER 41

Bess
October 26, 1872

With very little warning, Mother accepted an invitation to the home of one of the most prominent citizens of Fall River. We spent the day in preparation for an evening of music and a formal dinner. Father's law firm worked closely with many of the corporate mill owners, banks, and real estate businesses. So, with a gleam in her eye, Mother mentioned that in addition to business matters, we would be able to make ourselves known.

"You must remember the importance of the art of good conversation, Bess," Mother said. "And, be a good listener as well. If you should happen to engage in a discussion about music, whatever you do, do not use foreign words or phrases. Even if you think that the others are musically trained or well-traveled, it's a clear mark of ill breeding.

"Why are you mentioning this now?" I winced when Tempy wrapped a strand of my hair around the curling iron. "Don't you believe that I know how to conduct myself?"

"I feel it is my responsibility to remind you of the rules of etiquette, should they slip your mind," she said, and then marched out of the room.

"Do I need constant reminding, Tempy?"

"It's not for me to say," she said.

After weaving a simple black satin ribbon into my hair, Tempy saw to my wardrobe. With much deliberation, I selected a long-sleeved, low-necked, dark blue, silk dress, trimmed with lace and ribbons. She assured that the details of every point of my dress were tended with perfection. Although often viewed as minor points, even the smallest articles were made neat. My lace gloves were trimmed to match the dress, and I wore black satin slippers with fine silk stockings. With my curls set and glossy, my skin pure and refreshed, all articles of dress proper, clean, and harmonized, I was well suited for the occasion, appearing as ladylike as Mother required.

As expected, we showed up well before the appointed time. For as Mother reminded us, lest we ever forget, it was better to be early than late. I would not know of that firsthand, because I had never arrived anywhere on time. In our family, arriving on time meant that we were late.

The wind whipped up the hill with gale force, a hint of winter's impatience. Holding tight to my heavy woolen cloak, I followed my parents up the front steps. There were no disappointments to be had. The house was grand, with the most exquisite decor, and servants at every turn.

Once greeted by the doorman, we were taken to the ladies' room, which was well-lighted and spacious. Upon one bureau, was a charming basket filled with a good supply of hairpins, and a sewing box furnished with all that was necessary to repair a dress, in the event of an unfortunate accident. Along with eau-de-cologne, was an intricately carved mahogany apothecary box, lined with purple velvet. The assortment of essentials included at least two dozen bottles of various balms, oils, and powders, including; rhubarb powder, lavender oil, spirit of rose-hips, mullein balm, mint water, elderberry flower extract, and spirit of hartshorn and salts for unexpected faintness.

I was marveling at the plethora of small, carefully detailed bottles when a maid—an older woman with a kind, round face—drew near to help us remove our cloaks and hoods. A younger maid then approached, rolled them all into a neat bundle, and set it on a table with the others.

"Your name?" she asked.

"Adams," Mother said while the older maid assisted her. "You may combine our belongings together."

The maid nodded and found a card with our name printed on it, pinned it to our bundle, and set it aside.

After the older maid smoothed out the wrinkles in our dresses and straightened the part of my hair that was slightly mussed, we were escorted by a servant, who took us down the long hall, where the hostess waited to greet us.

She was gracious, genuinely pleased that we accepted their invitation. Mother met her at a reception when we first moved to Fall River, so she acted as if they were longtime friends. Father was already engrossed in conversation with the men who smoked cigars, never to look up again, until it was time to move to the dining area.

We entered the parlor to be met by the melodious sounds of a string trio. I imagined myself running over to the musicians, throwing myself at their feet, and taking in each note to imprint upon my soul to see me through the winter.

Instead, I crossed the room slowly, and because of my insistence on remaining calm, was able to identify the composer. It was definitely Vivaldi, one of my favorites. It had been some time since I heard the pure beauty of strings. I refused to allow myself to dwell in sorrow of what once was, and celebrate the moment that I was in. I delighted in the fact that they were in tune, and as Mr. Carver would have noted, played with effective dynamics.

I stood before them, drinking in the rich harmonies that quenched my withered soul, catching that which dribbled down my chin. For wasting one single note, was indeed a sin.

"Bess," Mother said, just loud enough to reach my ears.

"Aren't they divine?" The color crept into my cheeks.

"I was embarrassed when you crossed the room completely unattended."

I sighed. "When I heard the strings, I couldn't help myself."

"You attract too much attention when you act without thinking."

"Be careful not to be so concerned about my actions that you miss the opportunity to make new friends."

"You are—"

"—look at that piano. I wish I were invited to play, but of course, it won't happen," I said.

"Don't look at it so longingly; it's rude and selfish. Your time will come. After the recital, when it is known that you are an accomplished pianist, perhaps you will get a chance to play at such events. Remember, we are no longer in Boston."

"How could I forget? You remind me every day." I crossed my arms.

I was taken aback when in through the side door, entered Mr. Carver. He looked quite handsome in his well-tailored suit. He gave a nod to the string players, who were at rest, yet attentive. He approached the trio and spoke quietly. They shuffled through their music as he sat down at the piano.

"This is so exciting, Mother," I said. "I had no idea that Mr. Carver was going to be here, and to hear him play is a treat."

"Perhaps he will invite you to play," she said. "If he does, remember to only play one piece and to quickly get up off of the stool."

Choosing to ignore her gloomy tone, I didn't respond. I focused on his posture, the gentle arch of his fingers over the keys, and how, with an air of confidence, he made eye contact with the violinist.

The resonant sound of the strings traveled directly to my heart. In an attempt to prevent me from exhibiting my humanness, Mother grasped my elbow and led me to a group of chairs that lined the wall.

"It's best for us to be seated."

Without taking my eyes or ears away from the music, I sat beside Mother while she continued to point out the faults of others—their dress, posture, hair, or what she had learned from the shallow pool of gossip that she had already dipped her toes into.

At the end of the third movement, I clapped quietly, so not to get Mother going about attracting attention and being ill-bred. Mr. Carver made his way over to me. When I started to stand, he insisted that I remain seated, and he asked permission to sit beside me. I did not pay attention to Mother nudging me with her elbow. I saw nothing wrong with engaging in conversation with my piano teacher.

"That was lovely," I said. "It was so balanced and blended nicely."

"Thank you," he said.

"It was Mozart, correct?"

"Yes, "Piano Quartet No.1 in G minor," better on a harpsichord, but it is fine with a piano. Would you like to play?"

"Oh, I don't know."

"I have a copy of the piece that you are playing if you would like to play the first movement."

"Shouldn't I save it for next week?"

"No, if you were to play the entire piece, and we were handing out a written program, I would discourage it."

"Then I gladly accept the invitation."

After the string trio finished their set, Mr. Carver escorted me across the room, where I stood off to the side.

"Ladies and gentlemen, I present Bess Adams. She will play for you this evening."

The talking and movement ceased while all eyes were on me. I positioned myself on the stool and waited for him to place the music before me.

I took a slow, deep breath, and in heart and spirit, lifted up to play as God would have wanted me to play, as divine as the angels above.

Chapter 42

August
October 26, 1872

In our constant race against darkness, we finally reached the end of our route, the grandest house of all, perched high on the hilltop. One by one, the carriages passed by and entered through the iron gates, where the rich folks were greeted and escorted into the house.

Each time the door opened, I heard faint music. I was tall enough to see over the wall and recognized the carriage from the music house. A servant assisted two women and a man. The younger woman was covered by her hood, so I was unable to see her face. The older woman had all the signs of a proper upbringin', but had a sour look about her. I wondered if either of them played the piano.

Finn leaned against the wall, gobblin' a fresh piece of sweet bread given to us by a friendly woman on our route. In fact, her braided bread was the best I ever had.

I motioned for him to come with me. We walked for a bit and stopped at the pump for a quick washin' up. When we rounded the corner, I caught a glimpse of a young man in Sarah's window. I stopped. It seemed I had seen him somewhere before. As far as I knew, it was frowned upon for men to visit unmarried girls in their rooms. I s'posed that he sneaked in.

I tried to get a closer look, when the candle was extinguished, leavin' me to wonder. Then, I noticed that Finn was a ways down the street. I had to run to catch up with him. My heart hammered inside my chest. *Who was that man in Sarah's room?* Maybe it was her cousin. Clara said that she had visitors. She wasn't a harlot or a prostitute. I knew plenty of girls like that.

Chapter 43

Bess
November 2, 1872

It was a full house, a larger audience than expected. In fact, with the elaborate architecture and decor, we could have been in Boston. Many of the dignitaries that sat in the front row were at the dinner that we had attended the week before. I was confident that I would make my mark.

I waited in the wings, fanning myself with the program, and marveling at the brilliance of a handsome young violinist's performance of a Paganini Caprice. Much to my surprise, the participants were rich with talent and had traveled from Boston and New York to settle in Fall River. As Mr. Carver mentioned, there was talk of a music academy being built. If that were the case, there would be a need for instructors, and every good music academy had an orchestra. With the rising population and so many immigrants, it seemed to be a wise decision. Unless, of course, most of the immigrants were millworkers.

The audience roared when the violinist took a deep bow. He walked off stage, brushing past me, his after-performance radiance propelling each step. Mr. Carver placed my music on the piano stand and waited for his introduction.

I made my entrance. Mr. Carver assisted me at the bench, before taking his place as page turner. A hush fell over the crowd. I took a calming breath and began my performance of "Mozart's Piano Sonata No. 8 in A minor."

With an appropriate pause between each movement, I played with confidence and complete dedication to the intention of the piece. No note was more important than another, for each was an equally vital part of the whole.

I found that whenever I played the second movement—the Andante—a profound sensation stirred from within. Perhaps it was because there were enough spaces, stillness between phrases, where the perfection of the composition could be realized. I knew not where the seat of this emotion dwelt, and I had no intention of denying it.

This night was no exception. When I came upon that passage, a few tears rolled down my cheeks, onto my forearms, and fell upon my dress. It did not cause me to stop or lose my focus. I had learned to accept the emotions brought forth when inhabiting deeply layered compositions. Soon after the tears dried, and I arrived at the final movement, a quick burst of energy emerged from each note. I reclaimed my balance.

At the end of the piece, I rose to my feet and curtsied. The applause and shouting of "bravo" fluttered within the walls of my heart. As I turned to walk off the stage, Father approached with a red rose. Together, we exited the stage, where Mother waited in the wings.

"Well done, Bess," she said. "Your dress is spoiled in the front, but we can have it cleaned."

I brushed past her and made my way over to where Tempy and Davis stood in an unlit corner.

I threw my arms around Tempy's neck. She hesitated before hugging me back. "You're a gift from Heaven, child," she said. "And, you gave it a chance."

Mother came up from behind and fussed with the bow on the back of my dress. I ached for her; there were certain times in one's life when an embrace was essential.

Chapter 44

Sarah
November 3, 1872

Every time my head drooped forward, Norah jabbed me with her elbow. It was hard to imagine that I had become like one of those old folks who fell asleep durin' the sermon. As much as Mother protested, my sister and I poked fun at them.

Once he started in on Eve, I perked up. Ever since I was old enough to understand the hypocrisy of it, I rejected what everyone tried to teach us about her. We learned about her in Sunday school and at church. Even Mother referred to Eve when it came to matters of bleedin' or childbirth. It was Eve's fault for everything.

I was quite disappointed in my sister for believin' in the curse. I asked her what kind of God would punish his own creation for seekin' wisdom? For eatin' an apple? If it were so, he was not a kind and compassionate God, but one created of and for man, a tyrant that condemned for no reliable or valid reason, an action that would continue to resonate unless we became her ally.

Pastor Leighton used his sermons to castigate the sinners in our church, or the ones that he suspected were less than perfect. However, for some reason, in the face of women, he stuttered. I did not want to pick a fight, and I could never do so. It was unacceptable behavior for a young woman or any woman for that matter. But, he knew. He knew that I would not take part in blamin' everything that ever went wrong, since the Garden of Eden, on Eve.

I returned my attention to the reverend—flushed and heated—as he pointed up to the Heavens and exclaimed, "Then the Lord God said to the woman,

What is this you have done? And the woman said, The serpent deceived me, and I ate, Genesis 3:13."

I was saved by the hymn. I so needed to stand and sing.

Unlike Mother, singin' was not my favorite thing, especially hymns. I preferred to sing them in small groups, relishin' the harmonies, not in with a wild crowd who were just wakin' up from the sermon, pretendin' to have a musical bone in their bodies.

My sister and I were accustomed to makin' sure that Mother was praised whenever she sang. All the way home, she talked about her singin'. She would ask, *Are you sure I sounded good, and you're not just sayin' that?* We had to convince her. She knew but was afraid to believe it. The truest part of her was quite proud and for good reason.

My mind had a tendency to wander, bringin' me to the fact that I hadn't seen August around. I feared that I may have discouraged him by never showin' up at the same time or by shoutin' at him while runnin' off with a groundless explanation. Mother always said, *there are many flowers in the garden. You're not the only one.*

I hurried down the steps, quickly scannin' the street, only to find no sign of him. I tried to keep on the sunny side, not permittin' my heart to sink. Clara reached over and wrapped her warm hand around mine, and we walked quietly towards our tenement. I fancied the idea of an afternoon of cookin', launderin', and brushin' up the room.

After our chores were done, and while the girls were either readin' or playin' a game of cards, I entered the room holdin' my braid up high in the air.

"Look at what I did!" I exclaimed.

"Oh my," Clara said. She dashed over and took it from me.

"You're not in ya right mind," Ruby said.

Clemmie gasped, while Norah and Addy were speechless.

"Yes, I decided that it was too much of a risk to have my hair get caught in the machinery. Look at what happened to Clara. She could have lost her life. And then, last week at Durfee's, one of the girls had a similar experience, but not quite as bad as what happened to poor Clara," I said.

"But you're not careless like the others. You wear a snood," Addy said, purposely avoidin' Clara's pained expression.

Mercy and Rebecca stood in the open doorway.

"What's all the fuss?" Rebecca asked.

"Sarah went and cut off her braid," Addy said.

"I wasn't careless," Clara said, crossin' her arms over her chest.

"You were young. It's okay that you were careless," Addy said. "But, everyone knows that you were careless."

"What? You cut your beautiful hair?" Mercy snatched the braid from Norah.

"Why did you do that?" Rebecca asked.

"She's afraid that she'll get her hair caught in the machinery," Norah said.

"Can I have your braid?" Mercy asked.

"What? What are you talkin' about?" Rebecca whipped it away from her.

"I can coil it around my head," she said.

"Your hair is brown and frizzy. It would look ridiculous," Rebecca said while wrappin' it around her own head.

"You won't be suitable for courtin' with hair like a boy," Mercy said.

"Who has time for courtin'?" I asked.

"You do! I see you with that boy… August? And, you're always goin' off, like Cora did. I know you're meetin' up with him, but I won't tell no one," Mercy said.

"Just because we're friends, doesn't mean that I'm courtin' him. We have a lot in common," I said.

"What have we got here?" Mary moseyed in and snatched the braid from Rebecca.

"Sarah cut her hair," Norah said.

"I wish that you would all settle down," I said. "And besides, it's hair. It will grow back."

"Abigail would never cut her hair," Mercy said. "Are you gonna tell her when you write?"

"She will see me when I return to New Hampshire. She won't mind at all," I said.

We sat together, drinkin' tea, and discussin' the men who worked in the mills—which ones were not taken and worth a second look, and which ones were horrible. I hadn't noticed that Clara was no longer present until she burst in.

"Clara, what have you done?" I shouted.

170

She pushed her way into the middle of the room, holdin' her messy blonde braid. "I don't want to ever go through that again. I think that havin' short hair is a good idea."

Before the end of the night, Clemmie, the youngest and quietest of the group, cut her curly brown hair too. To prevent Mercy from stealin' our hair, we decided to hang our braids above the door of the sink closet.

Although in my usual tired state, I managed to steal at least a half an hour on my cornet. As long as the babies cried, the women shouted at their drunken husbands, and the girl across the hall played her concertina, I was fine.

Chapter 45

August
November 3, 1872

I THOUGHT IT was a dream when Finn cried out from across the room. I found him shakin' and feverish, so I covered him with my blanket and gave him the last of the bone broth.

He started coughin' on Saturday, but he seemed to be alright. Ignorin' the fact that the temperatures were droppin' fast and that he could get sick from a sudden chill, I made the mistake of sittin' outside of the music hall to listen to a concert. We stayed 'til about ten o'clock.

I knew that he was tired, but I couldn't pull myself away. At the time, I was glad I waited. Someone played that familiar song on the piano. I heard it so many times at the music house, I could hum right along with it.

I decided to give him some of the whiskey that I'd been cartin' around. I had it for a while, but whiskey didn't spoil. That's what Smitty gave us boys durin' the sickly season.

When I tried to get him to drink it, he made a big mess, chokin' and spittin' it out all over the both of us, so I rushed off to the drug store.

I stood in line and waited my turn. Some pushed and squeezed ahead of me, while others gave up and left. I had to stay.

All of that made me think of Billy. On the most frigid nights, we crawled up into the iron chute that ventilated the basement of the hotel, and we'd nestle down into the grates. Billy had been coughin' for a whole week before that mornin'. I went to wake him, and he didn't move. A strange light fell upon his pale blue face, and his skin was ice-cold. I screamed when I touched it.

I pried myself out of the chute and ran down the street, shoutin' for help. Course, no one listened, until I came across a policeman. I told him about Billy, and he went and got a fireman to help. No one understood that I didn't want them to take him away. No, I wanted them to rescue him and maybe rescue the both of us. But they didn't listen. They took him away in the poorhouse hearse.

Maybe it was because he was like a brother to me, the best friend I ever had, but I couldn't let him go, not like that. I chased after him for a bit and fell down in the middle of the street, cryin', tears frozen onto my face. Carriages swerved, people shouted, and for a long time, no one bothered to stop. Finally, a very good, a very decent woman, ran out and dragged me away from harm.

Other memories fade, but her old, craggy face stayed with me, and knowin' that other than her spirit, she had nothin' to offer. She was poor like me, but she had enough kindness to spare. She was richer than those who rode by in their elegant carriages, stole from their tenants, and worked in the merchant's block.

Billy and I left the Children's Aid Society when I was about eight or nine. As far as we knew, he was a year younger than me. We stuck together, sortin' bones at the West Nineteenth Street dump, usually stayin' right there, only runnin' from the ministers that wanted to take us to the island or put us on a train.

I often thought that if I had somehow gotten medicine for Billy, he would have lived. He too was worth redemption. So, no matter what it took, I would always try to get medicine. Bein' poor didn't mean you didn't have the right to take care of yourself. That's all I ever knew. But, after Billy, I learned to never give up. I would try not to be unprepared or go without.

It was finally my turn. At the advice of the chemist, I bought a bottle of Dr. Walker's Vinegar Bitters, a jar of honey, and rose water. He told me that I would see an improvement overnight. I hurried over to Tiago's to let him know that we wouldn't be stoppin' by for our usual Sunday visit, and he gave me a hefty beef bone for broth.

I looked in the direction of the Methodist church but kept on goin'. By the time I got home, the folks were already in church, and the streets were quiet. I stoked the fire, simmered the broth, and gave Finn his medicine. After coverin' him with both of our quilts and coats, he went back to sleep. I had to go to work without him, somethin' I hadn't done.

That night, I managed to juggle the ladder and carry everything. I was glad to get home. Francis Murphy offered to help, but I thought I could do it. If Finn was still sick, I would take him up on his offer.

Just as I left the outhouse and was about to gather my tools, I heard music in the distance. I wasn't sure what it was, so I followed it. Then, I realized that it wasn't in the distance at all. It was comin' from Sarah's tenement. I stopped and listened. It was a quiet song, perhaps played on some kind of horn. A soft light streamed through the attic window, revealin' the blurred shadow of a man.

CHAPTER 46

Bess
November 9, 1872

LIKE MARCH, NOVEMBER lacked commitment to any particular season. The bright hues of autumn faded into death, as grayness spread over the entire landscape. Trees, once an indication of life amidst the dreary mills and drab people, became nothing, not alive or dead, enduring the tension, the stillness that begged for answers.

"You must get up and face the day, child." Tempy entered my room and pulled the curtains back with one great swoop.

"There's no reason to get up so early. It's Saturday. It's cold. It's dark. Please, let me sleep."

"You know how your mother is," she said. "You must get up and practice, work on your needlepoint, or read. She might be goin' to market."

"You can tell Mother that I'm sick," I said.

"But that would be a lie. Don't be lazy," she said.

I turned down the bed cover to see a dark red stain. I should have known that it was my time. I dreaded it so but always let it take me by surprise.

Mother didn't care about the predicament of women. She made sure that I had the proper cotton rags and approved of Tempy brewing her special tea. While never seeming to be afflicted, Mother called it the curse. In fact, she was so disinterested in women's issues, that the first time I bled, I cried all night trying to comprehend how I had become wounded without knowing it. It wasn't until Tempy responded to my crying, and told me about the unpleasantries of menstruation, that I understood what was happening and what I could expect for many years.

"I'm tired and have cramps," I said. "Will you tell Mother that I'm with the curse and will get up later?"

"Don't worry, child. Once you bathe, dress in clean clothes, and have some mugwort brew, you'll feel better," she said. "I'll tell her that you'll have breakfast later and to go to market without you."

"Thank you, Tempy." I tucked the blanket under my chin, tryin', yet failin' to ignore the warm stickiness. "Tell me when my bath is ready. I shall wait here."

I was usually pampered during the first few days of bleeding. Mother was clearly uncomfortable, acting rather odd, and looking on from a safe distance, not quite having the heart for it all, while Tempy addressed my needs.

CHAPTER 47

Sarah
November 9, 1872

THE COLD IN Fall River was different from the cold in New Hampshire. The wind from the ocean cut through to the bone. Once summer was behind us, I was able to embrace the fact that it was warmer in the spinnin' room than anywhere else. The men did not strip down, and except for one of the bobbin boys, we were no longer barefoot.

All of a sudden, Mary showed up at the station beside me. I did not have the heart to ask how she got Mr. Aldrich to agree. I was simply grateful that she was nearby. We shouted back and forth until I thought that my voice would give out, so I smiled while she kept right on talkin'.

Fearin' for her soul, I continued to pray for Mary because she returned flushed and late from lunch on more than one occasion. When she attempted to bring it up, I pressed my finger to my lips. I wanted to know nothin' about it. If she had listened to me, I would have tried to reason with her, but without thought, she was determined to give away her virtue to the vile Mr. Aldrich.

As far as spinnin', she was good at it too. Addy, who was happy that Mr. Aldrich had shifted his attention elsewhere, even if it were Mary, told us that we were both naturals. Oddly, hearin' that seemed to help.

"Do ya wanna go with me to the dance house tonight?" Mary shouted.

"Dance house? What's that?" I asked.

"It's a place where we can go dancin', meet people, and have a rum or two," she shouted, as the machinery stopped for the full spindles to be collected and replaced with empty ones.

Everyone heard. Some giggled, many could have cared less, while others looked shocked and dismayed. I put my hands on my hips. "No, I haven't an interest in such shenanigans."

She laughed. "You're so prudish. Ya might have a lil' fun if ya just let go once in a while."

"What kind of a place is that? A place where there is spirituous liquor is not a place for a lady." I brushed the lint off of my face.

The machinery started up with a kick and a roar. I tried to forget about the impossibility of Mary, how odd it was that I loved her, yet accepted her deviant behavior, and turned my attention to the onset of winter. Jonas needed a warmer coat.

When the Saturday evenin' bell rang out, I dashed ahead of everyone. They were beginnin' to think that my relationship with August was gettin' serious, but no one dared to press. I pushed my way to the head of the crowd and got upstairs ahead of the others.

I ripped off my snood and slipped into my band attire. I had two uncooked carrots and a piece of ham to gobble up, before oilin' my hair. Just as I was puttin' on my new cap, the door slammed, and the laughter and chatter from the girls filled the hallway.

It was time. They were all in their rooms, takin' off their cloaks and hoods, before goin' to prepare dinner. I sped down the stairs and out to the street. I could already see my breath, and it was early November. I picked up the pace and thought about how much I enjoyed the new music. I never dreamed that I'd play with such talented musicians.

Along with the others, I arrived at the auditorium right on time. There were a lot of handshakes and greetin's that I managed to avoid. We got into our seats and began tunin' up. I was always a little sharp but had no trouble. I didn't want to fuss, so I tried to do it ahead of time by listenin' to the proud and boastful cocks in the barnyard. Without callin' too much attention to myself, I got by with a simple nod and a word.

My eyes lit up when Mr. Daniels placed "Listen to the Mockingbird" on our stand. This was a piece of music that Uncle Edward played for us, to demonstrate the importance of a fluid trill. *You want to sound like a bird, like a real mockin'bird,* he would say. And he truly did. We didn't have the music then, so it was one of those pieces that we listened to, and eventually, I learned how to trill from his example.

"Jonas!" Mr. Daniels shouted.

"Uh, yes?" I looked up, realizin' that by the sounds of the cocks cooin', he must have called my name before, and I didn't answer.

"Would you mind playing the solo?"

Mind playin' the solo? Just like that? No time to practice or anything?

"It's fine if it isn't perfect the first time through, we haven't played this one yet. So, it's sight reading for us all," he said.

It sounded like somethin' Uncle Edward would say. I realized that I could put myself in Edward's place. He learned in a settin' like this. I cleared my throat. I couldn't say no. "Y-yes, I'll be happy too," I said, damnin' the blush that raged in my cheeks.

I skimmed over the music—a lot of ink on one page. My breathin' quickened. If I failed, I would have been forced to leave in shame. Every other man in the room would have died for the opportunity to play a solo. Accordin' to Uncle Edward, cornetists tended to believe that they could play anything better than the next one. And even if it weren't so, puffed up like an ole rooster. He said that's what drove them.

We played it slowly at first, which was actually a bit of a challenge with that particular piece. I remembered the trill and imagined that Uncle Edward sat on one shoulder while the mockin'bird was perched on the other. It was as if he had prepared me for that moment.

I forgot who I was. Jonas? Sarah? It mattered not. I was lost in the brilliance of the piece. I had a lot to work out, but I did reasonably well.

"You did a great job," Frederick said. "It's not easy to read pieces like this on the spot."

"Thanks," I whispered.

He smiled and looked right at me. His smile faded, but his stare did not waver.

He knew that I was a woman. He had to know. Men didn't blush all the time, at least not a man's man. Sit up straight. Act like a man.

I cleared my throat. "It was nothin', really." That was better. I resisted everything that my mother taught me. I had to be bold, conceited, and quite unmannerly.

We ended the night with "Red, White, and Blue," a quickstep that I remembered well from the parades in Ossipee and when Papa mustered with the Sixth. My sister and I used to wave our pocket-handkerchiefs when the bands played such upliftin' pieces.

It was near the end of the song when I felt it—a gush of warm blood between my legs. My face had surpassed any blush previously known to me, and my soul was about to faint. I knew not what to do. Surely, I could not stand up with a feminine stain on my trousers and a puddle of blood on the chair.

The room began to spin. The men were packin' up, laughin', and jokin'. I remained completely still, afraid to move or even exhale.

The alto horn player approached. "Nice job," he said. "Your trill was as close to a real bird as anyone could get."

"Thank you. I learned how to trill from that piece," I said, suddenly realizin' that not only was I bleedin' through my trousers and onto the chair, but I also spoke in a thin, high-pitched voice.

"Well, it was good. I liked it," he said.

I pretended to shuffle through my music. I dropped the entire stack onto the floor. Usually, men would fall over themselves to help me. *God, show me the way. I will do anything You ask of me.* I froze. After what may have been several moments, I pulled my coat from the back of the chair and dropped it on top of the small pool of blood. Keepin' my legs pressed tightly together, I squatted down, picked up each piece of music, and crammed them into my sack. Most of the men had left and were out the door.

"You played well tonight, Jonas," Mr. Daniels said.

"It was nothin'," I said.

Oh, how I hated myself at that moment. For the first time in my life, I accepted a compliment without blushin' and was sinfully discourteous. It was too late to act otherwise. I had pushed myself further into the barnyard. For the first time, I had grossly primped and preened and groped to maintain my balance. The slight thread that held me together was about to break.

"Well, you're a valuable addition to the band," he said. "Have a good evenin'." He finally walked away.

I scrambled to my feet and wiped the blood off the chair with my handkerchief. With all my belongin's packed, I raced towards the door, almost bumpin' into the pot-bellied, white-haired man, who had come to put out the lamps and lock the doors.

In bloodstained trousers, I stood on the steps, with my horn and satchel in my arms. *Breathe.* I focused on remainin' steady while my heart threatened to stop altogether. *What's takin' him so long?* I watched. I bled. I waited until the drummer boy—the last of them—was almost out of sight before headin' home.

I didn't care that I was so cold that my whole body shook. I just wanted to rip off my clothes and hide them until I could launder them in secret. I had no towel or rag. When we bled at the mill, we often threw straw upon the floor. There would be no such thing for Jonas. He could never bleed.

I heard a noise and broke into a run. I stopped, thinkin' that I might vomit, but didn't. It was gettin' dark early as it did in November—a reminder of the long, cold winter to follow. Bein' out on the streets in a strange city was frightenin'. But then again, as a man, I had less to fear. I slowed down and caught my breath. I had to be prepared to turn around, and if need be, raise a fist.

Act like a man. I spun around, ready for it, whatever it may have been, and there was no one there.

Chapter 48

August
November 9, 1872

With all the medicine and bone broth that I made him drink, Finn came around. I was glad, because Francis Murphy had to accompany me with the ladder, and it just wasn't as much fun. I also hated worryin' if Finn would recover or not. Without takin' notice, I had to keep passin' by the music house on the hill. I didn't expect him to understand or even approve. Besides, I had found someone else. Although I had to strain to hear, the fella that played music in Sarah's room was quite good.

After the last lamp, Francis Murphy went one way, and I went another. Of course, I stopped at the dance house when I heard the fiddle, accordion, penny whistle, and pipes. I always liked those old Irish tunes and had to give it a listen. Even though whiskey and a fling would have been fun, I knew better than to go inside. Those houses were often raided, and I wanted to keep my job. If I got taken in, they would have sent Finn back to the children's home.

I had two cigarettes left, so I lit one and sat on the sidewalk, but not for too long. It was gettin' cold, so I thought about goin' home to stoke the fire and check on Finn. I was about to leave when two police wagons arrived, and a half dozen officers entered the dance house. The music stopped, and there was a lot of commotion. One time I was arrested at a dance house, locked up, and charged with disorderly conduct. That was enough.

I left the screamin' and hollerin' behind and hurried home, followin' in the footsteps of a man, who had bolted by me earlier. He stopped. Perhaps he had fled from the dance house just in time. His slender build led me to believe that he may have been the man that I saw in Sarah's window. I tried to get a good look at him, but it was too dark. When he turned, I slipped out of sight, into a store entryway. I didn't want to start a ruckus. Then, he took off and rushed into the tenement.

I waited. Within a minute or two, he lit a candle and sat with his back to the attic window. I tried to dismiss the heaviness in my chest. I thought that Sarah and I had somethin' special, but I was wrong.

Chapter 49

Bess
November 28, 1872

It was our first Thanksgiving in Fall River. In the past, it was customary for our servants to spend several days in preparation, as Mother insisted on having a large gathering. In an effort to avoid a woeful heart, I kept busy.

Usually, Father's brother, Chase, and his family traveled down from New Hampshire. In turn, we celebrated the Fourth of July at their lovely home on the lake, staying for at least three days.

Father's former associate and his family used to join us as well. After an elegant dinner, we played games, and weather permitting, walked along the Charles River. I was particularly fond of Madelene, and although a bit younger, she was quite jolly. We enjoyed each other's company so much that we faithfully promised to get together throughout the year, a promise never kept.

We expected Father's new partner, his wife, and their three young boys to come. I met them once before, and the boys were full of the devil. Spending an entire afternoon with them was unimaginable. I tried but was unable to find the patience necessary to tolerate such rowdy behavior. Their mother was a timid thing, too mild to raise three sons.

The previous day, during my lesson and at the last moment, Mother barged in with a red face and heightened frazzled look about her.

"Mr. Carver, would you like to join us for dinner tomorrow?" she asked.

He raised an eyebrow and fiddled with his beard. I had learned that he was not one to respond in a timely manner. He preferred to ponder each word and review his options before offering a reply. When we first met, I thought that he didn't hear me, but it was the opposite.

"I'm honored," he said.

We stood in painful silence, unsure of whose turn it was to speak while wondering if it was an acceptance or regret. I was about to say something when he finally came around and completed his sentence.

"I would like that very much," he said. His smile brightened the room. "What time would you like me to arrive?"

I was greatly relieved that we had come to a conclusion, somewhat concerned that we had just mixed business with pleasure, and surprised that Mother had broken her own rules—a sure sign of ill breeding.

My piano teacher coming for dinner was a perfect distraction. Occupying my mind with such nonsense, instead of pining away for Boston, had its value. It was odd to think of Mr. Carver sitting at our table and not beside me at the piano. Other than music, I didn't know what we would talk about.

I got up earlier than usual. As always, Tempy tended to my bath, arranged my hair, and prepared my dress and accessories in time for us to attend a special Thanksgiving church service. I preferred to stay home, as the sky threatened snow, and I had no desire to bundle up and go out in it, but none of that mattered. It was not debatable.

By the time we returned home, the house was quite cozy and filled with the aroma of spices, roasted meats, vegetables, and baked goods.

I had to convince Mother that my desire to help arrange flowers was a creative, artistic activity, and not a chore or servant's job. I was not trying to ease their burdens, but I actually loved flowers. After a stern word, she said yes, but just that one time.

When the guests arrived at two o'clock, I was more than ready. The women were handsomely dressed, and the men wore the usual dinner attire. It would be impolite for me to speak about the three boys, for I hadn't a nice thing to say. In trying, I could mention that they were charming to look at, but my temples throbbed within moments of their arrival. I tried several times to give Mother a look, but she purposely avoided making eye contact with me.

Dinner was to be served at four o'clock. From three o'clock on, I began to fret. In anticipation of Mr. Carver's arrival, I found myself checking the clock and looking out the window.

"Bess, I wonder where Mr. Carver is?" Mother asked.

"You invited him, Mother. I am not his keeper," I said, noticing that I was biting my fingernails, a disgusting habit that I had long outgrown.

"We'll have to start without him." She stormed out of the room.

I followed her into the dining room, where everyone was waiting to be seated. Mother whispered something to Siobhan, one of the newest servants, who quickly took away the extra place setting.

Our dinner began with oyster soup, followed by fresh cod with a special egg sauce. Of course, we had boiled ham, chicken pie, and a plump roast turkey with chestnut stuffing.

As she did every year, Mother raved about the cranberry sauce. Her relatives owned a well-known bog in Plymouth and shipped a crate to us for the holidays. We also had an assortment of pickles and fruits, such as mangoes, candied peaches, apples, nuts, and raisins.

Except for the corn, which came in a can, all of our vegetables were fresh. Our newest cook created delights, such as mince and pumpkin pies, apple tarts, and my favorite, Indian pudding with cream.

Just as I was about to taste the pudding, there was a rap at the door. With my spoon in midair, I stopped and looked towards the hallway, where Davis was escorting Mr. Carver into the room.

"Come in, Mr. Carver," Father said, rising to his feet.

"Forgive me for being late," he said. "There was a fire at the house next door, and I had to wait to be cleared."

I became quite blushful and stared down at the table. I twisted my linen napkin in my hands and became noticeably shaky when he stood beside me. Davis prepared his setting and pulled a chair up to the table. He sat down, his arm touching mine. I felt as if I would faint and had no understanding as to why.

"Is the fire out, Mr. Carver?" Mother asked.

"Please, call me Joseph," he said. "Yes, the fire is out. It was a kitchen fire, and luckily it was contained."

All of the talking resumed as everyone wanted to know more about the fire, the engines, how many people were evacuated, and why they did not hear the fire bell.

I sat quietly and watched as he politely answered questions while remaining calm and self-assured, even though he was grievously late for dinner. When he stole a glance at me and smiled, my heart could not resist. No longer known solely as Mr. Carver caused an uninvited stir. Being Joseph had changed everything.

CHAPTER 50

Sarah
November 28, 1872

DESPITE THE AGE-OLD belief that workers rested on holidays, in truth it mattered not. I fidgeted throughout the night, wide awake long before the first bell sounded. There was no such thing as sleepin' late. Our habits, both good and bad, ruled the day. Because we agreed to help with special dinner preparations before church, Addy, Norah, Mercy, and I arose before the others.

In the dark, I made my way through the maze of beds and crates. The days were not only gettin' colder, but they were shorter as well. I wasn't one to complain, but with our long work hours, I could get a glimpse of daylight on Sundays, or if I sneaked out of the buildin' durin' the workday, which was not worth the risk.

As much as I convinced myself that bein' far away from home, playin' music, and bein' independent was good, I couldn't help but question the bitter fact that I had left my sister behind. She was courageous and of fine stock, this I knew to be true, but I was concerned. I had not received word of a weddin'. Her letters were about the failure to reach the father of her unborn child and a disturbin' level of acceptance of her fate. I continued to fret about her dreary future.

We were dissimilar that way. She believed that everything that happened was accordin' to God's will. Instead of puttin' up a good fight, she bowed her head in submission. She had blind faith, which made our mother proud. I took matters into my own hands, asked for divine guidance, and gave thanks when necessary. I was careful not to sin, and I was charitable and kind.

I wrapped my cloak around my shoulders and entered the hallway, where I heard others rattlin' about. When it got too cold, I fetched the water, and then I dumped it out the window like the others, keepin' the offal cart busy.

Once dressed and washed up, I made my way to the kitchen. Just like Mother, the Irish women took charge. Old Maggie stoked up the stove and pecked as expected. As crude as she tended to be, and after losin' her only daughter to influenza, she was like a mother to us.

Enjoyin' the quiet and the warmth of the kitchen, Mercy and I peeled carrots and sliced onions, which didn't help my eyes after a lack of sleep.

I smiled at Mercy. Much to Rebecca's dismay, she took to wearin' my braid as if it were her own. The hair color was off, but she made it neat, and if you didn't look too closely, you wouldn't have known if it were her hair or not.

After our preparations, we returned to our room and got into our Sunday best. The mothers who stayed home with the babies and young children finished up in the kitchen. I tried to ignore thoughts of Mother bakin' merries and roastin' the finest turkey imaginable. She got special cranberries from Mr. Tibbets, who claimed to get them from his family's bogs in Massachusetts.

All through the service, I wiggled in my seat. When it ended, I wasted no time leavin', eager for our Thanksgivin' feast. There, standin' across the way, were August and Finn.

"Hello," he said, wonderin' if I'd come up with a reason to run.

"August, it's nice to see you," I said, wavin' for Clara to go on ahead. I tried to speak to Finn, but he was engrossed in a coin that he held up close to his face.

"I haven't seen you for some time," he said. "How have you been?"

"Uh..." I looked up at the sight of real snowflakes, a refreshin' change from the lint that swirled about recklessly and stuck to you. I was wordless—not good, not bad. What was good in my life was a secret, while millwork was hard and tirin', not worth mentionin'. "I'm well."

"You don't sound so convincin'," he said.

"It's not that I'm unwell. There just isn't anything new to say," I said, instantly regrettin' it when I saw his look of disappointment. "Well, I'm thinkin' about bein' a drawin'-in girl. That has crossed my mind. The pay is better, and it requires more skill."

He looked as disinterested as one could possibly be. He placed his hand on Finn's shoulder and started walkin'. "Can we walk you home?"

"Yes, of course," I said. "Are you cookin' a special dinner today?"

"We're goin' to visit my friend, Tiago. He's a butcher. He invited us over."

The wind picked up, and it started to snow harder. August grabbed my arm, and we hurried to the tenement. I liked his touch. It was such a simple thing, not like an embrace or a kiss, but it meant somethin'. I paused. Not too close, because he could never know about Jonas. I kept at a distance.

As I watched them walk away, I caught a whiff of cigar smoke.

"Ya keep lettin' him go," Mary said, "such a foolish girl." The smoke curled around her face, and she looked as if she could laugh at any moment.

"What am I supposed to do?" I asked. "He can't come in, and I have no desire to go crawlin' into that shed where he lives."

"I don't know. But ya gotta' do somethin', before he finds another one," she said.

"Come on, put out your smoke; let's go in," I said.

Surprisingly, she did. And, together we went into the kitchen, where all was abuzz, and everyone wanted to be in charge.

We sat at three separate tables, each providin' more food than I had seen since my arrival.

As always, Mrs. O'Leary said the prayer.

"O Lord our God, thanks for providin' meat and drink for the nourishment of our worn and tired bodies, made weak from our hard work. Give us Thy blessin's so that we may be comforted and sustained. We give thanks that we don't hunger and thirst for food and drink, and that it's on our table today, and that we have our health, Amen."

Suddenly Mary rose up, causin' quite a clatter. "I got somethin' to say."

She cleared her throat. "God, Watch over the children of Ireland, scattered around the world. May the little ones be mothered, as they should be, and all of us raised up from the deeps, Amen."

After a pause, and without unity, we managed to say, 'amen.' Mary plopped down into her chair, tucked her soiled linen into her collar, and dug into the food.

We enjoyed hunter's pie, very much like the stew that Mother made when we were children, only the spices were more pungent. It consisted of the best end of a neck of mutton that was trimmed of any fat, smoked tongue, alternately layered with potatoes, onions, and mixed herbs, baked in an earthenware pie dish. The top layer of potatoes was neatly scalloped around the edges and carefully glazed with eggs. On each table was a pigeon pie that Mrs. O'Leary personally prepared, a half a loaf of soda bread, and steamed apple puddin'.

Chapter 51

August
November 28, 1872

Due to stormy weather and the wanin' moon, I passed on the wine and thanked Tiago's family for the hearty dinner. All bundled up, Finn and I set out to light the lamps. The bug cranks had long packed up for the winter, and other than the occasional stragglers, the streets had become quiet. We used to go much slower when it was warm. As it got colder, we tended to rush through the night. Sometimes challenged by the wind, it took a while to learn how to keep the torch burnin'.

I missed the music that I used to hear at the house on the hill but solved the mystery of who was playin'. More than once, I saw a young woman sittin' at the piano. I could only guess that she was the one. I never got to see her face. And, like most of the people on the hill, she was the fancy type.

CHAPTER 52

Sarah
December 4, 1872

THE NIGHT HAD fallen, and though my pocket-handkerchief was soaked in tears, they continued to fall from my eyes. There was no end to it. They had just begun. I had not been so low-spirited and sick at heart since Mother's death.

I re-read Abigail's letter, starin' at the words, "county farm." It was as if I had learned of her death.

How was it possible? Although I suspected Mrs. Blake to be an old biddy, I saw how she looked at my sister. She was jealous and greedy, but I thought that Moses could be trusted. I could not stand the idea of her in that wretched place. Mother told us how cruel it was. She warned us, tellin' us that we must be good and work hard, or we might end up there.

Most people were hooligans or simple-minded. Some were just kindly old folks, who had no one to care for them as they waited at death's door. Of course, there were the ones like Abigail, who went there in shame, carryin' a child with no man claimin' to be the father. A place where such a man would be the poormaster, overlookin' my sister while unwillin' to shoulder the burden of fatherin' his own child, was hellish indeed.

I went from sadness to anger, and then disbelief. My sister, again, threw herself at the mercy of God, not lookin' to blame Silas and that fancy tart that he chose over her. She always accepted her fate without a fight. I could not understand her tellin' me not to worry. How dare she expect me to be like her, a frail flower, wiltin' under the pressures of the wieldin' sword of men?

I stuffed the letter back into the envelope and looked out over the amber lights of the city, stunned to spot August on the street lookin' up at me. I blew out my candle. It was my fault for not checkin' to see if he was there. It had become a regular activity for him. I had to ask myself, and without an answer, if I liked it or not.

I sat in the dark until my rhythmic sobs emptied into a gentle flow of tears. I looked out, and he was gone. How I longed to be embraced. He must have thought me to be in peril at all times.

I knew that I could not go downstairs. The chatter and questions would have done me in. I preferred to sleep in the attic, but then they would have suspected that I was with August, who I did not see a fraction of the time that I had led them to believe.

I tried to pray, but it would not happen. I was angry with God. He did nothin' but disappoint, punish, and hurt innocent folks, seemingly opposed to women. If I opened up to Him, unlike my innocent sister, I would commit blasphemy, ensurin' my place in Hell.

To reach a level of comfort, and in search of spiritual refreshment, I closed my eyes and passed through the hidden door, the safe and private place that I went durin' such times, where I was never alone.

Chapter 53

Bess
December 4, 1872

Between Mother's meaningless chatter with the washerwoman, and my inability to think, the mere clatter of the door knocker took away my breath. It was all her fault. Everything was doomed because of Mother. Had she not invited him into our home as a guest, he wouldn't have insisted that we call him by his first name. It was easier to refer to him as Mr. Carver. Once it became personal, concentrating on the music was a challenge.

Yes, Mr. Todorov was charming and very handsome, and when I was younger, my heart craved him. From time to time, I fancied the idea of being in his arms but quickly dismissed such thoughts, as he was quite professional and strict as a teacher. Not that Joseph—Mr. Carver—was any less professional, but I just could not address him as Joseph and make musical progress.

When he entered the room, it became difficult to breathe. It was a moment that would not be forgotten, because it was no longer a mere possibility that I had fallen hopelessly in love. It had become evident, that if the opportunity presented itself, I would have surrendered. Not only did we share our passion for music, but we also strived for perfection. We recognized the light that shined in the other. He brought out the best in me without provocation. He even seemed to understand Mother and handled her with ease.

"Hello, Bess."

"Mr. Carver?" I nodded and immediately wondered why I felt such conflict over something as simple as a name.

He chuckled, causing me to blush.

"It's a fine day," I said, immediately ready to crawl under the piano bench and hide.

"And finer now that I am here," he said. "Shall we get started?"

Setting aside my fear for a moment, I looked into his eyes. How could I not have gotten lost in them?

CHAPTER 54

August
December 4, 1872

HER BLUE CAPE covered most of her face, but I could still see her eyes. They looked sad, not twinklin' like I remembered.

"Don't be sad," I said.

She hugged me and whispered a few words that I could not hear.

"What?" I asked. "Don't leave. Please, don't go."

I heard the footsteps, and although tempted, did not turn to look. I couldn't lose sight of her, not this time. She covered her face and wept, before vanishin' into the thick fog that crept in from the shore.

I cried. I cried hard. Through my tears, I looked down at my feet upon the church steps. There was a hole in the toe of one of my small shoes. I sat down and stared into the fog, not knowin' which direction she went in, or how she got there. Again and again, she was gone.

A loud clatter jolted me out of my dream. After wipin' a tear from my cheek, I sat up and watched the dim outline of Finn sittin' in his new bed crate, fiddlin' with somethin'.

I paid him no mind and got the coal hod. We were runnin' low, and the cold had set in. It was time to move into the cellar of a nearby tenement. Throughout the winter, it would protect us more than the old splintered shed. A cellar wasn't bad. Anything was better than an iron chute, the alley, or a narrow canvas cot, strung up between rough beams. I wasn't pleased about movin', but even with the little stove filled and ablaze, I couldn't keep our place warm.

I stood in the alleyway, relievin' myself in the heavy, wet snow. I knew that we had enough for breakfast, but I had to go to the market. The last of the oats set overnight in the pot. I'd add our remainin' apple, a few raisins, and a touch of brandy to our stirabout.

When I went to get my tobacco tin, it wasn't on the table. I looked over, and there was Finn, proudly combin' his own hair. It brought a smile to my lips. At least he was tryin' to take better care of himself, but I didn't want him takin' things without me knowin'.

His cheeks were flushed. He looked right proud. Before I took away the comb, I waited 'til he was finished. At first, he tried to hold onto it, but he decided to let go. I tossed it down on the table.

"I'll keep it here," I said.

I searched for my tin, which was under the corner of his quilt on the floor. I held it in front of him and shook my head. "No, don't take my tin," I said.

I had hoped to get a reaction, but his face was blank. When I returned to makin' the stirabout, he tugged on my sleeve and then dropped the blue cloth into my hand.

"What are you doin' with this?" I shouted. "What else do you have, you little thief?"

I emptied the coins onto the table and counted them. Seein' that they were all there, I traced my finger over the stitched letters, A-U-G-U-S-T, and tucked the cloth back into the tin.

CHAPTER 55

Sarah
December 21, 1872

ALTHOUGH THE NIGHT was exceptionally bitter, I was grateful that the snow flurries in our midst were real. Each player stood before a small puddle of frozen spit. I hadn't played my cornet out in the cold for such an extended period of time. Once, as a surprise for Mother and Abigail, I stood outside and played "O Holy Night" and quickly returned inside to sip hot chocolate by the fire.

It was not a woolen cloak and hood, but my winter frock coat made a difference. I was no longer shiverin' for hours after returnin' home from rehearsals, but standin' in one place with a cold mouthpiece pressed to my lips was unbearable. Instead of our regular rehearsal, the band gathered in front of City Hall and performed traditional Christmas music. I pulled my hat down, almost coverin' my eyes, but I was still able to see Mr. Daniels, the bandmaster.

I rushed home from the mill just ahead of the girls, knowin' that they would eat supper early so that they could attend the concert. I finally told Clara that I was meetin' with August, and she promised to seal her lips in silence.

In addition to keepin' an eye on the music, I kept track of the people who stood in small groups, some singin' along, and others huddled together wearin' a familiar deadened expression, a look of longin' that only the mill people seemed to have.

My heart leapt when I spotted August and Finn near the outer edge of the crowd. They set everything down and took to listenin'. Luckily, they weren't any closer to me.

Breathin' had become an arduous task, so I focused harder on the music, rememberin' that Jonas was a good man, one who presented himself well. I agreed to stop feelin' faint and to enjoy what I set out to do, to play music. I made it. That meant even more to me than bein' a drawin'-in girl. My sister would love to have been anywhere other than locked up at the County Farm. I had no right to be distraught.

When the crowd cheered, I heard her. Over and above all, Mary shouted, "Bravo! Encore!"

I knew it was her. I didn't have to look. She seemed to know everything, but that could not be true, for someone with vast knowledge wouldn't make so many bad choices. I swallowed my fear and played.

We were near the end of our little concert when Clara and Clemmie—deep in conversation—walked behind Mr. Daniels. They stopped. Clara looked right into my eyes and smiled. Before that night, I would have thought it hardly possible to sweat in such frigid weather conditions, but I did.

I looked down at my music, refusin' to make eye contact with her. So that was what it felt like when a girl made inappropriate advances. I would remember that the next time I felt inclined to flirt. I was disappointed in Clara. I believed her actions to be quite forward, to smile at a man like she did, and a complete stranger no less!

At the end of the song, I blasted a stinger. One note! It echoed far beyond the crowd, beautiful and bright, but dreadfully wrong. Mr. Daniels raised an eyebrow. His expression of shock and disapproval could not be disguised.

Leanin' in close, Frederick said, "That girl fancies you. If she wasn't so damaged, you could have your way with her."

I wanted to slap him. I assumed that he was a gentleman. My face flared up in defense of Clara. How could he speak of her with such disregard? If it weren't for her scars, she would have been lovely to the outside world.

The other cornet players elbowed each other and openly snickered. I had seen cocks like this in the barnyard, struttin', peckin', and sometimes even fightin' to the death. They puffed and preened at the expense of others. That one erroneous note was all it took for them to get a gleam in their eyes. I imagined what they thought, "Jonas made a mistake, not just a minor mistake that could be buried somewhere in the music where few people would even know about it. No, he made a mistake that hung over us all like an ominous cloud. That fella' was a disgrace."

CHAPTER 56

Bess
December 21, 1872

ARM IN ARM, mother and I strolled through the crowded square. To some, that could have been charming, and I'm sure that many believed it to be so. She squeezed my elbow, steering me this way and that, talking under her breath about those who were brash and unladylike, reminding me to stand up straight, not make eye contact with others, and to wear a fixed smile. She warned me about walking too fast. There was nothing more ungraceful than a girl darting across the street in front of carriages. She even slapped my hand when I raised my skirts to avoid soiling them. She said it was better to be badly soiled than to lift them too high, appearing to be a nothing but a raw country girl. She would not tolerate that kind of disgrace.

She paraded me about as if I were livestock at one of those county fairs in New Hampshire that she often spoke of. When we were visiting my uncle and aunt, I always asked if we could go, but the answer was a firm no. As odd as it was, our visits were restricted to the lake house. I loved it there and didn't complain. I did not have to be so modest and quiet, dignified and graceful. At times, I longed to be rough cut and free, to throw away the rules of etiquette. I wanted to misbehave.

Earlier in the day, after church, we went to a Christmas social at the home of the mayor. It was very well-attended, and many faces were becoming familiar to me. It was evident that my concert debut left quite an impression, as I was asked in advance to play at least one piece on the lovely piano in their great room. Knowing that this might happen, I revisited J.S. Bach's "Christmas Oratorio," and Mother arranged for a courier to deliver the music to the mayor's home the day before.

Father insisted that we show our support for the mayor and other dignitaries, by attending the holiday festivities. There were people of all stations milling about, some singing along with the brass band as they played Christmas carols, others swaying, singing in a foreign language, or looking vacant and spent from working long hours and lack of sunlight.

We finally came across Father and some of the men who smoked cigars. We stood behind them with the other women, waiting for the mayor to give his speech. He didn't have much to say, just that Fall River was a splendid city, one of the largest textile cities in the world, boasting over one million spindles. After wishing all a Merry Christmas, he gathered his family and departed.

"The music is good for a brass band," Mother said.

"I didn't really pay attention," I said. The snow came down harder, and the wind picked up. I pushed my hands deeper into my rabbit muff. "Perhaps we should leave now."

"Let's listen to one more song," Mother said.

Father joined another group of men who smoked cigars, and they turned their backs to everyone, fanning their arms about, making plans for more mills—bigger and better.

The band was actually in tune, and I found myself enjoying the harmonies. However, I couldn't stand out in the cold and play music like that. The slender, young cornetist at the end of the first row caught my attention. He wore his hat pulled down, almost completely covering his eyes while his face continued to redden. Struck by his discomfort, first scanning the crowd, and then looking back at the conductor, I moved in closer. He stood out, and his apparent vulnerability reeled me in. I wanted to rush over and save him, from what, I knew not. Of course, that was a silly, wild thought.

"Bess, now let's find your father, and get Davis to bring us home," Mother said.

"Oh, Mother, now I am captivated by this brass band. Like you said, it's very good for a brass band. I usually feel overwhelmed by brass, but this is lovely," I said, keeping my eyes on the cornetist.

She pulled her hood tightly around her neck. "We never seem to agree; do we?"

I didn't answer. I even tapped my toe, which was a compliment to them and highly unusual for me. "No, I suppose we do not."

As usual, the mill girls behaved poorly, hollering while the band played, knowing only the rules of the street. It was hard to tell them apart; they all looked alike in their ragged clothes. It was such a shame that they passed along their poverty and ignorance to their children. Even the lamplighters—crude and uneducated— knew enough to stand politely by the fence.

When the song came to an end, the young cornetist that I had my eye on, played an awkward, loud note. He looked up in astonishment. Despite the cold, tiny beads of perspiration glistened on his face. I was horrified on his behalf.

"There, we really must go now," Mother said. "My feet are like ice."

"Wait," I said, not sure what I was expecting.

"If they aren't finished now, they will be very soon. We must go. Davis is waiting!"

The other musicians were openly laughing at the young man. I feared that the snow around him would melt from his shame. How dare they laugh. Most, if not all, of the people in the crowd, were unaware of his mistake. It was his comrades, his fellow musicians, who humiliated him.

CHAPTER 57

August
December 21, 1872

WE WERE NEARLY late showin' up at the Street Department, but we made it on time. I took pride in bein' reliable. We rushed, because earlier in the day, we moved what little we had into the cellar of a nearby tenement. It happened to be next door to Sarah—not too close, but close enough. The shed wasn't built for warmth, and Finn was sickly. We had to squat somewhere else.

Sean, a fellow lamplighter, helped us move. I was worried about gettin' caught but took a risk. With most folks at work, other than a few girls mindin' the children, we went unnoticed.

There was plenty of room for Finn's crate, and I would find a new one for myself. A former squatter left a small pine table with a chair. Fortunately, there was a large stove in place, so we left ours in the shed.

Had it not been for the clouds, the remainder of the moon would have shined through, and Finn and I could have gone to the Christmas festivities in the city. Francis Murphy told us that we could go if the weather was clear.

When we reached the end of the last street, we heard the brass band. The festivities were still goin' on, so we decided to stop by. There were more people than I expected. Finn wanted to join some kids sleddin' down a small hill, but I didn't want to lose sight of him.

The music reminded me of the Children's Asylum Band. I never joined them or any other, even though one of the ministers offered to give me a battered old horn and said he'd teach me how to play. I wanted to, and I tried, but I couldn't make a sound. Jimmy did though, and he was pretty good. He carried that horn with him everywhere. After I left, and for quite some time, Jimmy played alongside the organ grinder and tambourine girls. Then one day he was gone—maybe to one of the islands, or he was placed out.

I wasn't plannin' on stayin' too long. I wanted to return to our new home and make stirabout while there was time. I tapped Finn on the shoulder and was about to leave, when I noticed one of the musicians in the band. He looked awful familiar. I collected my gear, and with Finn close behind, went to get a better look. Because he kept his head down, it was hard to see him. He was a twig of a man, and other than the drummer boy, was the smallest of them all. His appearance was careless and disordered, and he could not sit still. Then he looked up. It was him—the man who played in Sarah's attic.

He was not as he was in the window, quite the opposite. His distress caused me to squirm. Finn and I returned to the back of the crowd, and I let Finn take a turn on the sled. Once everyone started to leave, and the band members went their separate ways, I decided to follow him.

He headed towards the market and Tiago's shop. Rather than takin' a chance at Finn gettin' sick again, we went home. Even though he didn't go to the tenement, I knew it was him, the man in the window.

CHAPTER 58

Sarah
December 25, 1872

IT WAS WELL before daybreak, and the girls slumbered well. I was alert, and my nose was cold. I stared up at where I knew the boarded-up window to be and imagined a snowy day. I wondered if my sister had made her first snow angel and if the County Farm even permitted such activities. I thought of her in with the aged, the hungry, the sick, and those who suffered from senility. I heard that they also housed criminals.

I sat up. *I cannot do it. There's no snow for an angel.* The streets were filled with sour, rotted food, and half-frozen puddles created by the sinks, outhouses, and overflowin' chamber pots, dumped carelessly out the windows. All of the buildin's were crowded together. I questioned my sanity, for I came from a world of vast openness—fields, mountains, and woods—and suddenly, I was unable to find a patch of clean snow.

Blessedly content, Mercy rolled into my space. How naive she was, eternally happy and inquisitive, runnin' around with my messy old braid somehow pinned to her head. With a conflicted heart, I pulled the blanket over her shoulder.

Instead of bein' pleased to be with her sister, Rebecca pecked at her, always tryin' to embarrass her in front of others. If only she knew what it felt like to worry, to pray that her sister was well while knowin' that she was in a horrid place filled with danger and darkness.

Rebecca's callous behavior was unacceptable and invited a certain longin' that I tried to push away, but since leavin' Abigail, I could find no peace.

I nudged Mercy back to her section of the bed and nestled up against her. We could sleep late. It wasn't just any Wednesday. It was Christmas. I didn't need to get up and tromp through the dirty, gray slush on my way to the mill. I should have been happy. Typically, the holidays delighted me so, but I had no interest in stringin' apples or singin'. Norah and the others baked ginger cookies while I sat in my alcove overlookin' the city. I had my fill of Christmas carols when I played in front of City Hall and disgraced poor Jonas. The thought of it caused a fiery blush.

Then there was August. I did fancy him, but there was no time for such things. The drudgery of work each day was a challenge in itself. However, keepin' such a vital secret caused my spirit to wilt. I started to purposely avoid him; I was tired of makin' excuses. It was easier to try to forget about him than to face him.

I was proud. Even without Mother around to keep me in line, I managed to adhere to my Christian values. Surrenderin' to him would have ruined everything. I needed to save money so that I could fetch Abigail from the County Farm, maybe send for her and the baby. Sortin' it out had become a chore. No matter where he was raised, bein' fatherless would leave an ugly mark and follow him everywhere.

With both love and sorrow, thoughts of our farm weighed heavily upon my heart, for I missed the cleanness of the countryside. Everything had changed. Christmas was so special with the tree, music, and merries. Even after Papa died, we were festive and cheerful.

Determined to make it work, I wouldn't allow self-pity to enter into my existence, especially when I knew that it was much worse for others. I tried to be bright. It was not home, but we did our best to make our room pleasant. One of the older women crafted a wreath out of straggly branches, decorated it with scraps of red yarn from the mill, and hung it in the kitchen.

Returnin' to New Hampshire was out of the question. I set out to be independent, and not nearly enough time had passed. It was hard. But, it was a matter of perspective.

I was meant to be in Fall River. It was possible to escape my grief where there were no physical reminders. However, I had to find a way to bring Abigail home, but there was no longer a home to speak of. Besides, I didn't know if I could have handled the shame surroundin' our blackened name. I may have murdered Silas for not bein' a man of honor and found myself hangin' by the neck. It seemed highly possible that I too would have ended up at the County Farm.

I also learned that Weston Jones, the only boy interestin' enough to win my heart, did not only reject that sentiment, but he moved to Maine. It seemed best for me to stay put.

Although I could have slept longer, my thoughts marched into my head like an army of ants. I dreaded gettin' up and leavin' Mercy, who was always warm. Barely makin' a sound, I inched my way to the closet to find the chamber pot.

When I was in the hallway, someone from another room brushed by, almost knockin' me off my feet. I lifted my lamp but to no avail. She was gone.

I followed the scent of unsavory food. Once in the kitchen, I looked out the window. The clouds passed quickly overhead, and the street lamps illuminated the snow flurries. I believed that if I looked hard enough, I'd find a clean patch of snow.

When I turned to get the coal hod, I caught a glimpse of the one who pushed me earlier. It was Mary! I was concerned about her smokin'. She always sneaked out, and I thought it to be even worse for her health in the cold weather.

I was about to return to the chore at hand, when I noticed her bent over, clutchin' her stomach. I slipped on my cloak and dashed out into the cold.

"Mary!" I shouted. "What's wrong?"

She turned away.

I stood by anxiously, watchin' her all hunched over in her oversized calico blouse, frayed petticoat, and mismatched shoes.

"Do you need help?" I asked.

She dragged her sleeve across her chin. "I'll be fine."

"You're ill. You should see a doctor," I said, ignorin' the echoes of conversations with my sister just a few months before.

She started heavin' again. "People like us don't see doctors."

"Perhaps somethin' you ate was spoilt," I said. "More than once, I caught you eatin' from the dinner pail after it should have been emptied." I was stunned at my ability to find excuses for the obvious.

She leaned against the fence. "It ain't nothin' like that," she said. "It's a baby. There's a baby inside of me." She pulled out a stub of a cigarette.

"What?"

"Ya heard me," she said. "Why are ya so surprised?"

I went to hug her, and she turned away to light her cigarette. I continually tried to help people who did not want my help. Mary was one of those people, the first on the list since movin' to Fall River. I thought that she too would end up in the almshouse—the poor farm in Fall River.

"Ya don't need to take pity on me," she said, drawin' long and hard on her cigarette.

"Don't tell me what to do," I said, sick of these women bearin' the responsibility of motherhood without support from the men involved. "You have to tell Mr. Aldrich."

"Why do I have to tell him?"

"Because he must own up to the consequences of his behavior."

"What makes ya think it's him?" she asked, throwin' the cigarette on the ground and crushin' it with the heel of her good shoe.

"What do you mean?" I asked, ignorin' the rumblin' in my own stomach.

"Brown—ya know, the weaver from 'cross the way—caught sight of me with Mr. Aldrich and decided to have his way with me."

"What? How could you do that? I know who he is. Mr. Aldrich was bad enough, and now you tell me that you lifted your skirts for him too?"

"No, I did not consent."

"What?"

"I love Mr. Aldrich, and he loves me," she said, wipin' a tear from her eye. "Brown chased me down and forced himself on me in violence." She came undone.

"Why didn't you tell the police?"

"Do ya think they'd believe me? Brown is one of the men from England. And, if Mr. Aldrich found out, he wouldn't want me anymore. I'm sure that when I tell him about the baby, he'll take care of me. We might leave together. I know that he loves me. I'm not like my mum, I don't sell my body to buy bread, and then trade it for whiskey."

The Angels' Lament

She fell into my arms and watered my cloak in tears. Her whole body shook. She was no longer a woman, but a scared little girl. We both knew that Mr. Aldrich would not leave with her, that she would give birth, and continue workin' at the mill while one of the girls in the tenement watched the baby.

At the sound of the patrolman's approach to extinguish the street lamps, we returned to the tenement. She sat at the kitchen table while I stirred the coals and emptied the hod. The silence ached to be filled.

"Did you ever make a snow angel?"

"Did I what?" she asked.

"You know, make snow angels," I said.

"Do I seem to be one for the likes of it?"

"No, I mean you never know, Mary. Just about everyone makes them in New Hampshire, includin' the boys. You fall back into the fresh snow, and by movin' your arms and legs just so, leave an imprint of an angel."

"There's plenty of snow here for that," she said.

"No, no there is not. It has to be deeper than what is on the streets, and clean. Angels need to be made in fresh snow," I said.

"There's more snow here than anywhere else," she said and laughed.

"No, you have never been to New Hampshire. The snow is fresh and very white."

"But, it snows almost every day here, even in the summer," she said.

I shook my head. "You don't understand."

"I s'pose I don't," she said.

I found a bit of soft ginger root, enough to make us tea. We sat together in quietness, waitin' patiently for the daylight to come.

After a breakfast of Mrs. Brennan's best Indian meal stirabout and soda bread, we attended church. As always, Mary stayed home, avoidin' the House of the Lord altogether. Oh, how her spirit must have craved refreshment, but she would not hear of it. She promised to help Clemmie, Bridget, and the others prepare for Christmas dinner.

211

Although my heart did feel a slight jab, I kept an eye out for August but didn't see him. It was safe to say that he was finally discouraged, and I no longer had to worry about lies. Hand in hand, Clara and I traipsed along, excited to get back to the others.

Of course, I was prepared for a skeleton of a feast, knowin' that it would be nothin' like home. There would be few, if any, presents exchanged. I planned to focus on the fellowship of kindred spirits—bein' grateful for what I had, not sorrowful for what was lost. I could not continuously occupy my mind with thoughts of Mother, Abigail, or the County Farm. I had to remind myself to pray more, even though it meant to stop bein' angry at God. I realized that in order to maintain any form of goodness, and rather than ignorin' Him altogether, that I would pray to the Divine Mother. There couldn't possibly be only a Father, there had to be a Mother in all of it.

We stopped as many carriages and sleighs headed up the hill towards the homes that I had yet to see. "Clara, would you like to take a walk?"

"I don't see why not," she said.

"Dinner won't be ready for a while, and too many hands spoil things," I said.

Surrounded by an assortment of delightful aromas waftin' out of kitchens, people callin' out to one another, and amidst the sound of sleigh bells, we made our way up the hill.

It was the first time I had seen so many magnificent houses. I mean, there were many nice homes in Wolfeboro, and one or two right in Ossipee, but all of the houses before us were grand. They were not all crammed together but had what looked like courtyards with gardens, statues, and fountains.

We stopped. "Clara, this is almost a castle," I said.

"Yep... sure is pretty," she said.

"Look! There's a big yard," I said.

"There are big yards everywhere," she said and smiled.

Without warnin', I ran through the bushes and stopped right in the middle of a large open space. The snow was well above my ankles, but not quite as high as my knees. Clara stood far enough away to watch and not get caught. I fell back into the fluffy snow, makin' a perfect snow angel. Careful not to disturb it, I got up and looked. *There should be another.* I fell back again, makin' another one while catchin' snowflakes on my tongue. I wanted to fill the yard with snow angels.

"Clara!"

"I'm stayin' right here. I don't wanna get in trouble for trespassin'," she said.

"It's Christmas," I said, ploppin' myself into the snow again, makin' yet another angel.

"Hey, you!" A colored man shouted out from the carriage house. "Go on! Get out of here!"

I pulled my hood down so that he couldn't get a good look and report me to the authorities. I scrambled to my feet and barely made it to the bushes. We giggled and ran down the street—down, down, down—not stoppin' until we reached the thick, dark slush that surrounded our yard, where men gathered in vice and misery, and ill-tempered women argued with the world.

Chapter 59

Bess
December 25, 1872

After devouring Vienna chocolate and hickory-nut macaroons with pineapple ice cream, I joined my parents in the great room, where we exchanged gifts. I was beside myself with glee when Mother and Father gave me a golden locket. It was delicately engraved with my initials and had a photo of both of them in it. I treasured trinkets and enjoyed wearing jewelry.

I gave Tempy another embroidered pocket-handkerchief to add to her collection. Other than playing the piano and getting settled in a new city, I had done little else with my creative time. Soon we would be painting china, but I never seemed to get a lot accomplished when we did such activities. It was more about sharing gossip with the other women, and only a few truly cared about the quality of their work. Mother often reminded me that it was a time of leisure, not a time to compete. I wanted to do my best or not bother at all.

I thought it appropriate to give my parents the gift of music. I saw no point in buying them something that they could easily get themselves when they wanted or needed to. I would be using their money, so was it really a gift? I think not. A gift is from the heart.

Mr. Carver recommended that I work on Schubert's "Piano Sonata in A minor." So, my gift to them was a framed copy of the music title page. Mr. Carver frowned upon separating the cover from the whole piece, but it was my decision. I was about to give it to them when Davis began shouting from the carriage house.

Mother pulled back the curtain in time to see a woman running from the garden and out into the street.

"Those ragamuffins need to stay in their own neighborhood," Mother said.

"Where would that be?" I asked. "What kind of trouble is there in a long-dead garden?"

"Oh, just someone looking for scraps, I suppose," she said, walking away from the window with her head held high.

I smiled. Whoever it was had made three lovely snow angels right in the center of the garden. I hadn't even thought about snow angels since that snowy Thanksgiving, when along with a lop-sided snowman, Madelene and I made them in the park.

Chapter 60

August
December 25, 1872

It snowed heavily throughout the night and into the day. Finn started to show signs of bein' sick again, so we stayed put. He wanted clam soup for dinner, but we had to wait until spring for that. We dug up clams now and then, but that stopped when winter set in. We shared a piece of pork steak with cabbage, onion, and leftover bread from a kind lady on our route. There was no need to go anywhere until it was time to light the lamps. I collected enough coal on the side of the road to keep our fire goin' for at least a week.

Chapter 61

Christmas Day, 1857
The Orphans' Home and Asylum of the Protestant Episcopal Church
New York City

"Elizabeth! Hurry! Come quickly!"

"What?... Another one? We've already had four throughout the night. We need more beds. Tell Father that we need them soon, or we cannot do this. Do you hear me? Margaret?"

"Don't fret. Of course, we'll do this. We always manage. Once you've been here for as long as I have, you will see. Besides, some of the older ones are going to Randall Island in a few months, others will go on the trains, or simply run away. Let's get him inside. It's cold."

"I ran as fast as I could when I heard the bell. Oh, just look at him. He's shivering. I'll fetch another blanket. Let's bring him into the kitchen and warm him by the fire. How could anyone leave such a beautiful boy?"

"Out of necessity, Elizabeth, out of necessity. In time, you'll become accustomed to it. Is there a note?"

"Here it is, pinned inside of his coat. He has a fabric patch too."

I am leeving my sweet son on your dorstep. His name is August. He is 3. Im not a bad mother. I love him more than aneything. I need help. Once I find his farther, I will send mony. This is why I am leeving August here. I cannot rase him on my own.

Once I find his farther, I will come backe for him. I pinned a blue fabricke with our inishalls inside of his coate. I have the other halfe, which is identicle so that I can come backe for him. I will return. S. Wood

"Hello, August. Don't be afraid. God will guide us. They're typically stunned for the first day or two."

"My heart crumbles for every child and mother who ends up in these circumstances."

"Mummy?"

"Mummy has gone away for now. We shall take good care of you."

"He's such a beautiful boy. Lord knows that we are crowded, but we always find room for one more. He is a Christmas blessing for some family. A boy this handsome will not suffer here for too long."

"Wipe away that tear, Elizabeth. You can never let them know that you are distressed. We must make them feel safe. With more experience, you'll learn to view him like all the rest of the children that reside in your soul. You will find a compartment for them, a place that is safe from pulling you under. You must harden and become strong. Not that caring too much is a weakness, but in an orphanage, tears will do you in."

"But, he's so young and innocent, and there are so many of them, I can't—"

"—Just remember, one is not better or worse. They are all the same—God's children. We do good work, and for that, we will be rewarded in Heaven. Who knows the fate of little August? The Lord knows. And, be prepared to accept that his mother will not return. Until then, we are the guardians, the keepers, and we will carry on as needed."

CHAPTER 62

Sarah
February 15, 1873

PROPELLED BY MY own fear, I sprinted all the way home. The brittle month of February showed no mercy upon us. The urine froze in our chamber pots, the inside of the cracked and patched window in our room was encased in thick yellow ice, and sickness waited at the door. I had resorted to keepin' my feet warm by tuckin' them into the patched mail-bag that Mercy gave to me as a Christmas gift. I learned that without kindness, a soul will droop rapidly, especially durin' the reign of cold. With so much sadly broken, I lacked strength for future woes.

Mrs. Brennan warned us about the dangers of not wearin' a warm cloak to and from work. Tragically, many had been laid in a coffin—victims of fever or consumption—from rushin' out of the heated mills, flushed and eager to get home, with only light protection against the frigid night air or dampness from a storm.

I was careful to wear a warm cloak over my work dress and a heavy overcoat to band practice. Rehearsals were a welcome change from the daily routine of the mills, but the lack of sunlight caused my spirits to wilt. Had I not been able to play music, I would have failed the Fall River experience, for we departed in the mornin' before sunrise and returned home after sunset. I missed the sun. By nature, winter was dreary, but it was far worse when workin' in the mills.

Bein' closed off and inward worked well. My fellow bandsmen gave up tryin' to engage in conversation and thought of me as odd. Whenever I tried to speak, my words piled up like a derailed train, and I blushed like a girl. Silence was my ally. As long as I played my part, kept my head down, and went out into the back room durin' our break, I could sustain the lie and Jonas would live on.

I always ran home. My fear of the dark plagued me. Even when I reminded myself that I was a man, I continued to run. I knew that if we had a race, I could have beat any boy back home.

Once again, I managed to slip into the tenement and up the stairs without bein' noticed. I went to the attic alcove to change my clothes and jumped when I saw Mary.

"Sorry, I know this is ya secret spot, but I had to get away from everyone," she said.

"You scared me!"

"Why are ya dressed up like that?"

"I can't really talk about it," I said.

"Ya look like a boy." She started in laughin'.

"It's none of your business."

"Wait! I saw you in front of City Hall. You're in that band, ain't ya?"

I sat down and placed my hands on her knees. "Listen, you cannot tell a soul."

She laughed again, only this time it was a wicked laugh, and it was loud.

"Shh…" I looked around the room.

"I can't help it. This is so damn amusin'. Ya dressed up like a boy, and I'm sittin' here with a fat belly. We're a pair of scamps, ain't we?"

"It's nothin' to laugh about," I said.

"So, this is really why ya cut off ya hair, and everyone who cannot think for themselves followed suit."

"I have always wanted to play in a band. They won't allow women, and I really wanted to—"

"—never mind, ya handsome bloke."

"Stop. Just stop."

"'Tis true. We ain't supposed to laugh. We need to be in misery and despair," she said.

"No, I'm tired. Please, promise me that you'll keep this a secret."

"I will," she said, lookin' out over the moonlit city. "You're my best friend."

"What about Mr. Aldrich?" I asked, unable to validate our friendship.

"What about him?"

"Is he leavin' his wife?"

"I don't know. He said that we could talk about it when the time came," she said.

I could not tell her my real thoughts and cause her hope to sink. I watched her icy breath and the candlelight flicker in her eyes. "I'm goin' to change into my skirt, and then let's find comfort in a warm room, the kitchen, where we can share a cuppa by the stove."

"If he doesn't leave with me, I will find a way to leave on my own, just the baby and me. We won't stay around here to suffer. There is always a better place."

Chapter 63

August
February 15, 1873

The Leblancs came down from Quebec to join the others in the mills. Pierre, a mule spinner, didn't speak much English, but his wife tried. Their daughter was about four years old, and there was another one on the way.

How could I put up a fuss? Finn and I were squatters ourselves, and with this cold snap and all, we had to let them in. Every day, I expected the landlord to either charge us for rent or kick us out. I wondered what was takin' so long.

Doin' his best, Pierre explained that they had been livin' with his sister's family, when there was an outbreak of measles, so to spare their daughter and unborn child, they left. Ruby, one of the weavers who lived next door, told them about the cellar.

We hung a ragged blanket between our sleepin' quarters, open at one end so that we could still get the heat. Pierre had some tools, and his wife had kitchen utensils, a good oil lamp, and a washtub that she set up in the corner beside her chamber pot.

As long as I remembered the narrow canvas cots, the cellar was not so bad. And, it was much better than any other place at Five Points, where we were overcrowded with wretched drunks, degraded women, Italian rag pickers, and even the organ player's monkey—the vilest of all—crammed together so tightly that we often couldn't move freely when we slept. Many people were sick, as we were surrounded by death.

Yes, the cellar was good. I liked it. There was room to move around. Sure, it got smoky, but I aired it out when I could. I was prepared. If more folks showed up, I wouldn't turn them away.

Chapter 64

Bess
February 15, 1873

I ADMIRED THE courage of the wayward girl, the one who left snow angels in our winter garden. After each storm, I tended to them, carefully recreating them. I liked that they were there and that with each revision, they became more imperfect. It was as if they were my secret friends in this new, dreary place. I hoped to feel more cheerful in the spring, but until then, the angels would do. Mother thought it silly and worried about me catching a cold, but I had to do something out of the ordinary, or I would have curled up and died.

"Tempy, what would I do without you?"

"Oh child, I'm sure you'd do jes fine," she said.

I looked out over the barren yard once more, before climbing into my freshly warmed bed. February was exceedingly dreadful. With the house so drafty, were it not for Tempy and the others tending the fires, we would have frozen to death.

In the morning, I preferred to linger in bed, but Mother wouldn't hear of it. There was no end to her complaints. She did not winter well at all. She badgered me until I got up, played the piano, did needlepoint, and read at least one chapter of classic literature.

For penmanship practice, and to remain connected and cordial, I penned a weekly letter to my cousins in New Hampshire. Mother wanted me to perfect the art of letter writing, saying that it was a sign of good character to send and receive letters with regularity. She deemed it to be productive and the foundation of much refined and social happiness.

It was a challenge to write to the same people every week, trying to conjure up a message or measured words of love while carefully avoiding long, tedious details of boring trivialities. It was required that my letters be gracefully worded while never revealing confidentialities. Not only did Mother inspect my letters for proper content, charm, and grammar, she was a stickler for neatness. If there was so much as one small blot, the entire letter was tossed into the fire, and I was to begin again with a fresh sheet of paper.

She considered it bad taste to express oneself honestly, use flowery language, or quotations. When asked why she did not write the letter herself, she became highly insulted and sulked for the rest of the afternoon.

A good daughter would have chased after her and begged for forgiveness, but that was not our way. I tried many a time to feel sympathy or regret when I injured her spirits, but she was comforted in the depths of her own misery. Secretly, it was what she craved. The few times I did try to console her or offer an apology, she plunged deeper into her gloomy state. Even showing the smallest indication of soothing her sorrows brought about harsh punishment to me, the offender.

Although there was nothing new to mention, and it was unacceptable to write from my heart, again, I sat with pen and paper, trying to write according to her rules.

I was never allowed any leisure time. When I took an interest in baking, Mother thought it to be frivolous and beneath me. Life was so unfair.

Chapter 65

August
April 12, 1873

We didn't have to light the lamps. The moon was full with nary a cloud to be found. Even when it was as plain as could be, I had to check in with Francis Murphy, but he finally trusted me.

Winter hung on tight right up 'til the first week in April, when we got a blizzard. The snow was meltin' quick, makin' a real mess. It was a good afternoon to walk about and gather coal. I knew where to look for the droppin's, and I checked once a week. Finn was back to collectin' bugs and moths with the bug cranks, so he didn't have an eye out for coal.

Before we got started, we were gonna head over to see Tiago. Sometimes he had work for me, not for money, but for barterin'. If I helped him with the smokin', I'd get a cut of meat.

Just as we approached the outhouses, I saw Sarah's friend Mary. She didn't bother to stop. I talked to her a few times, enough to know that she was trouble. Her doomed condition was right clear and, other than the man in the attic window, I never saw another man around.

I could tell that she had spent a fair amount of time on the streets, and without knowin', our paths may have crossed. She cussed, smoked cigars, and had that feral look about her. She put up with those things that others couldn't grasp. I'd been there so many times before—beyond pain, clingin' fiercely to survival.

Chapter 66

Sarah
April 12, 1873

MARY DID NOT return to her station after dinner. I could barely wait until ring out, but I did not want to be penalized. Mr. Aldrich was more twitchy than usual, and he avoided lookin' at me. It was apparent that he no longer paid attention to routine matters. When one of the doffers dropped a full tray of bobbins, we all stopped in dreaded anticipation, but he didn't take notice.

I made it a point to glare at him whenever I had the chance. I wanted him to know that he did not fool me. Why Mary continued to listen to his lies was hard to understand. I begged her to forget the notion that he would leave his wife, but she sincerely believed that he loved her.

"Where's Mary?" Norah shouted.

"I don't know. She left at the dinner bell, and I haven't seen her since," I said.

"She was distraught. She and Mr. Aldrich had words," she said.

"Oh no! He's an evil man. We've got to hurry home after ring out. I hope she's alright."

"Stop talkin'! Get back to work!" Red-faced and wide-eyed, he limped in our direction.

"Or you'll do what, exactly?" My heart jumped when I spoke without thoughts of consequence.

"Did you talk back to me?" He was so close, I could see beads of perspiration on his brow.

"I suppose I did," I said, continuin' to spin.

"Well, you better watch yourself, or I'll put you on notice!" he shouted.

"Is that what you did to Mary... put her on notice?" I asked, ignorin' Norah's pleadin' eyes.

He mumbled and stormed off. I paused and gathered my wits about me. All I needed was to be blacklisted, and I would have to move away to Lowell, or just change my name and get another job in Fall River.

"I'm shocked at how sassy you were," Norah said.

"There's no such thing as ignorin' him. How dare he fornicate with the girls here, only to let them suffer and bear his children, without takin' responsibility. Mary swears that he loves her while he is already off with another girl. I think she's only thirteen, and to make matters worse, he has a wife and children at home."

"Who is the girl? How do you know?" Norah asked.

"I went to the cardin' room and saw him with the little blonde girl. I think her name is Sophie. She comes in with her mother and is usually by her side. They live next door."

"Sophie? Oh no!" She wiped her brow with her hankie. "Did he see you?"

"Of course he saw me. He doesn't care. He likes that there's nothin' we can do about it," I said. "Besides, he gets pleasure from us seein' him simply because he is morally corrupt."

"Does her mother know?" she asked.

"What do you think? They work beside each other. How could she not know?"

"I would kill him if he did that to my daughter."

"And, you would be without a job...out on the streets starvin'," I said.

The sweeper came over and quickly brushed up by our feet. I was both stirred and exhausted from worryin' about Mary, Sophie, Sophie's mother, and all of us in general. My hatred for Mr. Aldrich was beginnin' to take a toll on me.

The spindles whirred, and the lint floated around us in a threatenin', unearthly manner. I squeezed my eyes shut, only for a moment. "Heavenly Father, Protect us—sisters, mothers, and daughters—from Mr. Aldrich. Why do You let him harm the innocent? What kind of a God are You? Please, shine Your light. I cannot see my way out. Without guidance, I shall turn away. Have mercy on us, Amen."

"Sarah!" Addy grabbed my arm.

My ears were ringin'. Sweat poured down my back, soakin' my dress. My feet were swollen, and I felt faint. So, this is what happened when one threatened God.

"You're pale. You don't look well. Clemmie, fetch some water!" Addy shouted.

I sipped the water, and the room came back into focus.

"What happened?" Addy asked.

"I'm a bit weary. I'll be fine," I said.

It was nearly time for the day to end. I returned to my station.

Mr. Aldrich stayed away from our part of the spinnin' room for the remainder of the day. It seemed as if the afternoon bell would never ring, but it finally did, and because it was Saturday, it rang early. I was grateful that it was not a rehearsal day, and I could tend to Mary.

Norah and I wasted no time dashin' out ahead of the others. When we turned the corner, we were met by Mrs. Brennan.

"Come quickly. It's Mary," she said, scurryin' down the hallway.

Passin' by the wailin' babies and tongue waggin' mothers, we followed her up the stairs and into the room that Mary shared with seven other girls.

A pale stream of light made its way through the only clean spot in the window, into the dark corner of the room, where she lay on her bed. She had sunk deeply, almost disappearin' into a stack of blankets. Her face was pale and bloodless, her lips blue, and her damp, scraggly hair was pressed flat against her forehead.

At first, no one spoke. It was as if the air rushed out of the room, leavin' me disordered and queasy, but it was no time to faint. I stared at her chest and couldn't tell if it rose and fell.

"Is she dead?" Norah asked.

"Stop," I said. Usin' the word dead when referrin' to Mary was not permitted.

By that time, the doorway and out into the hallway was crowded with girls, peerin' over each other, tryin' to get a good look.

"We need to call a doctor," Mrs. Brennan said.

"No one can afford a doctor here," one of the girls said.

I knelt down beside the bed and put my ear to her mouth, tryin' to detect a breath. I could not. My heart thumped wildly in my chest.

"Mary," I said in a low-pitched, unrecognizable voice.

She remained perfectly still.

"Mary, it's me. It's Sarah," I said in that same voice. I reached down for her hand. It was cold—ice cold. Then, I caught sight of a stream of blood flowin' steadily towards my feet. I ripped the blanket away and gasped.

I shook her. "Mary! Mary! Wake up!" Her head fell forward.

Norah climbed onto the bed and embraced us both.

"This is not happenin'," I said.

Mrs. Brennan lifted Mary's skirt. "Oh, Dear Lord!"

Between Mary's legs was a small baby covered in a mixture of blood and a film of whitish oil, with the cord still attached.

I vomited into the half-filled chamber pot that Addy was holdin' onto.

"Somebody, go get a doctor, the one on Bedford Street," one of the girls said.

"She doesn't need a doctor. She and the baby need a hearse," Addy said.

"It's a girl. It's a baby girl," Mercy said, almost as if it were a joyous occasion.

"Be quiet, Mercy. You're not helpin'," Rebecca said, pullin' Mercy away from the bed.

"What are these?" Addy asked, holdin' up two empty bottles.

"I don't know. Read the labels." I said.

She handed them to me. "I don't read."

I held the smaller one under the light and read aloud, "Ingredients: Tansy Oil, Pennyroyal." The second bottle was smudged, but I could make out, "Rue, Ergot, Opium."

"Tansy Oil is what they use to start the bleedin'," one of the other girls said.

I covered Mary and her baby with a blanket and sat on the edge of the bed. "Someone get the doctor. It has to be reported, and they know what to do," I said, chokin' back tears.

I stared at her, expectin' her to move, or laugh, or say somethin' crude that in the past would have shocked me, but no longer did. It was because of her that

I was able to ride the train safely to Fall River. She taught me about courage and tolerance. She showed me how to laugh at myself and my limited, rigid ways. It was because of her that I questioned everything, even God. It was Mary who jolted me out of my sleep, to set me free.

One at a time, the others retired to the kitchen or left the house. I stayed with Mary, caressin' her forehead and allowin' my tears to spill from my eyes. Then, I lay down beside her until the doctor came.

With great reluctance, I got up and stood beside the bed while the doctor examined the bottles. He sniffed the smaller one. "This was likely the cause of death. Even a small amount would be lethal, and the entire bottle is gone. She didn't need both bottles to end her life."

Within moments, two other men arrived. They placed Mary and her daughter on a stretcher. I accompanied them out to the street and watched as they loaded Mary and her baby into the poorhouse hearse.

My tears stopped. I looked upon my friend one last time. "Yes, my dearest Mary, you and your daughter left without him. You did it. You went to a better place."

I sat at a table in the kitchen with a bowl of simple porridge before me, lookin' out at the settin' sun. Usually, I would have eaten what was before me, ravenous from a long day at work, but there was no hunger in me. I was dead inside. The unbroken stillness was shattered by those who seemed to possess no feelin's— the mothers who stirred the bubblin' pots with their unkempt children pullin' at their skirts.

All I could think of was that I missed Mother, Abigail, and the pine-clad hills of home. With sorrow so frequent in and around Fall River, I wondered why I believed Mercy and Rebecca in the first place. Had it not been for August and the music, I would have gotten on the next train to New Hampshire. The County Farm had to have been better.

"Here, this is for you," Norah said, handin' me an envelope.

I stared at the familiar handwritin' before openin' it.

Dearest Sister,

I write to tell you that my son, Samuel Josiah Hodgdon, was born on March 21. I will not lie. I had a dificult time of it. Had it not been for Nellie, the Indian woman, we mighte not have lived. I know that he was born of sin, but I must tell you that he is a blessin from God. He is beutiful & I love him so. Do not worry about me dear sister, for I remaine strong & acsept God's will. I work hard. There is no time for idle hands. Samuel is a good baby & with help from the others, I cary him with me at all times. I am lerning about plants from Nellie. I wish to help the ones here who fall sicke. Mother would be proud & glad to know that she is no witch. She cares for me as if she were my own mother. I hope that you are well & hapy & that you still play your beloved cornet. Until we meet agin.
Your Loving Sister,
Abigail Hodgdon

Chapter 67

Bess
April 12, 1873

It was a pretty day. The greening had begun, and everything around me was dripping and splashing. The grass and leaves sparkled with jeweled dew, capturing a vast array of colors and holding onto them for as long as possible.

Despite Mother's insistence that I avoid the sun, I simply could not. It was delightfully warm on my face, begging me to sit at the edge of the garden and be in it. I was prepared, for at night, she would sit on my bed and count the freckles across the bridge of my nose. I only had a few, so few that she could keep track.

I turned my attention to the garden and how it would soon be filled with heady blossoms. It was time to honor the passing of the torch, from winter to spring with summer waiting patiently.

It was down to the two of us, the last snow angel—refusing to give in, safe in the small patch of snow beneath the shadow of our house—and me. Gradually, the other two surrendered to a clear, deep puddle. Throughout the entire winter, I tended to them. With all of the snow piled up around us, it had become an unintended commitment. I didn't give it much thought. It just happened.

CHAPTER 68

Sarah
April 14, 1873

No matter how many times I heard it, the sound of the first bell rattled my bones. I hadn't done so before, but I stayed in the attic all night and didn't care. After the initial shock of rememberin' where I was, and the thoughts of Mary set in, I tried to move. The bitter cold caused everything in me to ache.

When I looked out the window, a wave of despair rolled up from my stomach and stuck in my throat. I crashed my way through the room. Of course, there was no chamber pot, and the window was jammed. I thought about breakin' it, but at the last second, it opened. I stuck my head out in time to vomit on the street below, where the first stragglers headed for the sinks and outhouses. I coughed and gagged unmercifully, and no one was bothered. I collapsed into my chair, cryin' as if there were no end to it. Then, I slowed down my breathin', like Mother always told us to do when we required strength to endure.

I was calm until I spotted somethin' under the other chair. At first, it looked like a spider, and I pushed it with my toe. It didn't move. I examined it closer, raced back to the window, and expelled the remainin' bile from my stomach.

Unable to hold back my tears, I went back and picked up the half-smoked cigar stump that Mary must have dropped and put it in my pocket.

Goin' to work was unthinkable. I imagined puttin' my hands around Mr. Aldrich's throat, watchin' him take his last breath. My violent urges terrified me. I wondered if I was capable of indulgin' in revenge. He was strong and would end up killin' me first. And, if I did survive and go to trial, a judge and jury would laugh. No one would care to hear a spinner's grievance. I would die by his hand or a noose around my neck. I got to my knees and pushed through my prayerless state.

Dear Lord,

You have become my soul's enemy, and faith is not possible. Mary was right, it's how you live, not when and where you go to church. Yes, I am needy. I confess my greatest sin —the lie—so that I may fulfill the desire for music that You instilled in me. But, my spirit is generous and does not reflect a cruel God that punishes the friendless, wayward, and less fortunate.

Although my humble soul was bowed in gratitude, and I surrendered, You have shown me no mercy.

Who are You to punish Mother, Mary, and Abigail—the most faithful of us all, clay in Your hands, willin' to drink from the bitterest cup?

I am lost and unworthy, but it is You who made me. I grieve, for those I once loved have suffered a cruel fate. I cannot find comfort when You slay me. Should You restore peace in my heart, it will be then and only then, that I will consider returnin' to faith unshaken, Amen.

I closed my eyes and retreated into my world. The essence of calm wrapped itself around me, holdin' me in the palm of its hand. I had never felt it so powerfully before. It wasn't good or bad. It was as if I were suspended out over the world with no intended direction. Havin' lost track of time, it was impossible to say how long I remained in that much-blessed state.

Then the calmness ended. In its absence, I knew that I must stay home. I wanted to hide and cry and scream, but Mary would never have stayed home. If she found me as I had found her, she would have done exactly what I decided to do. I rushed to do whatever it took to carry on.

"Where were you?" Clara cried.

"I was away. Never mind. Please, leave me—"

"—Sarah, stop. It's not just you. We were all there, and we too loved Mary," Addy said.

In my state of uncertainty, I was grateful, and I needed someone to stop me. I had never snapped at Clara before, so who knew what I might have done.

"Sorry," I said, reachin' over to take her small hand in mine.

We walked in silence, which was usual for us in the mornin'. I didn't bring my dinner pail. I had nothin' in the way of nourishment, but eatin' was not essential at that time. My recently trimmed hair was stickin' out and not covered with a hat. I was outside of myself and didn't care.

When we entered the yard, I told Clara to go on without me. There were many people huddled outside of Mr. Colby's office and in the lobby, where the jobs and rules were posted.

Like an earlier version of me, the new people—perplexed, fresh-faced, and naively optimistic—stood together, unknowingly leanin' on each other, readin' the posters. The others, who had already been in the mill system, stood quietly with slouched shoulders and dark circles beneath their eyes, wearin' their hunger like a badge.

Mr. Colby entered and met me with a scowl. I started to speak, and he continued to walk by with a group of potential spinners behind him. I waited. Both late and out of place, I deliberately broke the rules.

The ones who were to work in the spoolin' and weave rooms were the last to go, and it was finally just Mr. Colby and me.

"What is it that you want, Miss—"

"—Hodgdon. Sarah Hodgdon," I said.

"Why are you here and not at your station?" he asked, the loathin' evident in his tone and posture.

"I am here to request a transfer," I said, knowin' that I could no longer govern my tongue.

"Now? On a Monday morning?" He smirked and started to walk away.

"Stop!"

He stopped but kept his back to me.

"I know that I should have come to you after the workday, when everyone is so tired that all they can think about is goin' home. That is why so many of us keep on doin' what we do. We are just plain exhausted, and there is no time for stoppin'. We might stop for good if we do, so like the well-oiled machinery that we work with every day, we must keep goin'."

He turned to face me.

"I know that the men and women here mean nothin' to you, the overseers, or the owners, but we are human. We have wants and needs, we were all once innocent children, born into the wrong families, endin' up like this."

The sweat rolled down my back; my temples throbbed. Suddenly, I wished that I had my long locks, that I was dressed in one of my lovely dresses sewn by Mother, and that I looked beautiful so that he would consider what I had to say.

Although not as powerful as a man's, I did have a voice. I am aware that like the others, I was expected to remain silent, which is why bein' Jonas meant so much more than playin' a horn. But in truth, I was not a refined, elegant woman, and in the mill, unless you were an overseer or some such thing, a man did not have a voice either.

It was absolutely undeniable. I was no one. I stood before him with puffy red eyes, mussed up short hair, a ripped and ragged dress that was soiled from work and rain. In less than a year, I was a shell of my former self, without a trace of beauty, and to most, not worth hearin'. I carried on in spite of it.

"Did you know Mary Grace O'Connor?"

He shook his head, no.

"If you saw her, you would know who she was," I said.

"There are hundreds of people passing through here each day, how—"

"—it matters not what the numbers are. We are not any less human because there are many of us." I began to shake uncontrollably.

"What is your point, Miss Hodge?"

"Hodgdon. Please say it right. My point is that a young woman named Mary Grace worked here with me, in the spinnin' room. She was a good hard worker. One of the girls that Mr. Aldrich had his way with—"

"—We will not discuss such private matters." His face was about to burst.

"It is no longer private when she is pulled away from the loom for all to see," I said, "and taken out by the stairwell durin' workin' hours."

He looked up at the clock and crossed his arms.

"He is our boss? He is despicable. He said that if she didn't cooperate, he would make her life miserable. He promised to leave his wife and children, knowin' all along that it was a lie. She would have to take care of it on her own—Mary, a sixteen-year-old girl, alone, livin' in our slum of a tenement with others like her, to work and raise a child!" By then I was no longer thinkin'. The words spilled out of my mouth, purely unfiltered.

"Well, uh…"

"I am here to tell you that she took her own life… last Friday, after Mr. Aldrich told her that he had no intention of takin' care of her. When his lies came to an end, so did the lives of Mary and her unborn daughter!"

"Here she is," he said, pointin' to a crumpled list in his hand.

My eyes fell upon her name with the word "deceased" written beside it.

"So, you knew not to look for her. I suppose it is your job to distribute the list?"

"I was about to do that when I had to stop and talk to you," he said.

"Well, I am sorry to inconvenience you."

"It's not an inconven—"

"—never mind. I am not apologizin'."

"I am askin' to be transferred to the attic. I want to be a drawin'-in girl."

His eyes opened wide as he fumbled with his papers.

"It's either that or I leave for one of the other mills and will do so with a good report," I said.

"This is not customary," he said.

"Mary was not customary. I cannot face Mr. Aldrich without the thought of violence, which is not of my nature. Surely, you can understand the bind I'm in. I want to continue workin'. I'm an excellent worker. Most of my roommates work here as well. If I return to the spinnin' room, I may act on my feelin's, which are based on Mr. Aldrich's sinful and predatory behavior."

"There are others who have been waiting," he said.

"I don't care. I'm not fragile and come from a long line of fiery women who do as they say," I said.

He remained quiet. The deafenin' mill sounds pounded into my chest.

"Very well then, you leave me no choice," I said, and headed for the door.

"Miss Hodge, wait!"

I stopped. My heartbeat clashed against rhythm of the machinery. A source of unusual strength swelled inside of me. I finally turned to look at him.

"It's Hodgdon," I said.

"Miss Hodgdon, I cannot honor your wishes. I'll spare you the punishment of being late today and dismiss your violent threats. You will not speak of this to anyone. His wife is a relative of the owners of this corporation. Your accusations would be troublesome for all involved. If you cause a scene, you will be discharged and blacklisted. If you return to work without further unruliness, you will have an opportunity to be a drawing-in girl. I'll put your name on the list. You must wait your turn."

"I cannot guarantee what will happen next," I said.

I was usually obedient, but somethin' inside of me had changed. I would never again ignore my instincts. I would only follow them.

With all eyes upon me, I walked to my station. Mr. Aldrich wasted no time headin' towards me when Mr. Colby cut him off. They spoke for some time, before goin' in different directions.

I had no memory of carryin' out my duties. My motions were automatic, and I was powered by an unknown source. When others attempted to speak, I looked beyond them.

At last ring out, I dawdled, waitin' for a handful of sweepers and doffers to leave. Mr. Aldrich was finally alone, tendin' to a spinnin' frame. I stood behind him and waited.

He turned and dropped his wrench. "Bloody hell! What are you doin' here?"

"I will only say this once and never speak to you again. May you burn in Hell for killin' Mary Grace. I will decide whether or not to tell your wife of your lecherous behavior—havin' your way with the young girls, impregnatin' them, and then shruggin' it off as if their lives are insignificant. If I see you carryin' on like you have been, you will regret it."

He grabbed my arm with great force and pulled me close to his face. "Don't you dare threaten me. I will destroy you." He laughed hard, barin' his yellow teeth. "Besides, you're all tramps. No one will believe you."

"Oh, everyone will believe me. I do have friends in high places but have chosen to work here on my own. I could leave at any time," I said, tryin' to extricate myself from his grip.

He raised his hand as if he might strike me. "Watch yourself." He released me with a push.

I stumbled back but caught myself just before crashin' into a frame. I collected my wits about me and watched him leave the room.

"Do you need a hand, ma'am?" One of the sweepers, wearin' a red cap and a genuine look of concern on his youthful face, approached me.

"I'll be fine. Thank you for askin'—"

"—Patrick," he said.

"Patrick, I'm fine. Shouldn't you be goin' home? It's after ring out," I said.

"I'm leavin' now. I had to finish up."

Without the need to share a word, Patrick and I left together. He walked with me until I got to the tenement, and he kept on goin'. I didn't know where he lived and didn't ask.

I went straight to the attic and reached into my pocket for the cigar stump. I smiled when I finally struck the match. I drew in the smoke and coughed hard. It was a foul tastin' thing. I couldn't understand why anyone smoked. But, I smoked Mary's cigar, until it was too hot to hold in my fingers.

Chapter 69

Sarah
May 9, 1873

Usually done in by the end of the week, the girls were excited that P.T. Barnum's circus was in town, and at the risk of penalty, took early leave. Ever since our episode, Mr. Aldrich and I exchanged long cold stares, each determined to outlast the other. I always won. Without question, there was a part of him that feared me. He knew that I could slay him with my tongue and possibly crush his reputation. He went pale the day that his wife came to the mill. He couldn't shoo her away fast enough. She was a frail, little thing, a wisp of a woman whose silhouette all but vanished in the side view

He was a coward, but not just any coward. He wielded power that he could not handle. It was too much for him, and his fear streaked madly across the lines on his forehead. I was aware that our silent battle would not last, and I was the one at risk. He had an unrestrained evilness about him. I needed to get out.

Deep, murky puddles did not deter the girls. I chased after them, thinkin' of how easy it would have been to swear. There was so much about Mary that I didn't appreciate, until after she abandoned this world.

I managed to hold my tongue. The last thing I wanted to do was slosh through the rain and muck to stand in long lines to see a circus. When I moved to Fall River, I did not think to bring my over-shoes. Until witnessin' the sight of people wallowin' in the mush that surrounded the circus tent, I hadn't thought of them.

"Come on... run!" Clara shouted.

Run? Not only did I refuse to run, but I also stopped right in the middle of the most significant crowds I had ever seen.

Stoppin' may or may not have been an error on my part, as she was swept away by the rapid flow of people, and I was bumped from all sides. Rather than resist, I slipped back into the current, hopin' to reunite with at least one of the girls. If I did not see them, it would have been a valid excuse to go home.

I finally had a reason to smile. Up ahead, I spotted a red hat, and sure enough, it was Patrick with another sweeper. He was often the reason that I was able to endure. His true innocence stirred up my pure mind, savin' me from the dangers of a cold heart, filled with nothin' but hatred for the man who killed Mary.

The depth of my grief for her was unexpected, oddly more unbearable than it had been for my mother. I supposed it was because I was with Mary under different circumstances. I saw death upon her face and felt the warm blood of both her and her daughter. I was able to escape all reminders of Mother, but Mary stayed with me.

Each night, when I closed my eyes, I saw her face and that of her tiny, perfectly formed baby girl. When I found an old soiled prayer book in the kitchen drawer, I decided that she needed a name. I called her Grace. *Hail Mary, full of grace, the Lord is with thee; blessed art thou amongst women and blessed is the fruit of thy womb, Jesus. Holy Mary, Mother of God, pray for us sinners, now and at the hour of death, Amen.*

I stood on my tiptoes and looked for the girls. With thousands of people tramplin' through the mud, pushin' their way towards the entrance of the tent, it was hopeless. I lacked both the strength and ambition to continue and thought it best to go home.

"Sarah!"

I turned to see August, pullin' Finn along with him. They wove their way through the herd, comin' in my direction.

I patted Finn on top of his rain-soaked cap. "Hello."

He smiled up at me.

"So many people here, eh?" August asked.

"Too many for me," I said. "I was thinkin' of goin' home. I'm not much for crowds."

He laughed. If one disliked crowds, the last place to be was at a circus in a city that craved distraction from the hardships of everyday life.

"I know. Why are you here, you ask?"

"No, well… yes, sort of," he said.

"I let the girls persuade me, and now we're separated."

"Let us accompany you." He held out his arm.

With my dress soaked through to the skin and rain streamin' off my straw bonnet, I stood before him. It was too late to brood over my drizzly appearance. I smiled and gladly took his arm. When I was with August, I had a happier heart.

I had never been to the circus. A few years before, when the circus came to both Wolfeboro and Conway, Mother did not want to spend money on such things. *We have fairs in Ossipee, not circuses,* she said.

After some time, we finally made it to the entrance of the enormous tent. He reached into his pocket, pulled out a tin and counted enough money for all three of us.

"That is so kind of you, but I will pay for my ticket," I said.

"I would never want you to do that. The pleasure is mine."

As soon as we stepped inside, I feared that my heart would faint within me, as there was a cornet band playin' at an alarmin' tempo. Not only that, they weren't makin' mistakes. They were exquisite. I had heard that circus bands were amongst the best, but in my imagination, it was about clowns, odd people with unusual features, a feast of peculiarities.

As we walked along, we saw cage upon cage of animals—tigers, lions, ostriches, and a massive rhinoceros. Then, there were the majestic elephants, camels of all sizes, and clown-like dogs. Situated on the far side of the tent were more ferocious animals such as a puma, black leopard, and Russian bears. I was very much amused by the monkeys. Of course, there were the superhuman feats by the man with the iron jaw and his female partner—the female Sampson—and a vast collection of curiosities, both artificial and human.

Addin' to the intrigue, was a band with an automaton trumpeter, bell ringers, drummer, and organ grinder. The show was unlike anything that I envisioned.

I was not disappointed when August mentioned that he had to leave early to light the lamps. In fact, I was relieved. The eye can only take in so many new sights at once.

With our clothes still damp, we left the Hippodrome and went back out into the rain. Determined to get in, people continued to stand in the long lines that spilled out into the streets.

When August took my hand in his, I trembled. I didn't understand. I held hands with Clara every day. I couldn't go anywhere without her catchin' up to me and grabbin' my hand. As much as I told myself that I wanted nothin' more than friendship, it was a lie. I had secret thoughts of surrenderin' my whole heart.

We stopped in front of the tenement. When he looked deeply into my eyes, I wanted to look away, but could not. He touched my cheek.

"You really are a beautiful girl," he said.

"Oh, please… I look dreadful. You're much too kind," I said, lookin' at the attic window, thinkin' of how safe it was there.

"No, you should accept a compliment. You're a beautiful woman. At least to me, you are."

I took a quick breath. The truth was right there. I looked dreadful. If he considered me to be beautiful in such poor condition, he would have been beside himself to see me in my best dress, with fixed curls, and clear, clean skin. I could not bear for him to look at me any longer. I had lost weight, and like the others, I had become haggard and sickly. He did not know that my hair was gone, as I hid beneath a scraggly bonnet. I could not go on. I had one Sunday dress that was beginnin' to fade, just as Addy warned me that it would. I was savin' money to return home, to get Abigail and find somethin' else for her, for us. My spirits shattered at the thought of Abigail's son. I could not spend money on a new dress or bonnet to look good for a man.

"I have to go," I said, and stepped back. "Thank you for takin' me to the circus. I'll always remember it."

"So will I."

I left him standin' on the street with his little brother, who was completely unaware, and I felt his eyes on me as I dashed past the outhouses. I raced up to the attic, careful to stay away from the window.

I fished around in my pocket for a half cigarette that I had found in Mary's things. There was at least a dozen more stashed in her tobacco tin.

Daria, a girl from Mary's room, gave me yet another tin, somewhat smaller and not so rusted. I took it out of my other pocket and stared at the crude note wrapped around it with butcher's twine. She said that Mary asked her to write it about a week before her death.

I settled back into the chair and lit the cigarette, bringin' her essence into the room. I closed my eyes and thought about how we bickered and how much I missed it. We were different in many ways, but we cared for each other. There was no pretendin' with Mary.

I opened the tin. Inside was a small, fuzzy angel made from lint. I unfolded the note. *"Sarah —It snows 'most every day in Fall River. There's always enough snow for an angel here. Them angels are all around us. Don't forget. Yours truly, Mary."*

Chapter 70

Bess
May 9, 1873

I PRAYED FOR relief, and I got it. For most of the day, the rolling clouds hoarded the rain. It wasn't until Mother started a storm of her own that the heavens were willing to release a torrent of tears. And then it rained hard, but not hard enough to drown out her shrill voice. She went on all morning about the way I treated Jonathan Mitchell. By my standards, I was not ill-mannered, nothing more than indifferent. She did not hide her motives and insisted on attending so many gala events, I was becoming exhausted.

"He's a nice young man, from a prominent family," she said. "You must remember that rudeness will repel, and courtesy will attract. You are only polite some of the time. You should exhibit true kindness from the heart at all times, or you will end up a spinster."

"You don't understand. I'm not one for small talk. It lacks substance," I said.

"When he spoke to you, you didn't pay attention. You just sat and gazed around the room as if he wasn't there," she said. "I was horrified."

"I did not gaze around the room. I don't know what you're talking about."

"How do you expect to receive a proposal from a desirable young man in our circle, if you only offer a sour look and cold manners?"

"Mother, I'm not going to throw myself at the feet of every eligible man in Fall River. You must accept that I'm in no hurry to marry. I wish to play the piano. There's plenty of time for marriage and children."

"You can still play the piano and be a wife. Marriage does not mean that your interests die."

I could not talk to someone so intoxicated by her own ideas that she did not make sense. There was no room in my world for her vanity. If she wanted to live a thin, hollow life, that was her choice, but I chose something else.

"You know," she said, "all eyes are upon you—an up and coming woman in Fall River."

"I don't care," I said. "And, there are many up and coming women in Fall River."

"You should care, and it matters what people think. It's much more important than what you, yourself, think," she said.

"Why are you not proud of me for being sensible and using good judgment? Are you so miserable that you want me to be blinded by the first man who pays the least bit of attention to me? Do you wish for me to be as unhappy as you?"

"How dare you speak to me that way. I see how you look at Mr. Carver," she said.

"So, that's what this is about?"

"He's beneath us—a servant. We pay him to teach you."

I jumped to my feet. "It was you who invited him for dinner and started to call him by his first name. What is it that you want? Mr. Carver and I share a mutual love of music. He is of high moral character and doesn't exhibit affection. We respect each other—he as the teacher and me as his student. He did not offer a marriage proposal. There's more to think about than whether or not someone meets your requirements for being my future husband. It is your constant interference that causes so much unhappiness."

Of course, she left the room, slamming the door and sobbing all the way down the hallway. It was not new. The servants were aware of us. Father was not home, and when he was, she acted differently—less injured and more perplexed.

An hour passed before she returned. It was usually longer than an hour, but the circus was in town. She rapped lightly on the door.

"Do you want to go to the circus?"

"It's pouring rain. There will be scores of mill people and nothing but mayhem. I'd rather not be a part of that."

"But, we have a driver and umbrellas."

"Do you want to see the spectacle so badly that you would brave such elements?"

"Very well." Again, she slammed the door.

I detested being out in the rain and could not stand the thought of being amongst mobs of people. I had been this way all of my life, but Mother insisted on parading us around as if she wanted the commoners to see how well off we were. She could look down on them and attempt to feel good about her elevated station in life.

Besides, I wanted to practice the new music that Mr. Carver gave me. He told me that I was his best student. I did not want to disappoint.

Chapter 71

Annie Quinn Hodgdon
June 10, 1847
Cork Harbour, Ireland

I WANTED TO hold tight to her hand, but I thought that it might break. I remembered when her cheeks colored up, and her eyes sparkled. She was soft and round, as a mother should be. Even when I was eight years old, I climbed up onto her lap to draw in her scent and take shelter in her fullness as she sang to my brother and me.

To my sorrow, it had been months since she rose up to sing. There were few songs to be had, although Daidí still played his fiddle, but never again like before. Nothin' was the same. Together, we had shifted into a minor key. We sang and danced to remember who we were, clingin' to a faint ray of hope when the cries of anguish were unimaginable. The howlin' that came after dark continued to echo in my ears on many a long night.

We spent the previous winter huddled together with three other families in what was once a lovely rural cottage, much further away from the shore than what we were accustomed to. Daidí was a fisherman and did us fine until the trouble came.

We were not rich, but we were content, imperfect, and lovingly frayed around the edges. Like the other fishermen, Daidí fished along the shores in his currach, where it was safe, for the deep waters were much too perilous for small cowhide boats. The fish that he caught were bartered daily for our needs and were enough to pay the rent, and in spite of it and like the others, potatoes were our primary source of nutrition.

Had he not sold his tackle and nets to settle with the landlord and obtain food, we might have found a way to stay in our own cottage a bit longer, for he could have continued to fish. It had become a devastatin' riddle, choosin' between rent or food, because of the risin' cost of both, Daidí could afford neither.

There was nowhere to turn. Knowin' that ships filled with home-grown oats, barley, and Indian corn were berthed in Cork Harbour, and off limits to us all, caused our hunger to deepen and tempers to flare. If we were not careful, the last of our strength would have been consumed by our fury, further strippin' the meat from our bones and stealin' the will to survive. We had quickly become like the ones that we saw at crowded soup kitchens or standin' in lines to enter the workhouse, in the fields—animal-like and feral.

Daidí even risked his life by joinin' an uprisin', which did not help. Some were wounded, and others died, makin' us a little more afraid. The ships stayed in port, not intended for the ravenous folk with empty bellies and rattlin' bones—until the cost of the food was finally lowered, but we hadn't a shillin' to our names. Therefore, the fully loaded ships set sail for England, or the provisions sat in warehouses within our sight, resultin' in death from abandoned hearts and famished souls over hunger and disease.

Mam urged Daidí to stay away from the fights, to find work layin' down black rock for the roads that led to nowhere, but Daidí couldn't hear a word that she said. It wasn't that he was unwillin'. No, the art of genuine hearin' had been lost. He might have tried. At another time, he would have heard her, but his ears no longer took in words like they used to.

He said that if they could only confiscate one ship—one boatload of oats—that we would survive another few months. Livin' on nettles was not enough. His main bent was to save his family and, of course, himself. He tried to make the bitter choice between life and death, for there was not enough food for both. If he starved, he was too weak to work. If he ate, we starved.

People talked about how the ones workin' on the roads just died right there along the way, only to end up in a shallow grave, not quite deep enough to keep away the rats and dogs. Who had the strength to dig a proper grave beneath the green sod without layin' down in it as well?

Daidí was a fighter. He would not succumb. He would raise a fist and join any uprisin' that he could, even if it meant throwin' rocks, yellin' into the wind, and maybe even bein' shot, wounded, or worse. He would die tryin'. That was Daidí.

After months of seein' people dyin' of road fever, layin' in the fields, and sittin' on the edges of the fences in front of their hollow gardens, before bein' driven out of their cottages, Daidí thought it best to accept kindness from Father Tierney. We stayed at the lice-infested dwellin' of the O'Sullivan's.

Winter came and went. God had turned away from us, as the winter before our departure was the worst one that anyone could ever recall. Relentless blizzards buried us so deeply in the snow, it blocked the windows and reached the roofs. The icy winds from the Southwest howled at night, bringin' frigid gales of sleet and hail that froze onto the surface of the snow, makin' it so hard that it was impossible to leave a house that had become more like a prison with each passin' day.

I had reached a point where bein' unfed, cold, or with fever, was not my greatest concern. We lived with it, unless of course, we died, and then it didn't matter. However, I could not bear to see another mother carryin' her dead infant in the street, beggin' for money for a coffin.

We stood together in the long line that led to the medical inspection required before boardin' the ship to Liverpool. My feet became heavier with each step. By the time I left my last footprint upon the soil of my native homeland, I was barely able to walk. I stopped and closed my eyes as the fresh northerly breeze cooled my cheeks. I turned once more to look at the majestic shoreline and clear blue skies that hardly resembled the blackness that threatened to consume all that remained.

Yes, Mam had become fragile, but I trusted that she would not break. I finally took a chance and squeezed her hand.

Chapter 72

Sarah
June 13, 1874

It took over a year for me to reach the point where I no longer felt the need to run all the way home from band rehearsals. I was comfortable bein' Jonas, at least more so than at first. I accepted that folks passed me on the street as if they were passin' a man, and I was in no danger of bein' accosted.

My fellow bandsmen knew me as a peculiar young man, somewhat distant and of few words. It was very awkward when I was at a concert, and the sister of one of the tenor horn players expressed an interest in me. I was able to dissuade her with my unwelcomin' behavior.

How funny it was that as a man, when I could have spoken up, I refrained, yet as a woman, I often spoke my mind, landin' me in more trouble than I could manage.

It was a miracle that the girls at home didn't pester me. They believed that I was stealin' away with August, and some even frowned upon it, especially Norah. She thought that I had lost my virtue, and I let her think so.

No one bothered goin' up to the attic. Mary was the only one who was curious, bein' the smart one and all, but the others were too busy frettin' over things that didn't matter or were just tryin' to keep up with the frantic pace of our dismal lives.

It had been nearly nine months since I was advanced to the position of a drawin'-in girl. I liked it much better. It was still quite demandin', but the pay was slightly better. I did not have to set eyes on Mr. Aldrich, unless our paths crossed on the stairwell, or if he came to our floor for any reason. Addy told me that he had taken up with Bridget, but she refused to speak about it, and I knew that it would not do me or anyone else any good to confront him.

The worst that had happened, other than losin' Mary, was that I started smokin' cigars. It was a terrible habit, and I thought that I would switch to Egyptian cigarettes, like some of the others, but the cigar was Mary's choice.

I spent more time in the attic than I used to. I practiced there and found that sleepin' in a bed that I fashioned out of some old blankets and a bedtick was better than havin' Mercy crowdin' me every night. I also loved to look out over the city while I had a smoke.

The unravelin' began.

CHAPTER 73

Bess
June 13, 1874

THERE WERE TWO performances, one in the afternoon and one in the evening. I thought of the one in the afternoon as nothing more than a warm-up. The tickets were less expensive, and the commoners were encouraged to attend. The local elite showed up in the evening when playing your best mattered most. I loved the pressure and excitement of a polished performance.

As always, I was well prepared, and the afternoon performance was effortless. I sipped my lemonade backstage while the string trio performed.

"That went well," Mr. Carver said.

"I think so too," I said in a moment that meant everything. I realized that I had been starving all along and that I never knew love. Before me was a feast. I only imagined that my heart was beating, when it was merely tapping its way through tangled barriers, trying to crack itself open.

He sat across from me, took the lemonade glass from my hand, and stared directly into my eyes.

"What is it?" I asked.

"I just wanted to tell you how proud I am. You learned the Brahms in such a short period of time."

"I did."

We had run out of ways to hide the truth. Mother threatened to fire him and find a new teacher if I did not stop carrying on so. As far as I knew, I did nothing improper. I simply practiced diligently and kept to myself. She tried tirelessly to find a suitor for me, but I did not act in a manner that pleased her. She complained about me becoming an old spinster and that she would not approve of romance, or even worse, marriage to a lowly piano teacher.

If it weren't for Tempy, I would have been hopelessly lost. She taught me about patience, but even that started to wear thin. Therefore, I learned to take small steps in my daily life and leave the rest to chance.

"Bess?" he asked.

"What? What is it?" I could not lift my eyes to meet his.

"I love you."

His words came precisely when the trio played the final note. The audience gave a standing ovation. With Mother and Father at the market, for that small passage in time, we were alone.

I couldn't speak. The applause thundered around us as we sat together in a darkened corner backstage. When he kissed me, I couldn't quite breathe, and I felt as if I were someone else. I had been kissed once before when I was only fourteen. Every part of me was awakened as we kissed, making up for the many months that we longed to touch.

"Mr. Carver?" I looked straight into his eyes when I spoke. The applause died down. "I love you, too."

We kissed again. Beethoven, Bach, Mozart—none of those boys would ever be the same.

Chapter 74

August
June 13, 1874

It was a dark night, and we finished work early. Before goin' home, I stopped by the house on the hill, in case that young woman was playin' her piano, but it was quiet. Between her and the man who played the cornet in Sarah's attic, I was fortunate.

Since Francis Murphy started havin' heart trouble, my route was expanded, and I was in line for a supervisor's position. For the first time in my life, I would matter, which was an accomplishment in itself. I dreamed of it, but never thought I'd see it.

With the money that I saved, we were able to move into a tenement. There were still too many people, but it was always better than Five Points. Even though I hated it there, and almost died more than once, it gave me the chance to appreciate everything else.

Besides, we had no choice but to move. The cellar had gotten too crowded, and the landlord finally came around and collected rent. Stayin' there was cheap, but when one of the children came down with smallpox, we couldn't leave fast enough. There was talk about the parents not reportin' it to the authorities and how they could even be prosecuted. I was just thankful that we didn't get sick.

I was still close enough to Sarah's tenement to keep an eye on her. She stopped goin' to church, so I was able to see her earlier on Sundays. The man that frequented her tenement continued to come around. At first, I thought that he was Sarah's friend, and then Mary's, but after Mary's death, he still showed up.

I couldn't stand it. When I saw him that night, I decided to at least find out his name and tell him that I was an admirer. He sensed that I was behind him, and though he didn't run, he picked up his pace, windin' his way through the deep passageways, away from the street lamps.

I caught up to him and grabbed his arm.

"Don't be afraid," I said, feelin' a strange sensation in my stomach. He was skinnier than I expected.

He stared at me and attempted to back away. I tightened my grip, realizin' that it wasn't a he at all. I could never mistake those eyes. "Sarah?"

Again, she tried to pull away, but I grabbed both of her shoulders. "What are you doin?"

"I can't talk right now." She looked away.

I led her to a nearby bench.

"What's goin' on?"

"Damn," she said. "I can't…"

"Take a deep breath," I almost wanted to laugh, but she was beside herself.

"I don't know where to begin."

"Well, try."

She held up a small leather case. "It's a cornet. I'm a musician."

"A cornet? Of course."

"Yes, I'm in the Fall River Cornet Band. I've been playin' the cornet since I was a little girl. I auditioned last year and made it. The only way that I can do it is as a man."

I pulled her into my arms. "I've been listenin' to you all this time? I thought it was someone else. I suspected that he was your secret boyfriend, and then I s'posed that he was there to see Mary. I've been watchin' and listenin' to him—to you—for a long time." I couldn't contain my laughter.

"You have?" she asked. "It's not funny. I tried so hard to hide from you, from everyone. I even play with a rag in my bell."

"You did manage to hide. But, I was curious and so impressed. You're very good, and I can hear you, not well, but I can."

"I don't know what to say. Mary was the only one who knew, and she swore to secrecy. When she first found out, it bothered me, but for some reason, it was a relief. The business of keepin' a secret can weigh on you." She fidgeted with her case.

"And, the others?"

She smiled."Well, they think that I'm carryin' on with you," she said. "With the babies and children bein' quite noisy at suppertime, no one seems to notice. You can never tell a soul. Can I trust you?" She looked at me with her clear blue eyes and black smudged face.

"Of course. Of course, you can trust me." I knew that I cared for her before, but right then, I realized that I had fallen in love.

CHAPTER 75

Annie
June 13, 1847
Somewhere out on the Atlantic Ocean

DAIDÍ MANAGED TO save the ship fare settlement that was given to him by the landlord upon our eviction in November. Because of this, in Liverpool, we could board a ship that was headed straight to Canada, and not have to stay. So many others had to find a way to earn their passage, never makin' it to North America.

When we settled with the barrister, and he accepted the fare for the family, we were told that we would be greeted by an agent in Canada, who would have food, money, and resources for our resettlement. He promised to pay between two and five pounds, enough, as Daidí said, for a good start.

We held onto each other, followin' Daidí in the long line until we were aboard the brig. There was much confusion, somethin' between relief and fear, as we waited to hear what was to follow. Sailors rushed about with perspiration tricklin' down their soot-covered faces. Some men were given bricks for the fireplaces on deck for cookin' food. Because we had no food to bring, we were promised an allotment of a pound a day, which had to be enough to see us through.

When we went below, we passed by a lower deck, where surrounded by their rags and food rations, people huddled together on the floor. I tried to take deep breaths—a trick that Mam taught us when we were overwhelmed—but the smell of vomit hung in the air.

I shielded my face with my skirt as we made our way to an area that would be our home for as long as it took to get to Canada. Daidí said that it would take three weeks, no more and no less. Mam corrected him, tellin' us that it was dependent on the weather.

Although we had but a few items, we carried them over to the bare wooden bunks that would serve as our beds. A very old woman lay nearby, moanin' and callin' for her mother. I tried to look away. At least when we were in the open air, there was some distance between us and the others.

"Mam, I can't place my sack here. It's covered in filth," I said, forcin' my eyes away from the woman.

"Annie, this is only for a short time," she said. Her expression was stern, while her eyes were wet with tears.

I set down my sack and watched as the others, beyond hunger, almost naked, clad only in their protrudin' bones, claimed their bunks with the same reluctance as me. Already weak and ill, some lacked the energy to protest and just fell onto the hard frames. Another sobbed woefully for a dead child left behind—cries familiar to our ears and forever pressed into our hearts.

"Come now. Let's go back up," Daidí said, tryin' to keep us from givin' up before we even left port.

With his fiddle under his arm, and a sack containin' our daily rations to bring to the foredeck, we would cook and maybe sing a song or two. Because it had taken so long to get to the ship, it was possible for music to lift us up.

We went topside, where I gulped the fresh air as if I had been drownin' and finally reached the surface. There were many folks gathered around their little fires, and whether in merriment or quarrel, makin' too much noise. They cooked whatever they could in pots and pans of various sizes. Thick smoke billowed from the small fireplaces, mergin' with the scent of fish and bacon from the folks that had the means, and the burnt cakes, biscuits, and stirabout from the others.

We found a fireplace that was not bein' used and still had some hot coals. It was made from a large wooden case lined with bricks. Mam had brought one pot for us to use, and she made a large griddle cake that was blackened around the edges and uncooked in the middle.

"Eat this. We'll do better tomorrow," she said.

We sat together, tryin' to ignore a fight that broke out close by.

"Let us eat in thankfulness," Daidí said.

We ate and watched the sailors, some rushin' about tendin' to the heavy sacks while others sat tarrin' rope and mendin' sails.

We went to the afterdeck and looked out over the ocean. Daidí had never been out that far in his currach, so with whatever strength he had, delighted in the open sea. The two ships that sailed near us all day were far away, almost too far to see.

The favorable breeze carried us along, refreshed my spirits, and brought color to Mam's cheeks. My brother, Seamus, smiled for the first time in many months. We were on our way to Canada. There was hope for us.

Some of the older boys played games, and a few of the younger children laughed in merriment. Showin' his best face, a man played his concertina. Amidst their weakness, and in spite of the swells, his wife and children rose up to dance.

There were also those who could not hold back from vomitin' over the side of the ship, for as Daidí said, they had yet to get their sea legs. The swells did not bother me, but the seas were smooth that first night.

It wasn't clear to me whether we stayed up too late because we were optimistic to have set sail, or that we avoided goin' below deck, where it smelled of death, and the people groaned and cried out in despair.

Mam, Seamus, and I sat together and watched the night sky while Daidí paced the deck. I had never seen as many stars as I did on that first clear night. Other than the candles in the window of the mistress's cabin, it was quite dark on the ship.

We finally retreated down below, to the splintered bunks that Mam had covered with our clothes. It was warm, but because of the dampness, I shared a blanket with Seamus.

The first night was one without sleep, for all I could hear were mournful cries. A mother and daughter on the bunk across from us were up all night with the fever. It was as if we were still at home. Bein' out to sea was no different.

The mother cried when she tried to get water from a cask that had leaked. Although Daidí scolded her, Mam offered them a drink from one of the cans of water that we brought with us from Liverpool, only to find it spoiled and murky. Against Mam's warnin', they drank it, makin' them sicker. Mam was beside herself, askin' the Lord for forgiveness for makin' things considerably worse. I thought that mornin' would never arrive.

Together we stood in the open air. Until the sun rose high in the sky, it was cold and cheerless, but it was better than the foulness of the stiflin' decks below. We had our first breakfast—flour porridge—and we heated our other can of water on the stove. Daidí said that if we heated it, it would be safe to drink. He intended it to be for Mam, but she quickly took it down below to the mother and daughter.

The mistress herself looked quite pale, for each time she appeared on the deck, groups of sickly creatures crowded around her. The few water casks on board were leakin', and we had just started our journey.

Very few passengers boarded the ship in good health. We all looked forward to arrivin' in Canada, where we would collect our money and allotments from the agent and be on our way. Daidí knew all along that he didn't entirely trust the Canadians and said that we must leave as soon as possible. Canada was simply a place to stop on our way to America—the land of the free and home of the brave—like the song that the sailors used to sing after dippin' into the rum.

CHAPTER 76

Sarah
July 18, 1874

OF COURSE, I could not share it with the girls, but until my secret was revealed, I could not comprehend the toll that it had taken on me. Instead of runnin' frantically to and from band, August accompanied me, and we shared a pleasant walk. It was about our fondness for one another and had nothin' to do with protection.

I pushed him away when he reached for my hand. "You cannot show affection towards me. My bandmates already think of me as odd. I would have to quit if they thought that I liked boys."

He laughed. "I don't see why you can't just be you."

"Men only—it's a tradition. This band was together durin' the war. Most cornet bands are made up of men, but there are some that do allow women, but none that I'm aware of here."

"Why don't you start your own band? Then you wouldn't have to sneak around. The world is bein' robbed when they can't see you on stage, playin' your horn as your pretty self."

"I wouldn't know where to begin," I said.

"Hang a few posters to find out if any of the girls in the mills are interested."

"But then they would have to have horns, and the time to practice," I said. "And, I wouldn't know where we could practice or who would be our bandmaster."

"You should at least try," he said.

"You're a dreamer."

"You should be one too.

Chapter 77

Bess
July 18, 1874

"We must tell her."

"She won't give us her blessing. I'll be cut off from my family forever."

"You always talk about your mother. What about your father? What about him?"

"He doesn't care, as long as it doesn't interfere with business affairs. Although he might prefer merging his empire with another family of wealth. I don't know."

"Are you worried about money?"

"I wasn't, but perhaps I should be. Until now, it didn't occur to me that I would miss out on a sizable fortune should I rebel against them."

"Then you are worried about money."

"I'd rather not plan my life around their deaths. I don't care about money. I think that it would bother them more than me if they had to leave their estate to charity. Maybe they would leave it to my cousins in New Hampshire. They don't need it, though. My uncle is a doctor, and his wife comes from a wealthy Boston family. I don't know."

"Are you sure you want to do this?"

"Let's wait a while longer. Can you wait?"

"I think so."

"Fine. Let's work on the Beethoven. Let's just do that for now."

Chapter 78

Annie
July 18, 1847
Grosse Isle, Quebec, Canada

A STRONG WIND blew down river, takin' us out of the thick fog that had previously concealed all of the views around us. The early mornin' sun glittered on the surface of the water. I knew better than to have renewed hope. Once we reached the river, we stopped and started many times, either to pass by other ships or to cast off the dead.

For days, we sailed past islands and had seen land. Vessels of various origins, sizes, and purpose, passed by us in both directions. Although the fresh air felt good on our faces, and it seemed as if the sick and dyin' had a chance at some sort of recovery, it was short-lived. For many, the illnesses were already present when we began our voyage, and others fell ill along the way.

Earlier, I would have been captivated by the beauty of the tall fir trees on the shores, or the lighthouse and small cottages, but nothin' would soothe the pain from such frequent death and wretched conditions. All that survived were weak at best.

"Would you like this?" A kind man, not one of us, who slept in a cabin beside the captain and his wife, handed me a Bible.

I looked at Daidí as he continued to stare out at the shoreline. He had not spoken more than three words since that awful night.

"Daidí, this kind man is offerin' me a Bible," I said.

I broke the spell. Daidí looked at me with eyes that would never be the same. He saw too much. We were different. I saw too much as well, but I knew that I would carry on. Daidí was lost.

"Do you want it?" he asked.

"Yes, I would like it very much," I said.

"We have no money for it," he said. "Nothin' to trade."

"I am giving it to you to keep as a gift," the kind man said.

Daidí returned his gaze towards the horizon.

"Thank you," I said.

I spent the rest of the afternoon readin' Psalms, finally gettin' used to the sound of massive, grindin' chains as we stopped and started, pullin' up and droppin' down the anchor. For several hours, we floated motionless on the water. It wasn't until the break of day when we set sail once again, and the wind favored us.

Since Daidí stopped speakin' and eatin', I did my best to cook my own food with what was left of the rations. Even though the sailors added charcoal and alum to the remainin' water in the casks, it was foul, so many tried to drink the river water. The captain warned us of this because we were in a place in the river where there was still too much salt.

We were headin' towards our destination, Grosse Isle, when a lovely schooner pulled alongside us. A man, clumsy in appearance yet of high importance, came on board. When he saw the general state of the emigrants on our ship, he looked frightened, as if he wanted to flee. With a cloth over his nose and mouth, he spoke to the captain in broken English. He left a pamphlet, rules I s'posed and quickly exited.

Before reachin' Grosse Isle, where many vessels awaited inspection, we passed through intricate channels and saw several picturesque islands, as we sailed along the wooded shores of Canada and Maine. It would take weeks to navigate the river.

We hoisted our ensign—a signal for the inspectin' physician to board. We thought that we would sleep in our berths for another night. We were told that on the followin' day, a physician would come aboard, durin' which time, three more people died and their bodies committed to a watery grave—an experience witnessed but not wholly comprehended.

As individuals and between us all, there was not enough strength to sort it out. We needed to breathe. We craved clean water. We lacked sleep, and the pain in our empty bellies had reached beyond the hunger that we carried with us on the beginnin' of our voyage. Daidí wasn't quite certain of it, but we needed to live another day.

To pass the time, we cleaned as much of the filth as possible. Women washed the clothes with river water, men shaved for the first time, and some of the weak and sick showed slight signs of improvement. Daidí did not respond to any of it. I made him eat the flour porridge and drink a bit of water boiled on the fire.

I was close enough to hear the captain answer the physician's questions. How many on board? How many dead? How many ill? And, if there were any births, for which the answer was five. I did delight in seein' the tiny babies, although two of them didn't make it for long, they were very sweet to look upon. I was stunned to learn that the brig before us had suffered much higher losses and that the physician was not surprised at the number of dead on our ship. Other ships that sailed with us were quickly discharged and passengers released, as they had fewer dead and dyin' on board.

The time came for us to get in line and do our best to stand. In our cleanest rags, we waited to be reviewed. A decision would be made about who would be taken to a hospital and cared for, and who would be permitted to wait on the island. Those goin' to the island would board a steamer headed for Quebec to meet with the agents and receive promised provisions.

Whenever a boat came in our direction, we surged with an unexpected source of energy, only to wilt as it passed by, goin' to another brig for inspection. It was too much to bear. We had been at sea for over a month, and then we were in the river, only to wait endlessly at our destination just to disembark.

The tide brought in many fine vessels that sailed straight through, as they had no passengers on board, while others hoisted their signals only to wait as did we. Two brigs sailed past, and we watched as passengers by the hundreds were left on the island.

We had finally gotten far enough away from the ocean where the salt was gone, but because of so many ships and the amount of waste, debris, and corpses, we still could not drink the water. The remainin' filthy water in the last cask had run dry, leavin' nothin' to boil. Finally, the Canadian priests rowed up beside our vessel and came aboard.

After speakin' in French to the pilot, who translated for the captain, they went down into the hold. They were down there for what seemed like hours, administerin' to the sick, givin' an old man his last rites, and then baptizin' two infant boys.

When they came back, they told us that our ship was better than some of the others, some were so vile in the lower decks, folks stood ankle-deep in filth and excrement. They also praised the captain for the burials that took place out to sea. Because some ships had passengers herded together with no room to spare, and amongst them both the sick and the dead, there was more illness and death.

They mentioned that we should be thankful because even some of the nuns and priests were in tents and fever sheds with cholera and typhus. The priests were well spoken and said that we were fortunate to have escaped a worse fate like others in our midst. They bowed and thanked the captain one more time and got into their boat and rowed away.

In the meantime, the old man who had received his last rites died. Just as the sailors were about to throw his corpse overboard, the captain stopped them. He told them to put his remains in the hold, and he would be taken to the burial grounds on the island instead.

In the distance, what we could see of Grosse Isle looked as if it could have been beautiful, but instead was lined with white tents and small buildin's. As far as the eye could see, there were bodies wrapped in canvas or placed in haphazard boxes, made out of berths and random wooden scraps, bein' carried off the ships and over slippery rocks by well-intentioned sailors. Ship after ship unloaded their dead cargo, bringin' with them a handful of mournin' survivors, and the ghosts of the ones who were dumped in the sea.

First, the sickest ones were taken—a skeleton mother ripped away from her screamin', soon to be orphaned children, lookin' upon them one more time. A little boy clung to his emaciated father before bein' taken away to a strange land, an unendin' funeral.

Again, Daidí kept his eyes fixed ahead, gazin' into nothin'ness, where it was safe, or so he thought. He was still at the rail of the brig when they came for us, the healthy ones.

"Hey, you, come now!" One of the sailors shouted.

I took Daidí by the arm, and we left together. We walked past all of the stacks of coffins and bodies, and those bein' taken to the white tents and sheds, and we went to a small buildin' where Daidí signed his name. We were instructed to go to one of the sheds, where the people were crowded together like cattle. I knew Daidí's limitations, so we continued to walk. Even though we were in the river for a spell, we had sea legs, as one of the sailors had warned us that we would.

I missed the coolness of the wind at sea. The sun scorched my once fair skin, havin' peeled and blistered many times. I lost my shoes, so the rocks burnt my feet, but we had to walk. There were swarms of mosquitoes stingin' my skin, addin' to my discomfort. The ones on the Isle who were settled and not so sick, were nearly naked, washin' their clothes in the river and layin' them on the rocks to dry.

Together, we walked away from the shoreline, until we reached an ash grove. We found the biggest tree and sat beneath its shady crown. There was no agent, no provisions, and no money. We were hungry, thirsty, and what remained of our spirits was crushed, but we made it.

I owed it to the stars. When the others were below and asleep in their berths, I managed to find my way up to the open deck. The snorin', cries, groans, and creakin' noises of the ship made it quite simple. I came to know my way around by the feel of my hands.

I liked the moon, but it was too revealin', and I risked gettin' caught, so I went topside on the darkest nights, when there were so many stars that it almost did not seem real. We had many stars at home, but they stretched further across the sky over the open sea.

The Angels' Lament

I carried with me a grieved heart. When I left my homeland, I had a mother. When I stepped foot upon North American soil, I did not. However, I knew that I was stronger than most, and if anyone could have survived bein' an unmothered child, it was me. What choice did I have? I got my strength from Mam. Daidí did as well. He could not live well without his wife.

However, I had not thoroughly awakened from the dream of losin' Seamus. To me, he was not really gone, but, yes, I did know the truth. I did, but I could pretend with him. When Mam was given to the sea, she made such a big splash, but Seamus slipped under the waves so quietly, barely makin' a ripple, leavin' room for unreasonable hope, that perhaps he was not really gone after all. Yes, I knew… He was gone.

Daidí and I were on our own.

CHAPTER 79

August
September 19, 1874

I BOLTED FROM my bed when the bells rang for fire. Surrounded by disorder—folks hollerin' and tramplin' through the streets—I made my way outside. Fire engines raced through the mayhem, headin' straight for the clouds of smoke that billowed up into the sky.

The fire signal was intermittent and unclear, bringin' about more panic to an already bewildered crowd. After precious moments lost in confusion, and by followin' the smoke rather than the lost engines, we discovered the source.

"Granite Mill! Number One is burning! Granite Mill!" People hurried down the street, some carryin' blankets, and others only half dressed. Surrounded by mayhem, I stood still, starin' at the smoke.

Sarah! I couldn't move fast enough. I ran inside and dragged Finn out of bed.

"There's a fire. We have to go get Sarah."

Although not quite awake, he sensed my urgency. He dressed quickly, and we ran with the others towards Granite Mill.

The mill was fully ablaze, with flames explodin' into the sky. Fire ladders reached only partway up the buildin', and people were jumpin' from as high as the sixth floor, just to hit the ground with an awful thud. I couldn't think. Sarah was up there somewhere.

Glass flew everywhere when women smashed windows, and flames and smoke raged behind them as they waved their bloody arms, screamin' for help, and fightin' to breathe. Some men made their way down with either ropes or strong coils of warp. They descended for a few stories, only to let go when they were still a ways from the ground.

Helpless, we stood together on the sidewalk while our fellow workers, brothers and sisters, children, parents and friends, burned, suffocated, or leapt to their deaths. A young girl jumped from a window, only to get caught on a ladder, where her limp body dangled until the firemen were able to retrieve her, at which time she was already dead.

There were many attempts made to aid the terrified workers, scorched right before our eyes, blinded by smoke, and silenced by the cracklin' blaze. A huge, muscular man happened to catch a small blood-covered boy in his arms, and then he carried him to a nearby company tenement buildin', where doctors treated the wounded.

An older woman worked tirelessly with her friends, draggin' mattresses close to the buildin' for people to jump on, and quilts to cover them. Others got together with hand-held blankets to break the fall of those who summoned the courage to leap.

The smoke and flames continued to rise up to the sixth floor, where I searched for a sign of Sarah. The roar of the fire competed with the harrowin' screams that came from within the inferno and down on the ground.

One at a time, men emerged to lower themselves with ropes. I recognized a man who lived across the hall from me. He slid down, almost gettin' to the second story, when he let go. His injuries appeared to be minor, maybe a broken leg. Another man grabbed the same rope, only he held onto it for a bit longer, and his fall wasn't as bad. It seemed as if the women and children had the impulse to jump.

I still didn't see Sarah or any of her friends, so I headed for the buildin'. Before I got to the door, a red-faced policeman charged out in front of me.

"Where do you think you're goin'?"

"I'm goin' inside to help!" I attempted to shove him, but he was twice my size.

"You can't go in there. Only firemen can, and it's too dangerous now for that. Get outta' the way!" He pushed me.

I stopped when I heard shoutin' in the background.

"Hold on! Don't let go! You can do it!"

I looked up to see a woman holdin' onto a rope, swingin' back and forth, hittin' the buildin'. I ran closer to get a better look.

"Sarah!" My voice was muted by the howl of wind-driven flames and constant cries around me. "It's me! Don't look down, Sarah! Go slow and take your time!"

She hung on, not makin' any progress, as the rope swirled. A wisp of a woman draggin' a threadbare quilt approached me. "Here, hold this. She can jump."

"No, no, she can't. She can take her time and come down on the rope," I said.

My eyes watered and my throat burned as I stood by and watched Sarah dangle way above me for what felt like hours. Even though it seemed pointless, I shouted just the same.

"Hang on, Sarah!"

Just as she slowly inched her way down, a woman shrieked and plunged from a window on the sixth floor, bumpin' into her, causin' her to spin and crash into the buildin'.

"You're fine! Take it a little bit at a time!"

She looked down at me. "I can't!"

"Yes, you can! You can! Keep your eyes on the buildin'. Go slow!"

A man brushed by me with a woman wrapped up in a bloody gunny sack while two more girls jumped to their deaths.

Even though I could not hear my own voice, I continued to scream as loud as I could, so loud that I thought that I would lose consciousness. Once again, I was surrounded by the stench of death.

Chapter 80

Sarah
September 19, 1874

The rope seared the flesh of my palms while the flames spun me around in circles, slammin' me into the buildin'.

"If I die, remember that I love you!" Clara screamed, hangin' out the window, and wavin' her bloody arms.

Every time I focused on her face, she was quickly swallowed up by the black smoke that rolled out from behind her.

"You're not gonna die. You're not gonna die..." I could only whisper.

Someone called out my name. I tried to look, but when I opened my eyes, I started to fall. I had to close my eyes to stay safe.

Sarah, you climbed up there, you can get back down. It was Papa talkin'. I always went too high. Abigail was better at climbin' trees than I.

Papa, I'm gonna fall.

No, you won't fall. You'll be fine. You have to trust yourself.

I can't. Catch me, Papa!

You can, Sarah. Take one small step at a time.

I'm scared.

Don't be. I'm right here.

"Sarah!"

It was August. Screams and cracklin' flames drowned him out, but I just knew it was him. I could only think of respondin'.

Then, a woman jumped from above, collidin' with me, takin' away my breath. I tried to see through my burnin' eyes, but nothin' was possible. My soul had fallen prey to an unrelentin' sense of desertion and sorrow. Although utterly forsaken, and with greatly diminished faith, I considered prayer. However, I feared that I could not. He abandoned Mother, Abigail, Mary, and now me. He had no mercy. Therefore, I had no choice but to seek guidance and comfort from within. Perhaps it was this radical change that beckoned such dire consequences. If blind faith was expected, I wanted no part of it.

I almost lost my grip and started to fall, but struck the buildin' instead. My face was scorched, and my hands were numb and bloody. The only face that I recognized was that of the apple woman, standin' beside her cart, lookin' up in horror.

I closed my eyes again, wrapped the rope around my ankles, and slid down a few feet, cuttin' deeper into my palms, and gettin' closer to August. He sounded like Papa. I couldn't sort them out.

If I could forget one face, one harrowin' moment, it would have been when a young girl dove head first from an attic window. Time was suspended in a vacuum of silence. We locked eyes. I think I could have touched her. With the hem of her skirt engulfed in flames, like a shootin' star, she fell to the earth. I held my breath and watched. It wasn't until a group of people rushed to her aid that the shrieks of devastation resumed.

I exhaled and almost let go. Chokin, spittin', and fightin' for air, I imagined the fall. Tears and saliva ran down my face and neck, and I couldn't lift my head. Death called my name, and it didn't seem so bad.

Sarah!

You want me to join you now, Mother?

Within her own sacred fire, she was before me, calm, serene, and whole.

No, not now! You know what to do.

I loosened my grip on the rope.

White hot flames licked the edges of her body, closin' in until all I could see was her face.

Be brave. You are not alone.

I held on tight and began to spin. I waited, stopped, and stared into the fire. As expected, she was gone. I screamed so loudly that it hurt my chest and lungs. No one could hear. Not even me. Then, I hung in silence, causin' me to wonder if I had perished too.

"Lord, how unworthy I have become! I come to You in my darkest hour, yet You still forsake me. My soul is bowed deeply before You as I face death. If You spare my life, I will never more offend or grieve You. I will live in servitude, uplifted from my spiritual poverty, mournin' my past offenses. I dare not ask a favor, as I have departed from the right way, and 'tho You slay me, and the women I loved so dearly, from the sorrow of my heart, I beg for forgiveness. I will trust in Thee, Amen!"

I slowly opened my eyes to see that I had not reached Heaven. Instead, I was near a window on the fourth floor. I looked beyond the blaze where a group of men and women—two spinners that I knew well— struggled to reach a ladder bein' held by a group of firemen.

I calmly slid down the rope, makin' it to the second story before lettin' go.

When I crashed into the unforgivin' earth, the pain that exploded in every part of my body was accompanied by one loud crack and a series of smaller ones. Instead of burnin' to death, I shattered to pieces. How many? I did not know. In spite of my curiosity, I was relieved.

I woke up in August's arms with a blur of faces lookin' down on me. When I spotted Mr. Aldrich, talkin' to one of the firemen, I tried to sit up. My anger for him had survived. I fell back and surrendered into the safety of darkness, tryin' to find the peace and tranquility that I relied on durin' unspeakable times. I managed to be removed from the events in the outer world, but this time, I was truly alone. The comfort, usually present in my hidden world, was out of my reach.

Then came Mercy—her face blackened with a blend of blood and soot. "Thank the good Lord you've been spared," she cried.

"Mercy." I longed to hug her, but could barely mouth her name, for breathin' had become burdensome.

"We're lookin' for Rebecca! We're lookin' for Rebecca! Oh my God! Did you see her? No one knows where she is!" she screamed.

A kind man put his arm around her shoulder, and together they walked away as she sobbed uncontrollably. I caught sight of a red hat—Patrick's hat. There he was in a motionless heap, his legs twisted grossly beneath him, and eyes fixed in death's vacant stare.

"Patrick… Not you," I whispered before slippin' into darkness.

I was taken to a physician who had set up temporary quarters across the street from the mill. Along with cuts and bruises on my face and body, I had severe burns on both of my hands. My right leg was shattered in several places, and my left elbow, along with at least two ribs, was broken.

Many of the wounded had sustained injuries that would take many months, years, and even a lifetime to heal. This was not considerin' the internal trauma wounds that would afflict us for the rest of our days. I was grateful for the ones who made it out alive, yet I knew many of the dead.

Clemmie had a broken arm and burns over most of her body. She escaped from the fifth floor by way of rope.

Bridget had several broken bones and a sprained back. The word is that she was not at her usual station on the fifth floor and had a time of it in the stairwell. Her injuries were not fire related.

Clara's arms were severely bruised and cut from broken glass, and her face and neck were badly burned. It is said that she helped some of the children escape before climbin' out of the window and usin' a rope to make her way down.

Addy was missin' for many days. They were finally able to identify her after she gained consciousness. She suffered many broken bones, and a head and back injury.

It so happened that Rebecca's face was scorched beyond recognition. She ended up in a room down the hall from me, under the care of the same physician. It would be months before either of us could leave.

Because she was home with a dreadful sore throat, Ruby avoided it all. She was in turmoil about whether or not she should miss work, as it was customary to work through our illnesses. Her decision to take care of herself saved her life. Most of the workers on the lower three floors escaped with minor injuries or none at all.

My heart plunged into the depths of despair when I learned that dear, sweet Norah lost her life. She vanished from my sight when the room quickly filled up with smoke. We all dashed about frantically, tryin' without success to break through the door to the stairwell.

Oh, how I grieved! The world wouldn't be the same without Norah in it. I left her behind, trapped on the sixth floor, where just two weeks earlier, she was finally able to join Clara and me as a drawin'-in girl. We even celebrated. Mrs. O'Leary baked a fine meal cake to have after her first day on the new job.

Chapter 81

Bess
September 19, 1874

STRUGGLING TO REMAIN buoyant in the last light of day, I sat alone in the garden. Although long over, the smoke from the mill fire hung heavy in the air, and blackness mingled with the orange clouds on the horizon. Unsure of its roots, I stood face to face with profound melancholia, and I reluctantly invited it in.

Even Tempy could not brighten my spirits, but she did try by offering me a glass of cool cinnamon water and butter cookies. I needed to be alone. Joseph was going to come by, and together we were going to tell my parents about our plans to get married. Ours was already a risky situation, and after such a monumental event at the mill, it would never do. The mood was much too somber. Father was only interested in saving the corporation, nothing about me or anyone else was of importance. I knew my place.

Unlike me, Joseph had friends who worked in the mills. When stopping by, pretending to give me a book of music, he was filled with anxiety. He provided a detailed account of the horrors of the disastrous fire. He was a spectator for the duration of the tragedy and was quite shaken. We both knew that given the circumstances, with Father's position in the corporation, it would not be advisable to even entertain the idea of dinner or an announcement of our pending engagement.

Shortly after the fire broke out, the men who smoked cigars were at our home. After much shouting and general alarm, Father left with them. His torment wasn't connected to the pain and anguish of those who were maimed or lost their lives in the fire at Granite Mill. No, no, he was only concerned with the consequences, if any, that all of this would have on the corporation.

I had been watching him and the others since I was old enough to get a basic idea of what mattered to them. It had nothing to do with the happiness and well-being of others. It was solely about finances and money. Workers were only as good as the machines that they sweat and toiled over every day. They were not even human to people like my father.

My thoughts about his selfish ways caused an ache in my bones. Mother only cared about how it would spill into her life. She cared even less, because she did not bother to understand Father, let alone all of the humans that suffered due to his part in it. It was his job to protect the corporation, nothing more, nothing less.

At that moment, I realized how vital it was to help those who were less fortunate. Together, Joseph and I would share our gifts with the world.

CHAPTER 82

August
October 25, 1874

"You're almost there."

"I can go further."

"I know, but overdoin' it causes more harm than good."

"I'll never be able to walk without these crutches if you keep pamperin' me."

We found our way to a bench and sat down. The sun felt nice, but the crisp autumn breeze was a reminder that winter was soon to follow. She rested her head on my shoulder. I was worried about her leg. It was healin' but broken in so many places. She was determined to get back on her feet too fast, causin' her leg to swell. Her elbow was broken too, and when she leaned on the crutches, I could see her pain. I didn't want to discourage her, but I tried to get her to slow down.

"Have you given any thought to what you want to do after your injuries heal?"

"I was thinkin' of Patrick and the others—all of the children who don't have a mother or father, and somehow end up workin' in the mills. I want to be there for them."

"There are thousands of them. They aren't only here. They're everywhere. I should know. I was one of them, and Finn too."

"At least you managed to stay together," she said.

"Well," I shifted my position on the bench, "Finn isn't really my brother. I mean, he's like a brother, but he just happened to show up, and I didn't have the heart to turn him away."

She studied my face. "You lied to me?"

"I don't think of it as lyin' really. When we first met, I didn't know much about you, and I couldn't explain how it all came about without you judgin' me. Also, I was tryin' to protect him."

"Protect him?"

"He had run away from the children's home or almshouse, and I was sure they were lookin' for him. I hoped for somethin' better. He and others like him, who aren't quite right, are considered beyond hope of redemption. I know this to be true. It wasn't a secret."

"What are you talkin' about?"

"When I was growin' up, we were forced to go to awful places, islands where there was almost no way to escape. Or, they took us away on trains to be placed out, to work for couples out west who were buildin' their farms. There are places like this everywhere, professin' to care for children, but it doesn't always end up that way. Sure, some families adopted the children from the trains and gave them a good home, but for the most part, we were just workers.

Boys like Finn didn't have a chance. And, most of the girls who were placed out were nothin' more than housekeepers, but it was better than bein' in the Magdalen asylum. There was no escapin' from there."

"I had no idea. In New Hampshire, we have the County Farm, where my sister is, but no islands or trains takin' them away."

"I started out in an orphanage in New York. My mother left me there when I was about three years old. I remember her in my dreams. She wears a blue cape and has green eyes. I have a note that she left. I don't know why I keep it. I s'pose it's all I have left of her."

"Of course you kept it," she said.

"Like all the other orphanages, this one was overcrowded. As far as I know, they saved my life. It didn't stop me from leavin', though. When I was nine, I ran away with Billy, who was like a brother to me," I said.

"For a few years, we lived on the streets in a place called Five Points. We sorted bones with the others at the street dumps. There were lots of children like us. Billy didn't make it." I was surprised that after all this time, I still choked up.

I rolled up my sleeves.

"What happened to your arms?"

"Along with a lot of other boys, I lived with a man named Smitty. For shelter and a bed—a strip of canvas strung between two attic beams—he taught us to go out and pick pockets. I was terrible at it. I tried, but could only do it when he was watchin' from a distance. Whenever I was out on my own, I got scared and returned empty-handed. One day, he brought me home and told me that he would fix it so that I could get some money. He burnt my arms several times with a hot iron, and then he poured acid on them."

"What?" She traced my scars with her finger. "I can't believe this. It's horrible."

"I was ten years old at the time. He sent me out on the streets with my ravaged arms to tell folks that I was injured at a steel factory. I got lots of money, more than the pickpockets, and I gave it to Smitty."

"But, all of that ended when I was rounded up with some of the other boys and taken to Randall's Island. We stayed in the House of Refuge, and if you were bad, and even if you weren't bad, they hung you up by your thumbs.

I hated it there. That's where the idiot's asylum is too, you know. It's better suited for the dead than anyone still takin' a breath. I managed to stay there for a few years, only to get right on one of those trains headin' west. I figured out pretty quick that it wasn't for me. After only one meetin' with a family, I escaped. I've been travelin' ever since. I've been at Fall River longer than anyplace else. I made up my mind that I would have a real job and earn an honest livin'."

A tear fell from her eye.

"This is why I want to help children. To hear of your tragic childhood leaves me without words." She buried her face in my chest.

"Don't cry. It made me strong. Together we can do somethin' that matters. Our meetin' was not an accident."

We sat on the bench longer than usual. There was no need to light the lamps right away. The skies were clear, and the full moon rose early.

Chapter 83

Sarah
October 25, 1874

A DAY DID not pass without August by my side. He only left to go to the market or to light the lamps. Because his boss's condition had worsened, August had more responsibilities and received an increase in pay.

Since the fire, I stayed in a tenement with about a dozen other girls, all under the care of Doctor Wilder. I was bandaged up quite well and had made significant progress with the crutches. Within a short time, I was expected to walk again, and I would be on my own.

The mill paid for the funerals of those who perished and the short term medical expenses of the injured. There would be a trial to determine the corporation's legal obligations based on an investigation of the conditions of the mill and other safety matters. We could only pray for a fair outcome.

Poor Rebecca! Of all of us, her wounds were the worst. I feared she was on a path to the grave. Unable to sleep, she whimpered day and night and swore that she would avoid a lookin' glass for the rest of her days. I tried to console her, but she refused any kind words. In truth, her face was so badly burnt that the doctors and nurses had to cut away the dead skin and treat the blisters on a daily basis to prevent infection. Her nose was all but gone, and she was so disfigured that had it not been for her voice, she was unrecognizable.

She cried for her mother, but there was no room for her in the recovery house. Mrs. Porter planned to come to Fall River and stay with Mercy until Rebecca was able to travel, and then the three of them would return to New Hampshire.

Mercy stopped in every day on her way home from work. I was concerned about her, as she had become fragile and afraid. She had lost much weight, and her clothes hung off of her in the most unbecomin' manner. She and some of the other girls from our house went to work at the Durfee Mill, although her heart was not in it, she managed to get a position in a lower room.

August gathered my belongin's from the tenement, and except for my cornet, which was tucked under my bed, kept them at his place. I decided that even after a full recovery, I would never work at a mill again.

I didn't think of August as the religious type. In fact, he scoffed at my suggestions of goin' to church. But, ever since the fire, he was involved with Father Brennan of St. Mary's and the citywide relief committee that helped to organize benefits to raise money for the victims of the fire.

The French Canadians and the Irish Catholics made a pledge to join together to assist the victims who would never be able to work again. It didn't take long for the aged workers to be sent to the poor farms, elder homes, and wander about on the streets. The children were sent to the local aid societies, poorhouse, and some were said to have been taken away on trains to be placed out.

Initially, I decided to keep the horrific details about the fire a secret from Abigail. With her own grim circumstances, she had enough to worry about. I did not want to burden her with my woes. However, I feared that with Mrs. Porter knowin', and the way that news traveled, she might find out. There were many millworkers from New Hampshire, and I was sure that it would be published in the newspaper. Therefore, I had no choice.

My Dearest Sister,

I write to you with distresing news. This time it is to report a tragic fire that hapened at the mill where I worked. It was devastateing, and many lost their lives. It is because of the greatness of God that I am alive, Abby. I admit that my faith had been shaken, but I owe my life to Him.

Mercy is fine and had no injuries. I am recovring from a broken arm and leg. We are the fortuneate ones. It is Rebecca who was hurt the most. She suffered very bad burns and will be laid up for a long time. When we are together again, I will share the perticulars. I think of you and baby Samuel and yearn to meet him.

I have a bit of good news. I met a wonderful man. His name is August, and he is kind and careing. He is not a millworker. He is a lamplighter. Who would have imagined that I would fancy someone like him? Mother would have aproved. I still think of how you and I will be together again one day. Pray, sister, and it will come true.
Affectionately,
Your Sister, Sarah Hodgdon

Chapter 84

Bess
October 25, 1874

It was not about a polished performance, but drowning out the rage of the men who smoked cigars. We were in an undeclared duel. The louder they shouted, the harder I played. I matched their fury with my own, which was beyond working to my advantage.

Unable to resolve their inconvenient catastrophe in a typical day at the office, they stormed in and out of the house at all hours. I had never seen Father so worried and distracted. He had so much to hide. Mother just paced up and down the hallway, stopping now and then to press an ear to his office door, which was hardly necessary since they rarely spoke in polite tones.

I couldn't touch another piano note. With the truth scattered about in helpless disarray, the ivory moon—radiant and willing—showed up, begging me to sit beneath its unflinching eye.

Chapter 85

Annie
October 6, 1854
Ossipee, New Hampshire

I STOOD BENEATH the unveiled moon. The harshness of it—full and white, lackin' any trace of magic or purity—was too much to bear. Illuminated in my surroundings, yet weighed down by my own vileness, I could only give way to discouragement. Nothin' was truer than that which shone in the moonfield. Although my heart did know itself, I lacked sufficient strength to take refuge under the shadow of its wing.

The trees, once my protectors, had become eager witnesses. Rather than marvel at their boldness and beauty, I cursed them for mockin' me, for standin' in their noble perfection. Preferrin' darkness over the light of judgment bein' cast upon me, I walked hand in hand with my lamentable sins. I could not look upon anything but the stony road beneath my feet.

I dismissed the ghosts of townspeople standin' before their houses with pointed fingers and sharp tongues, and I focused on each step. My heart pounded too hard and too fast to care that the Indian woman, who lived in the back of the store, followed me, hidin' behind the trees.

So much time had passed since I left the barn, yet I continued to fight for air. I knew where the truth was, but could not get a hold of it. Even the moon pushed it upon me with brutal insistence. There was no escape from my woeful and humble condition.

The cold night air drove me. Like a false angel, I glowed in wicked radiance from the dried sweat upon my skin. If I could have prayed, perhaps it would have been different, but I could only run from the stubborn righteousness that I once clung to, a flaw in my nature.

I heeded the call of the serpent, followin' the desires raised in my heart, fallin' into a careless state. Tears stung my eyes, as droplets of blood abandoned my virtue, leavin' a stain upon my garments and dampenin' my unworthy soul.

Chapter 86

Sarah
December 18, 1875

Mrs. Brown was a talented seamstress and kind enough to let me borrow a weddin' dress. Even though it was not new, and worn by a few others, it was charmin' and fit well. With great concentration, I walked steadily down the aisle. It had been at least a month since I last relied on the crutch. And then, I only used it at the end of a long day.

Clara was quite happy to be my maid of honor. More than anything else, I missed walkin' to and from the mill with her warm little hand in mine. In the face of all obstacles, her smile remained eternally bright.

It had been over a year since the fire, and there was nothin' but conflict in Fall River. The trial favored the mill, absolvin' them of any wrong doin'. The labor troubles continued to mount, leadin' to an increase in workers' discontent. The streets were often filled with violent crowds that required prompt action from the police. Many people sustained injuries durin' these riots. Had I not suffered greatly in the fire, and maintained my position at the mill, I would have joined in the uprisin'.

Ever since the fire, August had become involved with St. Mary's church, and although I was raised as a Methodist, I felt at home amongst the Irish Catholics. My awareness of Mother's childhood trauma in Ireland was heightened. She did not express the degree of famine and pestilence present durin' this harrowin' time, but she consistently ensured that we never wasted so much as a crumb and that we always helped those in need.

Because she kept her stories to herself, I only knew fragments of the awful occurrences that led to her perilous voyage across the Atlantic Ocean. I learned more about her homeland from my friends in Fall River than I did from her.

Her beloved Daidí passed away when we were so young, I had no actual memories of him. What I remembered may have been what I conjured up from her stories.

She spoke of her Mam and brother briefly, always cautious when she did. She kept her secrets tucked away safely in the darkest part of herself. I stopped askin', for I knew that she would not speak of anything other than what she had already told us.

I was somewhat surprised at August's devotion to the church. He claimed that he was grateful for the women at the orphanage, where he was dropped off as a baby, and that he had learned the Catholic ways durin' his time there.

I was quite moved that the French Canadians and Irish had come together in solidarity for the good of the people. It was because of their determination to see to it that folks were treated right, especially followin' the fire, that I was able to do my work at the Fall River Children's Home. The pay was minimal, but the need without end.

After the weddin', we rented a small cottage. It was perfect for the three of us and had room for at least one baby. August was eager to start a family. I was perfectly content to rise up to the challenge of motherhood when it was meant to be. Until the time came, we had two additional boarders—mule spinners—hardworkin', likable fellows from Quebec.

Besides, we weren't goin' to be there forever. August promised that someday we would return to New Hampshire to fetch Abigail and Samuel. We weren't sure if we would live there or Fall River. I personally had my fill of bein' away from home. I craved the mountains.

CHAPTER 87

Annie
December 4, 1854
Ossipee, New Hampshire

I USED TO dream of the world beyond the guarded embrace of the mountains. Down in the deeps, I knew that I had no business goin' away. My travelin' days ended when I was nine years old. We had gone far enough. I knew my place, where we took root after we left our homeland.

So, when the mills of Lowell called to me, I dismissed the urge to go. It was a natural choice, as I had given my heart to Samuel. Had it been a year sooner, I may have married the loom instead of the man that I so loved. For this, I gave thanks to God.

I thought of Mam and Seamus in their dark, watery grave, the burial place of my childhood innocence. I tried to imagine what it would have been like if she were fussin' with my hair and tendin' to my dress, and if my brother's smile continued to charm.

Although I often hungered for them, my true recollections of Mam and Seamus had faded fast into dreams, somewhere hidden but not completely gone. Perhaps the Lord took them so that they would never know of my weakness and imperfection. It was upon my shoulders that they were called to join Him.

It was a comfort to know that Daidí was just beyond the closed door. In spite of his tendency to waver durin' restless times, I held fast to the belief that he would rise up to the challenge of givin' away his only daughter.

I looked out the window and caught sight of the moon smilin' down on me and smiled back. Daidí said that folks never considered the power of the full moon that appears in the light of day. *It's a sign of good luck,* he said.

I tried to eat some soda bread and jam, but due to all the excitement, couldn't keep it down. I'd say that I was hungry and full at the same time; so it wouldn't hurt to wait 'til our weddin' breakfast to take nourishment.

I studied my reflection in the lookin' glass. I was just as trim as ever with my corset pulled tight. No one would have known. Samuel was disturbed when I told him that I missed the bleedin'. Our plans to marry enabled me to hide the evidence of our sin. The math was close enough to diminish doubts of my worthiness. His concerns were with his folks.

As much as I loved Daidí, we rarely, if ever, reached beyond the boundaries of our endearin' little farm. When he was not staggerin' from the hard cider that he packed away, he was workin' hard, indeed. I smiled when I thought of him, how he sometimes twirled me around and sang a ditty from the old country. I would remember to sing them to my children, although I knew that Mam would have preferred hymns.

My fidgetin' was about to get the best of me. I opened my sack and looked through the sheet music that Daidí had found at the old meetin' house. Someone was about to throw it all away before they moved to the new place. I lacked the skills to read all of the notes, but I tried to learn on our piano, and over the years had at least four full lessons. It didn't matter whether or not I fully understood the notes on the page. I liked to look at them and know that Daidí spoke the language of my heart. I hoped that he would play his fiddle one last time.

CHAPTER 88

Bess
January 7, 1876

IN ADDITION TO the elite of Fall River, there were distinguished guests from nearby towns and other parts of the country. There were at least fifteen hundred people in attendance. After all were seated and had quieted down, we were escorted to our seats in the front row, where we stood facing the audience.

"Ladies and gentlemen, please give a warm welcome to the board of directors and faculty members of The Academy of Music!" the announcer shouted from the podium.

When the applause died down, we took our seats. It had taken years for the opening of the academy to come to fruition. Because of the number of Joseph's students and his participation in many local recital and concert series, he was asked to be the director of teaching. After much discussion, he persuaded me to teach. I did not think of myself as incapable. I wished to focus my attention on performance only. It didn't take long for him to bring a new perspective to my role as a musician.

Yes, many dream of spending all waking hours performing and playing, but to be an actual ambassador of music, it is essential to plant the seeds of the future. It is possible to do both—perform and teach. In fact, teaching inspired and motivated me to be more aware of myself. It expanded my limited view.

"Here is your program, Mrs. Carver." Mr. Beyrent's words rattled within the walls of my chest. I still wasn't accustomed to my new last name. Even though Joseph was a well-respected member of the community and The Academy of

Music, for which we were celebrating, he was not well-bred. It was because of my parents' response to him that I was alert, prepared to defend him.

It had been only three weeks since our simple wedding took place. Mother and Father had ample time to accept our marriage but chose to remain distant and aloof. I regretted that I did not allow them to provide a lavish wedding for us, but neither Joseph nor I wanted such frivolity. Had I comprehended the potential depth of their emotional injuries, I would have gone along with their need to overindulge.

I was warmed to get a glimpse of dear, sweet Tempy, sitting in the third row with a blanket on her lap. Beside her sat Mother, who stared at me with her usual look of bewilderment, while Father, no doubt, was pouring over numbers in his head, not really seeing me at all. He was always far off in his thoughts, but since the strikes, he had also become exhausted and defeated.

Excitement filled the air as the orchestra entered onto the platforms. With the concertmaster in the center, they tuned up. By quarter past eight, they were all in place and opened the program with Wagner's "Overture of Tannhäuser." The second piece was different, yet equally as powerful with "Invitation à la danse" by C. M. von Weber, accompanied by Hector Berlioz on the harp.

When the orchestra began "Beethoven's Symphony No. 5," Joseph reached over and took my hand in his. Right then, I let go of Boston once and for all. I never dreamed that I could ever be satisfied in a place as vile as Fall River. When we first arrived, I intended to return home as soon as possible, but I was wrong. There were endless possibilities in all circumstances.

Intermission was filled with dizzying conversations and lines of people waiting to speak with us. I was relieved when we finally returned to our seats. The orchestra continued to lift our spirits as they performed "The Overture of William Tell," by Rossini, and "Traeumerei" by Schumann. I feared that my head would burst.

Following the last piece, and before the people in the audience began to leave, the mayor got up to speak. He thanked the audience for their support while crediting the benefactors of The Academy of Music—the notable men from the Borden family.

After a surprisingly rowdy "three cheers" for Simeon B. Borden, Esq., the crowd called upon him to speak. For the first time all evening, Father perked up as Mr. Borden took the stage. He gave a short speech, expressing that his friends were pleased with the outcome, and how it was appropriate to make such notable progress when entering into the centennial year, making the city proud.

CHAPTER 89

Sarah
January 7, 1876

WHILE AUGUST BROUGHT light to the city, Finn slept soundly, lyin' in fever, and I sat alone by the kitchen fire. I tried to hide my disappointment, but my heart was heavy with regret. Ever since I heard about it, I looked forward to attendin' the grand openin' of The Academy of Music. Because of August's new position, we were given general admission tickets for standin' room.

It had been over a year since I played with the brass band. I never returned after the fire. With such crushin' injuries, it took months to heal. I missed it greatly, but I managed to play as often as I could. Livin' in the cottage offered a more pleasant practice experience. Without hidin' in the attic, or pretendin' to be Jonas, I was free. Because the cottages were tightly packed together, I continued to stuff a rag in the bell. I longed for the full band. Playin' alone was unfulfillin', but Father Brennan said that he would think about gettin' a band together at church. Until then, I was grateful to have had the opportunity to play with the Fall River Cornet Band, and that they never discovered my real identity.

I thought about returnin' to the band but couldn't muster the necessary strength. It wasn't that I was any less brave, but I possessed a different kind of courage before the fire. It took time to heal after comin' completely undone. I didn't think of sendin' a letter to the bandmaster, and by the time I did, too much time had passed.

My hair had grown out, and durin' all the commotion, I lost my limited man's wardrobe. So, I entered a new season in my life, and there was no swervin' away from the truth. Without regret, I quit the band, quit smokin, and left dear, Jonas behind.

Chapter 90

Annie
Winter 1855
Ossipee, New Hampshire

The icy rain drummed against the roof, and it was as dark as night. I stumbled across the room and fell into the chair. Samuel was out, and I needed to gather my wits before his return. I prided myself on a well-kept house and preparin' a hearty supper each night. The bouts of weakness, nearly faintin', and wretchedness in my stomach had been worsenin', but I usually managed to feel right before nightfall. I did not complain.

Samuel was a kind man, and he would worry to no end if I told him of my true condition. Of course, he knew that I was with child, but he was not aware of the trouble in it.

Slowly, I rose to my feet, countin' my breaths and leanin' on the table. I finally made it to the stove to stoke the fire. When I lifted the cover from the pot, I had to look away. The smell of beef stew overwhelmed me, but I managed to stir it and rush back to my chair.

My hands shook when I unwrapped the dark, spicy root. I nibbled on the corner of it. I had to at least try. The mornin's were rough, and I enjoyed little rest.

The last time I was at the store, Mr. Burrows and I had our usual idle talk. While I settled my bill, the Indian woman, who sat in the back room makin' dolls, approached me. By then, Mr. Burrows had already turned his attention to Elsa Copp.

Without takin' her eyes away from me, the Indian dropped two parcels into my sack. One was the root, which, when taken in tiny amounts, brought about calmness. The other was a tangled ball of earth-encrusted leaves, wrapped in a crude note, held together with twine.

I finally unfolded the note. In thick, shaky letters, the word "TEA" was scribbled across the top.

Under usual circumstances, I was afraid of the Indian woman. Many of the town folk claimed that she was a witch. Fear is my soul's enemy, and I could not allow such notions to occupy my mind. Although she was not a Christian woman, and I believed it possible that God took offense, from time to time I did pray for her, as she seemed to have endured a life of many cares.

At first, I didn't know what to do with the root. I was worried, but the look in her eyes drove away my suspicions. I decided to secretly trust her. A small taste would do no harm. Come to find out, it was a miracle that brought about calm.

I broke off a piece of the twisted earth matter and stuffed it into my tea sack. In case I missed further instructions, I looked at the paper again. I had to rely on my instincts. I immersed the blend into the hot water inside of my teapot and watched as the water quickly turned a dark shade of amber.

After a few moments, I smelled dirt. I wondered if I had made a mistake, and that perhaps she was a witch after all. I recalled her look of determination. She knew; therefore, I did. I added a small bit of Father Will's honey, to take away any possible bitterness.

The more I stirred, the darker it got, and the more it smelled like tilled soil after the rain'. I was quite prepared for the unpleasantness of it all. When I brought it to my lips, yes, it tasted like dirt, but not as I imagined or as my nose would have tricked me into thinkin'. It was warm, buttery, spicy earth. It was as good as diggin' your toes in the mud and wigglin' until you cannot help but laugh.

My thoughts flew about the room, and I was both near and far at the same time. It appeared to be unsound, but I was all things. Such thoughts would cause Father O'Hara to request that I pray and seek guidance. I couldn't even consider tellin' the church folk here, or anyone else. The Indians were not honored. However, at that particular moment, I could not reject the overwhelmin' rush of love that washed over me. I savored it, knowin' somehow that it might vanish if I did not pay close attention. Blindness to such powerful wisdom was a loss, indeed.

It was reassurin'—an unmistakable indication that all of my troubles were in the hands of somethin' greater than me, but not necessarily God as we knew Him. Perhaps it was proof that God had a Mother, one who would guide, guard, and protect me, and call for my attention. It was the feminine face of God. I found myself questionin' everything and knowin' the answers all at once. A tear slid down my cheek. I knew that I would be fine, and my unborn child as well, for we were in the arms of Mother.

All of my senses had fully awakened, eyes opened. I found it necessary to pace myself, because, with each swallow of the rich earthen brew, I craved more. I straightened my posture. Anything that was previously blurred came into sharp focus. Along with any fear of the Indian woman, the flurry in my stomach had vanished. It was unnecessary to suffer. I was puzzled as to why I waited so long to trust her.

The spinnin' stopped, and I was no longer on fire. I approached the stove, boldly removed the cover from the pot, and stirred with vigor.

I knew that we could never turn back, but I tended to dwell on my unworthiness. Perhaps bein' with child wouldn't have been so wearisome, had it not been conceived in sin. I was offered a vision that day but could never speak of it. All I could do was pray, pray for Him to shine his light on me, and beg for redemption.

Chapter 91

Bess
April 25, 1878

NOTHING COULD HAVE prepared me for the shock of knowing that the separation would last forever. Hard as I prayed, somewhere within the confines of my soul, I almost always believed that he would not be accepted into the gates of Heaven. There was a time when I deemed such thoughts as nonsense, but throughout the years, I reconsidered my faith.

It was not that he did anything outwardly mean or horrible, but it was how he aided those who did. He made it clear that he would stop at nothing to protect his clients, and in doing so, he exceeded my expectations of his disgracefulness. After all, it was not Father who embezzled the funds, but he was tangled up in the wicked web of deceit by association. It was his people. Therefore, it was him.

Poor Mother! To find her husband hanging in the bedroom, was more than she could bear. She would never be the same. Her typical look of bewilderment became one of vacancy and sheer terror. I was unequipped to deal with her before Father's untimely death, and she made even less sense after. I regretted that my stubborn nature seemed to never make allowances for her shortcomings. She had reached a point where she was silent most of the time, and when she spoke, it was gibberish. Even Tempy could not understand her. After consulting with the physician, it was determined that she was in need of constant care in the asylum, for which I felt quite guilty. I knew that I could not help, and her remaining family members were not up for it.

Unable to play a single note, I sat before the piano. In many ways, I had lost both of my parents. My head was crowded with visions of that raw, dismal day when Father was laid to rest. The thought of the men who smoked cigars and their dutiful wives—pretending to care deeply—was quite afflicting. I could not erase the image of the remnants of his pale and emaciated self, lying in his casket. And, rather than his favorite suit, Mother selected an ill-fitting jacket that he once complained about and refused to wear. There he was, dressed in it for eternity, the last time anyone would see him, validating the fact that no one actually listened to each other. If it weren't for her lack of good judgment in everything else, I would have been convinced that she chose that suit out of spite. Everything about him, about his death, about Mother's reaction, and about me, was wrong.

I tried to return my attention to the piano. It was almost time for Joseph and me to go home. I was more upset by my lack of sorrow than I was about his gruesome death. I could not even summon a tear at his funeral but was able to hide beneath my veil. Tempy was the only one that I could trust. My relatives were vague and far away, and when they showed up, it was only out of duty. It was the last time for everyone and everything.

Suddenly, I was moved to play. I closed my eyes, and my fingers gracefully danced over the keys as I played a tarantella from my childhood days. It was sweet and melodic, nothing complex or intricate, a pathway back to a time of innocence—a time when I was unaware of the full extent of my father's capabilities.

A great change came over me. I was ready for the tears that needed shedding, but they remained locked within. Try as I may, I couldn't conjure up a tender memory of him. He was consistently aloof and detached. I accepted it. So why, at the time of his death, would I expect to fall apart and wail inconsolably?

My sense of longing shifted when the once spirited tarantella became grave and deliberate—a death march that demanded the participation of every atom within.

It must have been the heat of shame that caused one to sweat so. It was only April, but it seemed more like August. I wanted to bang my fists on the keys, to shout at him, and scream his name. The agony that I wished to conceal would not be quieted, for when he was dropped into the grave, I felt relief.

CHAPTER 92

Sarah
April 25, 1878

I DID NOT weaken. I continued to walk with a noticeable limp and suffered considerably in the damp weather, a common occurrence in Fall River. At first, I thought it silly, but August failed to see the humor in his invention. It took several months for him to build a special cart, and he took great pride in it. He used an old bicycle, spare wagon parts, and oddments from the Street Department. Situated at the front, he pedaled, pullin' the small cart behind him.

Most places were within walkin' distance from home. However, from time to time we liked to go further than what was comfortable for me with my weak leg, and we didn't care to spend hard-earned money on a hired carriage.

"I have a surprise for you," he said.

"Ooh, I love surprises."

He scooped me up into his arms.

"Where are you takin' me?"

"I can't tell you." He placed me in the seat of the cart.

"Where is Finn?"

"I'm gonna meet him later. I have meant to take you here for some time now."

I gripped the sides of the cart while he pedaled hard and fast, flyin' through the perpetual blizzard of lint. The crisp air felt good. He skillfully wove in and out of the crowded streets. Within moments, we were in front of The Academy of Music.

"What are we doin' here?" I asked.

"You'll see," he said as we came to a stop.

We walked around to the side of the buildin', where lovely piano music filled the air. He motioned for me to join him on a stone bench.

"I noticed that at about this time on most afternoons, someone plays the piano. I thought that we'd enjoy a private concert," he said. "I never mentioned it, but whenever I hear music like this on my route, I always stop."

It was beautiful, indeed. It had been a while since I had heard anything so exquisite. Listenin' to it was bittersweet, for it reminded me of what I missed—my cornet and the company of other musicians. Even as Jonas, I missed it.

"I want you to see somethin'," he said.

"What's that?" I asked.

"Follow me."

We went around to the front of the buildin'. He dashed up the steps and opened the door.

"Come on," he said.

"We can't just go in, can we?"

"I don't see why not."

Almost afraid of my own steps, I hurried after him, and together we entered a large reception area. The strains of many different instruments filled the air, and there was a flurry of activity—doors openin' and closin'.

"We need to leave, August. We have no business—"

"—Stop. Look at this." He led me to a bulletin board and pointed to a notice.

WANTED—SOLOISTS FOR THE FOLLOWING INSTRUMENTS: VIOLIN, CORNET, EUPHONIUM, TROMBONE, CLARINET AND OTHER REEDS. ENQUIRE WITHIN.

"See? This might be a chance for you to play as yourself. No more Jonas," he said.

Thoughts swarmed about in my head. *What kind of soloists were they talkin' about? Could I really audition as a woman? What was it for?* I fled from the buildin'.

"Wait. Where are you goin'?" He chased after me.

I returned to the shady area where we had listened to the piano, which had become quite passionate. I paused. "I'm sorry. I don't know what to do."

"Just relax for now and listen to the music. Think about what you want to play, and prepare for an audition. We'll come back, and you can talk to someone in charge."

"Relax? I can hardly sit still knowin' this. I would have to find out more details. I hope that I don't run into anyone from the band. But, I'm not Jonas anymore."

He laughed and pulled me into his arms. "Of course, you aren't Jonas. You don't need to be."

I rested my head on his shoulder. I wasn't quite ready to tell him that I had missed the bleedin' for over two months. It was best to be positive before makin' such bold announcements.

CHAPTER 93

Annie
April 1855
Ossipee, New Hampshire

THE SUN SPARKLED through the window, bringin' with it the greenness of spring. Samuel and Daidí were at the Blake farm breedin' the pigs. If it weren't for my discomfort and the peril of a rough ride, I would have gone into town with Miriam Blake. We needed supplies, and I secretly wanted more tea from the Indian woman. I ran out on the previous Wednesday. I dared not tell my husband because he and the others judged her harshly. What they failed to realize is, unlike the doctor's remedy, her tea offered considerable relief.

I lay in bed with both hands on my stomach, feelin' the baby move. It had become very active. I never thought that it would be so difficult. I felt sick most of the time, and walkin' had become a challenge. With great effort, I finally rose to my feet. I was not up for more than a few seconds when I was overcome by a fierce pain in my abdomen. I tried to drag myself to the bed, but I fell.

I don't know how long I had been on the floor before I heard the quiet knockin'. I waited. The baby continued to kick. I still couldn't move. The door finally creaked open. It was her—the Indian woman. She helped me to bed and put the kettle on the stove.

In peaceful silence, she held my hand and helped me drink the tea. It was stronger than before. The pain and tension eased more with each sip. She stayed with me until I finished the hot brew, gently strokin' my forehead the way Mam used to do. I was about to surrender to sleep, when she left my side, placin' a parcel on the table, before slippin' out the door. I watched her vanish into the heart of the woods.

CHAPTER 94

Bess
May 23, 1878

JOSEPH PACED THE room. "How can you think like that?"

"Like what?"

"That some people might be unsavory."

"We don't know who will come in off the streets. Especially here, where there are so many urchins and grubby millworkers. We just don't know, Joseph."

He hesitated and looked me in the eye. "It doesn't matter, Bess. Remember how you dislike your mother's judgmental ways? You're acting like her."

"No, I'm not. I think that we should limit our players to the students and known professionals of Fall River."

"There you are, using the word limit again. Will you please reconsider? You don't have to do it, but I think that you might like it." He left my practice room and slammed the door.

It was one thing for Joseph to sway me to be a teacher, but his latest request was that I collaborate with others as an accompanist. It was fine to do so with my students, to play simple duets and watch over them, but to actually accompany other instrumentalists was something that I never envisioned.

He supported the idea of showcasing local musicians in weekly performances, featuring those who were not students, but had the talent to share. Of course, this meant inviting unrefined musicians in off the streets and from undesirable neighborhoods. With all of the riffraff that I had seen going to and from the mills, I could not imagine the outcome. Did he entertain the thought of a tambourine girl or an organ-grinder? Perhaps the monkey would show up too. It was offensive at best.

CHAPTER 95

Annie
May 1855
Ossipee, New Hampshire

"Samuel, it would be best if she came to stay at our home, where she'll get constant care. She's had difficulties for some time and is very uncomfortable. I would hate for something to happen. She needs someone to be ready to assist her."

"I understand. I don't know how we'll pay for it, for bein' under your skilled care. It seems that most folks don't have to leave home like this."

"We'll worry about that when the time comes. You can't take the risk with her. If the worst should happen—Heaven forbid—at least we can save the baby. You live too far out, and her condition is worsening. We could lose both if she doesn't get the proper care."

"I don't know—"

"—it isn't usually like this, but she's losing strength."

"I can go see her? I mean, when I want?"

"Of course you can. She could have the baby today, or it could be a month from now."

He wasn't like any other doctor. I was safe with him.

Chapter 96

Sarah
May 24, 1878

"Would you like a glass of water?"

"Yes, please."

Mr. Gibbons—the program coordinator—was a very tall man, with thick white hair, and startlin' blue eyes. He stared at me with such intensity, I blushed and kept a close eye on the door. After too much time had passed, he finally left the room.

In case I had mistakenly exposed myself in some way, I checked the buttons on my dress, but everything was in place. I could not permit his behavior to distract me from the reason I was there. I blew into my horn. Even though I played for a good hour before August brought me to The Academy of Music, I had to warm up properly.

I never thought of myself as superstitious, but I felt significantly stronger when I wore the amulet that August made from Mary's snow angel. I rubbed it and stared out the window. I wondered why I endured such trials. I could have stayed on at work, mendin' garments and tendin' to the babies, but I chose to plunge into a world of doubt and worry.

He returned quickly and handed me the glass. "Please, take your time to prepare. I'll be back in fifteen minutes with the pianist, and we'll go from there."

"Thank you."

"You're welcome. Oh, and do you have the piano music for your piece?"

I handed him the piano part of "Haydn's Trumpet Concerto." He looked up at me.

"This is ambitious. Are you planning on playing the entire piece?"

"No, just the first movement," I said.

"Very well." He turned and left.

Suddenly I felt queasy. Where did the truth begin and end? I happened to know all three movements, but my fear kept me from admittin' that I could do such a thing. It would have been a shame to frighten them away. I was grateful to play one movement.

I waited for over a half an hour, and although startin' to fret, I was careful not to overdo it. I stood with my back to the door when Mr. Gibbons returned with the accompanist.

"Mr. Carver, allow me to introduce Sarah Wood."

Chapter 97

Bess
May 24, 1878

We didn't speak much over breakfast, and our carriage ride was quiet as well. Our disagreements were rare and trivial, but this one was significant. He would not back down. I finally told him that I would accompany one instrumentalist and that I preferred a child.

I was in the middle of a lesson when he burst into the room. Had he not looked so distraught, I would have had words with him. "What is it?"

"Excuse me, Bess, but I would like you to come with me for a moment," he said.

"Can it wait for ten minutes? William's lesson will be finished then."

"Well, I suppose I can wait for ten minutes, but you must come to my practice room when you're done," he said.

"Very well." My stomach churned, and I wished that I didn't insist on waiting for ten minutes. I wondered what could have been so urgent. I tried to turn my attention back to William, and completely forgot where we were. After playing a few meaningless scales, and me writing in his lesson book, I dismissed him.

I hesitated. For Joseph to behave in such a manner, something was amiss. I stood for a moment beside the open door and listened to the delightful sound of a cornet drifting down the hallway. Surely, it couldn't have been something like that. It did sound quite polished, but it was not necessary to interrupt me.

I sipped my water. If he were trying to prove a point, I would have a word with him. There was no reason to cause such tension. I decided to wait. I would not be manipulated. If it were a real emergency, I would know.

Unable to ignore the exquisite music coming from his room, I closed the door and waited for my next student. He would have to tell me all about it when I was ready. How dare he be the boy who cried wolf.

My student came and went. In spite of being tempted, I remained faithful to my stubbornness and did not rush to him. He too stayed in his practice room. The cornet music started and stopped.

I was not particularly fond of the brasses, but this was appealing to my ear. I needed to take a look. Having softened my thoughts, and wanting nothing more to do with quarreling, I set out to see what could have been the cause of my husband's unusual behavior.

I followed the strains of surprisingly bright music. I was about to enter the room when the music stopped. There stood a woman dressed in a faded green skirt with her back to me, fiddling with her music. She turned slightly, and my soul stopped in perfect astonishment.

Chapter 98

Sarah
May 24, 1878

Both men stood at the piano and stared at me. I wanted to pack up and leave. I had never witnessed such unbecomin' behavior. Mr. Carver, who was supposed to accompany me, up and left the room. Mr. Gibbons turned away and fidgeted with the metronome.

Then it dawned on me, someone remembered me as Jonas. That was it! They knew that a few years before, I was an imposter. Mr. Gibbons mumbled somethin' inaudible and hurried out into the hallway. I was ready to pack up and leave when he returned.

"I apologize," he said while takin' his place at the piano bench. "Now what tempo would you like to play this?"

I stared at him, thinkin' that I had overreacted, and I hummed the first few measures. As he played the introduction, I ignored everything that felt odd and out of place, and I concentrated on the music.

When it was time for my entrance, I played with all of my might. Somethin' wasn't right, but I refused to surrender.

After we warmed up to each other, it started to come together. I was able to concentrate and dismiss any fear. I stopped when we reached a passage that I suspected we would have to practice more than once. Right at that moment, Mr. Gibbons gasped and looked towards the door. I wanted to look, but I kept my eyes to myself.

"That went well. You're a fine player," he said, returnin' his attention to me.

"Thank you."

"Did you fill out the form so that we can contact you?" he asked.

"Yes, I did," I said while packin' my cornet in its case.

"You'll hear from us soon. I will recommend adding your name to the list," he said on his way out the door.

What an odd man he was. I was relieved to be alone for a moment before facin' August. I knew that I passed the audition, but I had no idea what had actually taken place.

Chapter 99

August
May 26, 1878

I was somewhat concerned when on Friday, Sarah bolted out of her audition. She was deeply disturbed, but would not speak of it. I asked her how she did, and she said that it didn't really matter; she passed.

Because she suspected that she was with child, I was more worried than usual. It wasn't healthy to be so emotionally wrecked. When we were in church, she didn't seem to be listenin' to the service but was deep in prayer. She was quiet all mornin', which wasn't like her.

Soon after we got home, someone rapped on the door. I opened it to see a well-dressed courier.

"Sarah Wood?"

"Sarah's in the garden. Is somethin' wrong?"

Without sayin' a word, he made his way to where Sarah was gatherin' dandelion greens.

"Mrs. Wood, this is for you." He handed her an envelope and stepped aside. She read aloud:

"Dear Sarah Wood,

    I request the honor of your presence this afternoon at our family estate at 630 High Street. It is urgent that we speak. It is not necessary,

but advisable, for your husband to accompany you. A carriage will fetch you at three o'clock.
Yours Truly,
Bess A. Carver
The Fall River Academy of Music."

"Ma'am, this is short notice. Are you able to attend?"

She paused. "Yes… we will."

"Very well then, a carriage will come by as noted."

Clearly, she was puzzled. Every time I started to question her, she hushed me up, assurin' me that it must have been a very good thing, or they would have sent a notice by mail.

Up until the carriage arrived, she tried fiendishly to smooth out the wrinkles in her Sunday dress and arranged her hair. At precisely three o'clock, a proper black carriage stopped in front of our cottage.

"Are you ready?" I asked.

Without a word, she dashed past me, out the door, and through the gate. I was surprised to see the familiar face of a negro driver from the estate on the hill. The address was in my old territory, so I knew where he was from.

He helped us into our seats. It was the first time I had been inside such a fancy carriage. I sat across from Sarah and held her hands in mine while she stared out the window.

There it was! I was stunned when we pulled into the carriage house. It was the estate where I sat by the garden wall and listened to piano music so many times. I couldn't believe that I was actually goin' inside.

The man who drove the carriage also accompanied us to the house, where there was a full staff of servants. The entryway was grand, with high ceilin's and mahogany trim. The furniture was showy and ornate.

We followed him down a long hallway and entered the room with the piano. I stopped in the doorway and took in the sight that I had previously only viewed from a distance.

An elderly negro woman sat quietly in a rockin' chair, and a tall man about my age came over and shook my hand.

"Hello, I'm Joseph Carver. You are Mr. Wood?"

"Yes, I'm August Wood. It's nice to meet you." I felt quite ashamed of my scuffed boots and threadbare pants. Although mended and clean, my shirt was quite worn out as well.

"And yes, Sarah, we have met," he took her hand and bowed. "Please make yourself at home. My wife will be joining us in a moment."

Chapter 100

Sarah
May 26, 1878

I SAT ON a perfect settee surrounded by things I had only seen in books and magazines. The house was brimmin' with magnificent artwork, paintin's, sculptures, and tall bookcases that reached the ceilin'. There were sparkly crystal chandeliers, table lamps, and elegant rugs beneath our feet. Every table was adorned with a hand-crafted doily and vases filled with fresh-cut flowers. The scent of lilacs and apple blossoms wafted in through the immense windows. I blushed when I looked out into the abundant garden and recognized the place where I made snow angles when I was with Clara. It seemed like it was but a dream.

I smiled at August, who appeared childlike in the giant, over-stuffed chair. The centerpiece of the room was the grand piano. I had never seen a real one before. It was so shiny, you could see a clear reflection of everything in the room.

One of the negro servants came in with a tray of beverages.

"Please help yourself to some cool cinnamon water," Mr. Carver said.

I had never tried it before, and although my stomach fluttered too much to try somethin' new, I thought it rude to decline.

We sat and sipped our drinks when, like a queen, she entered the room.

Chapter 101

Bess
May 26, 1878

I STARED INTO the looking glass one more time. Even the pressed powder could not conceal my swollen eyes. I had stayed up with Tempy throughout the night while she comforted me, and as always, shined a torchlight on the truth.

Mother—tucked away behind closed doors—was utterly oblivious to everything around her. It was a matter of weeks before she would be committed to the asylum permanently. Until the unfoldment of recent events, I was tormented about this decision. However, it had become a clear and accessible choice. *As you sow, so shall you reap.* The harvest was upon us.

I took a deep breath and entered the parlor, where our guests were sipping cinnamon water and waiting patiently.

I stood in the doorway, composed on the surface, but unraveling inside. My eyes rested upon her. It was too late when I realized how unfair it was to bring her into these circumstances in a room full of strangers. I tried, but could not pin down any one emotion as they fluttered around my heart, each begging to take the lead.

She gasped. I ignored my wobbliness, held my head up high, and walked in her direction. It seemed as if I couldn't get to her. We were suspended in a state of disbelief, but Sarah most of all.

Her eyes drew me in. I had never before seen my own hopes and fears. I realized that the looking glass did, in fact, lie.

She froze. *You can do it.* I resisted the urge to help her to her feet. I knew that she was strong enough. I recognized her courage as we looked straight into the other's soul.

She was clean, yet clothed in little more than rags. Her look of sadness screamed of a lifetime steeped in overwhelming affliction. To embrace her was to embrace me. I was unable to speak. *Was there a need to? Or, was it better to remain silent for a bit longer?*

"Sarah Wood?" I asked, surprised at the abruptness in my tone.

"Yes," she said.

Her voice was so small and frail, I had to strain to hear her. I found myself leaning in close enough to feel her warm breath. The ticking of the clock—the only sound that stood out clearly—hammered into the silence. I questioned if anyone else was breathing, or even in the room anymore. When I feared that I might crumble into a heap, I felt Tempy's eyes on us. I straightened my posture and carried on.

"Bess Carver," I said. "I'm Bess Adams Carver."

"I don't believe we've met." Her voice had gained fortitude, and a solitary tear slid down her cheek.

"Perhaps we have," I said. "Although, it has been a long, long time."

I turned to face the others.

"Thank you so very much for coming," I said.

If I were looking upon us from afar, I would have thought it to be a stellar performance. I was self-assured and well-spoken. I had assumed my late father's gift of captivating the men who smoked cigars when I really wasn't sure what would come next. It was a sort of trick that I didn't know I had mastered until I was in that extraordinary situation.

I approached the very handsome, yet scruffy, young man sitting in Father's chair. "Are you Mr. Wood?"

"Yes, I'm August... August Wood." He scrambled to his feet and bowed his head.

"Please sit, August. It is nice to make your acquaintance," I said, concerned about his paleness.

"The pleasure is mine," he said.

"You look familiar. I have seen you in and about the city," I said.

"I'm a lamplighter, and this was my route for a long time. I remember the beautiful music that came from this house," he said. "I used to look forward to it."

"That may be where I've seen you, on the street."

Joseph gave me a warning look that I didn't need. I honestly recalled seeing him with a boy, near the garden, and on the street.

"I would like you all to meet Tempy. She's a part of the family and has been with us for a very long time," I said.

Tempy nodded in agreement and continued rocking in her chair. My heart melted. She looked so old. Had it not been for her wisdom and calmness, I would not have survived any aspect of my life, including the one that we were facing.

"I understand that this is awkward, shocking, and highly unusual. I came home last Friday evening and spoke with Tempy. She has always been here for me."

I started to break. I couldn't look, or not look, at Sarah. My mind was blank. Rattled and not knowing what to do, I just stood there feeling as if it were my turn to almost faint.

"Here, Bess, come and sit down." Joseph guided me to the chair beside him.

I sipped his cinnamon water and continued.

"Before that night, I never knew any of what she shared with me. Possibly, deep down, I sensed that something was missing, or off, but I had no idea what. I know that without Tempy, I would be lost."

I paid no attention to Mother throwing things and shouting in the distance. She must have sensed what had emerged, as she adamantly, without being charged with a crime, proclaimed her innocence.

"So, on this momentous day, we acknowledge the truth, breaking through a veil of unforgivable wickedness that will resonate for future generations."

CHAPTER 102

Annie
June 29, 1855
Ossipee, New Hampshire

LIKE A FRESHLY sharpened knife, the pain sliced through my insides, takin' my breath away as a wave of warm, sticky blood surged from between my legs. "Get Samuel! Someone, get my husband!" I screamed.

The doctor had visitors, and I hadn't seen him for a few days. The ones left in charge quickly fetched him.

"He needs to be here now!" I gulped for air. "Please get me the Indian woman's tea!"

He rushed into the room with his wife, Iris, followin' behind. "Dear, dear, sit back and let me give you these drops. You'll feel better. Tilt your head back." His voice was deep and calm.

I opened my mouth, and the pungent drops burned down the back of my throat. I choked. His wife tried to give me water, but I spit it out.

"Get Samuel now, or I will leave here!"

"I know that it hurts. Try to take a deep breath," his wife said.

Darkness consumed me. The shadows of people comin' in and out of the room were part of my dream. Although some of it was real, I could not tell the difference. Sometimes, I only thought that I screamed, while other times I knew that I actually made a sound.

Several hours passed, and I only remember them shoutin' at me to push. I pushed for what seemed like days. Just when I believed that I could push no more, scream no more, and bleed no more, the doctor came in and gave me more of the black drops. Again, I lost consciousness, completely.

It wasn't until much later when Samuel arrived. "I'm here. I'm here, Annie."

"Where am I? Am I still here?"

He held my hand while they washed up the blood.

"Am I goin' to bleed to death?"

"No, you'll be fine," Samuel said.

"What about the baby? Did I hear a baby? It's quiet now. What's happenin'?"

I tried to concentrate on Samuel's voice, and then his face, but the doctor returned with somethin' else, somethin' darker and more bitter than before.

I couldn't hear anything, 'cept for what sounded like waves gently rockin' the ship. I closed my eyes and smiled when I saw him. "Daidí."

I rolled onto my side and vomited. I could no longer see Samuel, just the dark silhouette of a woman in the golden candlelight as she rocked in the chair, singin' a sweet lullaby. I tried, but I was too weak to call or reach out to her.

Chapter 103

Sarah
July 26, 1878
A Northbound Train

I NESTLED BACK into the plush seat, sippin' my cinnamon water, and lookin' out over Boston Harbor. I wondered what Mary would have said if she saw me in such a fancy train car.

Since leavin' Fall River, we had made the usual stops, but it wasn't as exhaustin' as bein' crammed into a common coach. Although I had too much on my mind to rest, we had a sleepin' berth that was much finer than I could have imagined.

At first, we intended to go to the County Farm and get Abigail and Samuel out once and for all, but God had another plan.

I was with child, and givin' birth in Fall River had no appeal, but we were unsure if August could find work in Ossipee. After only a week of inquiries, we learned that there were two positions at the sawmill. He had a steady job with the Street Department and had come so far. We had much to consider.

I also had the opportunity to play music as myself, out in the open. I didn't know how motherhood would affect all that. But, it was so dirty and crowded in Fall River, I could not decide what to do. With the ongoin' unrest, poor workin' conditions, and labor disputes, the circumstances in the city were worsenin'. It was no place to raise a child.

Lookin' back, I know that I complained about the simpletons in my hometown, but the folks there were honest and hardworkin', and it was clean and bright.

Against August's advice, Finn decided to go out West. He made friends with a young man, who convinced him of the great adventures and financial rewards of workin' in a silver mine. August didn't trust him one bit and worried about the dangers, but Finn was determined to go.

So, everything was in place. We were headin' back home to New Hampshire. However, a week before our departure, I received a letter.

June 30, 1878
Dear Mrs. Wood,
This serves as notification of the death of inmate, Abigail Hodgdon. She passed away on June 28, 1878, from complications of pneumonia.
As her next of kin, we are to advise you that adoption procedures may begin at a time when her son, Samuel Hodgdon, is adequately placed out. You have the first option to claim him, should you wish to do so. He will remain in custody at the County Farm until his outcome is determined.
Sincerely,
Emmett Smith, Josiah Warden, & Peter Rogers
Carroll County Commissioners

Silas was goin' to bring Samuel to the train station. I was eager to meet my nephew, but when it came to his father, I was still greatly conflicted. In my head, I went over the dialogue that we might have when I saw him. So much time had passed since Abigail tried to tell him that she was with child. I never understood what happened, and even though my sister made peace with it, I had difficulty findin' forgiveness in my heart.

I didn't know all the particulars, and I came to believe that all circumstances were set against them. Had he come forward and taken responsibility for Abigail and his own son, then perhaps none of this heartbreak would have happened at all.

CHAPTER 104

Silas Putnam
July 26, 1878
Ossipee, New Hampshire

I TRIED TO talk Jessie into stayin' home, but she would hear nothin' of it. The previous month, when I brought Samuel home from the County Farm, she weren't too pleased. In fact, she made me take him back 'til we had a proper discussion. She said that he could spend Sunday afternoons with us for the time bein'.

She asked why I had such an interest in him and not the others, and if I had lost faith in havin' our own child. At first, I was gonna fib a little, but I had to tell her the truth. Yes, I lost faith in us havin' our own child, but that we could have Samuel instead. She didn't have nothin' nice to say, mentionin' that he was a child of the devil and all. I told her to never say such words again. Ayuh, she was madder than a hornet.

I wanted her to know that he was my son and that I didn't know about it 'til it was too late. Every time I started to mention it, she quickly changed the subject. I weren't a religious man, but reckoned that I was given another chance. After all, I promised Abigail—may she rest in peace—that I'd take care of him. That coulda' meant lots of things. But, I knew it was time for him to come home. Jessie would jest hafta' behave properly. I s'posed I could get her to come around.

"It's such a fine day, a good opportunity to wear my new dress. I still say that I look better in yellow than most women. Mother knows me so well. And, how perfect is this straw bonnet? She was worried that it had too many flowers, but there could never be too many flowers on a hat perched upon my fair head." She laughed and fluttered her fan.

"Ayuh."

"You're not listening," she said.

"Here comes the train! Aunt Sarah! Aunt Sarah!" Samuel started to run towards the tracks, but I caught his arm.

"Please, must he make such a racket?" Jessie asked, rollin' her eyes like she always did.

"Oh simmah down, he ain't never met his aunt. Leave him be," I said.

"I have never met her either. I have a faded memory of her at her mother's funeral, but that was so long ago," she said, "such a plain girl if I remember correctly."

The brakes squealed, and the steam whistle blew. Folks got all excited and moved closer to the platform. I admit that I was lookin' forward to seein' Sarah. I knew she didn't care much for me, but we shared our love for Abigail.

The train finally stopped, and one by one, the passengers stepped off. A tall man got out of the first class car and turned to assist a lady. First came the parasol, and then she peeked her head out before steppin' down. I saw Sarah's lovely face and smiled. I didn't expect her to be so finely dressed. It weren't that she didn't deserve such things, but bein' fancy didn't seem to matter to them Hodgdon girls.

"Over here!" I regretted hollerin' and knew I shoulda' walked over to her instead.

"Is that her? I don't remember her having the means to dress so tastefully. I thought she was a mill girl," Jessie said, nearly droppin' her fan.

I took Jessie's elbow. "Come on, let's go meet her."

"I don't need your help," she said, pullin' away.

I had to run to keep up with Samuel. We stopped right in front of her as she continued down the steps and onto the platform.

"Sarah…"

She whispered somethin' into the tall man's ear, and they both laughed. I wasn't feelin' good about her not even botherin' to take notice of me. I knew that she was pretty mad at me, and rightly so, but she didn't know all the goin's on.

I was about to approach her when I caught sight of the bottom of a dress and the shoe of another woman comin' down them same steps. This dress wasn't so fancy, more simple than the likes of Jessie or Sarah, but right smart.

Not sure if what I was seein' was right, I watched her—identical to Sarah in every way—step off the train. She joined the other woman, and together they laughed, linked arms, and headed towards me.

It was clear that the second woman to step off of the train was Sarah. When she caught sight of me, she waved and ran in our direction. "Silas! There you are... And this must be Samuel."

"Aunt Sarah?" He reached towards her with outstretched arms.

"Yes, it's me." She embraced him.

"Mamma was right, 'cept she didn't tell me there were two angels. I only knew 'bout one."

About the Author

Before shifting to writing, Mj was a trumpeter and Civil War re-enactor, sporting a hoop skirt, and performing throughout the Northeast. Although the brass is a bit tarnished, she enjoys playing her cello.

Aligned with her passion for nature and exploring the ancient healing traditions, customs, and folklore of her ancestors, she lives on a farm in the woods of New Hampshire.

In addition to earning undergraduate degrees in social history, psychology, and music, Mj received an MFA in creative writing. For more information, visit her website: https://www.mjpettengill.com/

Made in the USA
Monee, IL
09 September 2020